The
Ships of Air

Also by
Martha Wells

The Wizard Hunters
Wheel of the Infinite
The Death of the Necromancer
City of Bones
The Element of Fire

The
Ships of Air

Book Two of the Fall of Ile-Rien

Martha Wells

An Imprint of HarperCollins*Publishers*

HarperCollins books may be purchased for educational, business, or sales promotional use. For information please write: Special Markets Department, HarperCollins Publishers Inc., 10 East 53rd Street, New York, NY 10022.

FIRST EDITION

Eos is a federally registered trademark of HarperCollins Publishers Inc.

Designed by Elizabeth M. Glover

Printed on acid-free paper

Library of Congress Cataloging-in-Publication Data

Wells, Martha.
   The ships of air / Martha Wells.—1st ed.
      p. cm.—(The fall of Ile-Rien ; bk. 2)
   ISBN 0-380-97789-3
      I. Title.

PS3573.E4932 W59   2004
813'.54—dc22   2004042051

04 05 06 07 08 JTC/QW 10 9 8 7 6 5 4 3 2 1

To Rory Harper

Chapter 1

So we made ready to leave the shore of the Isle of Storms, in hope of never setting foot on it again.

— *"Ravenna's voyage to the Unknown Eastlands,"*
V. Madrais Translation

Tremaine picked her way along the ledge, green stinking canal on one hand, rocky outcrop sprouting dense dark foliage on the other. She was exhausted and footsore and at the moment profoundly irritated. She said in exasperation, "All they have to do is get on the damn ship. Is that really going to be so hard?"

"It's the eyes," Giliead told her obliquely. He and Ilias were just ahead of her on the narrow shelf of rock, both men having a far easier time of traversing it than she was. The mossy water a few feet below was foul-smelling and stagnant, inhabited only by weeds and the occasional brightly colored snake. These canals cut through the rocky island in several directions, leading to and from the stone buildings that housed entrances to the deserted waterlogged city that wove through the caves below. The builders, whoever they were, had used black stones twenty or thirty feet long to line the watercourse, stacking them like tree trunks in the same way they built their underground walls and bridges.

"The ship doesn't have eyes." Tremaine struggled along, sweating in the damp air. The canal was overhung by the twisted dark-leaved trees; the overcast sky made it even more dim. For years the island had been a trap for seagoing vessels and the crews who sailed them; the whole place felt as if the corruption in the caves below had crept up through the roots of the stunted jungle.

"That's the problem," Giliead said, glancing back at her as he brushed a branch aside. "She just looks like—"

"A big blind giant," Ilias supplied, balancing agilely on the slick stones. They were both Syprians, natives of this world on the other side of the etheric gateway from Ile-Rien. They were brothers, though only by adoption, and they looked nothing alike. Ilias had a stocky muscular build and a wild mane of blond hair, some of it tied into a queue that hung down his back. He wore battered dark pants and boots with a sleeveless blue shirt trimmed with leather braid. Giliead was built on a bigger scale, nearly a head taller than Ilias, with chestnut braids and olive skin, dressed in a dark brown shirt under a leather jerkin. Both wore more jewelry than had been fashionable for men in Ile-Rien for many years—copper earrings, armbands with copper disks. Ilias also had a silver mark on his cheek in the shape of a half-moon, but that wasn't meant to be decorative.

Tremaine let out a frustrated breath as she ducked under a heavy screen of pungent leaves. She was the odd woman out, with short mousy brown hair and sunburned skin. She was wearing Syprian clothing too, a loose blue tunic block-printed with green-and-gold designs and breeches of a soft doeskin. Her clothes were a little the worse for wear but in better shape than the unlamented tweed outfits she had left behind in Ile-Rien.

At the moment all three of them were covered with bruises, howler scratches and patches of mud and slime from the walls of the underground passages. The last few days had been nothing but fighting and running and swimming and falling, and Tremaine just wanted everyone to quietly get on the ship so they could get the hell away from here. She had also gone to a great deal of trouble to steal the *Queen Ravenna* for just this purpose and she wanted her new friends to like it. So far they had stubbornly refused to share her enthusiasm. Even Ilias, who had actually sailed on the ship briefly.

"It won't matter how big the ship is as long as she sails by curses," Giliead continued frankly. "They're never going to get used to that."

Tremaine knew he was probably right, though she wasn't ready to admit it aloud. Syprian civilization was considerably more primitive than Ile-Rien's, and they regarded any mechanical object, from electric lights to clocks, as magical. Worse, Syprians hated magic, since all their sorcerers were murdering lunatics. It was a minor miracle that they had managed to get to this point, where a woman from Ile-Rien who was a friend of sorcerers could talk about this subject with Syprians at all. It helped that they were a sea people and fairly cosmopolitan, despite their prejudices. "But the *Ravenna* doesn't use magic," she pointed out. "The steam engines—" She stopped when she realized the words were coming out in Rienish. If there was a Syrnaic word for "steam engine" the translation spell that had given Tremaine the knowledge of the language hadn't seen fit to include it. "There's boilers, and you put water in them, and burn coal or oil or something, and the steam makes it go. It's not magic," she finished lamely.

Giliead and Ilias paused to exchange a look; Giliead's half of it was dubious and Ilias's was ironic. "They always say that," Ilias put in. He had spent nearly one whole day in Ile-Rien and now qualified as the local expert. "Wagons without horses, wizard lights, wizard weapons, there's an explanation for everything."

Giliead shook his head as he started forward again. "If that's our only way off the island, we're going to have trouble."

Ilias nodded. "It doesn't matter about me, I'm marked anyway," he said matter-of-factly. The mark he spoke of was the little half-moon of silver branded into his cheek. It was what Syprian law said anyone who had ever fallen under a sorcerer's curse should wear. "And Gil's exempt from the law because he's a Chosen Vessel, but it's the others I'm worried about. If the people in Cineth harbor see them come off that ship, they could all end up ostracized or worse. And some of the younger ones come from pretty good families, they could still have a chance of getting married."

Tremaine considered that, frowning. There were a lot of things she didn't understand about the Syprians yet. In many ways their society was a matriarchy; men seemed to hold the public offices like warleader and lawgiver but weren't allowed to own property, and family status was important. The Andrien, the family Giliead had been born into and Ilias adopted by, had had its ups and downs, mostly due to Giliead's being the local god's Chosen Vessel. The three female heirs to Andrien had all been killed by the sorcerer Ixion, leaving the family in danger of losing their land when Giliead's mother Karima died.

"They could end up ostracized," Giliead agreed. "But that's if we can get them aboard her in the first place." He didn't sound sanguine about the prospect.

It was the only way off the island at the moment and Tremaine didn't want to contemplate leaving anyone behind. "So you're not even curious to see the inside?" she prompted, trying a different tack. "Ilias did."

Giliead just looked back at her, not the least bit impressed by this technique.

Ilias snorted, swinging surefootedly over a gap in the stone. "I didn't have a choice."

Tremaine knew what he meant; the *Ravenna* had been the only way for him to return with the rescue party, to get back to his own world. She had been hoping the Syprians would like the *Ravenna* or at least get used to her. The way they acted toward their own vessels seemed to suggest ships were fairly important in their society. Ilias had become somewhat accustomed to the *Ravenna*, but he and Giliead were much more used to strange sights and magic than most Syprians. She said dryly, "I failed to notice your helplessness."

Instead of retaliating verbally, Ilias just grinned and deftly caught her when her foot slipped.

Recovering her balance with his help, Tremaine was glad she hadn't gone headfirst into the canal; once her clothes were soaked with water she didn't think she would have had the strength to climb out again, and that would have been embarrassing. She said reluctantly, "Nobody would necessarily have to see them get off the ship. We could send all of you ashore in one of the launches someplace nearby but out of sight." Tremaine was a little hesitant to suggest this idea, considering what she thought Ilias's feelings on the subject were. She knew that when he had been cursed by Ixion, no one but he and Giliead had known, and Ilias had still insisted on turning himself in to receive the curse mark. "Then you could warn the city that we were coming before we sail into the harbor."

"That might be best." Giliead had to crouch to duck under some dark trailing vines. Pausing to hold them up for Tremaine, he threw Ilias a thoughtful look, as if he had had the same qualm.

But Ilias just said, "There would be less trouble that way."

Ducking under the vines, Tremaine absently watched the display of flexed muscle as Ilias hauled himself up on a heavier branch to swing across another gap in the stone. She wasn't sure "less trouble" was a realistic expectation. But whatever happened, the *Ravenna* would be leaving this area soon, steaming through the unfamiliar waters of this world until it was safe to open the etheric world-gate again and bring the ship to port in Capidara, one of Ile-Rien's only surviving allies.

They still knew little about their enemies, except that they came from somewhere in this world. The Gardier used the etheric gate spell to reach their targets in Ile-Rien and Adera, something no one had realized until Arisilde Damal and Tremaine's father Nicholas Valiarde had somehow stolen the spell from them. After both men had disappeared, it had taken the Viller Institute sorcerers years to discover what the gate spell was and where the Gardier were coming from.

The spell needed two things to create a gate to another world: a circle of arcane symbols that no one properly understood and a sorcerer using one of the Viller spheres. Carrying her circle with her gave the *Ravenna* great mobility in traveling back and forth between worlds. As far as they knew, the Gardier didn't have circles on their ships or airships, and so could only create gates when they were close enough to one of their bases where a circle was located. Tremaine and the others had destroyed the Gardier spell circle on this island; hopefully that would keep the Gardier ships blockading the coast of Ile-Rien from coming through the gate after them. It would not stop attack by the Gardier already in this world.

A shout from above startled Tremaine. "Now what?" They were so close to temporary safety and she was so tired. The two men plunged ahead, splashing in the stagnant water. They were closer than she thought; only a few yards along was the break in the canal where a rough set of stairs led up the steep overgrown hill.

Tremaine reached the opening and scrambled up the steps after Giliead and Ilias, both almost at the top by now. The short scrubby trees and thorny vines clutched at her, and she clawed at the muddy rock to drag her weary body up. The stairs led into a flat-roofed stone building that was now filled with milling refugees, some whispering in anger or panic and others fearfully silent. She shouldered into the path through the crowd that the two men had already made, coming out of the square doorway into the plaza.

The little group of stone structures stood on a bluff looking out over the misty sea, all probably built about the same time as the underwater city; the stunted trees and thick carpet of vegetation had had time to eat away sections of the paving. Another flat-roofed building stood at a right angle to this one, concealing a shaft leading down to the caves.

Most of the freed prisoners had drawn back against the dark walls. They were all from Ile-Rien's world on the other side of the etheric gateway, a mix of Maiutans and other Southern Seas Islanders, Parscians, with a few Rienish. They had been captured and brought to this world by the Gardier as slave labor for their base in the island's caves.

Wrapped in a canvas tarp and lying on the pavement was the currently inert body of the former owner of those caves, the sorcerer Ixion. Tremaine stared warily at the bundle, wondering if Ixion had decided to rejoin the living and that was what had upset everyone. But Giliead and Ilias stood with Ander, Florian and the group of Rienish soldiers and Syprian sailors who had led the attack on the base, all looking out to sea. After a baffled moment Tremaine saw what had caught their attention: About three hundred yards from shore the low dark outline of a Gardier gunship moved silently through the mist.

Oh, no, Tremaine thought, her stomach clenching as she moved to join the others. It wasn't the gunship from the Gardier's harbor on the far side of the island, even she could tell that. This boat was longer than that one and had a second gun on the stern. "How long—?"

Florian glanced at her, her expression desperate. "We just saw it a few moments ago." She was younger than Tremaine, a slight girl with short red hair, dressed in stained khaki knickers and a dark pullover sweater. It had been Tremaine, Gerard, Florian and Ander who had first come through the etheric gateway, scouting the approach to the Gardier base, and been shipwrecked here. Gerard was back at the cove now where the *Ravenna* would be landing her launches in preparation for taking them all aboard.

Giliead must have already informed Ander of the situation because he turned impatiently to Tremaine, demanding, "It was the *Ravenna*? You saw it?"

Ander Destan was a tall dark-haired man, conventionally handsome. He was only a few years older than Tremaine but was already a captain in the Ile-Rien Army Intelligence Corps, or what was left of it. He had never quite trusted the Syprians the way she, Florian and Gerard had, but Tremaine could tell this wasn't disbelief of Giliead's truthfulness. It was pure relief; after seeing the gunship, a viable escape route probably seemed like too much to ask for. She nodded hurriedly. "Gerard's there with Niles now, the launches will be waiting for us in that cove where we met the *Swift*." She waved her arms. "We need to get moving!"

None of the Syprians gathered around could understand Rienish, and Tremaine heard Ilias rapidly briefing Halian on the situation. Halian was Giliead's stepfather and had been captain of the *Swift;* he was an older man than any of the other Syprians except Gyan, with a weathered face and graying dark hair. Halian turned to the other Syprian crew members gathered worriedly around, saying, "Break them up into groups and start leading them down the canal. There's boats waiting at Dead Tree Point."

Florian pressed forward, following the men as they scattered. "I'll translate for them." She and Ander were the only other Rienish besides Gerard and Tremaine who spoke the Syprians' language, Syrnaic. "Oh, here." She dashed back to hand Tremaine the battered leather bag that held the sphere.

Tremaine took it absently, hanging it over her shoulder as she watched the Syprians spread out to herd the freed slaves down the steps to the canal. The Gardier's prisoners had had to be in fair health to survive this long, but some of them were disoriented and shocked by their long captivity underground and the swiftness and violence of their escape. Some didn't speak Rienish, so that made it even more difficult. Getting them on the motor launches waiting in the cove would be less of a problem; once they saw the boats they would surely know it was their best escape. The Syprians were going to be the problem then. *I'm not leaving anybody behind,* Tremaine thought, taking a sharp breath. *Not this time.*

Ander's military team were gathered around the eleven captured Gardier; Tremaine moved to join them. The prisoners sat on the broken moss-stained stone of the plaza in a sullen group, their hands bound with the same chains they had used on their slaves. With pale skin and heads shaved to stubble, they all looked alike to Tremaine. Their brown coverall uniforms with heavy boots and close-fitting caps had nothing to distinguish one from the other. They were a different problem altogether. Tremaine eyed them, deciding it looked like a problem that could be solved by eleven bullets.

"The wireless?" Basimi, one of the Rienish soldiers, turned to ask Ander.

Ander squinted at the wireless that had brought them the *Ravenna*'s signal. "Take the box, leave the antenna." It was strung up across the two stone buildings and would be too much trouble to remove. And the Gardier knew they were here, there was no point in trying to remove any trace of their presence.

Ander stepped toward the Gardier prisoners, watching them carefully. He grasped the Gardier translator disk around his neck, saying, "Get up, follow us quietly and you won't be harmed." They had captured several of the translators, small silver medallions with an inset crystal that held the spell that converted the speaker's words to the Gardier language. They translated only Rienish, unfortunately, and didn't work for Syrnaic.

Most of the Gardier just stared at him but one spoke rapidly in a high light voice, the disk translating his words, "Free us and surrender. You will be well treated—"

Tremaine, her eyes on the long black shape of the gunship plowing through the gray sea, suddenly had enough. That a Gardier, sitting there in chains surrounded by Rienish, would still have the gall to try to dictate terms was too much. The slaves, the people fleeing Vienne knowing they had no control over their lives, poor dead Rulan's betrayal, what the Gardier had done to Arisilde, all came together in perfect clarity for her.

Basimi had set his captured Gardier rifle aside so he could pack the wireless box; Tremaine walked across the plaza to pick it up. Distracted and thinking she was just relieving him of a burden, he barely glanced at her.

Tremaine hefted it thoughtfully. The weight and stock felt odd in her hands and there was no safety. Crossing back to the Gardier, she pumped it to get a cartridge into the chamber. She stopped beside Ander, lifting it to her shoulder to aim at the Gardier spokesman. The man's expression went from stoic contempt to fear, his dark eyes widening in alarm. *Good,* she thought. *I'd hate to take you by surprise.* Then before her finger could tighten on the trigger a long arm reached over her shoulder and grabbed the barrel.

It was Giliead. Tremaine tried to hold on to the gun but had to give up before her hand got caught in the trigger guard. Ander was staring, startled. From across the plaza Ilias shouted, "Tremaine, stop that!"

"They won't move!" She gestured in frustration at the Gardier. She wondered if anybody else was appreciating the irony of the barbarian Syprians preventing the civilized woman of Ile-Rien from shooting the prisoners. Some of the ex-slaves had stopped to watch, probably hoping to see her do it. Ander and Basimi and the other Rienish military men were staring in disbelief. *Why do they all look like this is such a bad idea?* "We can't leave them, they know too much about us! What else are we going to do?"

"Not that." Giliead's expression was way too reasonable for her current mood. "They're not wizards," he said patiently. "And they're helpless." He held the gun away from his body, his distaste for what he thought of as a curse weapon evident, but there was no way she could get it away from him.

"Then let them loose and I'll pick them off on the run." But the moment of cold uncontrolled fury was fading. Tremaine knew she wasn't in touch with her own emotions at the best of times, but maybe this was a little much. She pushed her hair back, looking away.

Ilias rolled his eyes and turned back to helping one of the Parscian women to her feet, obviously leaving the situation to Giliead, who just watched Tremaine calmly. If he had said aloud, "I've given you my position on this and I'm not going to argue about it," it couldn't have been more clear.

"Tremaine, would you mind if I handled this?" Ander said with sarcastic emphasis. He was past astonishment and on to exasperated anger, the usual emotional state he and Tremaine communicated in. "Would that be all right with you?"

Tremaine folded her arms and told him, "Somebody figure this out right now or we do it my way." She couldn't back the threat up with Giliead standing ready to wrestle another gun away from her, but maybe in the heat of the moment nobody would figure that out.

The conversation had been in Syrnaic, and with Florian down on the stairs urging along the first group of prisoners, Ander and the Syprians were the only ones who had understood it. He turned to the Gardier again, grasping the translator, and shouted, "Get up! I won't ask it again!"

Maybe his grim face convinced them, though Tremaine thought it was probably her he wanted to throw off the cliff. Two of the Gardier stumbled to their feet and the others followed, the spokesman last and most reluctant, with the Rienish soldier Deric giving him a poke with a rifle to hurry him along. The other members of Ander's military team closed around them, shepherding them toward the stairs after the last group of refugees.

Ander stopped beside Tremaine. She expected another sarcastic comment, but he said reluctantly, "At least you got them moving. They really thought you meant it."

As he moved away Tremaine clapped a hand over her eyes. *It would have been worth it, just to show Ander.* He had known her for years longer than anyone else here except Gerard, and yet he didn't know her at all. She lifted her head to find herself sharing a look with Giliead. His mouth quirked, and she had the sudden feeling he understood.

Basimi, the wireless box packed in its case and tucked under his arm, pointed at the gun. "Uh, Ma'am, could you ask him if I could have—"

"Yes, sorry." Tremaine rubbed her face, trying to collect herself. She told Giliead in Syrnaic, "He wants the weapon back."

Giliead handed it over as Ilias came up to them. He gave Tremaine a pointed look, and she snapped, "Don't you start."

He ignored her, turning to Giliead. "You ready to take Ixion?"

Giliead let out a breath, his expression darkening as he looked at the canvas-wrapped bundle lying on the broken pavement. Moving the sorcerer's body wouldn't disrupt the ward Gerard had placed on it, but Tremaine wouldn't have had that job for anything, and Ilias looked as if this was as close as he planned to get to it. They both watched Giliead lift the body and heave it over his shoulder.

Tremaine hurriedly picked her way along the edge of the canal after Ilias and the others, the sphere's bag bumping her familiarly in the hip. *I feel like I just did this. Oh right, I did.* The overcast sky was darkening rapidly and the canal had become a dim gray-green tunnel as the overhanging vegetation screened what little light remained. Giliead, still carrying Ixion, had gone up ahead to talk to Halian, jumping down into the canal and wading through the waist-deep water past the line of refugees making their way along the stone ledge. Ander and the other Rienish were herding the Gardier prisoners through the canal up near the front of the line. Basimi was just ahead of Ilias, burdened with the wireless box and the rifle slung over his back. Tremaine had offered to carry the gun for him, but for some reason he had declined.

Most of the refugees were moving quickly, carrying the injured, helping each other along, spurred by fear of recapture. Occasional stragglers still fell behind, dazed by the suddenness of events or too scared by their long captivity to really understand what was happening. Ilias plunged into the water frequently to hand them back up to their companions or to just get them pointed in the right direction. "It's not the ones who are still trying to move you've got to worry about," he commented to Tremaine, hauling himself out onto the stone pathway again, dripping with the stagnant water and with his arms and chest stained with moss. "If they have to be carried, there's more chance they might go dead later."

Tremaine grabbed the shoulder of his shirt, more to steady herself than him, since he was far more surefooted on the slippery stone. "What do you mean 'go dead'?" Her knowledge of Syrnaic having come from a spell rather than studying the language, she found she actually did know some of the local idiom, but this one escaped her.

Ilias pushed to his feet, tossed the wet hair out of his eyes and moved after the others. "It's when someone's been caught or had their village cursed by a wizard, and they just never get over it. They won't talk, won't recognize their family, won't eat or drink unless you make them. You've seen that before?"

"Yes, I know what you mean." Tremaine digested that, not liking the implications. If the other Syprians were really that affected by exposure to magic, then that didn't bode well for a future contact between the cities of the Syrnai and Ile-Rien's government-in-exile. The Andrien family had accepted them, but then they had felt obligated by all the mutual lifesaving that had gone on between Tremaine, Florian and Ander when they had been stranded in the underground city searching for Gerard, and Ilias, who had been likewise searching for Giliead. And Giliead's mother Karima had managed to reconcile herself to having a son who was a Chosen Vessel, so getting used to the idea of wizards as allies probably wasn't as hard for her as the others. Tremaine had noted that Halian's son Nicanor, the current lawgiver of Cineth, had barely deigned to look at them.

"Anything I should know?" Basimi asked, glancing cautiously back at them. The conversation had been in Syrnaic and he hadn't understood it.

He was a hard-faced wiry man who was one of the few who had volunteered to follow Ander back to this world to infiltrate the Gardier base. Tremaine knew nothing about him except that he probably wasn't a traitor like Rulan. "Just chatting," she told him.

The first of the refugees must have reached the cove long before them. As they finally climbed up the canal's embankment near the bluff, Tremaine foundered in the sudden high wind. Following the last of the stragglers, Basimi staggered under the burden of the wireless. Ilias stopped, looking worriedly up at the cloud-heavy sky. "This isn't natural," he muttered. Tremaine was uncomfortably reminded of the spell-driven storm that had swamped the Pilot Boat when they had first been stranded on the island.

She stumbled around the rocks to see the little sandy cove and the even more welcome sight of two motor launches moored in the shallows. They were sturdy boats, each almost forty feet long, painted gray to match the *Ravenna*'s war camouflage, with steel hulls, diesel engines and canvas canopies to protect the occupants from the weather. The surf rolled in around them, white and frothy, and the wind lifted the sand in stinging sheets. Another boat already packed with people fought the waves between the tall rocks, heading for the safety of the larger ship anchored somewhere in the heavy mist outside the cove. At least Tremaine hoped the *Ravenna* meant safety. She couldn't see Niles, but Gerard and a couple of men in short jackets of the red-trimmed dark blue of undress Rienish naval uniforms were helping refugees onto the first launch. Florian was at his side.

Tremaine trotted across the sand, the wind tossing her hair, and got there in time to hear the other girl say, "Gerard, is this an etheric storm?" Florian squinted up at the streaming clouds overhead, her face white and strained, having to nearly shout to be heard over the roar of the surf.

"I'm afraid so." Gerard winced away from the spray as the waves broke around the launch's hull. He was a tall man in his early forties, with dark hair just lightly touched with gray. He was currently wearing Syprian clothing, battered dark pants and a loose mud-stained white shirt with a green sash; he was a sorcerer and had been Tremaine's guardian before she was old enough to assume control of the Valiarde family fortunes. "It's nearly impossible for us to call up weather magic so quickly, but we've seen the Gardier do it before."

Florian gave Tremaine a concerned look as she approached. "Is that all of them? Ander already took the Gardier on another boat."

"We're the last," Tremaine told her, looking around for the Syprians. They were gathered in a group over by the rocks, and Giliead, hands planted on his hips, was talking to them. Ilias had gone to stand at his side. *That doesn't look good,* she thought grimly. She noticed Giliead didn't have the canvas-wrapped bundle anymore. "Where's Ixion? Did they put him in the boat?"

"On the other one." Gerard nodded, indicating the launch wallowing in the surf a little further down. "That's the boat you'll be taking. I want the sphere to stay fairly near him."

"Are they coming?" Florian shielded her eyes from the spray, watching the Syprians worriedly. "I know they think the engines are magic, but it's their only chance."

"I'll go see." Stumbling in the wet sand, Tremaine went over to join the group.

Arites, a young man with wild brown hair who was a Syprian poet, was standing with Dyani, Gyan's young foster daughter. She was a slight girl with dark brown hair tied back in a loose ponytail. Gyan himself looked grave, and Halian was fuming with frustration and anger. Most of the others hovered between confused and rebellious. "I won't do it," one of them was saying stubbornly. He was big like Giliead, but with darker hair and a boxer's mashed nose. "It was bad enough letting them curse the *Swift,* and we saw what happened to her—"

"It was Ixion's curseling that did that," Gyan objected. Tremaine was glad he was on their side. He was an older man, with a heavy build and a good-humored face, balding with a long fringe of gray hair. He was much respected by the other crew. "And Gerard's curse got us out of that prison—"

"But you can't ask us to get on that wizard ship!"

"It's not magic," Tremaine protested helplessly. "The lights, the engines, it's steam turbines and—" She stopped in exasperation when she realized the words were coming out in Rienish because there were no equivalents in Syrnaic. "Dammit!"

"I've been on the wizard ship," Ilias began patiently. "It's not—"

"You've got nothing to lose," the man snapped at him.

Ilias's expression went stony and he stepped back, reflexively drawing away from the group.

That did it for Giliead. He looked the men over with grim contempt. "I'm going. Anyone who wants to stay, we'll send help back to you. If the howlers or the Gardier wizards leave anything."

"Wait." Halian fixed an eye on the objector and said, almost too quietly for Tremaine to hear over the rising wind, "So you're captain now, Dannor?"

"Maybe he ought to be," somebody else piped up.

Without taking his eyes off Halian, Dannor backhanded the offender in the mouth, saying, "When I want you to talk for me I'll tell you."

"Tremaine!" Gerard shouted from the launches. "We have to go!"

"Go on!" she turned to yell. "We'll take the other boat." *I hope.* She could feel the sphere shaking violently in its bag and wondered if it was responding to the argument or the growing storm.

"The thing is, Dannor," Halian said, still softly, "either you're making yourself captain, or you're not."

Dannor breathed hard, something flat and desperate in his eyes. Halian had been Cineth's warleader once, Tremaine remembered. Dannor looked like he knew why Halian had been chosen for that job and didn't want to find out all over again. He stared out toward where the *Ravenna* lay, obscured by the heavy mist and the black rocks that sheltered the cove. A scatter of raindrops pelted the sand around them and thunder rumbled. "Halian, I—"

Halian's grim expression didn't soften. "Do you really think I'd ask you to do this if it wasn't the only choice?"

Gerard had splashed back out of the surf and started across the beach toward them. The other boat was leaving, she could see Florian standing in the stern watching them, hanging on to a stanchion as it fought the waves. The last one, empty but for two Rienish sailors, still waited. Tremaine was turning to tell Gerard to go back when sand suddenly blew up in her face and something shoved her hard from behind. She hit the wet beach facefirst.

The next thing she knew Gerard was dragging her upright, the sphere's bag knocking her in the stomach as she got her feet under her. "Ow," Tremaine protested weakly. Her ears rang, her head pounded, her teeth hurt. After everything else, it seemed especially unfair. "What happened?" The Syprians were scattered around her, sprawled in the sand or struggling to their feet.

Gerard spoke urgently, but his voice sounded far away over the ringing in her ears. Giliead staggered upright, shaking his head, and Ilias rolled over, still stunned.

Tremaine gave up on trying to hear Gerard and looked around for the source of the explosion. She saw with shock that the big rock they had been standing near was missing a large chunk off the top. She could smell burning and the aftermath of a lightning strike. She pointed at it, tugging on Gerard's sleeve, trying to get him to look. "They're shelling us!"

Gerard gestured imperatively at the boat, shouting something that sounded tinny and far away. Ilias managed to struggle up and Giliead pulled Halian to his feet. He started pushing the others toward the beach. Tremaine reached to help Dyani, but Gerard grabbed the other girl's arm and hauled them both toward the water.

Something flashed overhead, lighting up the gray sky, and Tremaine flinched. "What was that?" she demanded again.

Gerard's voice still sounded too far away but this time she understood his shout. "It's lightning, etheric lightning. The Gardier generated this storm and the lightning is aiming for us."

Damn. Tremaine stared up, stumbling as another flash lit the sky. The men on the boat were waving urgently for them to hurry. "Us specifically?" She looked around and saw with relief all the Syprians were with them; no one was staying behind. Dannor and Halian were half-carrying Gyan.

"Anything human," Gerard clarified.

"Why aren't we dead?" Dyani asked, looking up in terror at the flashes shooting across the gray sky.

"The sphere is deflecting it!"

Dyani probably didn't understand what that meant, but Tremaine was a little reassured. Arisilde, locked inside the sphere, was fighting the Gardier spells for them.

They stumbled into the surf and the cool water shocked Tremaine out of her daze. Staggering in the waves, they reached the boat. Tremaine grabbed the railing and looked for Ilias. She found him when he caught her around the waist and lifted her over the side.

The floorboards were already drenched with spray. Others tumbled in, and Tremaine helped Gerard and Dyani steady Gyan as Halian boosted him up to climb the rail. The older man's face was red and he was breathing hard; Tremaine hoped he wasn't having a heart seizure. Then she saw the gray hair at the back of his head was matted with blood and realized he must have been hit by a fragment of the shattered rock.

Giliead was the last to scramble in. The engine coughed to life, making the Syprians flinch in alarm, and the boat began to plow forward against the waves, taking them away from the island.

Chapter 2

The wall rose out of the sea and the fog, up and up, bigger than a mountain, taking up all the horizon like another sky. . . .

— *"Ravenna's voyage to the Unknown Eastlands,"*
Abignon Translation

Tremaine thought the water in the cove was rough, but as the launch left the shelter of the rocks, the high waves flung it into a violent roll. She slid from her seat to the deck, clutching the bench and trying valiantly to keep her stomach down where it was supposed to be. She hadn't ever been seasick before, but the waves tossed the boat like a tin cup.

Gerard pushed his way up to the bow and held on to the rail next to the sailor wrestling with the wheel. Everyone else was clinging to the seats, trying to brace themselves. Ilias was beside Tremaine, gripping a stanchion, and Giliead was braced next to him. Even with the wind and the spray in their faces they were watching something with awed expressions. Whatever it was Tremaine didn't think she wanted to see it. The sudden onset of nausea had sucked any interest in staying alive right out of her; it was almost like being back home again. Then the wind died suddenly and she realized the sea was less violent, the boat's wild dips and sways less agonizing. She grabbed the rail and dragged herself up a little to look.

At first all she saw was a giant gray wall. She thought it was mist or a low cloud formation, then she realized it was the *Ravenna*, looming over the little boat like an avalanche. Ilias and Giliead must have been watching her advance and turn.

The pilot turned from the wheel to shout, "We're all right now! She's come to our windward side so we're in her lee."

Oh good, an optimist, Tremaine thought. "She's shielding us from the wind," she translated into Syrnaic for the Syprians, though being sailors they probably didn't need her to tell them what had happened.

The boat chugged rapidly toward the *Ravenna* now, making good progress over the still-rough sea. Peering up at the ship, Tremaine could see a few lights glowing along the upper decks and a searchlight sweeping the water, fixing on the launch to guide it in. The gray paint made the ship fade into the heavy overcast sky and her upper decks were draped in mist. It fell over the ship like a giant's shroud, catching in diaphanous streamers on the three enormous smokestacks. She didn't dwarf the island behind them in actual physical size, but she gave the impression she wanted to try. The *Ravenna* had been built to be a passenger liner, the largest in the Vernaire Solar Line, and she was far from home, just like everyone else from Ile-Rien.

Somehow approaching the liner by sea was more daunting than just walking up to her on the dock; the *Ravenna* was free now and all-powerful in her element. As they drew steadily closer to that great gray wall, Tremaine suddenly remembered the smashed warehouse and the sheared-off pier, victims of a miscalculation during the ship's leave-taking from Port Rel. It had seemed funny at the time; it didn't now.

The pilot brought the little boat alongside the wall between dangling cables, then worked frantically with the other crewman to get them locked in place at the bow and stern. With the others, Tremaine stared nervously at the huge hull so dangerously close that she could count rivets. Gerard stood at the wheel, holding it steady as the two seamen worked. She saw Gyan up toward the bow with Arites and Dyani; he looked a little better though his face was gray in the dim light. He was staring at the *Ravenna* with nervous astonishment. Halian shouldered his way back through the others, his face intent, leaning over to ask Tremaine, "What are they doing?"

Giliead and Ilias both leaned in to hear her answer. She swallowed to clear her throat. "They hook those cables to the front and the back and then there's an electric winch to haul the boat up to the deck where they uh . . . keep boats." She knew about the procedure in principle but had never gone through it herself.

Giliead and Halian exchanged a dubious look, and Ilias leaned back on the rail, craning his neck to stare up at the height above them.

Halian nodded in resignation, squeezed her arm, and said, "Don't tell anyone else."

Finally one of the seamen signaled to those waiting above and the lifeboat started to lift, moving a little in the wind. Some men shifted and called out in alarm, but Halian snapped at them to be quiet. It seemed to take forever, and Tremaine tightened her grip on the bench, reminding herself that if the Rienish woman who was supposed to be blasé about all this got hysterical, everybody else was bound to do it too. She saw portholes in the *Ravenna*'s side, then larger windows streaked with water from the spray, then suddenly the boat swayed in toward an open deck, bumping against the ship's railing.

Tremaine stumbled as she stood and Giliead caught her arm to help her. A seaman held a gate in the ship's railing open and she stepped up on a bench and climbed through it, finding herself on the *Ravenna*'s polished wooden deck in a milling confusion of sailors, freed prisoners and people she vaguely recognized from the Viller Institute. The deck was rolling, but it was nothing after being thrown around in the little launch. The wind was still harsh, but the other stowed lifeboats, their canopies flattened down, hung overhead in their curved davits, forming a sheltering partial roof for the deck.

A little dazed, Tremaine noticed some of the sailors were women, their hair cropped short or tightly bound back under their caps. Early losses at the beginning of the war meant there were now more women serving in the army and the fragments left of the navy than ever before in Rienish history. It didn't surprise Tremaine that the *Ravenna,* designated as a last-ditch evacuation transport when the Pilot Boat had failed to return with the sphere, had ended up with a lot of female crew. It also meant they would all have only a few years experience at most and that none had ever worked on a ship like this before.

Tremaine watched the others clamber off the boat, then Gerard appeared at her side, guiding her to an open hatch. A seaman stood beside it, motioning for them to hurry. Tremaine dragged her feet, looking back to make sure the Syprians were following, then ducked inside.

Getting out of the wind was an immediate relief; with everyone

else, Tremaine jostled down a narrow wood-paneled stairwell that
opened abruptly into a large area, brightly lit and teeming with
refugees from the Gardier base, more Viller Institute staff and crew
members trying to get them all to go somewhere. Voices spoke urgently in Rienish, Maiutan, Parscian; freed slaves who had held together throughout the battle and the trek across the island were falling
down on the tiled floor and weeping with relief. Tremaine stumbled
and leaned on a wall of finely polished cherrywood. Over the heads
of the crowd, she spotted green marble pillars and the top of a
glassed-in kiosk. "Promenade deck," she said to herself, relieved. Now
she had her bearings; they had come down a full level from the boat
deck above and were in the ship's main hall and shopping arcade. Past
the people clustering around she could see that the glass cabinets for
the shops along the walls were dark and empty.

"Gerard!" Someone forced his way through the crowd. "There
you are," he said, as if Gerard had been deliberately concealing himself. It was Breidan Niles, the sorcerer who had brought the *Queen
Ravenna* through the etheric world-gate to this temporary safety. He
had narrow features, fair hair slicked back and wore an exquisitely tailored country walking suit. Despite the appearance of a man who
should be lounging decoratively at one of the expensive and fashionable cafés along the Boulevard of Flowers, Niles had been working on
the Viller Institute's defense project as long as Gerard. As the other
primary sorcerer on the project, his role had been to stay in Ile-Rien
to watch over things there; this evacuation had been his first chance
to travel through the gate.

Before Niles could continue, Gerard interrupted. "There's a problem. We're holding an enemy sorcerer called Ixion." Gerard gestured
toward the damp canvas-wrapped bundle Giliead was just depositing
on the floor. "He isn't a Gardier; he's a native collaborator. He's apparently perfected a consciousness-transference spell that can take effect at the moment of his death. Now he seems to be in some sort of
comatose state. Giliead here is something of an expert on this subject
and he believes it's very possible that Ixion has another body waiting
somewhere that he can transfer into if we attempt to harm this one."

"I see." The crowd noise rose and fell around them, but Niles
stroked his chin thoughtfully, eyeing the quiescent bundle as if they
were standing in a quiet library. "No chance we could tempt him over
to our side?"

Gerard's mouth twisted in distaste. "I rather doubt it. From what our allies tell us the Syprian sorcerers are all quite mad. My experience with Ixion certainly bears that out."

Niles's frown deepened. He pulled a booklet with a printed cover out of his coat pocket and began to flip hurriedly through it. Tremaine stared. It looked like a tourist brochure. "What is that?" she demanded.

"A map of the ship for passengers," Niles explained. "There were bundles of them in the purser's office. They come in handy since so many of the crew were assigned here just yesterday." He glanced at Gerard. "Thorny problem. But this Ixion isn't resistant to our spells like the Gardier?"

"No, not resistant at all, fortunately." Gerard pushed damp hair out of his face. "Does the ship have a brig?"

"No, but there's a secure area meant for stowaways. That's where your Gardier prisoners have been packed off to." Niles's brows lifted as he studied the map. "The ship does have an extensive cold-storage capability."

Gerard smiled thinly. "That's a thought."

Giliead touched Tremaine's arm, asking uneasily, "What are they saying about Ixion?"

Tremaine started. Listening to Gerard and Niles talk, she had almost drifted off. "They've thought of a place to keep him," she explained, switching back to Syrnaic with an effort and trying to look alert. "A locked cold room somewhere."

He nodded, pressing his lips together. "I'll take him there."

"No!" One of the Syprians protested. Tremaine craned her neck and saw it was Dannor. *Of course.* "You brought us here, you stay with us."

Tremaine saw Halian's face suffuse with red. Ilias muttered something under his breath that hadn't been included in the sphere's translation spell. But it was obvious the others agreed, except maybe Arites, who was staring around in anxious curiosity. *It's a good thing they don't know Niles is a sorcerer,* Tremaine realized. Ilias knew from his brief visit to Ile-Rien, but he didn't look inclined to mention it. The Syprians had gotten used to Gerard, but there was no telling how they would react to another Rienish sorcerer, especially as unsettled as they were now.

Watching with concern, Gerard told Giliead, "It's all right, we can take care of it ourselves. I still have a ward of impermeability on Ixion."

Giliead hesitated, threw a dark look at Dannor, then said reluctantly, "All right."

"Very well." Gerard turned to Tremaine as Niles called over a couple of men to take Ixion. "Will you let me have the sphere?"

She nodded, handing him the bag wordlessly. The lights were too bright, and everything was taking on a surreal tint, probably a product of her exhaustion. As he pushed off after Niles, Florian appeared, saying, "Were you the last, did everyone make it?"

Tremaine stared at her blankly. Florian, with her red hair tied tightly back and her face pale, seemed oddly normal against the chaotic background. Tremaine shook herself and nodded a shade too rapidly. "Yes, we were the last. Everyone made it."

"Good." Florian relaxed in relief. "I've got to go, I need to help them get some people down to the hospital."

"Good luck," Tremaine managed as the other girl slipped away through the crowd. She looked at the Syprians gathered around her. Dyani had fetched up next to Tremaine and she anxiously eyed the light in the wall above their heads. It was encased in a smooth crystal sheath mounted in a brass base. It took Tremaine a moment to realize what was wrong, then she said hurriedly, "The lights aren't magic, they just look that way." *We need to get out of here*, she thought wearily. She stood on tiptoes to see over the heads of the crowd; her legs felt like rubber.

"This way," she said in Syrnaic and turned to follow the wall around. By this method she found the grand stairway at the back of the large chamber. She led the way down the carpeted steps, feeling the tension in her nerves ease as they left the noisy crowd behind. She glanced back to make sure the Syprians were following and saw Giliead and Halian both looking around, probably doing head counts. Gyan was walking by himself but holding on to the wooden banister with another man at his elbow watching him worriedly. Dannor, who had started the mutiny, looked wary, and she was glad to see Ilias was right behind him.

The next deck was the First Class Entrance Hall she, Florian and Ilias had passed through when they had boarded the *Ravenna* in Port Rel. It was brightly lit now, the fine wood walls and the marble-tiled floor gleaming, and nearly as crowded as the main hall. Tremaine continued down to the next deck, finding a smaller carpeted lounge, mercifully unoccupied, with one wall taken up by the steward's office. It was covered in sleek wood and had etched glass windows; there was a light on inside and the door stood open. Tremaine hesitated then decided not to bother them. If she did, it would just give someone the opportunity to give her a lot of unnecessary instructions and orders.

Four large corridors led off from here, two toward the bow and two toward the stern. She picked the nearest and led the way down toward what should be the First Class staterooms. The corridor seemed to run most of the length of the ship, the patterned carpet making her a little dizzy as her eye followed it. The doors were in little vestibules opening off the corridor; she picked one at random. There was only one doorway in this vestibule, so she hoped that meant it was a big room. "This is the place," she said over her shoulder, trying the handle. It was locked. She stepped back and gestured. "Can somebody open this?"

Halian stepped forward, took the handle and applied his shoulder to the fine-grained but light wooden door. Something cracked in the jamb and it swung obligingly open. It was dark inside and smelled dusty, unused. Tremaine stepped in, fumbling for the wall switches.

Behind her, Dyani whispered like a litany, "The lights aren't curses, they just look like it."

"It's all right," Ilias told her, managing to sound as if he believed it. "Really."

"Are there curses here?" somebody asked Giliead.

He hesitated an instant too long. "No."

Tremaine found two call buttons for the stewards before finally pushing the button for the lights. As the lamps flickered to life she saw she had struck gold. The lights were milky crystal lozenges set into cherrywood-veneered walls and the floor had a deep tawny carpet. If Giliead could sense spells it might be the concealment wards protecting the ship from the Gardier; or the staterooms in this section might have been warded against thieves at the commercial liner's commission. If they had, nothing had happened when the door was forced open. She walked through a small foyer to a sitting room with gold-upholstered chairs and two couches. The built-in writing desk, the silk pillows and the rich red drapes concealing the portholes in the far wall were all meant to make it look like the best hotel in Vienne rather than a ship's cabin.

The Syprians followed her with subdued murmurs of admiration at the furnishings. Gyan dropped down on one of the couches, clutching his head and groaning. Halian turned and in a grim tone that reminded Tremaine that he had raised at least two children, said, "None of you better break anything, I'm saying that right now."

Breathing space immediately formed around a delicate little marquetry table.

Muttering, "There's got to be beds somewhere." Tremaine shouldered her way through and fumbled at the latch of a sliding door in the other wall. She pushed it open to reveal a dining room with a fine wood table, more upholstered chairs, another built-in desk and chest of drawers, and another couch.

"Is it all like this?" Dyani asked in an awed whisper. Tremaine glanced back at her and saw the girl seemed to be over her fright. She looked more intrigued than afraid now. Ilias hadn't liked the ship much either, until he had seen some of the more richly decorated public rooms. The Syprians used a lot of color in the painted walls and floor mosaics of their own homes, and the rich fabric and decoration must seem comfortable and familiar to them, unlike the starkness of the Gardier base.

"Normally they charge a lot of money to stay here," Tremaine told her, stepping into the dining room. She knew there were even better suites available, forward on the deck above the Promenade, just below where the captain and the chief engineer had their quarters. Those were the ones meant for members of the royal family.

Pressing the switches for the lights as she went, Tremaine found two more unobtrusive panel doors that led into equally lavish bedrooms, with two double beds each and accompanying vanities and chests of drawers in the same cherrywood. There was also a smaller plainer bedroom that might be the maid's quarters though it was probably better than any of the Third Class rooms, and a large bathroom with gleaming taps and walls that looked like alabaster but probably weren't. She was momentarily stymied by the fact that all the beds had been stripped to the mattress covers; going off in search of the laundry, wherever it was in the bowels of the ship, was not high on her list of what to do next. But by opening all the doors and drawers she discovered a cabinet in the maid's room with neatly folded linens, towels and silk bedcovers, all in red or gold to match the curtains and carpets. They weren't musty because the seals on the cabinet doors were nearly airtight, and as she piled them into Dyani's arms the faint faded scent of lavender laundry soap puffed up from the folds. It was odd; the people who had carefully cleaned up after this suite's occupants on the ship's last voyage had probably never imagined that the next time she left port would be to carry refugees away from a devastated Ile-Rien.

In the sitting room everyone was finally starting to settle down. Ilias had shown the others how to get hot water out of the bathroom taps and Giliead was in there tending Gyan's head wound; Arites, deprived of paper and writing implements by the Gardier, was walking around muttering to himself, probably trying to memorize details; some of the men had just curled up in corners and gone to sleep. Tremaine found herself standing in front of the mural on the dining room wall, a surrealist mix of curves and angles. One of the men whose name she thought was Kias—big, olive-skinned, with frizzy dark hair falling past his shoulders—asked, "What is that supposed to be?"

"I don't know," Tremaine replied honestly. Her last dose of strong coffee had worn off far too long ago and the world felt distant and strange. The surrealist mural didn't help that sensation.

There was a knock at the door and several people flinched. "What now?" Tremaine grumbled and went to answer it.

Ilias followed her into the foyer, saying under his breath, "Did you steal this room too?"

Ilias had maintained that Tremaine's method of getting the *Ravenna* diverted to the Institute's use was stealing; that he was technically correct just made it worse. "How very helpful." Tremaine glared at him, then opened the door.

It was an older woman, slender, her graying dark hair neatly arranged and her face bare of cosmetics. She wore a plain but well-tailored blue-gray wool suit. Tremaine thought she might be one of the Institute's secretaries or administrators but didn't recognize her. The woman lifted her brows and said calmly, "Oh, it must be Miss Valiarde from the Viller Institute. They said you'd be somewhere with all these young men." She smiled admiringly at Ilias, who was leaning against the other wall, displaying more bare chest and arms than one usually got to see in Ile-Rien since the ballet, the opera and the more interesting demimonde theaters and dining establishments had shut down for the duration. He smiled engagingly back at her. Tremaine suspected the Syprians were going to prove popular, at least among the Rienish on board. "We're just trying to keep track of everyone," the woman explained, "So we can get all these poor people into rooms. I'll note down that you're in charge of this suite. . . ." She wrote rapidly on the clipboard she carried.

Gratified as she was to actually be recognized, Tremaine had a sudden qualm at being "in charge" of anything at the moment. "What do

I need to do?" she asked, shifting to lean casually against the door and cover the broken lock with her body.

"Just make sure the dead-lights—the metal covers over the portholes—stay fixed in place. There's plenty of freshwater for drinking but do have everyone use the saltwater taps for bathing. And here," She pulled one of the ship's map booklets from her pocket and showed Tremaine two areas marked in pen. "If anyone needs medical attention, Dr. Divies is set up in the ship's hospital with the army surgeon, and some volunteers are going to try to serve a hot meal in the First Class Dining Room in a few hours."

Tremaine took the booklet, finding herself smiling. "They're ambitious."

The woman caught her meaning and smiled back. "Yes, if there's any delay, it'll be because they've mislaid themselves in those huge kitchens." She checked her notes again. "Also, try to conserve the linens as much as possible. Getting the laundry operational is rather low priority at the moment. Oh"—the woman tucked her clipboard under her arm and extended a hand—"I've forgotten to introduce myself. I'm Lady Aviler."

Tremaine automatically shook the extended hand. The expensive but tastefully plain just-what-one-should-wear-to-an-evacuation clothing, the confident beau monde manner combined with the polite leer at Ilias all made sense; she was a member of Ile-Rien's nobility. The Aviler family had been highly placed in the Ministry as long as the Fontainons had been on the throne. She couldn't remember if it was Lady Aviler's son or husband or brother who had been minister in charge of the War Appropriations Committee. How had the woman ended up on the ship? Had she been in the group picked up at Chaire? And more importantly, did she know the orders Tremaine had brought to transfer the *Ravenna* to Colonel Averi and the Institute were forged? "This is Ilias," she managed, hoping to distract her.

Lady Aviler gave him a pleasant nod and a warm smile. "How very nice."

As Lady Aviler continued briskly up the corridor, Ilias leaned out to watch her. "Get back in here," Tremaine snapped, anxious to shut the door again. She was paranoid about her trick with the orders being uncovered. Not that it had been terribly well covered in the first place, but she hadn't had any time. *And really,* she told herself, *at this point there isn't much they could do about it.* Except, of course, throw her in the brig with Ixion and the Gardier. But the main thing was that it would be embarrassing and she knew it would tell too many people more about how her mind worked than was good for anybody, especially her.

Ilias stepped back in, giving her a wry look. "She was nice."

Tremaine grimly shut the door, heading back into the sitting room. "Sure she was."

Gyan was back out in the main room again, his head wound tended, resisting Halian's attempts to make him sit down. He demanded, "Do we know where we're headed, if the Gardier are still out there?"

Gardier. Oh, damn. Tremaine rubbed her forehead, trying to massage away the pounding headache. She needed to know what was going on out there too. "I'll go up and find out." She started for the door again.

Giliead stopped her, taking her by the shoulders and steering her back into the room. "No, you've done enough. You're about to fall down."

"I am not," Tremaine protested, stumbling.

"Yes, you are." Ilias took over, taking her arm and hauling her back through the dining room. Kias was still staring at the mural. "When's the last time you slept?"

"Don't ask hard questions." Tremaine rubbed her eyes. She wanted to say that she had to get back up to where the decisions were being made. The Viller Institute's money and authority meant nothing now, and she had only a toehold with the people who were running things. If she didn't hold on to it, she would lose even that.

Ilias steered her into the maid's room, and Tremaine gave in and collapsed on one of the narrow beds. The mattress was still bare but it was wonderfully comfortable. She was asleep in moments.

Ilias looked around for a blanket and Dyani handed him one out of the cupboard. She paused to run her hand over the dark red fabric, saying, "All the dyes match. And the weaving is so tight. How do they do that?"

"You should have seen their city," Ilias told her, covering Tremaine with the blanket. Her tousled hair and the shadows under her eyes made her look vulnerable and soft. When awake she was anything but, no matter what she seemed to think of herself. "And that was after the war with the Gardier."

Dyani took a deep breath, looking down at Tremaine worriedly.

"These people are so powerful. If they can't fight the Gardier with ships like these, how can we?"

Good question, Ilias thought grimly, but he squeezed her arm, and said, "We'll think of something."

Arites ducked his head in to whisper, "Halian wants to talk to you."

Ilias grunted an acknowledgment, having an idea of what Halian wanted. He stepped out past him. "How's your shoulder?"

"Good, see." Arites pulled the charred torn fabric of his shirt apart so Ilias could see the little round wound. "The wizard weapon sent a bolt right through me—there's a hole just like this on my back where it came out, but Gerard made the bleeding stop and a little later I saw the hole had closed up, like this."

Arites sounded rather pleased and enthusiastic about the whole thing, but then as far as Ilias could tell he had been born open-minded. Ilias absently flexed the arm he had broken in the wreck of the *Swift*. "Yes, they're good at that." The problem was, if everyone didn't keep quiet about it when they got back to Cineth, Arites might end up sentenced to a curse mark.

Ilias returned to the main room, seeing everyone was settled in the beds or collapsed in the padded chairs that looked almost as comfortable. Thunder rolled outside, distant and ominous; he could hear the wind trying to bore into the heavy metal hull, but not a hint of a draft came through. There was only the familiar sway of the deck underfoot to tell him he was on a ship.

He looked for Giliead and Halian and after a moment heard their voices out in the hall. He found them just outside the door, leaning against the dark wood walls of the little vestibule. The wizards lights out here, like those inside, were set back into the ceiling behind mist-colored glass ovals so they weren't harsh and bright. There was a carpet on this floor too, a gold-and-brown one with a pattern that dazzled the eye as it stretched the length of the corridor as far as Ilias could see, which was a pretty damn long way. By ducking his head a little he could tell it curved upward as it grew smaller with distance, until it vanished into shadow. He could hear voices speaking Rienish somewhere down there and saw a few men come out of a door, look around in confusion, then retreat.

Giliead saw he was looking at the curve in the floor and said ruefully, "It's hard to believe."

Ilias nodded, knowing what he meant. A building this large, espe-

cially constructed of metal, would have been enough of an amazement; that this was a living ship was almost incomprehensible.

Leaning against the opposite wall, Halian said in a low voice, "So?
Can we trust these people? And I don't mean our friends, I mean the
ones who give them their orders."

So Ilias was right, and it was time for this conversation. He glanced
at Giliead, who just looked thoughtful. Ilias leaned in the doorframe
next to him and said slowly, "Everything's as they said. I saw their
city. There were places that had been torn apart and burned to the
ground by the Gardier. The man who took Ixion away with Gerard is
another wizard." Ilias held out his arm, showing them the faded
bruises. "When the *Swift* sank I broke this, and he healed it."

Giliead took his arm, looking it over carefully. Ilias continued, "But
they have traitors, people who have sworn themselves to the Gardier
like the one who betrayed us on the island. Some captured Ander and
Florian and nearly killed them before we came back here."

Halian nodded, impatient. "That's to be expected in a wizard's war
like this." He stepped closer, his face serious. "I know you weren't
there long, but did they seem the kind of people we could ally with?"

Ilias stared at the floor. He didn't like this all being on his head; he
didn't want to mix what he wanted with what Cineth, let alone the
whole Syrnai, should do. In his gut he thought the Rienish would
make good allies; better than the Hisians, who made treaties only for
the pleasure of breaking them and thought everybody who looked
odd was a wizard. He told himself it wasn't just because the Rienish,
like the woman who had come to the door, never saw his curse mark
for what it was and that he liked being looked at like a man again. "All
I can tell you is that they treated me well." Glancing up at Giliead, he
added, "And it wasn't like the places here that fall under wizard's
rule." They had both seen what could happen to a village or town
taken over by a wizard: the people cursed into obedience and treated
like slaves. There were towns past the Bone Mountains in the dry
plains where wizards had held sway for generations, and the inhabitants were little better than cattle.

Giliead eyed Halian. "You're thinking of what to advise Nicanor
and Visolela." Nicanor was Halian's son by his last marriage and now
lawgiver of Cineth with his wife Visolela. It would be their decision
whether to recommend the alliance to Cineth's council or not, and
whichever way it decided, the rest of the city-states in the Syrnai were
likely to follow.

"We need an alliance." Halian pressed his lips together. "What they're doing now is just helping shipwrecked travelers, no more than any other civilized people would do. But when the Gardier return for vengeance we'll truly need their help."

Ilias shook his head regretfully. "They haven't been able to help themselves. When we left, their cities were falling," he said, trying to be honest. "But their god-thing can fight the Gardier in ways we can't. We'd be better off with their help than without it."

Halian looked at Giliead. When the cities of the Syrnai sent a representative to foreign lands, it was usually a Chosen Vessel, but they all knew this was different. "You agree?"

Giliead nodded, as if he had already made the decision sometime ago. "Yes."

Ilias took a deep breath. He had gone with Giliead to the Chaeans and to other lands, but he had the feeling that going with the Rienish would take them even further.

Halian leaned back against the wall, his face grave. He knew what this decision could mean. "Then we need someone to speak for us with them. Would Tremaine be a good choice?"

"She'd fight for us." Ilias snorted. "And I don't think she knows how not to fight dirty."

Giliead's mouth quirked. "That's true."

"All right." Halian stepped back, nodding to himself. This wasn't his first wizard war by a long stretch; Ilias just hoped it wasn't the last one for all of them. Halian already looked worn down and older than Ilias was used to thinking of him.

Giliead must have had the same thought. "Get some rest," he suggested.

Halian nodded wearily, clapping Ilias on the shoulder as he went back into the room. Ilias and Giliead looked at each other, then Giliead jerked his head down the hall, back toward the stairs. "I want to see what they did with Ixion."

Ilias nodded. He was tired, his head hurt from the storm and his scars ached, but he was too keyed up to sleep. Besides, it was their job to make sure there were no curses lying in wait so the place was safe for ungrateful bastards. As they started down the corridor, he said, "I'm going to kick the shit out of Dannor."

"He's an idiot," Giliead agreed grimly.

Dannor wasn't really an idiot and they both knew it, but Ilias was tired of his word being disregarded as worthless because of the curse mark. All his other years of experience at finding and killing wizards aside, a sane person might think that someone who had actually been cursed and survived would be the best judge of what was safe and what wasn't. *It's not as if you didn't ask for it,* he reminded himself. He took a breath, trying to look at it in perspective. "He was right."

Giliead gave him a sour look. "If you say that again I'm going to kick the shit out of you."

Caught by surprise, Ilias glowered back at him. "You think?" he said dangerously. They stopped, facing each other, but just then two Rienish women came into the corridor, and they had to step apart to give them room to get by. By the time the women had passed, glancing at them with nervous curiosity, the mutual urge to relieve their feelings by pummeling each other had faded. Still glaring at each other, they reached the room with the big staircase again and started up.

At the first landing Ilias stopped to get a better look at the Rienish-style painting mounted on the wall, forgetting his pique entirely. It showed a woman in a midnight black gown slashed with bloodred silk, a glitter of icy gems on her breast. She was sharp-featured but beautiful, with red hair coiled elaborately around her head. She was seated surrounded by a group of young men all in dark rich clothes, with long hair and beards. He had come across this kind of art when he had gone to Ile-Rien with Tremaine, Florian and Ander, and it was different from any type of painting he had ever seen before. "Look how they do this. It makes the people seem so real." He stepped closer to look at the brushstrokes.

Giliead put a hand on his shoulder and drew him back, adding matter-of-factly, "There's curses in that."

"Really?" Ilias fell back a wary step, startled. "Tremaine said the paintings didn't use curses."

"The ones in those rooms she took us to didn't. This one is different." Giliead held his hand over it, not quite touching it, frowning in concentration. "It doesn't feel dangerous. I don't think it was meant to be a trap. It's very old. Maybe it was painted by a wizard and his curses just . . . leaked into it."

"Oh." Relieved, Ilias stepped close again to examine the woman's image. "Maybe that's the woman the ship is named after." She looked like someone that would make Visolela feel threatened and defensive, so Ilias immediately wanted to like her. He jerked his chin toward the men gathered around her. "She had a lot of husbands." Warrior-husbands. They all wore swords, strange-looking ones with long narrow blades and rounded guards to deflect the sharp points. No one had worn swords when he had been to Ile-Rien, but he knew all the warriors must have been away fighting the Gardier.

Giliead nodded, studying the woman thoughtfully.

They went on up, finding the big room where they had first boarded less packed with people but still crowded, everyone babbling in unfamiliar languages. Ilias recognized some of the freed slaves by their ragged brown Gardier clothes. From here he could see there were round columns of polished green stone flanking colorfully patterned carpets and more of the cushioned furniture. There were glass-walled rooms along the sides, though they seemed to be empty.

"I don't see Gerard." Giliead let out his breath, sounding both resigned and annoyed. "This is going to be like looking for a pebble in a quarry. Any ideas?"

"No. . . . Wait, there's somebody." Craning his neck, Ilias saw a familiar sleek blond head bobbing through the crowd and started forward, shouldering his way through. It was the other wizard, Niles.

"Hey," he called when he was in earshot. "Niles."

The man turned, a little startled, and eyed them dubiously.

"We need to find Gerard," Ilias said. He was annoyed to find himself speaking slowly, as if that would help. The only word the man would recognize was the other wizard's name.

Niles lifted his brows, enlightened, and motioned for them to follow, turning to head for the opposite end of the big chamber. It was easier this time because people had noticed them and were moving aside, mostly so they could stare. It didn't bother Ilias since he had done his share of that in the Rienish city. And it wasn't unfriendly staring, like the Gardier or when he and Giliead had traveled to an enemy city or port; it was just honest curiosity.

Niles led them to the back of the big chamber, down a short corridor where the tile floor turned to rich green carpet. It opened into another stairwell, this one gently lit by cloudy glass panels in the walls, each etched with graceful waterbirds and plants. They went up a couple of decks, through an empty carpeted chamber, then a metal door that led to another stairway, this one narrow and without the colorful appointments of the others. The walls here were just the bare metal bones of the ship and as they went up Ilias caught the scent of damp outdoor air, as if a hatch was open somewhere. He wondered how far they were above the water. "How do you steer something like this," he said softly. It must be like trying to steer a floating city.

Giliead shook his head slightly. "The steering platform has to be in the bow."

"But how does that work?" Ilias protested. They came up into a short passage with four doors and Niles chose one, stepping inside. Ilias looked cautiously past him, seeing a room with wooden walls unadorned except for two small windows looking out into a cloudy gray sky. In the corner there was a long cabinet with narrow drawers, very like the one where they had found the maps inside the Gardier's flying whale. The men in the room were leaning over a big table spread with maps and papers, studying them intently. Permeating the air was the strong odor of that awful drink the Rienish seemed unable to live without. The Rienish sailors had identical clothing the way the Gardier did, but instead of dull brown they wore short dark blue jackets with bands of red on the upper arms, the front decorated with small round ornaments of bright metal. *The color of their clothes can't be the only difference between them and the Gardier,* Ilias thought, feeling a little uncertain in spite of himself. He glanced up at Giliead, whose brow quirked, as if he was thinking the same.

Then past the other men he saw Gerard, leaning over the table and looking reassuringly ordinary in his Syprian clothes.

"Gerard," Ilias said in relief.

"There you are." Gerard straightened up. He spoke to Niles for a moment in Rienish, then adjusted the pieces of glass he wore over his eyes and switched back to Syrnaic to ask them, "Everything all right? Oh, this is the shipmaster, Captain Marais."

One of the other men glanced up, studied them with sharp attention, nodding as Gerard repeated their names. Ilias was surprised to see how young he looked, though his face was reddened and weathered from long experience at sea.

Giliead nodded to the man, then asked Gerard, "Where's Ixion?"

"Ah, yes." Gerard's expression hardened as it always did at any mention of Ixion. It was one of the reasons Ilias trusted him. "We've got him stowed away in a specially warded chamber. Would you like to see it—him?"

Giliead let out a breath and glanced at Ilias. "Not really, but I should anyway."

"How do they steer this ship?" Ilias asked, only partly wanting to delay the visit to Ixion. He was really curious.

"Ah . . ." Gerard looked around absently. "I can show you the wheelhouse, it's right up here."

In Rienish he spoke to the captain again, who nodded and waved them on. Gerard stepped to the half-open hatch in the far wall.

They followed him into the next room and Giliead stopped so abruptly in the doorway that Ilias stepped on him. A little wary, he peered past him to see a big room, the opposite wall lined with large square windows.

Green-gray sea stretched out in all directions and they were so high in the air the heavy clouds seemed almost within reach. Ilias had seen the view from the bow before but they were higher up this time; in daylight, even the half-light of the storm, it was far more breathtaking. "A floating mountain," Giliead said softly.

The two men in the room turned to look curiously at them but didn't object to their presence. One stood before the center window, holding on to a wooden wheel mounted on a post. Gerard exchanged a few words with the other, who nodded and made an expansive welcoming gesture.

Giliead moved further inside, still caught by the view, and Ilias followed him, looking around. There wasn't much there he understood the use for except the windows. The other sailor stepped to one of the waist-high white pillars that studded the floor, taking hold of the lever that sprouted out of the top and pushing it forward. Baffled, Ilias glanced at Giliead, who shrugged slightly to show he had no idea either.

Gerard noticed and explained, "Those are the engine telegraphs. They're used to communicate the helmsman's instructions to the engineers in each of the four main engines." He indicated the squiggles on the pillar's side that might be writing. "Slow, full, stop, and so on."

Ilias exchanged a look with Giliead. Some of those words hadn't meant anything, but he thought he had caught the gist of it. It was more evidence that what all the Rienish were saying was true and that the ship didn't really use curses to sail. Wizards—the wizards they knew anyway—would have just cursed these men below to do whatever they wanted. Not require them to read their orders from signal flags or whatever these things did.

Gerard nodded to the man holding the wheel. "The helmsman steers from there. At the moment we're on a sort of zigzag course to avoid any Gardier airships that might be accompanying the gunship. Our advantage is that we're much faster in the open sea." He pointed to two glass boxes set above the center window. "That indicator shows the course heading, the other one shows the angle the rudder is making with the ship."

"You steer with that?" Giliead's expression was doubtful.

Gerard smiled wryly. "Yes, it's a little daunting to know that a ship of . . . Well, of however many tons is being guided by that. Supposedly it can be moved with one finger."

"She sheared off the end of the dock when she left port," Ilias told Giliead. "And smashed a house."

Giliead looked impressed. So did Gerard, for that matter. The wizard said, "Did she? I suppose accidents will— Anyway, let me take you to see Ixion."

They went down this time, past endless metal corridors and places where heavy pipes covered the ceilings. Except for the steady movement underfoot you could forget you were on a ship. The air had a slightly bitter metallic taint to it but it wasn't hot and moved as if there was a strong draft somewhere. The passages were as complex as the caves under the Isle of Storms. Ilias groaned under his breath, wishing they could leave trail signs. He kept telling himself if this ship was inhabited by anything other than people, the Ricnish surely would have mentioned it.

There were trail signs of a kind; down here they were painted on the slick gray metal walls or doors and on the decks above they were embossed in what looked like copper or brass. If they stayed here any length of time, learning to read the markings would become imperative, but right now Ilias couldn't see any pattern to them at all.

"How many wizards are aboard?" Giliead asked Gerard suddenly.

"Niles and I are the only Lodun-trained sorcerers on the ship that I know of." Gerard glanced over his shoulder as they left a stairwell for a narrow corridor. Before they had left the room at the top of the ship, he had picked up a familiar battered leather bag and now carried it slung over his shoulder; it held the sphere, the Rienish godthing. "There are a few others assigned to the Institute whose training was interrupted by the war, like Florian. The ship did stop to pick up more passengers at Chaire before creating the etheric world-gate; there may be some among them as well." He hesitated. "I was told that when the border fell, the Queen released all sorcerers from army service to flee to Parscia or Capidara. I'm . . . not certain how many would have made it."

Ilias glanced back at Giliead, who was unhelpfully wearing his stony expression. The thought of unknown wizards aboard made his nerves jump, but he reminded himself again it was different for the Rienish.

Gerard added more briskly, "I meant to tell you, I've spoken to Colonel Averi and Captain Marais and as soon as the storm passes and we're certain we've evaded the Gardier gunboat, we'll head back toward the mainland and put you all ashore somewhere near Cineth." He added hastily, "But not near enough to alarm anyone in the city. You'll have to let us know what would be a suitable spot."

Ilias hesitated, not sure if they should say anything about the idea of an alliance yet or wait for Halian. He felt out of his depth. Brow furrowed, Giliead said, "We were hoping you would stay to talk to Nicanor and Visolela."

"Really?" Gerard turned to regard them, his face serious. "We had assumed that would be impossible because of your beliefs."

Giliead shrugged slightly. "It's not . . . impossible."

Gerard gave him a thoughtful nod. "I see. I'll speak to the military commander about it."

As they moved on, Ilias exchanged a guarded look with Giliead. At least it had been suggested and Ilias supposed that was all he and Giliead could do without stepping on Nicanor's sensitive toes. Halian's idea seemed only common sense, but considering how much trouble the council had had with the very idea of wizards as allies, they had a steep hill to climb.

More sailors, men and women both, came and went down here, either dressed in the now familiar blue or stripped to brief white shirts stained with sweat and some dark foul-smelling stuff. They passed through a room where three men stood guard, all armed with the weapons that shot metal pellets to kill at a distance. The Gardier used these too, but the Rienish insisted they didn't need curses to work, but a black powder made from various metals. As deadly as the weapons were, they might as well have used curses.

"Here we are." Gerard stopped in front of a heavy door with a round glass window in the center. "The wards I placed around Ixion should keep him inside. Considering I used the sphere and that Niles has augmented my efforts with his own wards, it should be secure." Gerard rubbed his forehead, letting out his breath. "Of course, we also have the armed guards."

Giliead held out his hand to the door. "I can feel the curses—spells." He added the Rienish word a little self-consciously. From what he had told Ilias, Giliead and the others owed their lives to Gerard; if he hadn't given them a curse to immobilize Ixion, they would never have gotten out of the Gardier cells. Not without making a demon's bargain with Ixion himself.

Giliead stepped up to look through the glass and Gerard told him, "Niles and I believe your first instinct was entirely correct. Attempting to kill him would have been a mistake; I think if this body is still viable, the spell to transfer his consciousness won't initiate. Such a spell couldn't be cast in the usual way; it would have to be triggered by the sorcerer's death or severe injury." He hesitated, then gestured absently. "If he can somehow trigger it on his own, we won't know until he does it."

Giliead nodded thoughtfully. He held his hand close to the door without quite touching it. "It's cold. Is that part of what's keeping him inside?"

"No, that's actually not magic. This room is connected to one of the ship's refrigeration units. They create the cold." Gerard eyed the door. "We thought if we made it somewhat uncomfortable for him, he might be encouraged to break cover."

Giliead's mouth twisted ruefully and Ilias thought, *Won't that be fun.* He would have preferred it if Ixion never broke cover.

Giliead stood back so Ilias could look. Wary of what he might see, he stepped up to peer through the glass, feeling the cold radiating from the door. He saw a small metal-walled room, brightly lit. Ixion's new body, still clad in the brown Gardier clothing, lay on the bare floor. The skin on his face had a white waxy look and his features were blunt, like melted clay. From what they could tell, Ixion had grown this body in his vats, much the same way he had made the howlers, the grend, and the other creatures he had created to populate the island. It looked uncannily like his real body, the one Giliead had decapitated last year.

Ilias stepped back, ignoring the cold knot in his stomach. It was just a body, locked in a room and held helpless by Rienish curses, but thinking that didn't seem to help. "So when can we kill him? When we're far from the island?" He looked at Gerard.

Gerard glanced at Giliead and let out his breath. Ilias sensed he wasn't going to like the answer; Gerard looked exactly like a healer who was about to tell you that your leg had to come off. Giliead folded his arms and stared at the floor, as if he suspected what was coming. Gerard said slowly, "The problem is that this kind of spell is outside our experience. The books—and the people—who would be able to help are back in Ile-Rien, in the city of Lodun, trapped behind a Gardier blockade. And I suppose Ile-Rien itself has been overrun by now." He shook his head, as if just remembering, as if the idea was still unreal. He cleared his throat and his gaze turned thoughtful. "One solution might be for us to take Ixion back to our world."

Ilias ran a hand through his hair, looking away. *And if he escapes and finds his way back?* He knew Gerard was trying to help, but the thought of Ixion off alive somewhere, still plotting, with them helpless to do anything about it, was the last thing he needed.

Expressionless, Giliead said, "We'll think about it." After a moment, he added belatedly, "Thank you."

Ilias heard quick footsteps out in the corridor and Niles, the other wizard, leaned into the room, his face flushed. In Rienish he spoke hurriedly to Gerard, who answered in the same language, sounding exasperated. Niles replied and they argued back and forth for a moment.

Finally, Gerard turned to them, looking both harassed and enthusiastic. "Niles believes he has an idea for protecting the ship against the Gardier's disruption spell. It sounds unconventional, but— We can't afford to be choosy at the moment. Can you find your own way back?"

Giliead nodded, saying, "Good luck," as Gerard hurried away. Then he turned to Ilias, his face drawn in concern, taking breath to speak. Ilias interrupted him briskly with, "One of us should stay here. They don't know what he's like." He didn't want to talk about Ixion, not anymore, not right now. "I'll take the first turn, you go get some sleep."

Giliead hesitated, then obviously decided to accept the change of subject. He nodded, absently looking around for the door to the corridor.

"You know the way back, right?" Ilias asked, suddenly not sure if he did himself.

Giliead shrugged and gave him a farewell clap on the shoulder. "No, but I wanted a better look around, anyway."

Chapter 3

Gerard asked Gyan what the god was. He asks everyone that. Gyan said that didn't the Rien have gods of their own? Gerard said yes but that they didn't choose Vessels or give advice, and Gyan asked what they did with their time? Apparently no one knows.

—"Ravenna's voyage to the Unknown Eastlands,"
V. Madrais Translation

Tremaine woke from a dream about being on the train to Parscia with Florian's mother to find herself staring at an unfamiliar metal ceiling painted a cheery yellow. Through the bed she could feel the rolling movement and remembered she was on the *Ravenna*. The distant howl of the wind, muffled and rendered impotent by so much metal and wood, told her the Gardier's storm still pursued them.

She sat up in the narrow maid's bed, recognizing the warm lump next to her as Dyani. The girl was curled up around a pillow, sound asleep. Gyan was in the bed against the opposite wall, buried under a blanket and snoring faintly. There was a clock built into the paneled wall, but it was electric, powered by the ship's system. It would have started up with the generators and she doubted anyone had bothered to go around setting the clocks in the passenger cabins. Tremaine scratched her head vigorously and tried to get her brain to focus. She needed to find out what time it was, where they were, what the hell was going on.

She climbed out over the other girl and stood, stretching carefully. *Oh, God, I hurt.* She had been relatively fit and used to hard work after her stint with the Siege Aid, but after the past few days her muscles ached down to the bone. She felt bleary and incompetent as she opened the door and stumbled out.

Everyone seemed to be asleep, piled in the beds, with those who couldn't fit stretched out on the floor. Some of them had decided to shed their clothes and Tremaine, used to spending time backstage at theaters, regarded all the bare skin with bemusement. The lights she had turned on earlier still burned; she realized the Syprians wouldn't have wanted to touch the switches. It didn't matter as the electric glow, softened by frosted glass, didn't seem to be keeping anyone awake. The air was warm but not too musty or close, despite all the people in the suite. She stopped in the dining area, reaching up to adjust the small vent near the ceiling. It was a round bakelite orifice spewing air, with a metal lever to turn the inner ring to cool or warm, or to close it off entirely. The draft from it was strong; it might be outside air, funneled through the ventilation system by the ship's own movement. There were fans mounted on some of the walls as well.

She continued on, pausing at the raised threshold of the bathroom. It was the only room nobody was sleeping in. *You could have a bath,* she thought, tempted. *With hot water and soap.* She didn't think she was awake enough yet to make that serious a decision. She stepped in to get a drink of water from the tap, finding one of the small china tumblers still there though someone had carried off the matching carafe. Several pairs of boots were drying on the black-and-white tiles, the patched leather dyed in soft colors or stamped with fanciful designs. She leaned on the sink, looking into the mirror. Her mousy brown hair was getting shaggy and she pulled it back for an unobstructed view of her face. *No, still don't recognize that person,* she thought, resigned. Especially now, when she should be pale from the Vienne winter. Whoever that was in the mirror, her cheeks had a sprinkle of freckles and red patches from riding and sailing under this world's bright summer sun, as well as a nice patchwork of greenish yellow bruises. Giving up the unproductive self-scrutiny, she went back out into the main room.

In the sitting area Halian was stretched out on the couch, his face buried in a pillow. Giliead was still awake, sitting on the floor with his back propped against one of the chairs. His face drawn and thoughtful, he was staring absently into the foyer where the door to the corridor stood open. As he glanced up at her, Tremaine asked, "This is going to seem like an odd question, but is it day or night?"

"It's night," he told her, his voice low to keep from waking the others. "The storm is starting to die down."

She settled on the floor, cross-legged, and yawned. She wasn't sure how he knew that about the storm, unless he could tell it from the sound of the wind. She propped her chin on her hand, watching him. His long braided hair, the soft sun-faded colors of his worn clothes, made an interesting contrast with the smooth yellow upholstery and elegant lines of the armchair behind him. "Couldn't you sleep?"

"I did for a while. Too much to think about." He looked at the door again as two Rienish sailors passed in agitated conversation. "I was wondering what your people are like."

That was too abstract a concept to be discussing at this hour. But Tremaine found herself saying, "I don't know what my people are like anymore. I used to know, before the war. When it started, it seemed like the cities, the country just . . . stopped." Like Lodun, trapped inside its defenses by the Gardier's spells, perhaps not even realizing yet that Ile-Rien had fallen. "Things that were important to us just stopped."

Giliead accepted that with a nod, without demanding further explanation. This was probably the longest private conversation she had had with him so far. From his expression he was turning her words over thoughtfully. Did all Syprians accept people at face value or was it just the Andrien family, she wondered. They all acted as if not understanding you was their problem, not yours. She looked around, distracted. "Where's Ilias?"

"He's with the others guarding Ixion. He's worried about what we're going to do about him." Giliead shook his head uneasily and it was obvious Ilias wasn't the only one who was worried. "Even if we take Ixion far from the island before we kill him, we won't know if it's worked or not. Not until he comes back again."

"I hadn't thought of that." Tremaine felt a little chill settle in her stomach. It was the kind of problem Arisilde had been excellent at solving. But all they had left of Arisilde was what remained in the sphere. The other powerful sorcerers who might have helped were trapped or dead at Lodun, trapped or dead at the overrun Aderassi front, and if the Gardier had reached Vienne by now, trapped or dead there too. "Couldn't Gerard think of anything?"

Giliead's expression grew a little less distant. He shrugged slightly and said, "He's offered to take Ixion along when you go back to your land. And we appreciate the offer, but it would be better if we could get rid of him ourselves. If Ilias could see it was done and over." He hesitated, then added a touch stiffly, "He has nightmares."

And again, Ilias isn't the only one who'd like to see it done and over, Tremaine thought, watching his face. Under the worry, Giliead looked guilty. That had never been something her father had suffered from. *If you don't care for the consequences then don't commit the crime,* Nicholas had said once, years ago when she was too young to understand that he meant it literally. But not everybody understood what the consequences were likely to be. And not everybody had a choice. *And you don't know how he felt after your mother was killed,* some traitor voice said. She shook herself, pushing the uncomfortable thoughts away. "I have nightmares too, sometimes," she said, though her dream of the *Ravenna* sinking seemed far away now.

Giliead shook his head, ready to change the subject. "Gerard also said as soon as the storm clears and the Gardier leave the area, the ship will turn inland and they'll put us ashore where we can reach Cineth easily. Then you'll leave."

Tremaine frowned, rubbing her eyes. *I was afraid of that.* "Without stopping at Cineth?"

"Maybe." He looked at her, his face serious. "We told him we want an alliance, your people with ours."

Tremaine nodded slowly. As the Gardier had used the island as a staging area for raids on the Ile-Rien coast, it would make an excellent spot for Rienish troops to prepare to retake the country. They could use both spheres, Arisilde's and the one Niles had built, to open gateways to the coast or further inland, slipping spies, ships, armies through the etheric world-gates. If any Rienish armies had survived. They could still do it without Cineth's cooperation, but Tremaine didn't want to break that tenuous tie. "You think Nicanor and the others would go for this? An alliance with a world of wizards?"

Giliead looked away with a resigned expression. "I've given up trying to guess what Nicanor and Visolela will or won't do. But Halian seems to think so."

Tremaine frowned, trying to read his expression. "But we think Halian's an optimist."

A t first the Rienish guards tried to talk to Ilias, but realizing that was impossible, they fell to talking among themselves. He suspected they would like to ask about what they were guarding; he was just as glad they couldn't.

He had taken a seat on a wooden bench bolted to the wall and leaned back, stretching his legs out. He was beginning to get used to the feel of being underground, the metal walls, the strange noises and acrid scents in the air, though combined with the roll of a ship at sea it was passing strange. But as tired as he was, he didn't feel like dozing off. *Not with that thing only one wall away,* he thought, eyeing the door to Ixion's prison. One of the guards, studying him thoughtfully and perhaps too accurately reading his expression, went to the glass window to check on the wizard's sprawled body.

For years Ilias and Giliead had never known what Ixion looked like. The wizard had been too canny to ever face Giliead directly, sending creatures or laying subtle curse traps for him instead. Then the search had led them to a mountain village stalked by a curseling; the instant the survivors had described it they had known it was something Ixion was responsible for. It had fur and claws like an animal, but metal and wooden parts had been meshed with its flesh. It had killed the family of a man named Licias, one of the few who had been trying to hunt it. With his help they had destroyed the creature but Licias had been wounded. He was still suffering the loss of his family, alone in the village and not seeming to have many friends there. So they had taken him back to Cineth and Andrien House.

And he had been Ixion in disguise.

We should have asked more questions, Ilias thought, not for the first time, as he stared at the floor. *We should have found out he was new to the village, that no one saw the family he said the curseling killed.* But even if they had, would it have really made them suspicious of Licias? He had lived at Andrien in apparent friendship for months before he had finally revealed what and who he was.

Thinking about it, Ilias was beginning to wonder if the things the Rienish did, the way they used curses to build and cure and protect, was the way it was supposed to be. If Syprian wizards like Ixion had somehow looked at those things through a distorted glass, twisting them out of their original purpose into something terrible. It wasn't an idea he wanted to share with anybody but Giliead. Even Halian might think it was too extreme.

He glanced up as Gerard and Niles turned into the room, arguing animatedly in Rienish. Niles carried a leather-bound case over to the metal door that sealed Ixion's prison. Sitting on his heels to open the case, he took out several little glass pots and jars. Ilias sat up, feeling uneasy, but the containers seemed to hold various colored powders rather than anything disgusting. "What's he doing?" he asked Gerard.

Gerard sat next to him, holding the sphere in his lap and watching the other wizard critically. "If Niles is right—and of course he insists that he is—the chamber we've warded for Ixion will need to be excluded from this spell. Channeling the sphere's protective ability throughout the ship may interfere with the wards already in place. Those that shield the ship from view from overhead won't matter at a moment like that, but I'd rather not have the containment wards tampered with."

"Me neither." Ilias still didn't understand all the different Rienish words for curses, but he thought he had the idea. Niles took a sheaf of papers from his jacket and began drawing lines and circles at the base of the door, using the colored powders from the jars. As he added something from another container that looked like gold filings, Gerard made a critical comment in Rienish and got a sharp reply back.

Ilias eyed the sphere a little warily. "Is it really true there's somebody in there? Somebody you knew—know."

Gerard regarded the copper-colored ball with a kind of rueful resignation. "It seems so, unfortunately." He adjusted the glass pieces he wore over his eyes. "Arisilde was a very powerful sorcerer in Ile-Rien. He and Tremaine's father had been friends since they both attended the University of Lodun—that's a place for education, in history, law and medicine and many other things as well as for sorcery. He built this sphere after the design invented by Tremaine's foster grandfather, Edouard Viller." He took a deep breath, turning the tarnished metal ball over thoughtfully. Inside it something clunked. "Viller wasn't a sorcerer himself. He intended the spheres to allow a person with no magical ability to perform simple spells. But each sphere had to be charged by a sorcerer before it would work properly. The metal even seems to retain something of that sorcerer's essence. In the end Viller was never able to construct a sphere that would work unless the wielder had some small magical talent, no matter how slight." He shook his head, preoccupied. "Arisilde was the only one who could successfully duplicate the design, until Niles managed it with the sphere he constructed."

Ilias wet his lips. He was still trying to cope with the idea of wizards having friends, and presumably families, like normal people. "So he built it. How did he get inside it?"

Gerard absently rubbed at the tarnish with his sleeve. There was pain etched on his face as he contemplated the fate of the man he had known. "Arisilde might have been attempting to return from here to our world. Perhaps something happened during the transition, such as an attack by the Gardier, and the sphere he was using was destroyed. In an attempt to save himself, Arisilde somehow sent his soul and his consciousness into this sphere, which was stored at the Valiarde family home. This is Tremaine's theory, based on the sphere's responses toward her and its increasing abilities. It is just a theory." He glanced up, shaking his head grimly. "But after Gervas's revelation that the Gardier's crystal devices actually contain the souls of imprisoned sorcerers, it seems all too likely."

Tremaine decided to take that bath, then realized once she had wrestled her boots off that she hadn't yet retrieved her bag of belongings from the steward's office. The lure of clean underwear was too seductive to ignore, so she padded barefoot down the quiet corridor and up the stairs to the office. There she found it under the control of several women, some Institute personnel and some from the Chaire group of refugees, all apparently having signed on as Lady Aviler's minions. They offered to take the bag of Gerard's belongings to his cabin and Tremaine accepted, thinking that it would be interesting to see if Lady Aviler ended up leading a faction or being the power behind one. And Tremaine was certain there would be factions.

Walking back to the suite, listening to the quiet thrum of the ship, she decided grandly not to declare allegiance with any of them; it would be far more instructive to play them all against each other. She grinned to herself, giving up the fantasy. Attempting it in practice rather than theory sounded like a good way to get thrown off the boat.

As she passed one of the narrow cross corridors that connected the larger bow-to-stern passages, movement out of the corner of her eye startled her. Midway down the cross corridor stood two men, one in a civilian suit and the other in dark blue naval fatigues. Reflexes common to anyone who walked the less reputable parts of Vienne kept Tremaine moving with only a slight jerk of her head to betray she had noticed them; the set of their shoulders and the way they stood conveyed furtive activity, and she was fairly sure she had seen some object change hands. It might be nothing, and it was none of her business. War profiteering, the opium trade and other criminal pursuits had flourished in Ile-Rien since so many Prefecture officers and the sorcerers who had once assisted in investigations had been either killed in the bombings or gone into the military. It would be the same on this ship, which was going to be near impossible for anyone to police. She kept an ear cocked in case either man was foolish enough to pursue a potential witness, but neither came after her.

Back in the bathroom she started the water, then realized she had also forgotten to get soap. It didn't matter; the hot saltwater bath in the enameled tub felt incredibly luxurious. Her various cuts, scrapes and blisters stung a bit but it was worth it. By the time she got out and dressed again, Giliead had gone down to take his turn at watching Ixion and Ilias was back.

"How did it go?" she asked him, using one of their few precious towels to dry her hair.

"He didn't come back to life and kill us all," Ilias replied laconically.

Tremaine decided not to prod that sore point any further. The others were stirring and food was suddenly a priority.

In search of it, she and Ilias followed the map booklet back to the grand stair and down one deck, then through an elegant foyer to the giant First Class dining area. Dyani, who had loudly declared, "I'm not afraid. I want to see it," trailed along after them.

The room was huge with mellow gold wood broken along the base and top of the walls by silver and bronze bands. Silvered glass panels were set above the columns that separated the main area from the private dining salons along the sides. The light from the overheads was warm and the people sitting or wandering about were far more calm than the chaotic crowd in the main hall earlier. What must have been about half the room's original chairs and tables remained, and about a third of those were in use. The only reminder of the danger was the blackout cloth tightly tacked over the outside windows.

Lady Aviler was right and the volunteers had managed to produce food; trolleys were lined up near the baize serving doors and several women and a few older children were dispensing bread, soup, tea and coffee. Tremaine turned to Ilias to comment only to find he wasn't there. He and Dyani were absorbed in the set of embossed wall panels at the side of the big chamber. Going to join them, she saw the theme was "A History of Shipbuilding from Classical to Modern Times" and understood the attraction. She nudged Ilias with an elbow. "You think we can get the others down here to eat?"

"If they don't, they can go hungry." Engrossed in the images, Ilias didn't sound sympathetic to their plight.

"Did Dannor make any more trouble?" Tremaine started to ask, when someone shouted, "It's you!"

She looked wildly around, thinking *oh no,* but the woman who had jumped up from one of the tables and now hurried toward her didn't look hostile. She had dark hair tied back and wore men's pants and an oversized Rienish army fatigue shirt. As the woman reached her she caught Tremaine's hands and said in a Lowlands accent, "I thought it was you! You're the Ile-Rien spy."

"Oh, no, not really—" Tremaine managed. She did know this woman; she was a Lowlands missionary who had been taken by the Gardier on Maiuta. Tremaine and Florian had spoken to her briefly when they had been captured on the island with Ilias. She hadn't recognized the woman at first because the brilliant smile she wore now transformed her face and made her look years younger.

"I want to thank you." She wrung Tremaine's hands gratefully. "I thought we would never see the sun again. And you." She looked at Ilias. "I saw his people fight for us. Who are they?" she asked Tremaine, "I don't recognize their language."

"They're Syprians. The Gardier base was in their territory," Tremaine explained vaguely. "But I'm not really—"

The group at the woman's table was standing up to leave and one of the other women called to her. The missionary glanced over her shoulder. "I must go back, but thank you." She kissed Tremaine's cheek quickly and darted away.

Most of the Syprians who weren't still asleep ended up trailing reluctantly along to the dining room. Some of them eyed the food suspiciously, but when Halian, Gyan and Arites ate, they followed suit. The biggest problem seemed to be that since Syprian dining tables were only a foot or so off the floor, they found the waist-high Rienish ones awkward. Arites had found some old pages of ship's stationery and a pencil in the suite somewhere and sat on the floor, happily taking notes. Tremaine noticed he was writing with his good arm, a trace awkwardly.

Having gotten everyone else settled and approaching the food herself, Tremaine found her stomach in mild revolt, but a mug of tea settled it and she was able to eat one of the thick slices of bread moistened with rich brown onion soup. She had been expecting military metal plates and cups, but it was served on the ship's china, gleaming white with a band of antique gold.

Then one of the volunteers emerged out of the back somewhere to call out, "Is Tremaine Valiarde here?"

Tremaine set her bowl aside and stood hastily. "Yes?"

"There's someone on the line for you; it sounds important."

"On the line?" Tremaine frowned.

"The ship's telephone," the woman clarified as she led her back to the discreet baize doors. Just inside the first was a narrow little corridor that led to a sort of staging area of steel cabinets and wooden counters. Through another door Tremaine could hear pots banging and someone yelling in Aderassi. She started to make a jaunty remark about it being no different than any other hotel kitchen in Ile-Rien, then recalled uncomfortably that that was a way of life none of them might find their way back to again. Adera barely existed anymore and the fine hotels and Great Houses of Vienne were probably even now being turned into Gardier barracks. There was a telephone set tucked into a small cubby and the woman handed her the receiver.

Tremaine put it to her ear in time to hear, "Miss Valiarde? You've been asked to report to the ship's hospital—"

The thought that they had discovered she was crazy and were planning to lock her up crossed her mind. She brushed that aside in annoyance; it was an old defensive reflex from the time right after she had been kidnapped into a mental asylum by her father's enemies. Still, she demanded, "Why? Who wants me there?"

A little taken aback, the voice replied, "It's on Captain Ander Destan's request. I think it's something to do with the Gardier prisoners."

"Oh, Ander. I'll be right there."

The hospital was down on D deck, where according to the booklet the crew messrooms and workshops, one of the swimming pools, some of the Second Class cabins and much of the food storage areas were located. The corridor in this section was still decorated with wood paneling and carpet since passengers were meant to use it. As they approached the hospital they met Institute personnel coming and going, some leading small groups of ex-prisoners from the Gardier base. This caused a delay as many of them recognized Tremaine and Ilias as members of the group that had rescued them and they stopped to thank them in a variety of languages. Ilias seemed caught between gratification and bewildered embarrassment. Tremaine was embarrassed too, mostly because she had no idea how to respond, but she was surprised at Ilias's reaction. He and Giliead's daily life included risking death to defend their people from crazed wizards; didn't anyone ever thank them for it?

Then outside the door to the hospital area she saw two men, dressed in dark suits of an old-fashioned cut and archaic ruffled black neckcloths. Tremaine rolled her eyes. *God, Bisrans. That's all we need.* From their dress these two were members of the dominant religious sect that completely controlled the Bisran government. Bisra had come down in the world since it had near-successfully invaded Ile-Rien more than two hundred years ago; it had spent itself in pointless wars and had become a minor player in the game of nations. Easy meat for the Gardier, once they had finished with Ile-Rien.

The two Bisrans watched them approach, neither man losing the cold aloof expression worn like a uniform. "Who are they?" the younger one asked. He spoke Bisran, but that was one of the languages Tremaine's father had insisted she learn. One of Nicholas's many false identities had been a Bisran importer of glass and art objects.

The older man replied in the same language, "Some sort of native partisans, I heard one of the sailors speak of them. They're barbarians, worse than the Maiutans." He turned his head to hide a thin smile. "Perfect allies for Ile-Rien."

"At least the women aren't half-naked too."

Tremaine realized she was the Syprian woman in question; she was still wearing the shirt and pants Giliead's mother Karima had given her a few days ago. An astute observer would have noted her boots, scuffed and stained but with brass buckles and rubber heels, but then neither of these men had the perspicacity of the fabled Inspector Ronsarde.

Reaching the hospital door, she paused and said earnestly in accented Bisran, "I was naked but it's so cold up on deck." The older man stared and the younger flushed an unbecoming shade of red.

"Pardon me, you're in my way," she added in Rienish, stepping past them through the door.

Ilias eyed the men suspiciously as he followed her, then asked, "What's wrong with them?"

"They're Bisrans," she replied in Syrnaic, raising her voice a little, knowing the two men would hear the word "Bisran" and know she was talking about them. "They're idiots. Now laugh like I said something really witty."

Ilias laughed obligingly, then added, "I'm not doing this again."

A narrow corridor with green-painted walls led back into the hospital, which was a warren of wardrooms with a dispensary, operating theater and tiny cabin-offices for the doctor and nurses. It smelled like every hospital Tremaine had ever been inside, with the odor of carbolic that was an unpleasant reminder of the asylum. They passed an open door and she saw the room was lined with beds, all occupied. A pile of stained brown coveralls, the garments the Gardier had given their slave labor, lay on the floor. Voices murmured, a woman whimpered in panic and a harassed nurse she recognized from the Institute's infirmary passed, readying a hypodermic.

Tremaine felt her stomach clench and moved on past. Just around the corner was an office area, with desks and cabinets. Sitting perched on the edge of a table, Florian glanced up as they came in. "You're here," the other girl said in relief. She looked like she had had a bath as well and had changed into a clean sweater. She smiled a greeting at Ilias, then looked at Tremaine with concern. In Syrnaic she said, "Everyone says you tried to shoot somebody."

Oh, good. My reputation precedes me. "It was just a Gardier," she said, adding randomly, "Why are there Bisrans aboard?"

Dropping the subject with a reluctant frown, the other girl answered, "They were picked up at Chaire. There's a fairly big group of them. They'd escaped from Adera and had been stuck in Ile-Rien for the past month."

Tremaine lifted her brows, skeptical. "From Adera? From Gardier territory?"

Florian nodded grimly. "Ander said just the same thing."

"So you think they're spies?" Ilias asked worriedly. "You people have a lot of spies."

"I think that's why they wouldn't let them out of Ile-Rien." Florian turned to him, elaborating, "When the Gardier first invaded Adera, tons of people escaped into Ile-Rien and they sent most of them on through to Parscia or wherever else they wanted to go. My mother used to work with the Refugee Assistance group, finding clothes and things for them. Then the fighting along the border got very intense and the refugees stopped coming. But last month these Bisrans just found their way across."

"Found their way across when lots of desperate Aderassi who were native to the area couldn't?" Tremaine snorted.

Florian nodded agreement, her mouth twisting in annoyance. "I'm not sure why they were still in Chaire. I think the government must have been watching them."

"That's all we needed," Tremaine said, thinking of Rulan and Dommen and the other men the Gardier had suborned or bribed to work for them. They had had enough trouble with the spies they already had without taking on more.

Then Colonel Averi, Dr. Divies and Niles stepped in from the other passage. Niles was saying, "Individual Gardier aren't resistant to our magic, it's those devices they wear. We suspect they derive their power from disembodied sorcerers imprisoned within large crystals, but if the small crystal fragments contain individual spells—or if they're shards of the larger crystals, of—" He seemed to realize where that thought was leading and halted, his face hardening.

Dr. Divies was the physician assigned to the Viller Institute. He was about Gerard's age though his hair had turned gray early and he had Parscian ancestry showing in his coffee-colored skin. His face deeply troubled, he said what the others were thinking, "Shards of the imprisoned sorcerers. Broken-off bits of soul."

Niles took a deep breath. "It explains the siege of Lodun. We thought the Gardier must have teams of sorcerers working constantly to maintain pressure on the barrier, but with these crystals . . . it would be simple."

"Obviously their plan was to overrun Vienne, then destroy the Lodun barrier and collect the sorcerers at their leisure." Colonel Averi shook his head slightly, his lips thinning with disgust. He was older than most of the military personnel assigned to the Institute, with a habitually grim face and thinning dark hair. Startled, Tremaine thought he had aged at least ten years from the last time she had seen him; the skin of his face was pale and paper-thin, stretched over his skull like aging parchment. He and Tremaine had never gotten along and she hadn't thought much of him except as an obstacle to be worked around. Now for the first time she wondered if he had been sent to head the Institute's military detachment because he had been judged too ill for frontline service; he certainly looked it now.

"Don't count Lodun out," Niles said thoughtfully, hands in his pockets. "They've had a great deal of time to make plans, and they have access to some of the oldest and most extensive philosophical and sorcerous text collections in the world."

Averi looked away a moment, then said shortly, "My wife is in Lodun."

Tremaine folded her arms, looking at the floor. It made sense, but it was more than she wanted to know about Averi. Niles nodded, unperturbed. "I have a younger brother there. Not a sorcerer; he's in the medical college."

It was as if they were both admitting to sharing the same sort of chronic illness. Florian and Divies were watching them sympathetically, but Tremaine wanted to change the subject. "Have you seen the barrier?" she asked Niles somewhat desperately. She had only read newspaper stories about it, and seen a few grainy pictures that didn't really show anything.

"I have," Averi answered. "It looks rather like a wall of water." He turned to her. She wondered if the white around his blue eyes had always had that yellow tint. His expression enigmatic, he said, "Gerard is getting some rest, but he suggested you might help us. One of the Gardier is a woman—"

"Really?" Tremaine lifted her brows. She supposed there had to be female Gardier, but she couldn't recall seeing any on the base at all, much less in the group Ander and his men had rounded up. "One of the ones we caught? How did—"

Averi cut her off. "We want you to try to question her."

"Me?" Tremaine stared at him, startled that he seemed to be voluntarily asking her to do something.

"You and Florian have had the most experience with the Gardier," he continued, glancing at Niles. "We're not having much luck with the others yet."

"We have time," Niles said with a calm that had a hint of an edge to it. "There are some spells that may help."

Tremaine hesitated, biting her lip. She didn't want to do this. She didn't want to have a conversation with a Gardier, like he—or she—was a person. She turned to Florian, who was giving Ilias a low-voiced translation. "What about Florian? She knows as much as I do."

"I tried already with one of the men," Florian broke off the translation to explain. She didn't sound as if she had enjoyed the experience. She added in frustration, "He wouldn't talk to me at all."

Averi, Niles and Divies were all watching Tremaine expectantly. She pushed her hair back. She wasn't sure what was wrong with her; she could hardly give them a reason for her reluctance when she couldn't articulate it to herself. "This is hard," she said under her breath.

Ilias was watching her, his face concerned. "You want me to go with you?" he asked her. "You don't have one of those curse weapons, do you?"

Tremaine looked blankly at him and realized he thought she was afraid of losing control, of trying to kill the Gardier prisoner. *And he's right,* she thought, surprised to realize it. She nodded. "Yes. No. No, I don't have a pistol. Yes, I do want you to come with me."

The Gardier were being held in a part of the ship called the Isolation Ward. It was in the far end of the stern and walled off from the inside corridors, requiring you to go along the covered Promenade deck, leave its shelter for the open deck area off the stern, go down a set of steps to a lower open deck, then down a stairway and into a warren of small secure rooms with whitewashed walls. It was technically part of the ship's hospital system, a place for patients who came down with infectious diseases. In reality, it was a brig for stowaways.

To question the prisoners they were using a small treatment room that had a metal ventilation grille in one wall, allowing observers in the outer room to hear the conversation inside.

Standing in that anteroom with the guard, Averi gave Tremaine a Gardier translator disk. After what Niles had said about fragments of souls, Tremaine accepted it reluctantly. She hadn't noticed before, but the surface of the crystal set into the metal disk felt greasy, like a decomposing bone; she told herself that was just her imagination. Averi already wore one around his neck so he could follow the conversation behind the grille. He said roughly, "There's a guard in with her. I'm not expecting you to get their invasion plans for Parscia and Capidara out of her, just to get her talking."

"Right." She couldn't tell what Averi thought; he hadn't objected to Ilias's accompanying her. As the colonel turned to open the door, Ilias's mouth quirked in an encouraging smile.

The treatment room had been stripped to bare whitewashed walls.

A young man in gray Rienish army fatigues stood in the corner, one hand on his holstered pistol. His eyes went to Tremaine and Ilias as they entered, acknowledging them with a slight nod.

Tremaine's eyes went immediately to the other occupant; she had resolved not to make the mistake of showing shyness or diffidence even unintentionally. The Gardier prisoner was seated on a wooden chair, her hands bound with the manacles the Gardier had used for their slaves.

It was the one who had opened his—her—mouth, the one Tremaine had decided to shoot first. The Gardier was tall, lean and small-breasted, her face dirty from the battle, the skin on her cheeks reddened and raw. This didn't stir any sympathy in Tremaine's heart; the secure rooms for stowaways would have bunks with mattresses and bedding, sinks with hot running water and toilets. Compared to the conditions the Gardier had kept their prisoners and slaves in, it was practically the Hotel Galvaz. While Tremaine was still looking her over thoughtfully, the prisoner spoke first. "You were the one who wanted to kill us. I thought it was an act."

Tremaine felt her face move in a smile. "I'm not much of an actress." The Gardier's voice was husky but high in pitch. Tremaine had noted that on the island but not the other details; the smoothness of her throat and the shape of her hairline, visible now that her cap had been removed.

"Then why are we not dead?" The woman sounded bored and skeptical.

"You are. You're walking, talking dead." The words came out before Tremaine had a chance to think, but as she watched the Gardier's eyes narrowed, a faint trace of unease crinkling the smooth brow, and she knew it had been an apt impulse. *She spoke first because she wanted control of the conversation, she thought she could get information out of me.* She held her expression, keeping her smile from widening. You could do a lot with someone who thought that much of herself.

The silence stretched, and the Gardier finally said brusquely, "Then why are you here?"

"They made me come in to ask you questions." Tremaine shrugged, shaking her head, still with the faint smile. "I personally couldn't care less whether you answer or not, but I've already had lunch and I haven't anything else to do right now." She leveled her eyes at the woman. "I just want to get to the part where we throw you over the side." Tremaine let her gaze turn abstract and thoughtful. "If you survive the fall, you'll probably get trapped in the bow wake. It'll carry you right into the propeller. I understand it's very large."

The Gardier tried to stare her down, then looked away. *Sincerity helps*, Tremaine thought. She hadn't a shred of sympathy for the Gardier, even where she could find some compassion for the Rienish who spied for them. Greed, desperation, good intentions twisted out of shape she could have some empathy for; she could too easily see how she could have fallen into the same trap. The people who set that trap were just so much garbage to be disposed of.

Ilias nudged her with an elbow, asking softly, "Did she tell you anything?"

"We're not at that point yet," she told him. It was handy that the Gardier had never bothered to add Syrnaic to their translator crystals, or at least none of the ones they had found so far.

"Oh." He leaned back against wall, folding his arms. "It looked like it was going well."

The Gardier woman watched this exchange with a kind of wary incredulity. She said, "You behave as if they are people."

Tremaine lifted her brows. Though Ilias's boots and clothes had mud-stained patches from their recent adventures, he had had a bath more recently than the Gardier. He had also rebraided his queue so his hair wasn't quite such a wild mane; he didn't look that savage. "No, I behave as if you are people. I wish I didn't have to, but it upsets the others. What makes the Syprians not people to something like you?"

The Gardier stared, insulted. "They are primitives. They don't— It is obvious," she finished stiffly.

Tremaine's eyes narrowed. Destroyed coastal villages and ships going missing were what had drawn Ilias and Giliead to investigate the island in the first place. "If it's obvious, why can't you explain it coherently?"

"They can't be used for labor. They don't use civilized speech. They won't stop fighting." She sneered. "If they do, they're afraid of the tools."

The welders, the lights. The Syprians would think it was magic and would find it terrifying, would consider themselves soiled by the contact. *They tried them out as slave labor, and when it didn't work they killed them.* Tremaine couldn't say she was surprised. "And sometimes they blow up airships. How do you make the avatars?" That was the closest the Gardier's translation spells could get to a Rienish word for the crystals and their imprisoned sorcerers.

The woman shook her head, caught off guard. "I don't know. That is for Command and the Scientists. I am in Service."

"Then you're even more useless than I thought."

Tremaine let go of the translator crystal and headed for the door. Following her lead, Ilias pushed off the wall and trailed after her.

She expected to have to argue with Averi, but as the guard shut the door behind them the colonel nodded sharply, motioning for them to go on through to the outer room. Once there she saw the usually grim cast to his face lightened by satisfaction. He said, "It's a start. We'll isolate her from the others, give it a few hours, then see if she's more receptive."

Florian had been waiting in the outer area too. There were only two small rooms for the staff, with a small desk for the lieutenant in charge and some comfortless wooden chairs for the other guardsmen on duty, two of whom were women. "Did she tell you anything?" Florian asked, curious.

"A little." Tremaine shrugged. "A very little." She was relieved that Averi seemed confident. It occurred to her that she also had Averi in a receptive mood and maybe even inclined to discuss things with her. She said quickly, "Where do you think the Gardier come from? The Syprians sail all over this area, they travel fairly far inland, and have contact with a lot of other people. But they had never seen the Gardier or even heard any rumor of them before."

Averi nodded, leaning against the desk and saying thoughtfully, "Those maps your friends recovered from the base show a Gardier stronghold close to where Kathbad is in our world. I think it's possible—"

"Colonel—" One of the women soldiers leaned into the room to interrupt them urgently. "There's a call for you on the ship's telephone."

Averi went to the other room, taking the receiver from the instrument mounted on the wall. Watching his sallow face redden as he listened, Tremaine exchanged an uneasy look with Florian. The guards in the room watched him too, caught by the growing air of tension.

Averi finally said, "Yes," and replaced the receiver, turning back to them. "Florian, can you find Ander? Tell him it's the gunship."

Chapter 4

Ixion had killed two Chosen Vessels that the poets know of, Lyta of Hisiae and Kerenias of the Barren's Edge. But Vessels often disappear without trace, their companions with them, no one knowing of their deaths until their god Chooses again, so Ixion could have accounted for many.

—Fragment of incomplete work, titled
"Journal for the Chosen Vessel of Cineth,
under Nicanor Lawgiver," Abignon Translation

The wireless officer has picked up coded signals from the Gardier gunship. When they were translated it was apparent they were instructions to a landing party." Averi glanced back at Gerard, his face sober. "A landing party in a native city."

They were on the forward stairs climbing toward the wheelhouse, Averi in the lead, with Gerard, Tremaine and Ilias following. "Are we sure it's Cineth?" Tremaine asked, her stomach twisting with guilt. "I thought the *Ravenna* could hear wireless traffic all the way to Capidara." The ship had the most powerful transmitters and receivers on the ocean, or at least that was what the advertisements on the map brochure said.

"From the heading they gave, it has to be." Averi was out of breath from taking the stairs at such a rapid pace. "They're searching for Rienish refugees—they seem to believe you all left the island on native transport, which means they haven't sighted the *Ravenna* yet."

The ship hummed around them like a kicked anthill; Tremaine could hear someone shouting orders as they passed an open corridor. The ship's telephone had found Gerard in his cabin, and Florian had hurried off to fetch Ander, Ilias asking her to bring Giliead too. Then Tremaine realized what Averi had said. "Wait, I thought we couldn't break the Gardier codes." It was common knowledge that wireless operators on the Aderassi front and along the coasts had always been able to listen in on Gardier traffic, but there had never been any progress in deciphering it.

"Ander recovered some Gardier codebooks from the island," Gerard explained hurriedly, glancing back down at her. "One of the books had transcriptions of our older codes. There was a direct translation into a Gardier code, and that's allowing our wireless officers to understand their traffic."

"He didn't tell me," Tremaine muttered as she climbed after him. Ander being a good Intelligence officer again, she supposed. She hoped it was just that. He had at one point decided she might be either a Gardier spy herself or just stupid enough to be passing information along to one. Since she and Ilias had caught the spies in Port Rel, she had thought he was over that by now.

As they reached the wheelhouse level metal creaked alarmingly, and the stairs swayed under Tremaine's feet, sending her careening into the wall. She fell back against Ilias, clinging to the handrail, suddenly aware how high up they were. "What the hell . . . ?" she gasped. It was like being at the top of a tall and unsteady tower in a hurricane.

"The ship's heeling over," Ilias told her, bracing his feet on the steps to keep them both upright.

She looked over her shoulder at him, trying to keep up a pretense of calm. "Is that another word for sinking?"

"Turning," Gerard explained, grimacing as he hauled himself up the railing. "Without slowing down." Recovering his balance, Averi reached the top, wrenching the hatch open.

With Ilias urging her, Tremaine managed to pry her hands off the rail and drag herself up. As they reached the hatch, the deck began to sway back to a more level plane. Following Averi and Gerard, Tremaine bounced off the opposite wall of the short corridor and stumbled into the officers' chartroom.

The room held a polished wooden chart cabinet in the corner, and there was a large table bolted to the floor, covered with maps and papers. The place was full of disheveled uniformed officers and worried civilians. Tremaine recognized the captain even though he was in his shirtsleeves and a younger man than she had expected to see; he was standing in the center of the room, hands planted on his hips, anger written in the tense way he held himself and the grim resolve on his windburned face.

He confronted an older man in a brown walking suit nearly as well tailored as the ones Niles wore. Captain Marais was saying, "And I'm telling you, we're not going to run again. We were forced to abandon Ile-Rien—"

"Your orders were to take this ship to Capidara," the man interrupted briskly. He was tall, sharp-featured, with carefully cut gray-white hair. "The civilians, the women and children on board—"

"I know what my orders say, I don't need you to repeat them," Marais snapped.

It's happening, Tremaine thought, not realizing she had been unconsciously expecting this until now. The reality of Ile-Rien's fall was starting to sink in, and the chain of command was breaking down. From her family background Tremaine might have been expected to be an anarchist at heart, and she was a little shocked to discover this was simply not true; Captain Marais's defiance worried her, even though she wanted to save Cineth more than he did. The other men in the room looked angry, determined, tense. She saw Niles standing back against the wall, arms folded, his lips thin with annoyance.

"Apparently you do need your orders repeated," the other man shot back. "No one wants to see an undefended city attacked, and I admit an alliance of some sort with the native people is imperative. But this isn't a warship." He threw a glance at Ilias, who stood near the door with Tremaine. Ilias's eyes moved from one man to the other, wary at the air of tension in the room. Tremaine knew he couldn't understand the conversation, but she didn't want to chance interrupting it with a translation.

"We're at war with an enemy that doesn't recognize the concept of noncombatants, Count Delphane," one of the other civilians pointed out, his voice acerbic. He was an older man, balding and somewhat stout, dressed in a battered dark suit and fanning himself in the warm room with a folder of papers. "And we carry weapons, so of course we're a warship. The conventions of international law simply do not apply."

A solicitor, Tremaine thought, pegging him instantly. *A solicitor on our side, more's the better. And the opposition is Count Minister Delphane.* And she had been unnerved by Lady Aviler's presence. Delphane gestured in exasperation. "Taking us into battle with the Gardier is as good as murdering everyone on board."

Marais's eyes narrowed. "I've lost three ships in this war, and watched countless others go down. I don't intend to lose this one. But I'm in command here. If you don't like it, my lord, you're welcome to get off at the next port."

Nobles in Ile-Rien, including the Queen, could be familiarly addressed as "my lord" whatever their title, but Marais made the honorific sound like a threat. *The problem is, Delphane has a valid point.* But Tremaine looked at Ilias standing next to her, his face tight with anxiety, and knew it couldn't matter. Cineth was helpless against an attack like this. Delphane regarded the captain with narrowed eyes, saying, "At this time the Gardier do not even know of this ship's existence—"

Niles cleared his throat. "But they do. Colonel Averi?"

Averi stepped forward, facing the count. "Unfortunately Gardier-controlled spies were present in the Viller Institute's organization. We took some of them, but we couldn't possibly have found them all." He glanced sharply at Marais. *If he's smart,* Tremaine thought, clinically interested, *Averi won't directly challenge Marais.* Pitting the crew, under Marais's command, and the remnants of the army detachment under Averi, against each other, with Niles and Gerard and the other Institute members as wild cards was the worst mistake they could all make. But Averi only said thoughtfully, "And I can't believe the *Ravenna* wasn't spotted at Chaire."

Delphane looked at him, his lips pressed together. "I was aware of that. But we're in an entirely different world. Are the Gardier communications between wherever we are and Ile-Rien likely to be that swift?"

"As swift as our passage here," Gerard put in.

"We aren't facing a fleet, just a single gunship," Marais said deliberately. "And we have every chance of taking that gunship by surprise."

Delphane watched him. "As long as they can destroy our engines, Captain, size doesn't matter."

Captain Marais consulted Niles and Gerard with a look. "Well?"

he demanded. "Is that true? Or can your new ward protect us from their offensive spell?"

Niles glanced at Gerard, lifting a brow. Gerard took a deep breath, and said, "We can't know for certain until we test the ward. But I think it will work. I've seen the Damal sphere," he stumbled a little over the name, perhaps recalling that the sphere wasn't just named for its creator anymore, "the sphere's effect on Gardier airships firsthand. It stripped heretofore impenetrable wards away effortlessly."

Delphane turned to Colonel Averi, saying quietly, "So you are going to allow this?"

Ander arrived in the doorway, breathing hard, halting when he saw the grim tableau as the ship's captain, the military commander, and the highest-ranking civilians confronted each other.

Averi let out a slow breath and met Delphane's eyes. "Count Delphane, as the Solicitor General pointed out, we know the Gardier consider civilian transports, hospital ships and anything else that moves as a military target. This is a warship, whether we like it or not." His gaze went to Captain Marais. "You've already changed course for the native port?"

"Yes. At full speed." Marais's words were clipped. His eyes fixed suddenly on Tremaine. "Ask him to describe the harbor."

Startled, Tremaine managed to realize he meant Ilias and turned to him, repeating the question in Syrnaic. Throwing a narrow look at Marais, Ilias asked, "They're going to help?"

Tremaine felt all eyes on her, but she wasn't going to push him. "They're still arguing about it, but we've changed course for Cineth."

Ilias regarded Marais for a long moment. Tremaine saw a great deal of suspicion in that look, as well as pent-up fear and guilt. *If he and Giliead hadn't brought us to Andrien, this might not be happening*, she thought, sick with nerves. Her part in bringing them to this point wasn't exactly small either. Then Ilias took a sharp breath. "There are cliffs to the west, and a stone breakwater . . ." Tremaine translated his description hurriedly.

Averi listened, the creases across his forehead deepening. "You want to attempt an attack with our forward gun?" he asked Marais, not bothering to keep the incredulity out of his tone.

The weapon mounted on the *Ravenna*'s bow deck was an antiairship artillery piece. Tremaine tried unsuccessfully to visualize it, wondering if it could even be used to shoot at something in the water.

Marais's face set in an even grimmer expression, though it seemed he was getting his way. "If we can lure the Gardier out into open water, we won't need the gun." He glanced at Delphane, saying with pronounced irony, "You may find, Count, that size—and speed—do matter a great deal."

Delphane shook his head slowly. He seemed weary now that he had lost the argument. "I don't want to leave a potential ally's city to a Gardier attack any more than you do, gentlemen. But I hope your decision doesn't kill all of us."

Gerard and Niles hurried away to get their supplies for the sorcery, Ander and Averi to organize a small military force to land and search for any Gardier left trapped onshore. Marais had more questions for Tremaine to translate for Ilias, then let them both go.

Out in the corridor, officers and crew sped past them, dashing in and out of doorways, yelling commands and questions at one another. Tremaine was impressed with Captain Marais; he was obviously an intelligent man, and the pressure and his nerves had wound him up like a top. She headed for the stairs just to get out of the way, but Ilias caught her arm. "But how soon can we get there?" he asked her, throwing a worried glance back into the chartroom. He looked just short of frantic. "I know we left the island heading east, but where are we now?"

The captain had said full speed, and Tremaine knew that as a passenger liner the *Ravenna* had been criticized for barreling along at twenty knots in the dark and fog, and thirty knots in and out of crowded ports. But there was no way to translate that into Syrnaic. She met his eyes and said deliberately, "This ship is very fast."

He nodded, though he didn't seem much reassured.

"We need to see what's happening," Tremaine said to herself. An officer, fresh-faced and surely younger than Florian, bolted past them. Tremaine managed to snag his sleeve. "Excuse me! Do you know where Gerard is, or Niles? The Viller Institute sorcerers?"

Startled, he halted, looking from her to Ilias. But she could see he was thinking that if they were up here in the wheelhouse, they must be Somebody. "They're on the cable deck. You can follow me, I'm going there now."

Following the man down the forward stairs, Tremaine found herself wondering how Count Delphane, Lady Aviler and other important personages like the Solicitor General had ended up on the

Ravenna. Delphane in particular was a High Cabinet minister; he should have gone to Parscia with the government-in-exile and the royal family. There was only one reason she could think of to account for the presence of such high government officials.

They left the forward stairs to thread back through a Third Class area and reach a passenger stairwell, taking it to the landing that opened into the forward end of the now uninhabited main hall. The officer left the stairs, saying, "This way, it's quicker." He led them down a passage toward a set of padded leather doors with bronze fittings. He fumbled in his pocket for a set of keys and unlocked them, revealing a room like a big dark cavern. As the man hooked one door so it would stay open, Tremaine fumbled for the light switches on the wall.

As she pressed the first button, small indirect incandescents over a long ebony bar sprang to life, casting light down on leaping dancers in a wall mural above the empty bottle racks. The young officer said sharply, "Just the bar lights, madam. Leave the overheads off. It's still light out, but we don't want to take any chances."

It was the Observation Lounge. There was just enough light to make out the dark wooden walls and the chrome pillars supporting the ceiling. Tables, chairs and curved couches of red leather were scattered around the lower half of the room; a few steps in the marble floor led to the upper half, set apart by an ornate metal balustrade with enameled pylons. The curved back wall was covered by floor-to-ceiling curtains of dark red brocade, and it was all windows behind them. If one looked out with all those curtains open, the view would be incredible; or looking in at night with all the soft lights lit.

Ilias took one look around, then plunged across the room after the officer. The man fumbled under the curtains, then managed to open a glass panel door. Ilias pushed out after him, and Tremaine fought her way through the heavy drapes to find they were on a curved open balcony, looking down on the bow, the sea stretching out in all directions. The sky was gray with the remnants of the Gardier storm, and the cool wind tore at her hair. At the far end of the balcony a narrow set of stairs led down to a small deck area where the base of the mast was anchored. The mast itself was circled by a cargo derrick that looked like a giant metal spider with its legs tucked in, and surrounded by an impressive array of waist-high electric winches.

Ilias threw himself against the railing so enthusiastically she grabbed wildly for his shirt, thinking he was about to plunge over onto the deck below. But he was pointing at a distant line of cliffs. "Look, we're nearly there!" He tore down the stairs and Tremaine hurried after him.

There was a gap between this area and the forwardmost section of the deck where Gerard, Niles, Giliead, Florian and several crew members stood. Tremaine followed Ilias across the short railed ramp that bridged it and through a minefield of giant cables, giant chains, and giant spindles to wind them up on.

In the shelter of the forepeak, a small raised platform in the very tip of the bow, Niles and Gerard were crouched on the deck, drawing symbols on the planking in white chalk. Niles clutched a sheaf of notes, referring to them as he took pinches of different powders and concoctions from the small jars and boxes scattered around him. Both spheres sat on the deck: the tarnished copper one that held Arisilde and the smaller brigher one that Niles had constructed.

Ilias stopped at Giliead's side, asking him in confusion, "What is this?"

"They're making a curse so the Gardier can't see us," Giliead told him, keeping his voice low.

Ilias threw a cautious glance at Gerard and Niles. "Like the *Swift*? That didn't work so well."

Florian, trying to look over Gerard's shoulder without getting in his way, explained, "This isn't just a ward, it's an illusion. All the Gardier will see is a distortion in the air. Like when it's a very hot day, and the air seems to ripple. They'll hear us, but that won't matter. We just need them confused about exactly where the ship is."

"What about deflecting the Gardier's mechanical disruption spell?" Tremaine asked, trying not to sound desperate.

Glancing up, Gerard explained, "Yes, the new ward Niles has been working on should transmit the sphere's influence throughout the ship." He added, not quite under his breath, "We hope." He turned to tell one of the sailors, "Signal the bridge that we're ready."

The man hurried back across the deck and Tremaine stood on tiptoes to see past the solid metal railing around the forepeak. The ship was still moving at full speed, and she could see the opening of Cineth's harbor now. It was sheltered by a high promontory, with golden cliffs falling down to the water, a pyramidal lighthouse of gray stone marking the far end. Those cliffs cut off any view of the gunship, but part of the little city was visible, sprawled across a series of low hills. The buildings were mostly white stone with red tile roofs, none taller than two stories, and a few round fortresslike structures crowned the hills. The whole was dotted with shade trees, standing in the gardens and market plazas.

Tremaine had liked the place the moment she had first seen it. The trees reminded her of those that lined the Boulevard of Flowers, though these streets were dirt instead of ancient cobblestones patched with modern pavement. If the trees, if the Boulevard itself, was still there. *The Gardier are in Vienne now,* she reminded herself coldly. Jerking herself back to the present, she wondered aloud, "So how do we get the gunship to come out—"

A sound assaulted her ears, a deep boom that set her teeth on edge and made her bones shake. She clapped her hands over her ears along with everyone else, wincing away from it. Both Giliead and Ilias recoiled as if they were in real pain. As it died away she demanded, "What was that?"

"The ship's whistle." The officer who had guided them here pointed up above the forecastle. Tremaine could just make out two trumpetlike projections mounted on the first smokestack. "To lure the Gardier out of the shallow water." He looked back toward Cineth, shading his eyes. "They have to come out sometime."

Ilias was at her elbow, impatient to know what the giant boom had been. Tremaine explained in Syrnaic, then they waited, staring at the mouth of the harbor. Tremaine felt her nerves jump with impatience. Giliead moved away from the spell circle to pace, and Ilias boosted himself up on the rails to get a better view past the forepeak.

"There!" Someone pointed, and Tremaine saw the black shape of the gunship emerge from behind the promontory. She stepped closer to the rail. The illusion masking the *Ravenna*'s exact location made the Gardier craft seem hazy, as if she were viewing it through a mist. When they had seen the gunship from the island, she had thought the long low shape, the guns mounted in the bow and stern, looked predatory and sinister. From this high vantage point it suddenly looked like prey.

"Here it comes!" Niles shouted, anxiously studying his spell diagrams. Tremaine tensed, and Giliead reached to pull Ilias back from the rail. Without etheric lenses the spell that was traveling toward them was invisible, a deadly wave of power.

Then Tremaine saw the glamour haze and weaken, the view of the gunship still steaming across their bow momentarily crystal clear. Then a bright light flared. She threw up an arm to shield her eyes, stumbling back on someone's foot. *It didn't work, that was the mechanical disruption spell,* she thought frantically, *we're going to sink.* An image of the dream she had almost forgotten flashed vividly behind her eyes: The *Ravenna* sinking beneath black water, her lifeboats still in place.

In the next heartbeat she was free of the dream and back to reality. Giliead held on to her arm, and Ilias was braced against the rail next to her. Her eyes were watering and dazzled by the light, and she could barely see Gerard, Niles and the others. "It worked," she breathed. "Hah." That wall of light hadn't been the Gardier's spell, it had been the sphere, deflecting the Gardier's attempt to destroy the ship.

Tremaine blinked hard as the dazzle faded, and she leaned forward, gripping the railing. The *Ravenna* was still bearing down on the Gardier craft and, though she knew the gunship must be traveling at full steam, it looked as if it was standing still. Tremaine saw the puffs of smoke above the barrel as it fired its bow gun; the blast reverberated over the water a moment later. She grinned, pounding her fist on the railing. The gun pointed several degrees off their bow, fooled by the illusion still concealing the *Ravenna*'s exact position. "We can turn the spell back on them; Arisilde knows it too. We can—"

"We don't need curses," Giliead interrupted quietly, his mouth set in a tight line. "We're going to ram her."

"Can we do that?" Tremaine eyed the fast-approaching gunship. "Without sinking, or anything . . . ?"

The Gardier seemed to realize their error; the gun swiveled, but too late. The *Ravenna*'s drive forward didn't falter as the smaller craft disappeared from view; Tremaine grabbed the rail but instead of a huge crash there was only a thump that shuddered up through the deck. Stunned by the ease of it, she peered down the side to see half the gunship flip up and vanish under the surface as shattered wood and bodies tumbled past in the *Ravenna*'s bow wake.

"And you said metal ships wouldn't float." Giliead turned to keep the wreckage in sight, leaning out to look down the side.

"I never did," Ilias protested.

Despite their attempt to sound totally unaffected, or maybe because of it, Tremaine knew they were both a little shocked by the *Ravenna*'s power. She knew she sure as hell was.

The ship's drive forward slowed, and Tremaine saw from the way the water churned below that it was moving into one of those insane turns. *Oh joy,* she thought with a sick sensation, contemplating the indignity of dropping flat to the deck to cling to one of the big cables.

She grabbed Ilias instead, wrapping an arm around his waist. Still watching the pieces of Gardier ship bobbing in the waves, he absently put an arm around her shoulders, bracing them both against the rail. The fact that Giliead, though he didn't look particularly worried, still felt the need to hook one arm through the rail and grab Ilias's belt with the other, was not reassuring.

The ship started that frightening lean toward the waves and one of the officers from the group around Gerard and Niles shouted, "Hold on!" Everyone scrambled to grab something, Florian huddling down near Gerard. Niles grabbed for the loose jars of powder, hastily dropping them back into his case.

"No kidding," Tremaine muttered, watching in fascination as the churning green surface below drew closer. But this turn was less dramatic, and the ship began to sway back upright long before she felt the urge to scream. They were heading back toward the wreckage, still slowing.

As the deck rolled to become more or less level Ilias let go of Tremaine and she lurched away toward Gerard. Before she reached him a seaman pounded across the bridge from the other deck, shot past her to one of the officers standing with the sorcerer, pulling both men aside to speak urgently.

Tremaine threaded her way around the cables, demanding, "What is it?"

Niles turned away from the discussion abruptly, his face ashen. "We have a problem." He was staring down at the spell circle, at the iron filings in the center. "The inner core didn't oxidize."

Giliead, Ilias, Florian and the other seamen were all watching, puzzled, and in the Syprians' cases, wary. "Niles, nobody knows what you're talking about," Tremaine said, a sudden qualm making her snap impatiently. "The spell worked."

"It worked, but the other wards were supposed to be excluded from the effect," he said tightly. "They weren't."

Gerard turned to them, his face hard and grim. "It's Ixion, the wards around his cell failed and he escaped."

"What about Ixion?" Ilias demanded. Gerard had spoken in Rienish, and he had recognized only the name.

Tremaine grimaced. *That's all we needed.* She turned to Ilias, saying in Syrnaic, "He escaped."

The moment was one of those long heartbeats that never ends as she watched their faces. Giliead's expression went absolutely blank, concealing any emotion and somehow worse than if he had actually showed his feelings. Ilias looked horrified for an instant before his face set, then both men were running across the deck, jumping over the cables.

Tremaine started after them. "I'll go with them, they'll need a translator—"

"Tremaine, wait!" Gerard snapped.

She thought he was going to tell her it was too dangerous, she would just be in the way, but he said hurriedly, "Give me something you're wearing. Niles and I can track your progress with it. We may be able to locate Ixion with the sphere, and that way—"

Items carried or worn for long periods of time took on the same etheric signature as the body of the owner; Arisilde and Gerard had often used this spell for her father, sometimes tracking individuals all over Vienne. Tremaine was already doing a rapid inventory of her possessions. She wasn't wearing jewelry, her outer clothes were too new for the spell to work, she was reluctant to give up her under-things. . . . "Here." She hopped on one foot, hauling off her boot. "This is all I've got!"

Gerard accepted it with a grimace but didn't argue. She ran after Ilias and Giliead, charging up the stairs and tearing open the door to the Observation Lounge. The awkwardness of trying to run like this was too much and she stopped to haul off the other boot and her stockings, dumping them on a table. Barefoot she was much faster and caught them on the passengers' forward stair.

They barely noticed her appearance, intent on reaching the place where Ixion had been held prisoner. They made a transition to a crew stairway down in Third Class, then turned off down a metal-walled corridor on one of the decks below the passenger areas, threading rapidly through a series of turns until Tremaine saw a group of worried crewmen and crewwomen gathered at a doorway. The group parted for the two Syprians and Tremaine hurriedly shouldered her way through in their wake.

The door to the refrigerated compartment hung off its hinges, the lock wrenched from the distended metal. The whole side where it had met the wall was scorched and melted. Three of the guards lay sprawled unconscious on the floor and another was sitting up, a bleeding cut on his temple being tended by a medical corpsman. A red-faced older man in chief petty officer's uniform stood by the doorway, snapping orders about search parties into the ship's telephone. Giliead surveyed the scene grimly, then turned away, pushing back out. Ilias snarled, "I knew this would happen," and followed.

Tremaine turned to go after them, but the officer stopped her with a hand on her arm. "Where are they going?" he asked urgently.

"We're going after him." Tremaine pointed at his sidearm. "Can I have one of those?"

He stared at her, then unclipped the holster from his belt and handed it over.

The trail led upward through a small stairwell near the center of the ship. There were only a few lights set back into walls lined with smoky dark wood, and with the dark green patterned carpet underfoot they might have been making their way through a dim woodland glade. Keeping his voice low, Ilias said, "This makes sense. He's making for open air."

Giliead nodded. "He may be confused. He'll know we're at sea, but—" His slight shrug took in their strange surroundings, so unlike a ship except for the movement underfoot.

A distant hollow voice spoke suddenly, shattering the stillness. Ilias flinched violently and Giliead swore under his breath.

"It's the same as before," Tremaine whispered from behind Ilias. "He's telling everyone to stay at their posts or in their quarters, and to call the bridge if they see anyone suspicious."

Ilias nodded. She had explained it was one of the crew, speaking into a talking box that let his voice be heard through other boxes all over the ship. It had had a more authoritative ring when they thought it was the ship herself speaking.

"Here," Giliead said suddenly, frowning. "There's something here." He stepped off the stairs into a small foyer.

"What?" Tremaine demanded. She had a small curse weapon tucked into the back of her pants under her shirt, which she thought they didn't know about.

"Ixion must have cast a curse up here," Ilias told her as Giliead cautiously pushed open the door.

It opened into a long room where the wizard lights weren't lit but it hardly mattered; the whole outside wall was windows, nearly floor-to-ceiling, looking out onto an expanse of roofed deck that ran along this side of the ship, allowing in enough cloudy gray daylight to illuminate the room. It was filled with cushioned chairs and couches, pat-

terned carpets in soft warm colors covering a floor of green-veined
marble. There were drapes over portions of the inner wall and a set of
double doors near the middle. As they moved further in, Ilias saw
there was a large arched entranceway at the opposite end, next to a
giant example of one of the Rienish paintings. It was a river winding
through a green valley, so real it looked as if you could get your feet
wet standing near it.

An earsplitting shriek rent the air and he and Giliead both jumped
violently, looking frantically around for the source. But Tremaine
waved hurriedly for them to relax and moved to a little table near a
chair. On it sat a small box; she lifted the curved part on top and held
it to her ear. Ilias let his breath out and exchanged a harassed look
with Giliead; another one of the Rienish talking curse boxes. "You'd
think," Giliead said deliberately, rubbing the bridge of his nose, "they
could make those things a little quieter."

Tremaine listened for a moment, her face getting that concentrated look Ilias had learned meant trouble. He could just hear the
tinny voice issuing from the box, but it spoke Rienish. She put the
piece down, setting it carefully on the table instead of replacing it on
the talking box. "Ah, that was Niles," she said in Syrnaic, turning to
them. "He says hello." Then she jerked her head toward the double
doors.

Ilias stared at the doors, feeling the skin on the back of his neck
prickle. They were heavily padded with a deep red leather. Giliead
stepped to them, lifting his hand but not quite touching, then shook
his head. No curses. He came back to Tremaine and asked in an almost voiceless whisper, "What's in there?"

She had already pulled out the little map of the ship, studying it
frantically. "There's a small ballroom, a lounge and a theater, a movie
theater."

"A what?" Ilias asked quietly. Most of the sentence had been in
Rienish.

"It's a room where they show movies, moving pictures." She waved
the map, as if trying to use it to illustrate what she was saying. "It's
not a spell, it's like the engines."

"Great," Ilias said under his breath. He didn't know what the engines were either, except that the Rienish said they made the ship
cleave the water without sails or oars. He hoped she didn't mean "like
the engines" as in powerful enough to move a metal ship the size of
an island at incredible speeds.

"Is there another way in?" Giliead asked softly.

Tremaine traced the path on the map. "Yes, just through here, there should be another entrance through the lounge." She looked up at them, eyes thoughtful. "Gerard and Niles are on their way here."

"We can't wait." Giliead consulted Ilias, brows lifted. His mouth set in a grim line, Ilias nodded. Doing this made his insides go cold, but he knew they didn't have a choice.

Giliead took Tremaine's arm, drawing her with him through the open archway. She went without comment, stuffing the map back through her belt, with one enigmatic glance back at Ilias. He stepped to the leather-padded door, waited until he was sure they had had time to find the other entrance, then pushed it open.

It was a long room, filled with soft shadows. The walls were the same polished wood as the rooms outside, but broken by giant glass panels etched with a garden of colorful flowers and strange birds that glowed with wizard light. The entire space appeared empty, but that meant nothing. Ixion had curses that allowed him to hide in shadows not much bigger than a bird's wing.

Ilias stepped inside, moving cautiously but trying not to look as if he expected to find anything, his boots making soft sounds on the fine wood floor. He was certain the lights in the glass panels shouldn't be lit; the Rienish kept all the bigger rooms dark unless someone was inside, but Ilias pretended not to know that either. Ixion wouldn't have had time to notice, and he would tamper with the Rienish wizard lights and anything else he could find.

There was a raised platform at each end of the room, the steps up to them bands of silver and bronze, and another wizard light overhead was a mass of prisms in colors Ilias didn't know the names of. Padded chairs in rich blue fabric were stacked atop small tables, obscuring the view and creating more pockets of shadow. He could hear a low metallic clicking that he thought might be coming from the double doors near the platform on the right. On the left an open archway showed another room more deeply shadowed, filled with couches and chairs shapeless under big white cloths; that must be the lounge on Tremaine's map.

Giliead would be there now, slipping softly in while Ixion's attention was on Ilias, as it was bound to be. Ilias went toward that darker portion of the room, as if to investigate it. The cool air that came through the little grilles in the walls stirred the dust more than it should, and he knew there was something else moving in here with him. Then something brushed past him.

Ilias glanced down, saw the dust swirl up around his feet, saw it start to opaque and solidify. He tried to leap away and half fell as his feet remained rooted to the floor.

He saw sudden movement out of the corner of his eye and kept trying to wrench free, forcing himself not to look; Giliead would need every moment he could buy for him. The thickening dust crept up to his knees when he heard a gasp and a thump behind him. The dust vanished abruptly and he staggered free.

He caught himself against the side of the archway, twisting around to see Giliead wrestling with a struggling form wrapped in one of the white drapes from the furniture. Ilias lunged to help, skidding to a halt when the floor around the two figures turned molten green.

Ilias hopped back before the stuff touched his boots. It could be an apparition or a flesh-melting curse; he saw it wasn't affecting Gil, but that didn't tell him anything. Then he saw that the green ooze was shredding the drape. The thrashing figures separated as Ixion managed to toss Giliead off. Both came to their feet, Ixion tearing the remains of the drape away.

The man crouched at bay, still dressed in the brown Gardier garments, was like a shadow of his former self, his features still faintly blunted and distorted. But the way he held himself, the wild hate in his eyes were all Ixion.

Then the green mist dispersed, swept away in a silent wind.

Ilias glanced back and saw Gerard and Niles standing in the open doors, both wearing grim expressions. Niles had the god-sphere tucked under his arm.

Ixion stared at them for a long heartbeat, then smiled. He turned and pushed through the doors behind him.

Giliead plunged after him, Ilias reaching the doors only a few steps behind.

Directly inside was a bloodred curtain, looped back to reveal a dark room filled with chairs that all faced the back wall. Giliead had halted abruptly just inside and Ilias smacked into his back.

There were moving images flickering on that far wall, the source of the metallic clicking he had heard. *Moving pictures*, Ilias thought in awe. *She meant that literally.* Cast in shades of gray and somehow flat, they didn't look as real as the paintings in the other rooms, but they moved, jerking and stuttering across the wall in imitation of life. People walking beside stone buildings, on horseback, riding in wagons that moved by themselves like the ones in the Rienish city.

Then Giliead took a step to the side and Ilias realized one of the gray forms on the wall wasn't moving. Ixion stood in the front of the first row of chairs, outlined against the flicker of images.

Ilias looked at Giliead, his friend's face hard to read in the fractured light. Giliead caught his eye and jerked his head faintly toward the figure. Ilias nodded and started down the aisle on his side as Giliead moved down the opposite wall. *He's strong,* Giliead had warned him earlier, *stronger than he looks. And fast.*

He had just drawn even with the still figure, was just able to see the man in profile, when Ixion spoke above the click-clack noise. "The Gardier had so much contempt for their enemies, I never expected them capable of something like this." His gesture took in the room around them, the whole ship. "A floating mountain, with so many wonders inside it."

"I wouldn't describe you as a wonder." Giliead's voice was cool and level, but he had encountered Ixion on the island. Ilias realized he was breathing hard, his heart pounding. It was the voice. *It really is him.* The last time he had heard that voice was right before Giliead had cut Ixion's head off. He wanted to leap over the chairs and rip Ixion's throat out. He wanted to run out of the room. He managed to do neither, waiting for a signal from Giliead as sweat ran down his back.

The image on the wall changed to a view of a storm-tossed sea from the deck of a ship and in the suddenly brighter light Ilias saw the corner of Ixion's mouth lift in a smile. "And Ilias is here. I'll say 'It's been a long time' and you can say 'Not long enough' and—"

"Shut up." The words were out before Ilias realized it.

Ixion hesitated, then said more softly, "I know exactly what you're thinking."

"I really doubt that," Ilias grated. He heard a soft sound behind him and realized Gerard and Niles now stood in the doorway.

"Well." Ixion turned to eye the Rienish wizards. "How did they do it?" He looked at Giliead, head tilted inquiringly. "You fought for them. You used the curse they gave you against me. You haven't been cursed. You're acting for them of your own will. How did they do it?"

He was trying to sound merely curious, but Ilias heard the strain in his voice. He really wanted to know. Giliead must have sensed that too because he didn't answer.

"Is it just because they destroyed my curse on Andrien House?"

Ixion must have realized he was betraying himself and looked away, smiling at the flickering images on the wall. "I'm still searching for allies. Perhaps I can offer my services to them as well."

"I'm afraid we aren't in the market," Gerard said in Syrnaic, his voice cool.

Giliead spoke, "You're nothing new to them. They have wizards like you in their land, and they destroy them like sick animals."

Ixion watched the flicker of movement on the screen. Then he shrugged. "Surely you realize you can't kill me. I'll just come back."

For a moment no one spoke. Then Ilias heard another metallic sound, weaving in and out of the clicking of the moving images. It was the noise the god-thing in the sphere made, he realized, when it thought something was dangerous.

"If that's such a great plan, why haven't you just killed yourself?" Tremaine's voice was so unexpected, Ilias flinched. He hadn't even realized she was in the room. "You've had all the time in the world to jump off the boat. Hell, if you do it from the stern, you'll drown in moments. Instead, you wander around, sightseeing, playing with the switches on the projector. Even if you've got this other body to jump back to, which I'm still willing to believe, I don't think you want to go there."

Ixion turned, staring at her incredulously. "Who in the netherworld's name are you?"

"You didn't answer her question," Ilias said tightly. It was, now that he thought about it, a damn good one.

Ixion looked at him, then at Giliead. He finally said, "Very well, I'm not eager to go to my new body. It will take months for me to grow into it, and by the time I do, the Gardier will have retaken the island and destroyed Cineth." He turned to Gerard and Niles again. "I spoke to one of their men of learning at length. He taught me their language so we could converse. I know much about them and have no particular loyalty to cause me to dissemble."

"You would trade your life for information." Gerard sounded skeptical.

"Yes."

They can't, Ilias thought. *We can't.* But was there any other way out of this standoff?

Gerard spoke to Niles briefly in their language. Niles answered in a dry tone, and Gerard shook his head. He said to Ixion in Syrnaic,

"And if caught, you would trade similar information about us to the Gardier."

Ixion smiled. "Then don't get me caught."

W aiting in the lounge outside, Ilias paced, his jaw set so tightly it was beginning to hurt. There were Rienish guards waiting by the doors, but he hardly noticed them. "I should be in there," he told Tremaine. He wasn't exactly sure why he had followed her out here, except that she had grabbed his wrist and tugged, and he had been too distracted to resist.

"No, you shouldn't." She was sitting in one of the cushioned chairs, her bare feet propped up on a little wooden table.

He stopped, planting his hands on his hips, snarling, "He'll think I'm afraid to face him."

Tremaine was unimpressed. "No, he'll wonder where you are."

Ilias took a breath to reply, then stopped, staring at her. That wasn't the argument he had expected. "What?"

Tremaine studied her fingernails calmly. "He wants your attention, he wants you to be in there glaring at him and hanging on every word." She paused to pick at a broken nail. "Let him wonder what you're doing. Let him wonder what you're thinking." She looked up at him finally, her face serious despite her preoccupation with her hands. "Let him scramble to get a handle on you, instead of the other way around."

He thought that over, hoping to find a hole in it, but it was too patently evident to argue with. And her confidence told him she knew she was right. He dropped down into the next chair instead, demanding in irritation, "Why do you know things like that?"

She shrugged, and nibbled at her broken fingernail. "Annoying people is something of a talent of mine. I gave it up for a while, but lately it's started to come back to me."

T hey had the parley at a table just outside the moving picture room. Giliead wouldn't sit but paced behind Ixion's chair, hoping his presence made the wizard as uncomfortable as Ixion made him. *But he probably enjoys it,* Giliead thought with sour resignation. Thankfully, Tremaine had somehow gotten Ilias to leave with her.

Gerard took a place across from Ixion, grim-faced and somehow managing to convey that he felt Ixion was contaminating the air he breathed. There were men and women armed with Rienish curse weapons at the back of the room. The other wizard, Niles, was waiting with them, his face utterly cool and emotionless. Giliead had no feel for what the man was thinking, but he knew Ixion wouldn't be able to read him either and that Ixion wouldn't like it.

Gerard said with cold contempt, "Our position is simple. If you attempt to leave the room where you have been confined again, we'll kill you and you can go on to your next body and be damned. If you give us the information you have about the Gardier and cooperate fully, you'll be confined, but you won't be harmed, and we'll keep you from the Gardier to the best of our ability."

The god-thing's sphere sat on the table near Gerard, and Giliead could tell it was anything but disinterested. Its clicks and whirs sounded displeased. For the first time, Giliead could also feel little spurts of curses coming from it.

Ixion folded his too-smooth hands, saying, "You could provide refreshments for this discussion."

Gerard lifted a brow. "Your needs are immaterial until you give us reason to think otherwise."

Ixion sighed. "You could also tell whatever it is you keep in that metal cage to stop trying to annoy me."

Intrigued by the sphere's activity despite the situation, Giliead concentrated on it, focusing as hard as he could. After a moment he saw a dim wisp of white light drifting from the tarnished copper surface. Fascinated, he watched the translucent wisp arch over the table toward Ixion. There was something about it that made him think of a scout trying to creep past an enemy sentry post.

Ixion was saying, "I realize now it was the other presence I detected on the *Swift*, which I assumed was another foreign wizard. It's a clever trick, but—" The wisp became a talon and dived in for a strike. He halted, frowning. Through gritted teeth, he said, "I told you, make it stop."

Still concentrating on the sphere, Giliead suddenly saw lines of faded blue light stretching out from it, connecting to threads of different colors stretching all through the ship. He started, blinking, and it was gone, as if someone had dropped a cloth over a lamp to conceal it. Gerard's talk of channeling the sphere's power throughout the ship for protection suddenly made sense. Giliead realized he had been deliberately allowed to see the tendril that had touched Ixion, that the personality in the sphere had shared it with him like a private joke. He was just as sure that the sphere deliberately shielded itself from him. He didn't mind; seeing that light constantly would have been unbelievably distracting. *So the Rienish do have gods,* he thought, lifting a brow. They just didn't know it.

Without looking away from Ixion, Gerard said, "Arisilde, please."

Giliead said calmly, "Ixion, the man in the metal cage is a god, and has bigger stones than both your bodies put together."

Ixion flicked a glance up at him. "Crude," he commented idly, but Giliead could sense the wariness in him. He turned to Gerard again. "If I give you the information, you will release me."

Gerard evinced surprise. "Are the innocent people you killed still dead? As long as they are, we won't release you." His expression hardened. "You are bargaining for your life, not your freedom."

Ixion regarded him for a long moment, then laughed softly. "The Gardier said their enemies were soft. You may be soft, but you don't lie when you deal, do you?" He sighed, making a gentle gesture with his pale hands. "Very well, I agree."

Giliead met Gerard's eyes. They both knew this was a temporary measure.

They put Ixion back into another warded storage room, not far from the first one. Tremaine noted that as a concession to Ixion's apparent surrender, it had been made more comfortable with a cot and chair and some bedding. They had chosen a compartment with an ordinary wooden door, locked but less likely to hurt anyone if Ixion decided to blow it up. With Gerard's assistance, Niles had also warded the door, the walls, deck and ceiling against ether, light, scent and liquid, which should cover just about anything Ixion could attempt to use to harm them. These were wards that hadn't been used in years since they were no use against the Gardier. She wasn't sure if the sphere had helped them or not; it sat on a desk in the outer room of Ixion's prison, clicking ominously to itself.

Giliead and Ilias had stayed to grimly watch most of the process, then went to join the other Syprians preparing to go ashore with Ander's men. It was an expedition Tremaine hadn't managed to join, something she blamed Ander for. She also knew lifeboats had been dropped to search for Gardier survivors among the floating debris of the gunship wreck, but the rumor was that none had been found.

The chances were good that some of the Gardier had stayed behind in the city. The *Ravenna* was making a slow approach to the mouth of Cineth harbor, though she wouldn't try to go inside. One of the sailors had commented that she probably couldn't, since it was unlikely a harbor meant for galleys had been dredged to accommodate a liner.

Niles was finishing the last symbols on the deck in front of the closed door, the chalk marks fizzing and vanishing into the metal as he wrote. Gerard stepped over to join him, his notebooks under his arm. "This should hold him," he said, sounding both resigned and determined. "Until we have to channel the wards through the ship again. I'm afraid it will still cause this set to fail."

Colonel Averi just nodded tiredly. He had been out in the corridor discussing the situation with the army sergeant in charge of the guard detail. He eyed the door, "Some of the men were injured, but nothing permanent. It's almost as if he didn't want to burn any bridges, as if he planned this as soon as he regained consciousness."

Tremaine knew he was right about that. "He's like a rat. Or something else that always comes out on top."

"Can he provide any real information, do you think?" Averi asked Gerard, as if Tremaine hadn't spoken.

Gerard frowned. "Possibly. I doubt we dare trust it."

"There is one thing we need him for." Tremaine folded her arms, studying the door. "Ixion grew a body, an empty one. At least we hope it was empty—" Now everyone was staring at her. She finished hurriedly, "Arisilde needs a body."

That got Averi's attention. He stared at her, saying, "Good God, Tremaine." Gerard just rubbed his forehead as if he had a headache.

"I didn't mean the one he has." At least, not if they were going to be that way about it. "But the spell to make one."

"But could we force him to give us the spell he used?" Niles said calmly, getting to his feet and dusting off his hands. "He seems rather obstinate."

Tremaine kept her eyes on the door. *I bet I could think of something.*

Chapter 5

Some of those who saw the Ravenna from the cliffs said they thought the Gardier wizards had caused a great black island to rise up from the sea, until she called the wizard's ship out to do battle and ate it. Some of them didn't believe our telling that she was a ship until the Ravenna's captain followed our custom and gave her eyes.

— "Ravenna's voyage to the Unknown Eastlands,"
Abignon Translation

Ilias stood as close to the bow of the *Ravenna*'s launch as he could get, holding to the rail as the wizard boat plowed across the harbor toward the stone piers below the trading Arcade. He had thought these boats fast, but now impatience and fear of what they might find made this one seem to travel at a crawl. The lingering bitter taste of the confrontation with Ixion didn't help.

The boat was packed with the rest of the *Swift*'s crew as well as Ander and a dozen Rienish warriors. "I can't see any fires," Giliead said in a low voice, standing next to him and anxiously surveying the shore ahead. "Not up in the town."

Ilias just shook his head. He couldn't bear to speculate. The boat sheds that housed the city's war galleys looked undisturbed, but many of the fishing boats tied up to the piers were sunk, the tangle of broken masts still visible above the waterline. Above the dock area was the long stone trading Arcade, six open-arched entrances leading into stalls for merchants and for factors to sell or trade cargoes. Some of the wooden market stalls built against the far wall had collapsed, but as Giliead had said, there was no fire rising above the red roofs of the greater part of the town.

Halian, standing beside the Rienish sailor who held the wheel, pointed toward the pier nearest the end of the Arcade. "Bring us in there," he said, his voice tense. The man might not know the words, but he understood the pointing; he nodded sharply and adjusted the boat's course by turning the wheel slightly. The Syprians were silent, apprehensive; but behind them Ander was speaking to his men in their own language, giving curt instructions, replying to questions.

The Rienish all carried the long black shooting weapons, though the Gardier had curses that could damage them. The Syprians had lost all their weapons when the *Swift* had sunk, but the Rienish had given them small wooden crossbows the Gardier couldn't harm. Using both weapons was the most effective way of attacking the Gardier the Rienish had found so far, but none of the Syprians were willing to touch the shooting sticks, effective or not. Even if they didn't work by curses, they looked like it. Ilias had one of the crossbows slung over his back and the knife that he had managed to hold on to through the trip to Ile-Rien and back. Swords would have been helpful, but the Rienish had none on board. Or at least that was what Ander had said.

Ilias wasn't sure he entirely trusted Ander yet; for a young man he was cagey about revealing too much of himself. It was still hard for Ilias to believe that he trusted the motives of Gerard, a wizard, and Florian, an apprentice wizard, better than those of Ander, a fighter and warleader. Maybe it was because Ander still seemed wary of the Syprians' motives.

Ilias saw figures running along the front of the Arcade, vanishing into one of the arched entrances. He could see they wore light brown clothing from head to toe—Gardier. He nudged Giliead with an elbow, and his friend nodded. One of the Rienish spoke urgently, pointing them out to Ander.

The boat slowed as it neared the dock, the low thrum of whatever powered it sputtering to silence. With the others Ilias climbed out as soon as the side bumped the stone, Arites helping the Rienish sailor tie off to the piling. Ilias scanned the docks but couldn't see any movement. Halian paused, then stopped at a small fishing boat. Leaning over to see down into it, he demanded, "How many are there? Which way did they go?"

Ilias stepped up beside him and saw there was a young woman in the boat, huddled next to the mast. She stood, pointing shakily to the road that started at the end of the boat sheds and curved up into the main part of town. "I didn't see how many. Most of them went up there." She looked up at Halian, her face pale. "But in the Arcade, there's a wizard! I saw him run inside."

Giliead's expression hardened. He flicked a glance at Ilias, then told Halian and Ander, "You go after the others, we'll take care of it."

Halian nodded sharply, clapping Ilias on the shoulder as he turned away. But Ander hesitated, eyeing them watchfully. "Are you certain? You don't want—"

"We're certain." Giliead pushed past him, breaking into a run. Ilias raced after him as the Rienish pelted down the dock, following Halian and the others.

As they neared the Arcade, Ilias saw four or five people crouched at the first archway. Giliead waved them back urgently. Recognizing him, they faded back into cover behind the casks and large pottery jars stacked on the dock. One of the women was Feredas, the portmaster. As Giliead mouthed the words, "How many?" Feredas held up two fingers.

Giliead nodded and stepped to the side of the entrance, crouching beside the body sprawled there.

Ilias stepped back against the patched wall, pausing to cock his crossbow and take a cautious look ahead down the wide corridor that led through the building. Large square doorways along each side led into shops and storage areas for cargoes. The place looked like a small army had bashed its way through. Copper cooking pots, baskets and broken pottery were scattered over the dusty stone. Three other bodies lay in the passage: two women sprawled in the middle, one with the bright fabric of her skirt tumbled around her, and one man slumped against the wall. A fallen bushel of pomegranates, crushed under the boots of those fleeing or fighting, made the floor look as if it was awash with blood and gore.

Giliead nudged his leg to get his attention, and Ilias looked down at the dead man. *Tersias, Calensa's cousin,* Ilias identified him with a sick sensation. *Damn.* He had worked for Tersias's family as a youth, unloading cargo. Calensa had been his first love. Giliead twitched aside Tersias's shirt, showing Ilias the blackened skin around the mortal wound in the man's chest; it stank of charred flesh. He looked up grimly, and Ilias nodded to show he understood the warning. This Gardier had a wizard crystal that could throw fire.

Giliead eased to his feet, cocking his own crossbow, and they stepped inside the Arcade.

Slowly and carefully, Giliead moved down the corridor. Ilias stayed at his side, keeping several paces between them. The stalls were open across the front, deserted. They passed a coppersmith's shop with its wares tumbled into the passage and a place that sold bolts of cloth and dyes, mostly undisturbed. Ilias adjusted his grip on the unfamiliar weapon, feeling his palms start to sweat on the smooth wooden stock. This was the worst way to root out wizards; he much preferred sneaking up on them from behind.

A scatter of distant pops, like stones cracking under heat, sounded from somewhere outside; Ilias flinched, recognizing the noise the shooting weapons made. The Rienish must have encountered the other Gardier. Then he froze, poised on one foot, as a rustling came from the next stall. He heard a footstep and a worried mutter in the Gardier's harsh language. From the items spilled into the passage, the stall sold bronze lamps and braziers.

Ilias threw a questioning glance at Giliead, who nodded, his mouth set in a grim line. Ilias stepped soundlessly to the wall, stopping just before the edge of the opening.

Giliead dived forward suddenly, landing and rolling past the open entrance. Ilias heard a shout from the stall as he whipped around the corner. The space was crammed with metal goods, lamps, stands and bowl-shaped containers for oil stacked unsteadily or piled atop wooden chests. He aimed and fired the crossbow by instinct, almost before his eyes found the Gardier crouched back against the inside wall. It was a young one with soot stains on his face, just aiming a long black shooting weapon at Giliead. The bolt slammed into the base of the Gardier's throat. His weapon went off with an ear-shattering report as the man staggered, collapsing against the wall.

Movement toward the center of the stall caught Ilias's eye; he ducked sideways, realizing the other Gardier was concealed behind a stack of wooden crates. Giliead was on his feet now at the front of the stall, aiming his crossbow. Blocked from getting further in by the tumbled metalwares, he shifted impatiently, trying to get a clear shot. Ilias saw the crystal flash as the Gardier moved; he shoved forward with a yell, slinging himself over a pile of braziers. He swung the crossbow, clipping the wizard in the head just before his foot came down on something that slid away with a metallic screech; he crashed to the floor.

Landing on his hands and knees, Ilias scrambled to get his feet under him, to get hold of a pot to throw. Suddenly he felt a burning heat erupt in his chest and looked up to see the wizard, the man's face a rictus of pain and fear, holding the crystal over him.

Ilias didn't have breath to yell in horror. He saw Giliead loom up behind the wizard just as the Gardier jolted forward. Ilias ducked his head as the wizard fell over him, then shoved himself free, slamming a kick into the man's side. Rolling over, trying to sit up despite the fiery pain in his chest, he saw a crossbow bolt sticking out of the wizard's back. Blood soaked the dun-colored jacket but the Gardier was still trying to push himself upright, to reach for the fallen crystal. It was a broken shard, colored a yellow-tinged white, much smaller than the one Gervas had threatened Ilias and Tremaine with.

Giliead desperately shoved the crates aside, but the wizard stretched, his fingers brushing the crystal. Pain shooting through his body, Ilias grabbed a heavy copper pot and lunged forward, smashing it down on the shard. It broke in fragments, light spraying from the pieces like droplets of water, vanishing into the cracks in the paving stones. The wizard shouted in despair, and Ilias slumped over the pot, relieved, the heat in his chest fading.

Giliead pushed his way through the debris to grab the wizard by the back of his jacket, awkwardly straddling him. The Gardier struggled silently, clawing at Giliead's arm. His face set in grim distaste, Giliead whipped his knife across the wizard's throat.

After a moment to make sure the man was dead, Giliead dropped the body, looking at Ilias. "You all right?" he demanded, breathing hard.

Ilias nodded slowly, pushing himself upright and away from the spreading pool of blood, rubbing the reddened spot on his chest. The sudden heat was gone, barely a phantom pain left behind. He took a deep breath and sat up on his knees, looking worriedly at his friend. "Did he get you too?"

Giliead shook his head, plucking at his shirt. Ilias realized the brown cloth had a singed black patch right below the leather lacing on his chest. "He tried. It didn't work on me."

Some curses worked on Giliead, some didn't. It was just luck this

Gardier wizard didn't know the right ones to use. Ilias pushed to his feet, staring down at the wizard, who was just a dead man now. It had been a messy kill, and he knew Giliead hated that. "Did you stab him with that bolt?"

Giliead winced as he stood, absently wiping his bloody hands on his pants. "The damn bow misfired." He kicked the copper pot off the remnants of the crystal, using his bootheel to grind the last few solid fragments into powder.

Ilias watched this, noting that the fragments didn't burst into water-light and trickle away. He wondered if that only happened when the wizard imprisoned inside the crystal was released into death. If there really was a wizard inside the smaller shards, the way the Rienish said there was in the larger crystals. Giliead's face was still grim, his mouth set in a hard line. Trying to lighten the mood, Ilias stooped to pick up his crossbow, saying earnestly, "You want to cut his head off to make sure he's dead?"

Giliead gave him a forbidding glare. "That," he said deliberately, "Is not funny."

Popping sounds from shooting weapons led them up the road from the Arcade and through the lower part of the town. The trail of corpses—Syprian, Gardier and one Rienish—told them they were headed the right way. It also encouraged them to stay close to cover to avoid making themselves even better targets than they already were.

Houses with white clay walls and red tile roofs rose on either side of the wide dirt track, wooden doors tightly closed. Ilias heard dogs barking behind the garden walls, and a few stray chickens skittered out of their path, but other than that the town might have been deserted.

As they reached the corner of a larger house Giliead suddenly stepped back against the wall, motioning urgently for Ilias to do the same. He flattened himself against the cool clay surface, taking a cautious look past Giliead.

Around the corner was a small plaza with a square fountain house in the center, the edge of the roof carved with sea snakes. Leaning out, Ilias could just see two Gardier and three Syprians sprawled on the dark-stained dirt near the little pavilion.

Giliead elbowed him back with the low-voiced warning, "There's a wizard up on the roof, just to the right of the waterspout."

Ilias crouched and leaned out again more cautiously, studying the square. There was a good vantage point in the goat pen in the corner opposite theirs, where the slant-roofed shed provided cover from the rooftops. He saw a head with Syprian braids bob just above the gate. He glanced up at Giliead, jerking his head inquiringly toward the goat pen.

His friend nodded approval of the plan. "Signal me when you're ready."

Ilias faded back along the side of the house, leapt to catch the top of the garden wall and scrambled over. He landed on the flagstones of a courtyard shaded by berry trees. The back portico of the house was empty, a shattered bowl of cooked grains on the blue-tiled floor the only sign of the sudden disturbance. Crossing the court swiftly, he climbed the vine-covered wall opposite. It was shielded from the plaza by the second floor of the house, and he was able to walk back along it to the open pen.

Six piebald goats clustered in confused alarm at the back of the hay-strewn pen. Ilias couldn't see under the roof of the shed where the defenders had taken cover, but he could hear a quiet murmur of voices. He hunched low on the top of the wall and hissed a warning that he was about to appear. After a moment of fraught silence there was a soft reply, and he jumped lightly down into the pen.

There was still a flurry of startled movement under the low shed. Two Rienish men, Halian, Kias and a few townies all crouched behind the gate. "Where's Giliead?" Halian demanded, keeping his voice low.

He didn't bother to ask if they had gotten the wizard in the Arcade, knowing that if they hadn't, Ilias wouldn't be there. "He's around the side of the next house," Ilias told him, ducking under the low roof and kneeling near the gate as Kias shifted to give him room. "How many here?"

"Just one left on the roof, up there." Halian pointed, confirming Giliead's instinctive knowledge of the wizard's position, though Ilias didn't need it confirmed. "He's got a shooting weapon and those curse crystals."

Ilias nodded, noticing that one of the Rienish had lost his weapon and had burned hands, a sure sign of the curse the Rienish feared most. One of the townies was bleeding from a wound in the shoulder and was unarmed, but the other had a goathorn bow. "Hey, let me use that."

The man shifted it off his shoulder, then hesitated. *Curse mark,*

Ilias thought. At the moment it was more an annoyance than a kick in the gut. Halian twisted around to eye the man with grim intent, and he flushed and passed the bow and quiver to Ilias.

One of the Rienish asked an impatient question, and Ilias shook his head to show he didn't understand, motioning him to wait. He leaned out a little to whistle a sharp signal. At Giliead's answer, Ilias eased to his feet, readying himself to move.

Giliead leapt out of cover, shouting, firing the little crossbow at the pitch of the roof just above the Gardier's position. Ilias saw a flash of brown clothing and slammed through the gate, darting across the open court to put his back against one of the fountain house's pillars. He notched the arrow as Giliead loaded another quarrel and cocked the crossbow. Then he saw something dark grow in the air just in front of Giliead, an amorphous shadow that abruptly went solid and slammed his friend to the ground.

Ilias whipped around the pillar, raising the bow and firing up at the wizard in one motion. He knew immediately he had missed the chest shot, but as the Gardier swung around he realized he must have gotten him low in the belly. The man scrabbled wildly at the roof tiles, then went over backward. He struck the packed dirt of the street with a thump, lying in a crumpled heap. Ilias reached him as Rienish and Syprians appeared from doorways all over the plaza. He hurriedly kicked the crystal free of the man's hand and crushed it under his bootheel.

Giliead was already sitting up, wiping black sticky strands off his face and chest as Ilias reached him. Relieved, he sat on his heels to watch, saying critically, "That's a little like the curse the Barrens wizard used. Did it try to go down your throat?"

"Not that I could tell." With a sour expression Giliead scrubbed black goo off his mouth and spit into the dirt. "And I didn't need to be reminded of that."

Ander slid to an abrupt halt beside them, staring incredulously down at Giliead. "You're alive."

Giliead, always in a bad mood when even a mild aspect of a curse worked on him, just cocked a brow at the young man and said nothing.

Ander shook his head, still confused. "I've seen the Gardier use that spell before, in Adera. It's . . . brutal."

"We told you he's a Chosen Vessel," Ilias said pointedly, beginning to take offense. He knew Ander didn't trust them fully but he hadn't thought it extended to thinking them liars.

"Yes, but I didn't think—" Ander cut himself off, pressing his lips together.

Giliead got to his feet, wiping his hands off. Ignoring Ander, he said thoughtfully, "The god's here."

Knowing the god's penchant for dark cool places, Ilias looked at the fountain house first. Sparks of light hovered above the surface of the well, glittering like fireflies.

Tremaine sat on the bench of the accident boat as it chugged across Cineth harbor toward the stone docks. The heavy cloud cover was breaking up, letting the afternoon sun show through in shafts and patches.

She shaded her eyes, impatiently scanning the damage. She could see the sunken boats still tied to the dock and the collapsed stalls to one side of the trading building. It had been three hours since Ander had used an electric signal from the dock to tell them that the last of the Gardier had been dealt with and that there had been one man killed, plus some injuries among the landing party. They didn't know the extent of the Syprian casualties yet.

For Tremaine at least the wait had been excruciating, but she had known it would take some negotiating for the other Syprians to let more of the *Ravenna*'s crew land. She didn't know how convincing Ilias and Giliead and the others had been, but at least nobody was pushing catapults out onto the docks. The god's visit to the *Ravenna* might have had something to do with that.

It had appeared first on the Sun Deck, badly startling the refugees and crew who had gathered there for a view of Cineth. Niles and Gerard had arrived immediately and with them Tremaine had followed the god on its brief tour of the ship. It had visited the ballroom with the spell circle that allowed the ship to create etheric gateways; ignoring the strange symbols of the circle painted onto the marble tile, it had seemed more interested in the crystal light fixtures. It had finally ended up in the room outside Ixion's cell, sparkling around the door as if it knew what was inside but either couldn't, or chose not to, cross the wards.

Captain Marais had come down to look at it in consternation. "What does it want?" he had demanded. "And what is it, for that matter?"

"It's just curious," Tremaine had told him, aware she wasn't quite answering the question. They knew Arisilde had some kind of connection with the god, either before or after he had been trapped in the sphere. When the sphere had been stored at Coldcourt, it had influenced her writing without her conscious knowledge, sending her images of Ilias's and Giliead's experiences from this world. Arisilde could only have gotten that information from the Syprian god, though they still had no idea where or how he had come into contact with it.

"Fascinating," Niles murmured. He glanced down at the sphere. "Arisilde doesn't seem to find it a threat."

"It might be some sort of elemental," Gerard explained, frowning thoughtfully as he watched the play of light around the door. "Whatever these 'gods' are, the entities provide some protection for the Syprians against sorcerers like Ixion."

Marais lifted his brows. "Well, I wonder what it would do if we let it in to him."

Tremaine stepped up to the door and lifted her hand, her skin tingling as the god's humming energy briefly touched her. "Oh, I bet it could get in if it really tried." She raised her voice, "Hey, Ixion, the god's here. It wants to say hello."

Ixion hadn't replied, and after a time the god sparked more faintly, then gradually vanished.

Ander's message to come ashore had arrived not long after. Gerard must have also told Captain Marais about the eyes painted on Syprian galleys; when the accident boat had been lowered and they were moving away from the *Ravenna,* Tremaine saw a small scaffold had been hung off the bow and a couple of crewmen in safety harnesses were putting the finishing touches on the white paint outline of a stylized eye. *It couldn't hurt,* she thought. And from what she could see, ramming the Gardier ship hadn't even left a dent in the bow.

"There doesn't seem to be much activity," Gerard said in a low voice. He was standing at the rail next to her, surveying the line of docks with a worried frown. "Wait, there's Ander."

"What's he doing?" Tremaine came to her feet, grabbing the rail. Ander's message had asked for her specifically, and she had no idea why, though she supposed he might need her for a spare translator.

"Watching us with field glasses," Gerard told her dryly.

Finally they reached the dock, the motor coughing as the boat slowed to bump awkwardly against the pilings. The seamen scrambled out to tie it off, and Tremaine was right behind them, Gerard grabbing her elbow when her foot slipped on the wet wood.

Ander met them at the end of the dock. His shirt was sweat-stained and he had a rifle slung back over his shoulder. "You were right," he said without preamble. "They are willing to discuss an alliance with us." For some reason his expression was grim.

Gerard nodded, holding up a leather file case he had brought with him. "Colonel Averi had a document prepared, a letter of intent. It's not binding until the government-in-exile ratifies it, of course, but it'll be a start."

Considering it was probably prepared by Count Minister Delphane and the Solicitor General, it will be more than a start, Tremaine thought. But Ander was eyeing her as if she had done something. "What's wrong with you?" she demanded.

He stared at her for at least a full minute, as if expecting her to break down and confess. Tremaine folded her arms and stared back. He finally said, "They want you to negotiate."

Tremaine frowned, not understanding. "Negotiate with them?"

"Negotiate for them," Ander clarified, still watching her. "With us."

"Me?"

"Tremaine?" Gerard echoed, startled.

Ander looked at him, exasperated. "I can't talk them out of it. These people are so stubborn—it's like talking to stone walls."

Tremaine's mouth was open to protest; the very idea of that much responsibility curdled her stomach. But Ander's tone stopped her in midbreath. *He doesn't think I can do it.* Well, she knew she couldn't. But she could fake her way along until she found someone else who could. She told Ander, "Then you can take that letter back to Count Delphane. The Syprians are not going to sign anything without the advice of an independent solicitor who is an expert in international affairs." A dimly remembered phrase from an old newspaper article surfaced, and she added, "And I want an arbitrator from a nonaligned nation."

Ander stared at her, pressing his lips together. Then he said, "Perhaps we can get you a Gardier arbitrator." He turned on his heel and strode away up the dock.

Good exit line, Tremaine thought, eyes narrowed as she watched him go. Yelling a comeback after him would be highly unsatisfactory. And she didn't have a comeback.

She looked at Gerard, expecting another grim expression, but he was smiling faintly. "Your father would be proud," he said softly. "He couldn't have done a better job himself."

It struck her to the core and her eyes stung. *No, he wouldn't be proud,* she thought, looking away. But Gerard was, and that was good too. She forced the emotion down, putting it away where she could examine it later. "If my father was doing this," she muttered, "the Syprians would end up with a long lease on Chaire and most of the west coast."

Ander led them up the dirt path through the town, and Tremaine saw people were beginning to stir, coming out to check the damage in the harbor or gathering around the little fountain houses in the communal squares to talk. Some of them were standing on top of their roofs, using primitive spyglasses to look at the *Ravenna.* They got many curious glances, or at least Ander did; Tremaine and Gerard were still dressed in Syprian clothing.

From what Tremaine understood, Syprians had come from two different peoples who had blended together along the coast, one tall like Giliead, with brown or reddish hair and olive skin, the other smaller and blond like Ilias. Most of the young men wore their hair in long braids or queues like Ilias and the others from the *Swift,* though many of the older men seemed to cut it off at the shoulders or crop it short. Their clothes were in soft colors, with leather and cloth dyed or block-printed with designs. The women wore long skirts or dresses or the same cotton pants and sleeveless shirts as the men. Many of the people who worked on the boats or near the water wore little more than cloth wraps around their waists.

They reached Cineth's central plaza, a large area of open ground where spreading trees shaded little markets of awnings and small tents, still deserted after the attack. The plaza was bordered by several long two-story buildings with columns and brightly painted pediments that formed a ribbon of color just under their rooflines. The large one with the pillared portico was the town Assembly, the smaller round one with a domed roof was a mint, and the one with a forbidding square façade was the lawgiver's house. The city Fountain House was next to it, a low square structure with what Tremaine now knew were anatomically correct sea serpents winding sinuously over its pediment. There were a number of men armed with swords or long spears on horseback, making a loose perimeter around the plaza. The horses were distinctly Syprian, with rough dun-colored coats and patterns of small spots along their backs and down their hindquarters.

Heading toward the lawgiver's house, Ander gestured warily toward the largest tree, an old oak with heavy spreading branches that had sunk to the ground under their own weight. "The god came into town during the attack. It's settled in that tree now."

Tremaine stopped to look, squinting to see past the shadows under the branches. She couldn't spot any light or movement that couldn't be accounted for by the gentle breeze. But near the base of the tree, someone had stuck up a post with a goat skull as a warning, a few colored ribbons tied to the horns to catch the eye. "It visited us on the ship too."

Ander glanced at her as if he thought she was insane, but Gerard nodded, asking him, "Did it appear to take part in the battle?"

Ander let out a breath. "Not that I could tell. Except Giliead caught a spell that should have slowly strangled him from the inside out." He shook his head, incredulous. "The Gardier could have done more damage hitting him with a mud clot."

Tremaine nodded. "He's a Chosen Vessel." Gerard just looked thoughtful but Ander stared at her again. "What?" she demanded. "We knew that. Did you think they were making it up?"

Ander snorted in annoyance and stamped away. Tremaine followed, feeling like she had somehow gotten her revenge for that comment of his on the docks but not quite sure how.

Ilias met them at the door to the lawgiver's house, where he had been pacing with his arms folded. He looked like he had rolled in the dirt a few times but otherwise wasn't the worse for wear. "How is it going?" Ander asked him, keeping his voice low.

"I think they've convinced Nicanor," Ilias replied, with a glance back over his shoulder at the open door to make sure he wasn't overheard. "Now they have to convince Visolela."

"Oh, lovely," Tremaine commented under her breath. Visolela was Nicanor's wife, the head of his household and a major power in the city. On their last visit she hadn't even wanted Nicanor to speak to his scandalous relatives and their wizard guests where anybody could see him.

Ilias gave her a rueful glance in acknowledgment as he led the way inside.

A rather dark stone-walled foyer opened into a broad portico around an atrium, which Tremaine realized must be standard for large Syprian houses. It was bigger than the one at Andrien House and had less of the kitchen garden look about it. The trees were cyprus, their roots poking up into the formal flower beds, and there was a square reflecting pool down the center.

In a room opening onto the portico, Giliead, Halian, Nicanor and Visolela sat on low chairs and couches with brightly woven cushions. Halian nodded in greeting as Gerard and Ander stepped in. Giliead looked up with a slight smile. Nicanor, broody and thoughtful, glanced at them but said nothing. Visolela, stone-faced, didn't glance.

Ilias stopped at the entrance to the room, standing back against a stone column painted with red-and-black bands. Tremaine stopped with him, a reflexive habit she had picked up from following him through the caves and the underground city on the island. He gave her a gentle push on into the room.

The floor was all mosaic, with stylized waves along the border and flowers and vines entwining through the center panel. Wine cups and a carafe of some delicate white pottery stood on a low table, but no one was drinking.

Nicanor was Halian's son from his first marriage. He had long dark hair, and the family resemblance showed in the shape of his face and eyes, though Nicanor wasn't quite as tall as his father. Visolela was a beautiful dark-haired woman with a heart-shaped face and, Tremaine saw now, ice-cold eyes. She wore a light sleeveless dress of dark red, a silk stole with black-and-gray square designs looped over one arm.

Looking at Visolela, Ander cleared his throat. "This is Gerard, and Tremaine."

Nicanor actually looked at her this time, with an appraising expression. Visolela's jaw hardened, but she still didn't look. Nicanor asked, "You agree to speak for us to your people?"

It took Tremaine a moment to realize he was speaking to her. "Uh, yes." She started to add *Until you find someone better* but realized in time that it wouldn't exactly engender confidence.

Nicanor accepted that with a glance at Visolela for confirmation. "It won't be easy to convince the council," he said. "And if we do, it will still have to go to the Matriarch's council in Syrneth."

Halian nodded. "Karima could speak for us there. Her cousin Ilyandra is still influential on it."

Her voice hard, Visolela said, "When she tells them that Ixion still lives, I doubt any amount of influence will matter."

Tremaine saw Ilias's gaze go to Giliead. Giliead, fortunately, said nothing, though a muscle jumped in his cheek.

Nicanor flicked a thoughtful glance at Giliead as well, but said, "They will have to be made to understand that the alliance is necessary."

Visolela grimaced, and for an instant the hard lines in her face were visible, the ones that would become permanent evidence of bad temper as she grew older. "If Karima fails to convince them of that, then all of Cineth could end up ostracized. And even if she does, when the Hisians and the Menelai learn we have made a treaty with wizards, they will stop sending their trading ships. The trade with the Chaeans isn't enough to make up the difference. It might not matter to us at first, but people will starve in the smaller towns along the coast."

Halian let out his breath and rubbed his eyes. Tremaine sympathized. It would have been easier to argue with Visolela if she was wrong, but Tremaine suspected that wasn't the case, and they all knew it.

"If the Gardier invade, there will be no trade, no cities or towns to starve." Gerard spoke quietly, and they all looked up, startled. "You saw what they did in your city today. They can't be appeased, because they don't ask for anything. All they seem to want is territory, and people to turn into slaves so they can build more weapons to take more territory. We've found out from Gardier prisoners that they won't make Syprians into slaves because they can't or won't learn your language and they know you consider their tools cursed and will die before you use them. So they'll destroy this coast just to get you out of the way."

Visolela didn't look at him, but her mouth set, and a flush crept up the olive skin of her cheeks. She stood abruptly, gathered her stole with a sharp gesture. "I must speak to the portmaster and the trading guilds."

As she strode out of the room, Nicanor looked after her with a frown. He said, "She'll agree. She just . . . doesn't like the necessity of it."

Tremaine saw Giliead flick a dry look at Ilias. She strongly suspected it represented a repressed sardonic comment that would have undone all Halian and Ander's careful work. With that out of his system, Giliead sat forward, telling Nicanor, "I'll have to go with them, to make sure of Ixion."

Nicanor nodded slowly, tapping his fingers on the table. "They agree to this?"

Giliead looked at Gerard, who cleared his throat and said, "We were hoping you would send some representatives with us. If all goes well, we'll be rejoining the government of Ile-Rien in exile, and they will want to establish formal relations. It will be an exceedingly dangerous journey." He shook his head with a slight rueful smile. "But I know you're all very aware of that."

Later, Tremaine paced out in the plaza. It was early afternoon, and the last remnants of the storm streaked the sky. Ander and Gerard were waiting there too, though most of Ander's men had gone back to the *Ravenna*.

Nicanor had gotten Visolela to agree to Giliead going with the *Ravenna* to keep an eye on Ixion, and also that she would receive representatives from Ile-Rien's government as soon as they could be brought here. Now they just had to convince the rest of the Syprians at their council meeting, where Tremaine would have to be present to answer questions. At least she wouldn't be stuck in the large town assembly, but in the much smaller council chamber that was part of the lawgiver's house.

Coming up to pace next to her, Ander said, "You have to make it clear, we can't sign a formal treaty with them. Only the government-in-exile in Parscia has that authority."

Parscia, their ally to the south of Ile-Rien. It had been under attack as well, and now that the Gardier had overrun Ile-Rien, it was sure to be next. *Maybe they'll stop to destroy Bisra and buy us some time.* "Yes, I know," Tremaine said. "As long as we don't promise anything stupid, the government-in-exile will probably ratify our agreement. If we make it back there before they're all dead too." She grimaced and glanced up at Ander's exasperated face. "I'm sorry, that part wasn't supposed to be out loud."

He swore under his breath. "Tremaine, you have to take this seriously. Don't you understand—"

"I am serious! God, what does it take?" she shouted. She saw Giliead beckoning to her from the portico. "I'm going now. If you're so convinced I'm going to wreck this, then you can always shoot me."

Leaving him glaring after her in frustration, she stamped across to the lawgiver's house, stepping up onto the portico.

"Are you ready?" Giliead asked, managing to sound more encouraging than concerned. Ilias was looking past her at Ander, frowning slightly, and she knew the argument hadn't escaped either of them.

She nodded, feeling the tension start to gather in her chest.

"Karima told me all the rules. And she said Halian would help." From what she understood it wasn't necessary to get the council to vote, as it would be in the Ministry of Ile-Rien; all they had to do was answer the objections of any council members and hope that any objections they couldn't answer were shouted down by the others.

Giliead frowned slightly. "Well, Halian isn't good at speaking to the council." At Tremaine's inquiring look, he added, "He gets angry."

"He was better as the warleader," Ilias put in.

"Oh." Tremaine rubbed her brow, wondering if it was too late to run screaming. "That's good to know."

Giliead led the way along the portico to a large double doorway. Tremaine darted a look past him to see a short hallway leading into a round high-ceilinged room that seemed to be completely crammed with people. Tiers of benches circled the room all the way up to the mosaic ceiling, where little square windows let in light and air. From her earlier briefing, Tremaine knew the lower levels were occupied by the male heads of household and the younger sons and daughters. The female heads of the household sat up on the top tier. Men, even the male heads of household, couldn't speak without the female head of household's presence. Giliead, as Chosen Vessel, was the only one exempt from the rules.

As they entered the room, everyone stopped talking and stared at Tremaine. Somehow she hadn't quite expected that. Ilias nudged her with his arm, not trying to get her attention, but in a Syprian way of showing support. She saw Karima, seated on the top tier and wrapped in an azure stole, wave at them.

Tremaine followed them to the only empty space left, a couple of tiers up where Halian was already seated. She shuffled into a spot next to him as Giliead elbowed room for himself and Ilias on the bench just above. People started to talk among themselves again, but more softly. Then, across the room, Nicanor got to his feet.

He spoke well, making the events of the past two days into a story for his rapt listeners. Listening to him describe Vienne and Port Rel through Ilias's eyes almost distracted Tremaine from the nervous clenching in her stomach. But hearing herself depicted as some sort of hero made her deeply uncomfortable.

The moment when he revealed the fact that Ixion was still alive distracted her from her own concerns. The room went deadly still, the horrified silence seeming to stretch forever. Wincing in sympathy, Tremaine sneaked a look over her shoulder. Giliead's expression was as revealing as a brick wall, but Ilias looked angry and defensive enough for both of them.

When Nicanor finished, Tremaine tensed, her stomach cramping with stage fright, knowing she would be called on next. Then at least ten people leapt to their feet, each clamoring to express an opinion.

"This is impossible. They are wizards."

"They're like the Chaeans, their wizards aren't mad."

"That's no recommendation, we've fought with the Chaeans for decades!"

"The light-keepers saw that giant thing, run by curses!"

"They saw it destroy our enemies!"

Repeat until blind with boredom, Tremaine thought sometime later. Visolela and Karima had both answered some serious questions posed by a few of the female heads of household, all the while warily eyeing each other. Nicanor only occasionally interrupted the confusion on the lower floor, to correct a point of fact or to slap down a particularly outrageous statement, but mostly he kept his seat with a politely interested expression. Tremaine's respect for him as a politician increased; this was taking forever, but nobody would be able to claim afterward that they hadn't gotten a chance to have their say. Halian, on the other hand, looked bored and annoyed and made an irritated huffing noise whenever anyone said anything too stupid. Giliead was wearing his closed, impossible-to-read face; it would have looked more daunting if Ilias hadn't nodded off and slumped over against his arm. The air in the room was warm, and Tremaine was starting to drift a little herself.

Then across the room a tall spare man with the lean face of an ascetic stood up. Several of the others standing and waiting to speak immediately sat down.

Halian sat up, suddenly alert, and leaned over to whisper, "That's Pella." Giliead didn't react as far as she could tell, but he must have tensed, because Ilias sat up abruptly, blearily awake.

The real opposition, Tremaine thought, eyeing Pella.

He surveyed the room thoughtfully, waiting until he had everyone's attention. Finally, he said, "What guarantee do we have that these wizards will deal with us as equals?"

"We don't." Nicanor got to his feet, unhurriedly but without implying that he was stalling for time. "There are no guarantees in any alliance, any agreement, between strangers."

Pella lifted a brow, managing to give the impression that he was reluctant to correct the lawgiver. "Between strangers, yes." His expression hardened. "But all here know that those who make themselves wizards don't think of us as strangers, but as cattle."

Tremaine was on her feet, saying, "Excuse me," before her wits caught up to her. The room was deathly quiet, and everyone stared at her expectantly. She realized she had inadvertently taken the floor from Pella, something only a woman could do in this council. Having the entire room's suddenly riveted attention was not a pleasant experience, but instinct told her she should field this question. Nicanor couldn't argue in abstracts forever, no matter how good a rhetorical speaker he was, Visolela was disinclined to argue at all, and Karima knew nothing about Ile-Rien except the little she had been told.

Tremaine cleared her throat. "Most of our people aren't wizards. I'm not. The captain of the giant ship is not. Our Queen—" She realized she had used the Rienish word; there was no Syrnaic equivalent. She substituted hurriedly, "—Matriarch and her heirs and the members of her council are not. There is nothing in our law anywhere that says a sorcerer's interest takes precedence over that of any other person." Finding herself unable to sustain the formal tone, she added with a shrug and a wry smile, "We're more likely to cheat you because we have politicians than because we have wizards."

A faint murmur rose as everyone talked that over. Pella eyed her for a moment, something she was beginning to recognize as a rhetorical device. He said, "If you truly mean to accept us as equals, then prove it. Prove it with a marriage alliance. Let her align herself with—" He hesitated, but it was a calculated pause, a tactical moment to sweep the room with a glance and make sure he had his audience's attention. "With the Andrien House. With Ilias."

Tremaine blinked. *Did he just say what I think he said?* She looked at the others for help. They were staring at Pella. Ilias was struggling to keep his expression blank, but the flush of red under his tanned skin laid bare his feelings. Giliead's face had suffused with anger, Halian's lip curled with contempt. A glance up at the top tier of seats showed her Karima, sitting up stiffly, her hands knotted in her stole.

Baffled, Tremaine turned back to Pella, who waited with lifted brows, inviting her opinion. Then realization hit. *Oh, I get it.* She smiled at him through gritted teeth. Ilias's curse mark made him almost a nonperson in the cities of the Syrnai; a Syprian woman would never have accepted this offer. The fact that it meant humiliating Ilias in front of the council and his family was obviously just an added bonus. The only thing that made it bearable was the enormous satisfaction she was about to derive from knocking Pella right off his self-congratulatory little pedestal. "Is that a serious offer?"

Pella's expression of calm confidence hardened just a little. Before he could reply, she continued, "It sounds like that would be the Andrien family's business. But if they made the offer . . ." She hesitated for effect, mockingly copying Pella's rhetorical pause. "I would be happy to accept it." *Oh. Wait.* Suddenly uncertain, she leaned down to Ilias, asking in a whisper, "Is that all right with you?"

He looked startled. "What?"

Nicanor was on his feet now. "Is that your condition, Pella? A marriage alliance between Andrien and—" He looked inquiringly at Tremaine, who supplied automatically, "Valiarde."

Pella's lips thinned, but he obviously recognized that it was too late for anybody to back out, especially him. "Yes, that is my condition."

Nicanor turned back to them. "Is it agreeable to Andrien?"

Giliead and Halian stared blankly at each other as if nobody had ever wanted to marry anyone in their family before, and they had no more idea how to handle it than Tremaine did. She knew Halian had been married at least twice; surely he remembered something of the details. Then she saw with relief that Karima had left her place on the top tier of benches and was determinedly making her way down, stepping on the people who weren't fast enough to get out of her way. She stepped over the last bench, catching Halian's hand to steady herself, and leaned over to Tremaine, asking softly, "You said Gerard can speak for your family?"

"He's not my guardian anymore, but he's a trustee of the estate, so, sure." *Stop babbling,* she told herself urgently.

Some of those words had no equivalent in Syrnaic, but Karima must have gotten the drift of it. She nodded sharply. "Let's go talk to him." She took Tremaine's hand, firmly leading her down the steps and away without a glance at anyone else.

Once they were out of the council chamber and into the corridor between the buildings, Karima released Tremaine so she could unwrap her stole and shake out her hair. Without looking at her, Karima said, "Is this just for an alliance?"

Tremaine felt sweat break out all over her body though it was cooler out here than in the council chamber. "No," she found herself saying.

Karima stopped to face her, her expression intent, guarded but hopeful. "You would want to take him back to your land?"

"I don't have a land anymore. Even if we drive the Gardier away—" Tremaine took a deep breath. She had the distinctly contrary sensation of her mind being blank but her thoughts racing. It was uncomfortable. "I'll have to stay with the *Ravenna* until we find out one way or another if there's a chance to go back. Unless they throw me off the ship, which is always a possibility." *You're babbling again.* "But one way or another—I wouldn't ask him to go back," she finished awkwardly.

Karima nodded seriously. She started toward the steps out into the plaza, saying, "If you decide to go back to your land, then he will still be better off. Men who have been married once aren't subject to the family laws."

Following her, Tremaine nodded, not sure she was taking it all in.

Gerard and Ander, sitting on the steps of the lawgiver's house, stood up as they saw Tremaine. Gerard frowned in consternation, and Ander demanded, "It's over? What's happened?"

Tremaine stopped in front of them, looking expectantly at Karima, who lifted her brows slightly. Tremaine realized she needed to do the talking. She braced herself, giving them both what she hoped was a confident expression. *First things first: get rid of Ander.* "Karima and I need to speak to Gerard alone."

Ander's frown deepened, and he threw a sharp look at Gerard, but he retreated back out of earshot without further protest.

Gerard lifted his brows, puzzled. "Tremaine?"

She cleared her throat. Her teeth wanted to chatter from nerves, and she had to clamp her jaw to stop it, which made it difficult to talk. "It's going well; well, there's a lot of arguing, but— They want a marriage alliance, so I'm going to marry Ilias."

Gerard blinked. "You . . . you what?"

"You have to give us something. A boat, land, cattle, something of value," Karima put in, her voice a little concerned. "It doesn't matter to me, but if it's too little, then it seems as if you don't value him."

"I see." Tremaine nodded, not sure she did see but willing to work with Karima. She did have land, a house and a lot of property not leased to the Viller Institute, but it was all on currently Gardier-occupied war-torn territory. She also had an art collection if the Gardier didn't find or destroy the hidden vaults. Then she remembered the gold coins she had taken out of the family deposit box at the bank to pay the forger. "I've got gold, Rienish gold reals. They're each four ounces of solid gold, or really about 90 percent gold with trace metals. You can melt them down, or you might like them just as they are. They have the royal seal on them, and they won't be made anymore, so—" *Stop it.* She should tell Gerard she was hysterical and ask him to slap her. "I don't have them with me, but they're on the boat. The ship."

Karima was nodding, smiling in relief. She drew her stole around her. "That will be perfect. We don't use gold, but the merchants from Argot will trade a lot of grain for it." She threw Gerard a look, obviously noting that he had something to say on the subject. "Come back when you're ready."

Tremaine watched Karima walk back to the council house, then turned reluctantly to Gerard. At least he looked more grim than incredulous. He said, "Are you actually seriously contemplating this?"

Tremaine gestured erratically. *Maybe I am out of my mind. But then, didn't I know that already?* "Yes. It's perfect. It's what they want. Actually they don't want it, but they've suggested it, and now they can't get out of it. I'm in there too. I mean, I think it's a good idea."

Gerard rubbed his face, possibly trying to calm himself. "Tremaine, you can't."

She nodded rapidly. "I can, actually."

He said tightly, "Your father entrusted me—"

She gestured, impatient. "Gerard, we both know if my father was alive, he wouldn't give a damn—"

"I'm afraid we both do not know that—"

"And if he did, we wouldn't know until it was too late. And by the way, I'm doing it anyway."

Gerard let out a frustrated breath and looked away.

Tremaine waited uncomfortably. If it was a tactic, it was working. Unable to help herself, she said, "What are you thinking?"

Gerard regarded her. "I'm thinking it's typical of you that you can't explain how a steam engine works, but you can give the weight and metallurgic contents of a gold real."

While she was trying to decide how to respond to that, Ander returned, his face dark with impatience. "Will you tell me what the hell the problem is?"

"I'll explain," Gerard said sharply.

"I'm getting married," Tremaine told him, suddenly enjoying herself.

The incredulous expression on Ander's face was classic. "What?"

"Tremaine—" Gerard began warningly.

"Wait, wait. Can I borrow your notebook?" As Gerard reluctantly handed it over, Tremaine told him, "We need to send for the coins." She thought for a moment about whom she trusted to go through her things, then wrote a note to Florian, asking her to take the leather document case out of her bag and send it to her.

"What is this?" Ander demanded, looking at Gerard. "What is she talking about?"

"I don't know, why don't you ask her?" Tremaine said. She tore the page out, folded it, and handed it to an unwilling Gerard. "I'm going back in." She made her escape before either man could object.

Halian and Nicanor had moved to the far side of the chamber, talking intently amid the babble of other conversations. Pella had not been invited to join them, and he stood watching, his face tight with tension and thwarted anger. To Ilias, he looked like a man who had realized he had made a fool of himself and was all the more determined to make somebody pay for it. He also noticed a lot of people were staring at him, and not for the usual reasons.

Giliead had gone off with Halian, but now came back to sit down on the step next to Ilias, asking quietly, "How do you feel about this?"

Good question, Ilias thought. He wished he had the answer. "We want an alliance," he said to avoid it. He shrugged. "Even if it's Pella's idea, it's the best way."

Giliead's lips thinned in irritation. "That wasn't what I asked."

Ilias rubbed his eyes. Everyone was still watching them, or at least it felt like everyone. Giliead, of course, wouldn't care. The laws didn't give the Chosen Vessel any special authority in marriage matters, but if Giliead decided to argue against it, there would be few who would oppose him.

Silk brushed his arm, and he looked up to see Visolela standing over them. She was trembling with anger, her lovely face flushed as she demanded, "Are you going to allow him to do this?"

Ilias stared at her. "Me?"

Giliead just looked at her. It was a badly timed question, since Giliead must be in the middle of deciding just that. He said, coldly, "Go away."

She stared down at them, the flush deepening, then gathered her skirts and walked back down the tiers.

Giliead watched her go. "This could turn out badly."

He wasn't talking about Visolela; they already knew that was going to turn out badly. Ilias snapped, "And I just wouldn't know what to do, since nothing bad's ever happened to me before."

Giliead's jaw set, but his expression said he knew exactly how conflicted Ilias was. Ilias looked away.

Halian returned, taking the seat just below them. He looked up at Ilias seriously. "Well? Do you want to do this?"

People keep asking me that. "Will they really agree to the alliance if I do?"

Halian persisted, "If you're just doing this for the alliance, tell Karima now."

"If I'm not just doing it for the alliance, when do you want me to tell her?"

Halian swore in frustration. Giliead muttered something inaudible but obviously not complimentary. Ilias told him sharply, "You can stay out of this now."

Karima returned, the muttered babble of conversations quieting as she crossed the room. They stood up as she reached them. Karima lowered her voice, reporting, "She said she wouldn't expect you to go back to their land."

Giliead let out his breath, and Ilias couldn't help feeling gratified at the relief on his face. He was aware of the knot in his chest easing. He told them, "Yes, I'll do it."

Chapter 6

The story changed depending on who told it and when, but Giliead said most often that when Ilias was a young boy, his father told him they were going to town, but they took a horse and went the long way through the hills. He put Ilias down and told him he would come back for him later. It was windy but Ilias was more bored than cold, and he started to build a fort out of rocks. Enough time went by for the fort to get fairly elaborate. He went to look for sticks to make the boats, and that's when he found the little bones and the skull.

— *"Ravenna's voyage to the Unknown Eastlands,"*
Abignon Translation

Tremaine returned to the council room to find everyone milling around, talking over the situation. Her nerves jumping at the prospect of facing Ilias again, she threaded her way through the crowd back toward her seat, only to find her path blocked by Visolela. The woman gave her a flinty stare.

With Giliead's sister and Halian's daughter both killed by Ixion, and Giliead an unmarriageable Chosen Vessel, the house, land and property of Andrien would pass to Visolela when Karima died. Since Ilias still had the curse mark, Tremaine didn't think any of that had changed; Ilias was a ward of the house, not a son, so she wasn't sure if his wife would have been eligible to inherit. Looking at Visolela, standing stiffly and trying to face down the annoying foreigner, Tremaine didn't think she was keen on the idea anyway.

Spurred by an uncharitable impulse, Tremaine smiled and said heartily, "So, I suppose we're going to be related now."

Visolela stared, her mouth whitening with tension. Tremaine continued, "I can assure you that the Valiarde family is really something back in Ile-Rien. Yes, really something. It's a shame about the hereditary insanity of course, but—"

Visolela's almond-shaped eyes grew dark with rage. "Why are you doing this?" she asked tightly.

Tremaine was struck by some reluctant respect for her directness. Maybe they could actually talk; it wasn't unheard of. "That's a question I ask myself about almost everything." She shrugged slightly, trying to look casual rather than frantic. "This was Pella's idea, but it's a good one."

With deliberate emphasis, Visolela said, "Ilias was the only chance the Andrien had for a profitable alliance. Before he was ruined, there were women who were willing to offer as much as two spring harvests for him. Now, he's worthless. Association with a Chosen Vessel made him worthless." Her eyes narrowed. "I ask you again, why are you doing this?"

Fine, scratch the talking option. Tremaine regarded her thoughtfully. "You're a very angry person, aren't you." She leaned forward, just a little too close, looking deeply into the other woman's eyes. "So am I."

Visolela stared at her, her delicate skin reddening, then turned and walked away.

Tremaine watched her go, still fuming. That probably hadn't been the most intelligent response to someone who held so much power in Cineth, but it was too late now. *Two spring harvests?* she wondered, starting toward their seats again. *Was she serious about that? Of course she was; she has no sense of humor.* She suddenly wondered if Arisilde's translation spell substituted the Rienish word "marry" for a Syrnaic word that had no real equivalent, like it had substituted the Syrnaic word "curse" for all the different Rienish terms for magic.

The crowd opened up in front of her and before she realized it she was standing next to Ilias. Badly startled, she fumbled for something to say. Before she could embarrass herself, he said wryly, "Visolela doesn't like this."

"You heard that?" Tremaine asked, desperately self-conscious and trying to remember exactly what it was she had said. He was acting as if nothing had happened, which made it a little easier for her to talk to him without feeling like a bundle of exposed nerves.

He nodded matter-of-factly. "She was upset when I got the curse mark because she wanted to make Karima marry me off to the head of a trading house in Pirus. That's more than thirty days travel inland."

Oh, yes, Tremaine thought as she followed him back to their spot on the tiers of seats. By "marry off" he meant "sell off," or maybe a strange and uniquely Syprian combination of both. *This could be awkward.* There was an old Bisran joke about how there weren't any prostitutes in Ile-Rien because too many of the inhabitants were giving it out for free. Tremaine reminded herself of Karima's comment that men who had been married once were no longer subject to family law. Now that made more pointed sense. If Tremaine left him, Ilias would be free to do whatever he wanted, to stay with Giliead, to start his own household like Gyan the widower or marry again for love like Halian. If he could find a woman willing to ignore the curse mark. "Why is she so against anything that might benefit you?"

He scratched his head and looked vague. "You'll be higher in the family than her."

She frowned, sensing that wasn't the only reason. "By marrying you I'll outrank her? How does that work?"

"You'll be closer to Karima in the family. If I was Karima's blood son, you'd be her heir, but since I'm her ward, you just get the responsibilities but none of the property."

"I see." That made a little more sense. Visolela didn't strike Tremaine as someone too concerned with wealth, but she was all about power. Her position in the family gave her a measure of control over the Andrien's lower echelons, and she didn't want to give that up.

Ilias sat down on the bench and admitted reluctantly, "Also, it's not me she doesn't like, it's Gil. He slept with her once, before she married Nicanor."

Tremaine lifted her brows, genuinely shocked. "And that causes women to start vindictive vendettas against his entire family?" The comment was a knee-jerk reaction, covering her very real surprise that Giliead had ever actually unbent long enough to do something stupid, such as sleep with a woman who had "heart-eating bitch" written on her forehead.

"It doesn't usually go that far," Ilias admitted.

Tremaine looked up to see Visolela, still stiff with rage, standing by the opposite side of the tier. "Let me guess—she wanted him to use his position to benefit her in some way, he got huffy and walked out on her, she can't do anything to him directly because the god might take offense, so she goes after you."

"Don't talk about it in front of Nicanor," Ilias said seriously. "It's one of the reasons they don't get along."

Tremaine rubbed her eyes. The Valiarde family might be no prize but at least none of her relatives were on speaking terms with her. "I'll avoid the subject."

There was more talking, with intervals of yelling, as the discussions got back under way, but the heart had gone out of the opposition.

Tremaine thought herself safe for the next few hours, at least until the council called a formal halt. But the individual members were breaking up into groups to discuss plans for defending Cineth against the Gardier, and there wasn't much point in remaining in the room until they finished. As if aware of this, Gerard cannily sent Dyani in to ask her to come out and speak to him. Tremaine moaned, got up and dragged herself outside to face the worst. Gerard had had time to come up with some good ones.

He was waiting for her under the trees in the market plaza. Gyan and Arites were sitting a little distance away. Gyan nodded gravely to her; Arites had his parchment and ink out and was scribbling rapidly.

Without preamble, Gerard said, "I've spoken to Gyan, who's explained Syprian marriage in detail. In a first marriage the man usually has few rights, unless he comes from a powerful or wealthy family. For example, it's Nicanor's mother's influence combined with Visolela's trading connections that makes him able to hold the position of lawgiver. A wealthy woman can also contract multiple first marriages with more than one man at a time, though in Cineth that's considered declasse. A family such as the Andrien, who don't have much status at the moment, could usually expect to sell its sons into low-status marriages where they are the second or even third or fourth husbands. It's only after divorce, which occurs when the groom is bought by another woman, or his family buys him back—"

"But afterward, he can do what he wants," Tremaine wedged the comment in before he could go any further. She had to admit it was worse than she thought. "Ilias will still be better off, no matter what happens."

Gerard paused, regrouping. He counterattacked with, "Do you think he is in love with you?"

Tremaine snorted. She wasn't lying to herself. "Of course not. If he loves anybody, it's Giliead. But we're friends."

Thwarted, Gerard pressed his lips together. "Building a relationship based on nothing but shared danger doesn't always work."

He sounded like he was speaking from personal experience. Tremaine turned that information over. She had never thought of Gerard as actually having the kind of relationships they were talking about. He had kept his personal life very close over the years, working first for her father, then for the Institute. She met his eyes. "It's a good basis for taking a chance." *God, I almost sound like I know what I'm talking about.* It was frightening.

Gerard watched her a long moment, the tightness in his face softening. "I've seen you go through relationships with feckless young men. I watched you go through a decline that I couldn't understand or affect." He let out his breath. "I don't want you hurt."

I'm already hurt, this is nothing. Tremaine ran a hand through her hair, muttering inadequately, "I won't get hurt." She saw Ander approaching. The last thing she needed was his assessment of her current sanity. She looked for help and saw Karima walking along the portico with Dyani. Council participants were not allowed food during the duration of the discussion to keep things from bogging down, but this would be a good time to ask Karima if there was such a thing as a public restroom. She told Gerard, "I think Ander wants to talk to you. I'll just get out of the way."

Ander called her name sharply, but she didn't stop.

Ilias and Giliead had come out for some air and Ilias spotted Gerard under the trees with Tremaine. He watched Tremaine bolt off after Karima, leaving Gerard looking unhappy. Ilias glanced up at Giliead, knowing he was the cause and uneasy about it. "Maybe I should go talk to him."

Giliead nodded equably. "And say what?"

Ilias glared at him. "I don't know. I've never done this before."

Giliead snorted at the obviousness of this, but followed Ilias over to the trees. Ander reached Gerard first, and Ilias stopped a polite distance away while the young man spoke to the wizard in Rienish. He caught a few words here and there, nothing that really told him what the conversation was about. Some people on the ship spoke the language with such different accents he couldn't make out the few words he did know, and the verbs were always impossible—he was willing to swear on his life that nobody ever used the same one twice. But it was easy to tell Ander was angry.

The young man stamped away finally, and Ilias approached Gerard with caution. Not having anything else to say, he asked, "What's wrong with him now?"

Gerard lifted a brow, watching Ander's retreat with an ironic expression. "I'm afraid he doesn't want you to marry Tremaine."

Giliead eyed Ander's retreating form, not favorably. "Why?"

"I'm not entirely certain. Ander . . . has always been a young man to whom good things came easily. Before the war his family was wealthy and politically influential, and he was something of a darling of society." Gerard shook his head, smiling ruefully. "I may be wrong, but I think he expects Tremaine to be in love with him because most young women are. Since she obviously isn't, he fancies himself to be jealous."

Thinking, *I knew there was a reason I didn't like him,* Ilias cocked a brow up at Giliead, who grimaced in silent agreement. Having been left on a hillside to starve by his natural family because they had more children than they could support, Ilias didn't have much sympathy for Ander's sore ego. "I don't understand. If he wants to marry her too, why can't he just keep trying?" If Tremaine thought her family was willing to accept Ilias, a foreigner with a curse mark, he wasn't sure why she thought they might balk at Ander. If they were Syprians, he would think that Ander didn't want to join a family that had someone with a curse mark in it, but that didn't apply to the Rienish.

Gerard sighed, contemplated the sky for a moment as if asking it for strength, then said, "We don't have polygamy. Tremaine can only marry one man."

"So by your law, if she has me, she can't have him?" Ilias considered that, intrigued. "Huh."

Giliead folded his arms, his expression suggesting that he had a headache. "This is going to be interesting," he said under his breath.

Choosing Syprian representatives to go with the *Ravenna* had turned out to be a political infight that rivaled the combined machinations of Ile-Rien's Ministry, the Council of Guilds and the People's Front of Adera, as far as Tremaine could tell. The dangers inherent in the voyage weren't a problem, as Syprians were used to the idea of all long voyages being dangerous. Most people were more afraid of the *Ravenna* herself, though there seemed an equal number who were unwillingly intrigued by her.

Giliead was going because of Ixion; Ilias, even before the marriage business had come up, had planned to go with him. Apparently Chosen Vessels often acted as envoys, and there was a Chosen Vessel in the nearby community of Tyros who had watched over Cineth in Giliead's absence before and could be counted on to do it again. Apparently, Tremaine reflected, Cineth's god and Tyros's god didn't mind the temporary substitution.

Halian wanted Gyan to go as Cineth's representative, but Pella and his followers seemed to think Gyan was an inappropriate choice. Karima had intervened, standing up to demand sharply what Gyan and through him the Andrien House was suspected of.

Since the only possible answer to that was of making a private alliance with foreign wizards in order to oust Nicanor and Visolela and take over the city, a scenario that would involve a personal betrayal of the god on Giliead's part, the god's willful ignorance of that betrayal, and a betrayal of his son and daughter-in-law by Halian, as well as attributing absurdly labyrinthine motives to a family who had apparently shown little or no interest in city politics for years, Gyan was duly chosen as representative. Visolela then added five others, led by her older sister Pasima, a tall dark-haired woman with an athletic build, who had entered the council chamber during the discussion. She didn't have Visolela's perfection of feature, but the family resemblance was easy to see in her high cheekbones and stubborn chin. From the disgruntled look Giliead and Ilias had exchanged, Tremaine suspected the suite was going to seem awfully crowded.

Now all that was settled, and they were outside on the steps of the lawgiver's house waiting for a woman with the alarming title of marriage broker. The process sounded like it was less complicated than registering at the local Magistrate's office, but Tremaine found herself pacing and sweating. A sailor from the *Ravenna* had brought her leather case, and she had been gratified to see that Florian had taken the extra precaution of tucking it inside one of the ship's Royal Mail dispatch bags.

The sun was going down and a warm purple twilight had descended over the city. Tremaine forced herself to stop pacing and sat next to Giliead on the steps. Gerard and Ilias were standing over by the trees, with Gerard cross-questioning him on God knew what. Tremaine rubbed sweaty palms on her pants, thinking that it was a good thing she secretly liked causing trouble, or every nerve would have shattered like glass. Surprising herself, she asked Giliead suddenly, "Is this a good idea?"

He didn't ask what "this" she meant. "Yes." He cocked an eyebrow at her to see if she thought he was going to stop with that unsatisfactory answer, then added, "Because Ilias thinks it's a good idea."

She turned that over. "Why does Ilias think it's a good idea?"

Giliead shrugged slightly. "He's always wanted somewhere to belong, since his family abandoned him. He belongs with Andrien, but . . ." He took a deep breath, sounding resigned. "It's hard to convince him of that, sometimes."

Tremaine found that prospect daunting. "I'm not going to tell him what to do."

"He's never listened when I've told him what to do." Giliead smiled dryly, then added, "He needs someone to tell him he's all right. He doesn't believe me. Maybe he'll believe you."

"Me." Tremaine rubbed her forehead. "Why me?"

He eyed her thoughtfully. "You wouldn't lie to anyone to make him feel better."

Tremaine lifted a brow at him. "Because I wouldn't care enough?"

"I just don't think it would occur to you," he admitted. "Why do you think this is a good idea?"

Still reeling from this accurate assessment of her character, she said slowly, "I don't know. I think, maybe, I'm going to need the help."

Giliead looked up, and Tremaine realized that they were being approached by Ilias, Halian, Gerard and an older Syprian woman she didn't recognize.

She got to her feet as Halian said, "This is Nelia of Pergammon House, the marriage broker."

Tremaine eyed the woman reluctantly, trying not to make a snap judgment. Nelia wasn't that much older than Karima, but the lines on her face had the look of dissipation rather than age or weather, and her flesh sagged. All Syprians seemed to favor bright colors but her orange wrap clashed with her red skirt, and the green-and-brown-stamped figures along the hem didn't go with any of it. "Marriage broker and the midwife," the woman added sharply. "I still have the office, even if your Visolela took away my right to do the job."

"How nice for you," Tremaine said, not trying to make it sound polite. She had the feeling her snap judgment was going to prove accurate.

Nelia fixed a critical eye on Tremaine. "You look a little old to be making a first marriage. I see why you're willing to ally yourself with the Andrien, especially the marked one."

"Look, old woman—" Tremaine began, but Halian interrupted, telling Nelia repressively, "If you had any objections, you should have taken it up with Karima this afternoon."

Nelia nodded, as if he hadn't just all but told her to shut the hell up. "Having brought these two into the world, and most of the other boys in this town their age, I have to take an interest."

"It's a wonder any of us made it out alive," Ilias said under his breath.

Giliead, who had been studying Nelia with cool contempt, said, "We're in a hurry."

Nelia turned to him but didn't have quite the courage to treat him as cavalierly as she did the others. "Very well, very well." She turned to Tremaine. "How much are you prepared to offer for this fine young man?"

Gerard winced. "God help us," he murmured in Rienish. Gritting her teeth, Tremaine started to dig a handful of coins out of the case. Leaning over to look, Ilias said, "Not that much."

He ducked away as Nelia slapped him on the side of the head with her fan, snapping, "You're not in her family yet."

The blow couldn't possibly have done more than irritate him. But Tremaine's nerves were already on edge and she caught the woman's eyes and said in a level tone, "You do that again and I'll break all your fingers." *You are obviously not the type for a career in the diplomatic service.* If they ever managed to reach the government-in-exile, she doubted they would ratify her status as ambassador pro tem to Cineth and the Syrnai, not unless they wanted a war with their prospective allies.

Nelia eyed her, trying to decide if the threat had been serious or not. "I'm just looking out for Andrien interests."

"Don't do us any favors," Halian told her impatiently. "And the tide isn't waiting for you."

Tremaine hesitated, not sure how much to offer. She glanced at Ilias, but he had retreated to a safe distance, looking annoyed. Then behind Nelia's back, Giliead held up three fingers. Apparently Nelia had eyes in the back of her head because she whipped around to glare suspiciously up at him. He turned the signal into an absent scratch at his chest, lifting a laconic brow at her expression. Relieved to have something to go on, Tremaine fished out three coins and handed them to the old woman.

"Done!" Nelia exclaimed. She turned the coins over curiously, rubbing her fingers over the raised images on the surface.

Tremaine let out her breath. In the future of Rienish-Syprian diplomatic relations—if the Gardier left enough of either place—this might prove a real sticking point. Ile-Rien had ancient laws against slavery, mainly because Bisra had had slavery at the time, and Ile-Rien was automatically against everything that Bisra was for. And there were strict laws enacted only in the last century against indenture. Tremaine was fairly sure she had just broken about three of them.

"Your mother wants to see you both before you go," Halian was telling Giliead, the way he half turned his back on Nelia suggesting that she had ceased to exist once she had fulfilled her function.

Gerard led Tremaine aside a few paces, telling her, "That's all there is, there's apparently no ceremony."

"Oh." Tremaine had thought things were being truncated because of the need to leave at nightfall. "That's very . . . businesslike."

"Yes." Gerard didn't say *I told you* so but Tremaine definitely felt it floating in the air somewhere. He eyed her a moment. "I'm going back to the ship with the others. Will you wait for them?"

"Yes, I'll wait."

He squeezed her shoulder and walked away.

Watching him go, she was still on the steps when Ander came out of the lawgiver's house with Nicanor and Visolela.

He spotted her and it was too late for anything but a hurried retreat, and Tremaine suddenly didn't feel like retreating anymore.

He came toward her with a firm stride, and for half an instant she thought he meant to grab her arm. Tremaine had kept the pistol the sergeant had given her after Ixion had escaped; the holster was clipped to the back of her tough leather belt, concealed by the flap of the loose Syprian shirt. Her sudden awareness of it was a reminder that she had made a little rule about not carrying firearms for a reason, though this time she wasn't thinking of killing herself.

But he stopped in front of her, saying in a clipped tone, "Can I speak to you for a moment?"

"Of course." Past his shoulder she saw Ilias watching them alertly. She remembered that Ilias had never liked the way Ander behaved toward her, not even during their first confused meeting in the caves under the island. It had to be a social misunderstanding, but it was interesting that there was something in Ander's attitude toward her that Ilias interpreted as insulting.

"You didn't have to do this," Ander said in Rienish.

Tremaine briefly considered forcing him to explain what he meant by "this," but she was more in the mood for a frontal assault. "Maybe, but it's moved things along faster."

He just looked at her for a moment. "I meant, you have other options."

That stopped the frontal assault dead in its tracks. She had no idea what he was trying to say. "I have other options?" she repeated blankly.

He took a sharp breath. "You don't have to throw yourself away like this."

She stared at him. Now she knew what he meant. "You think I'm so desperate for—what? A man? A marriage?" *No, he doesn't think that,* she realized suddenly. *It's just the nastiest thing he can think of to say to me.* She grinned, suddenly free of any emotional constraint. "Go ahead, Ander, I welcome your expertise on all aspects of my private life."

He eyed her narrowly, and she could tell he was disconcerted by her reaction, which was more satisfying than any amount of yelling and hitting. She prodded, "What, nothing else to say? I'm shattered. No, really."

He shook his head grimly. "You make it impossible for anyone to care about you." With that he turned and walked away, leaving her standing there with a set jaw and half a dozen replies she couldn't use.

Ilias came to join her, watching Ander's retreating back. "What was that about?" he demanded.

"Ander being . . . Ander. Unfortunately." A sudden wave of rage startled her, and she realized she was too angry to have a coherent conversation with anyone now. Especially her prospective in-laws. Actual in-laws. Better to leave Ilias and Giliead and the others to say their good-byes to Karima and Halian in peace. "I think— I'd better go down to the dock and make sure the boat is ready to leave."

Ilias gave her that look that said he knew what she was thinking and nodded. "We'll be there as soon as we can."

Karima met them in the foyer of the lawgiver's house, where the dust from the plaza made the colors of the floor mosaic seem dim and faded. She stopped Ilias, putting both hands on his face, and asking, "Are you truly certain?"

No, he wasn't. He wasn't sure if it was right for Tremaine or Cineth, but he couldn't tell Karima that. He took her hands and smiled. "I'm certain."

Halian came to put his arm around her, and they went through into the atrium. Visolela, Pasima and more of their assorted relatives were sitting on the porch.

If it had been a normal first marriage, there would have been congratulation and relief and speculation on what the alliance with the new family would mean. But Ilias had a curse mark, and they were allying themselves with foreign wizards in order to defend against more foreign wizards, and he could see everyone was wondering if they were all out of their minds and if this wouldn't end in unimaginable disaster. And he had to get out of here for a moment.

He slipped out of the porch and back to the atrium. Giliead saw him escape but said nothing, just shifting casually to block the view between two columns so the others wouldn't notice. Ilias went through the dining portico at the back to the outer court that faced the street behind the building. The flowers had overgrown the beds here and an old rain tree shaded the big stone cistern from the sun. Ilias took a deep breath and ran his hands through his hair, trying to shake off his tension.

Being away from the pressure of everyone staring at him helped. After a moment he decided to do something useful while he was here and lifted the cistern's cover to drop the bucket in. He glanced up as the gate to the street squeaked, thinking it was Gyan. Instead he found himself looking at his older brother, Castor. Ilias did the first thing that came to mind: he snarled, "Get out."

Castor took a step further in, leaving the gate standing open behind him. In their few encounters as adults, Ilias had never seen much in his brother to remind him of himself; Castor had a heavier build and looked older, gray hair showing through his light-colored braids. Years ago he had married a woman from the western end of the Syrnai, who had been a trader and now owned a small farm not far outside Cineth. Ilias knew there were children and a lot of sheep, though he had tried not to know more. Castor demanded, "Is it true?"

Ilias's eyes narrowed coldly, and he didn't answer. This was about all he needed. He turned his back, grimly hauling up the bucket.

Castor demanded, "You're really going off with those people? On that great floating—thing?"

Ilias slammed the bucket down on the stone rim of the cistern, turning to face him. "It's none of your concern, it's never been your concern." Castor had known the family had decided to turn Ilias out nearly a day before their father had taken him off to the hill. This was just more belated guilt.

Castor took another step toward him. "If they're forcing you to do this, the Finan could help."

Ilias had to laugh. "Oh, you want to help me? And you expect me to believe that?" He knew his mother was behind this; he didn't think Castor had ever had a thought that wasn't put into his head by someone else. "Tell me why you're really here."

Castor gestured in exasperation. "I heard they were selling you to wizards, foreigners. I couldn't—"

"Is that why she sent you?" Ilias interrupted, derisive amusement turning back to fury. The Finan had always claimed that Ilias had run away, since it was against the law to abandon a child. They hadn't tried to press the claim in years, but the gold Tremaine had given for him might be reason enough for this sudden show of sympathy. "I'd throw my marriage price in the harbor before I'd let her touch it. If you think you can—"

"That's not it," Castor snapped. "It's not the price. She would never— She knows the Finan owe you. You know that. She just wants to—"

"I don't want anything she or they have," Ilias interrupted furiously. "And I don't want your pity, or your help or your guilt. Go back and tell her if she wanted to collect three harvest-weights' worth of gold today, she should have picked you to throw away instead of me."

Castor stared at him, breathing hard, his face reddening. It was an unfair blow, and Ilias was bitterly glad to see it hit the mark. Castor was a farmer rather than a warrior and had never been sought after by the young women in town. His trader wife hadn't been able to give much for him, but she had been the only one asking, and the Finan had had to settle for a love match for their oldest son rather than the alliance with a prominent family they had been hoping for. Then Castor said with deliberate scorn, "First Giliead gets you marked, and now this."

Ilias rounded on him, grabbing him by the shirt and yanking him forward. He said through gritted teeth, "Get out of here while you can."

Gyan stepped into the court then, eyeing the situation. Castor threw him a wary look, backing away from Ilias. He slammed out the gate, leaving it open behind him.

Gyan came to take the bucket away from Ilias before he hurled it after Castor. He gave Ilias a penetrating look. "It may be guilt, but he means better than you think."

Ilias shook his head. He didn't want to hear it. Not now, anyway.

With a resigned sigh, Gyan clapped him on the shoulder and gave him a shake. "You know what's best for yourself."

Chapter 7

And so the voyage began at the evening tide, though I learn that tides are meaningless to a ship of such power. Curses or not, foreign wizards or not, I think Ravenna's name will go down with Beila, Starsight, Elea, Wind, Dare and all the other great ships of our history. Whether Visolela likes it or not.

— "Ravenna's voyage to the Unknown Eastlands,"
V. Madrais Translation

Tremaine walked through Cineth alone in the long warm twilight. Most people were behind the dusty white clay walls of their courtyards or houses, having the evening meal or still discussing the frightening events of the day. The odor of cooking and of horse and goat manure competed with the scents of jasmine and the flowering vines that hung over the garden walls.

Though there was little resemblance, she found herself thinking of Vienne in the summer. There had been a large park called the Deval Forest, where it was always cool under the heavy canopy of trees or willow arbors, even in hot weather, and winding streams led to waterfalls and dripping grottoes. There was a small lake for bathing and boating, and anchored in it an old café on two large barges, amid little man-made islands of flowers.

Tremaine scuffed her boots in the dirt, head down, suddenly missing home with all the pain of a punch to the gut. Not the dark cold battered place she had shown Ilias, where the smell of desperation and fear and defeat had lingered in the streets. She missed the home of her memories: the theaters on the Boulevard of Flowers with all their lights lit, the beau monde in their coaches and long black motorcars drawing up in the opera circle, the raucous cafés and clubs where sultry women sang and drunken artists and their models reeled into the streets laughing, the old leather and dust and calm silence of the libraries at Lodun, the noisy markets of the little villages and towns she and Arisilde had wandered through the year after her mother died. She knew she was going to remember all this, if she lasted long enough for memory to dim, with bright points emerging like lighthouses out of a fog of misery.

But Ile-Rien was dying and would drag Cineth and the Syrnai down with it in an effort to save itself.

Tremaine reached the docks just as Ander and his men were leaving in the accident boat. *Pity I missed him,* she thought dryly. One lifeboat remained, the one waiting to pick up her and the Syprians. She walked down the dock to it, scuffing her boots on the stone. The evening breeze was cool as it came off the water, heavy with the scent of the sea. There were torches lit along the front of the Arcade, where people were still cleaning up after the attack, flickering lamps casting warm shadows from the stalls inside. Merchants who had fled earlier were still arriving to see what was left of their stock. Some worked, some stood in groups, talking and shaking their heads. Someone was playing a drum nearby, maybe on one of the boats, the rhythm weaving in and out of the sound of water lapping against the docks.

Down at the other end of the Arcade the wrecked ships still lay. Here were moored small fishing boats, the bows all painted with the elongated eyes, the bare masts bobbing gently in the slow swells. The lifeboat, even with its engine, didn't look all that incongruous among them. One of the Rienish sailors had hung up a couple of oil-burning hurricane lanterns to throw a little light on their area of the dock.

As she reached the boat Tremaine saw Visolela's sister and representative Pasima arrive with Pella and a few other men and women Tremaine vaguely recognized from the council. Some were carrying leather packs or woven bags. Pasima wore a dark-colored wrap draped casually and pinned at her shoulder over pants tucked into boots and a shirt. Some of the others wore similar wraps, draped and pinned or tossed back over one shoulder; it managed to look both stylish and practical for adventuring. Tremaine looked down at herself, wondering why her own outfit didn't look that good. Even in another world, she was terrible with clothes.

The group didn't approach the boat but stood over by the torchlit façade of the Arcade, having a conversation that looked fairly grim even from a distance. Gyan and Kias appeared next, each with a small leather shoulder pack and a scabbarded sword slung across his back. They walked up to the boat and Tremaine helped them pass their belongings over to the sailors to be stowed away. Then Kias jumped down to explore the boat, to the mild consternation of the Rienish sailors. Gyan eyed the small group around Pasima. "That's Pasima's cousin Cletia, Cletia's brother Cimarus, and their second cousins Danias and Sanior," he explained to Tremaine.

Cletia was slight and blond, with long curls that fell past her shoulders, and looked delicate next to tall, raven-haired Pasima. Cimarus was the most striking of the three men, tall and dark-haired, his long braids neatly tied back, and he looked more like Pasima than he did his sister. Danias looked terribly young, his light brown hair tied back in a thick queue, and Sanior didn't seem much older, though his face was set in a solemn expression. Trying to resign herself to their company, Tremaine said, "I'm surprised they convinced so many to come along."

"Well, we don't like to travel alone," Gyan conceded. "And Pasima won't be looking to any Andriens or their hangers-on—that's me, Kias and Arites—for company."

"The more the merrier."

Gyan snorted amusement. "I don't think we'll be doing much merrymaking with them." He shook his head with a sigh, saying, "I'm off to be the peacemaker," and walked over to join them.

Behind Tremaine in the lifeboat the three Rienish sailors were talking about different ports they had visited. Two had Vienne accents and one had a thick hill country inflection, and their voices made an interesting backdrop for the scene. Watching Kias's explorations, one commented, "It's a damn sight better here than the southern Bisran colonies."

"That's certain. These people just avoid you; they don't throw garbage."

A lone figure came up the dock briskly with a bag slung over his shoulder. After a moment Tremaine recognized Arites. He grinned cheerfully at her as he reached the boat, saying, "Don't worry, they're on the way. They were saying good-bye to Karima and Halian when I left."

"I wasn't worrying." Tremaine rubbed her hands off on her shirt and realized her palms were sweating again. Maybe she was worried. Maybe she thought a rational man as Ilias seemed to be would take the chance to escape. It would explain what her stomach was doing up in her throat.

Arites dropped his bag on the stone and rocked back and forth on his heels, observing the dark water lapping against the pilings and the shapes of the other ships with apparent satisfaction. On impulse, Tremaine asked, "Arites, were you married?"

"No, I'm an orphan," he said, with no reluctance. "My family were inland traders, and they were killed when I was a boy."

"Oh." Tremaine nodded slowly, the wind pulling at her hair. "By wizards?"

"Yes. It happened frequently back then. Livia had been the Chosen Vessel for Cineth, and this was just after she died. The god had Chosen Giliead already, but he was still just a boy. The Chosen Vessel for the Uplands already had a lot of territory to cover, and Tyros didn't have a Vessel then. The gods can't be everywhere at once either." He looked down at her, his face calm in the light from the lanterns. "Just bad luck."

"But how did you— Who took care of you?"

"The lawgiver's family is supposed to adopt all orphans, but I ended up at Andrien village, even though Ranior wasn't lawgiver anymore. Most people with problems end up at Andrien village."

"Is that why you came? Because you owe them?"

"No." He grinned down at her. "I just want to see new places."

"That's why I came too," Kias volunteered from down in the boat behind them.

At the end of the Arcade, Ilias and Giliead suddenly pelted around the corner, running as if they were being chased by an army. Tremaine took a step toward them, alarmed. As they passed under one of the torches she saw their faces clearly and realized they were both laughing.

One of the sailors moved up beside her, asking sharply, "Something wrong?"

"I think they're racing." She pushed her hair back, feeling a flush of pure relief that made her face hot.

"Oh." He stood there a moment, watching with a smile, then shook his head, turning back to the boat.

Giliead trapped Ilias against a cart someone had left in front of the Arcade. Ilias feinted, dodging Giliead's attempt at a tackle, tripping him so the bigger man staggered into the wall. He bolted for the dock, pounding triumphantly down the stone pier with Giliead barely a step behind him. He banged into the boat, grabbing one of the stanchions to stop himself catapulting headlong into it, his earrings flashing in the lamplight. Giliead stumbled to a halt, grinning self-consciously.

"You made it," Tremaine said foolishly.

Ilias looked flushed too, but that was probably just from the run. "Karima sent for some things from the house this afternoon; the courier got back just as we were about to give up on him." He dropped a leather pack and a cloth bag down into the boat. He had a sword strapped across his back, the curved horn hilt sticking up over his shoulder. One of the Rienish sailors came to help stow the gear under the seats, and Arites jumped down to help. Giliead had a sword too and a couple of long cases of light wood, one almost as tall as Ilias, the other about half the size. They had both changed clothes and cleaned up: Ilias wore a rust-colored shirt, sleeveless to show off the copper armbands, and the wrap thrown over his shoulder was the color of red wine.

Gyan returned from the group around Pasima, giving Giliead a clap on the back and Ilias's shoulder an affectionate shake. Giliead jerked his chin toward Pasima, Cimarus and their companions, asking in a low voice, "Are they coming or not?"

"She wouldn't back out now," Gyan said, grunting as he grabbed a stanchion and swung down into the boat. "But by the look of the others, they want to," he added in a low voice.

Ilias hopped down, holding up a hand to help Tremaine as she clambered after him. "What's wrong with them?" he demanded impatiently. He seemed anxious to get on the way. Tremaine couldn't think of anything to say that didn't sound stupid, so she kept her mouth shut.

"Now, you two have gone out beyond the reach of the gods since you got your full growth." Gyan gave Ilias a look of mild reproof. "Those youngsters have never been farther than the next city for the trading days."

"Are we ready?" Seaman Vende asked Tremaine. The other sailors were preparing to cast off, one of them stepping back up onto the dock to take down the lanterns.

"Five more," Tremaine told him, having to think a moment to switch back to Rienish. She turned to Giliead. "Should we call them, or—" She stopped when she saw Pasima and her group walking toward the boat, the lamplight revealing their stiff set expressions.

This is going to be an interesting trip, Tremaine thought grimly. "We're ready now," she told Vende.

They survived being winched up the *Ravenna*'s side again though the Syprian newcomers shifted uneasily and looked green in the lamplight. Tremaine couldn't blame them since the experience filled her with terror too.

She was aware that the Syprian delegates' first close-up look at the *Ravenna* was not one guaranteed to impress. With a possibility of Gardier in the area, the ship was still in blackout, and the deck was unlit except for a few small handlamps held by the sailors. The upper decks and the great stacks looming above them were just shapes and shadows in the dimness.

They gathered on the deck in an uneasy group, Pasima and her companions separating themselves from the other Syprians and from the sailors working to get the boat swung up and locked down in the davit. Ilias drew Tremaine a little further away from them, and said, "Hey, an Argoti merchant already offered Karima a shipload of grain for two of those coins. She's keeping one for the family."

"That's great." Tremaine suppressed an urge to throw herself over the rail. She didn't know if it was a suicidal impulse or just a rational response to the situation. "Ah, one thing. I'd rather you not tell Ander about the details of the, uh, marriage settlement."

"Why? Will he be jealous?"

"He would be, if he had any right whatsoever to be, which he doesn't; we talked about that before, remember?" She managed to force herself past that thought and on to the next. This was as good a time as any to try to explain the difference in Rienish society. "It's just that in Ile-Rien, paying for someone to marry is not looked on very well."

Tremaine knew she shouldn't have said anything when Giliead made a faint noise in his throat, possibly an aborted, instinctive warning, then found something very interesting to look at on the deck between his boots.

She couldn't see Ilias's expression in the jerky light of the sailor's handlamps, but he stared at her for a full minute. Then he said in a clipped tone, "If that's how you want it."

"Tremaine, can you come here a moment?" Gerard's voice called from somewhere behind her.

Ilias walked away without another word.

Giliead stepped up beside her, and Tremaine said, "I shouldn't have said that, should I?"

He shook his head, said under his breath, "The amount of the marriage price is . . . important. I'll talk to him," and followed Ilias.

Tremaine clapped a hand to her forehead. *I have the feeling I'm not getting laid tonight, either.*

"Tremaine!" She looked around to spot Gerard, gesturing emphatically at her in the dim light from the nearest hatch. As she made her way toward him, he said, "I'm glad you're back. There's a meeting in the Third Class drawing room. You've been asked to attend."

"Oh, goody." She followed Gerard's lamp inside and up the stairs.

Tremaine winced as they turned into a dark-paneled interior corridor where the electrics were far too bright. Suddenly she found herself grabbed and hauled aside by Florian.

The other girl stared at her incredulously. "You got married!"

Tremaine nodded. "Yes."

Florian looked worried. "But it's a matriarchy."

"Yes."

"Did he have a choice?"

"I asked him—afterward—and he said 'what?' but everyone was talking. So maybe, no, I don't know." Tremaine rubbed her temples, feeling a headache coming on. "So who do you think did that, the flighty poet or the maniac?"

Florian let out her breath. "I think it was some scary combination of both."

"But I had to do it," Tremaine protested. "It didn't exactly get everyone on our side, but it helped."

"And you wanted to do it," Florian prompted hopefully.

"Oddly enough, yes."

Gerard came back down the corridor, saying impatiently, "Tremaine, come along, please."

"I'm coming, dammit!"

Florian squeezed her arm. "I'm sure it will work out. Well, I'm not sure, but you know what I mean."

Gerard led Tremaine to the doorway of the Third Class drawing room. It was relatively small, for a public room on this ship, and almost cozy. There were still overstuffed armchairs, a marble hearth, and a floor-to-ceiling mural on the far wall of picturesque Parscian fishing boats at dock in some sun-drenched seaside town. Tremaine didn't want to contemplate it too closely, afraid to recognize it as a real place that had been bombed to extinction by the Gardier.

Seated around the room, Tremaine saw Niles, his assistant Giaren, Colonel Averi, Captain Marais, Count Delphane and Lady Aviler, as well as other ship's officers and some members of the Viller Institute she didn't know well. Colonel Averi was at the front of the room, saying, "We proved one thing conclusively. It is the crystals that provide protection against our spells, not anything inherent in the Gardier as individuals. That explains why the only spells that have any effect on them are illusions and glamours and concealment wards. The crystals can defend against an outright attack, but passive spells don't provoke a reaction."

"Is it true about the crystals actually containing . . . the spirits of people?" Lady Aviler frowned, as if she felt odd asking the question. "Of sorcerers?"

"Unfortunately, yes." Averi nodded to Gerard. "We'll hear a more complete report on that later. The captured Gardier have verified it, though they seem to know nothing more about the subject. They are beginning to speak to us, though they haven't said much of strategic value yet. We were trying to get them to tell us where the Gardier capital is, or at least what direction their homeland lies in. They seemed unable to point it out on the maps we have. I say unable, rather than unwilling, because once we realized spells would affect them Niles made us a confusion stone to use during the questioning. We have heard some details of their society. Some of these men seem to have been soldiers from birth. None of them can read or write except for a few simple symbols. This certainly explains why we found so few examples of written records in the wreck of the airship the Institute examined. It's my belief that only the upper-level officers are literate."

And I thought Ile-Rien's Village School Authority had problems,

Tremaine thought wryly. "How very odd," Gerard muttered. "For a society that seems so advanced in other ways."

Averi continued, "Now the one female soldier admitted that she can read. So she may have some sort of higher rank than the other prisoners, and may have more knowledge of where their homeland can be found. We're concentrating our efforts on her."

The colonel took his seat, and Gerard took advantage of the opportunity to move up to the front next to Niles. Tremaine edged into the back of the room, groping for a chair where she could think and possibly doze, when she heard her name.

Ander was on his feet, obviously about to report on the negotiations with the Syprians. "There was one problem. Miss Valiarde instructed the Syprian leadership not to sign any agreements with us."

Gosh, thanks, Ander, Tremaine thought, trapped on her feet by a sideboard and a small table someone had shifted into the aisle.

Delphane turned in his chair to fix his eyes on her. "Why was that?"

Tremaine tried to conceal her irritation. "I was negotiating on their behalf. It wasn't in their best interests."

"You've caused trouble, young lady. If you think—"

Fine. If that's the way you want to do it, let's put all the cards on the table. "If we're going to have a meeting like this, don't you think we should ask the Princess Olympe to attend?" Tremaine leaned back against the sideboard, folding her arms.

Silence settled over the room. She saw Gerard cover his eyes with his hand. Lady Aviler's head turned sharply toward her. Tremaine watched Delphane's face as he made a startled effort to conceal his real shock with angry disdain. He gave a short bark of laughter. "What on earth are you talking about?"

Tremaine shrugged slightly, milking the moment for all the brittle satisfaction it was worth. "I just hate to think of her getting bored, up there on the Sun Deck in Special Suite 3."

Someone coughed nervously, and Delphane's gaze narrowed with suspicion and defeat. He said grimly, "How did you know?"

Tremaine shrugged, making it look careless. There was only one explanation for Count Delphane, Lady Aviler and the Solicitor General all taking the *Ravenna* when they should have gone to Parscia with the rest of the court and the government. "I think Niles's report on the success of the sphere at deflecting Gardier spells did reach the palace by the day we left. There wasn't much time to do anything with the information since the Gardier were so close to overrunning Vienne. But you must have realized how dramatically the chance of the *Ravenna* getting through the blockade had improved." She looked down, idly scuffing her boot against the tile floor. "Reynard Morane told me the royal family had already left Vienne for Parscia that morning, but there would have been time to telegraph ahead and suggest an alternate escape route. The Queen wouldn't take it; if she was going to abandon the government, she would have done it before now. But she might take the opportunity to send one of the heirs to the throne, along with suitable escorts who could help her negotiate with the Capidarans. If she had sent Prince Ilorane, there would be no reason for Lady Aviler to come along. That leaves the Princess Olympe. Oh, I knew the number because that's the suite that was built for the royal family. It's on the tourist brochure." She looked at Delphane, lifting her brows. "So? Should we telephone and see if she wants to join us?"

The room was quiet. Someone shifted uneasily, and someone else stifled a cough. Delphane's eyes met hers, cold, assessing. *You broke cover,* Tremaine told herself. *The clumsy diffident girl with the odd sense of humor shows her true colors.* The realization should have left her cold, but somehow it didn't. She gave Delphane a cool little smile.

Lady Aviler said quietly, "She's asleep at the moment." Her expression was thoughtful. "You know Captain Morane, Miss Valiarde?"

Tremaine knew she felt more at ease taking on Delphane than Lady Aviler; she suddenly recognized that as the self-preservation instinct it was. Delphane had a higher position in the court and the government, but Lady Aviler had organized the evacuees; until they reached Capidara she had more real power on the ship, possibly almost as much as Captain Marais. Tremaine deliberately softened her voice, dropped the challenge from her tone. "He's an old friend of the family."

Lady Aviler lifted a brow but didn't comment.

Captain Marais cleared his throat and got to his feet, taking control of the room. "This is all very well, but we need to discuss our immediate plans. Niles, if you would?"

Niles stepped briskly forward, taking a pointer off the mantle and indicating the map. "We've discussed prospective routes at length, using the captured Gardier maps. We'll travel through this world's ocean until we reach the approximate location of Capidara's coast.

Then we'll create a world-gate and cross back through to our world and proceed to the port at Capistown. There, we drop off the civilians and resupply and refuel, and pick up whatever troops are available. Then back through the gate to this world. We sail back in this direction but head further west until we're in the approximate location of Parscia's coast, create another world-gate and dock there, and make contact with the government-in-exile." He turned to regard his audience, his face serious. "We're in a unique position. The *Ravenna* is the only Rienish vessel currently capable of moving between this world and our own, and she can make that crossing at will. The Gardier airships can only cross between worlds when they're within a mile of one of their spell circles. The *Ravenna* can also easily make the crossing between Parscia and Capidara in four to five days, faster than any military vessel we have left, twice as fast as the Gardier's airships. She can also transport, if pressed, close to ten thousand troops, perhaps more. Even though the Gardier inhabit this world, they don't seem to have devoted much of their resources to patrolling these waters as they have in ours. If we can establish a corridor of transport between our two allies—"

Tremaine edged into a chair, glad for the respite, even if it was temporary.

Their boat had been hauled aboard at a different place than last time, much closer to the stern, so finding their way back to their quarters took longer. The outer rooms were kept dark for safety, so the Gardier wouldn't be able to see the ship's outline from their flying whales. "If you get lost," Gyan told Pasima and the others kindly as they blundered through a nearly pitch-dark chamber, looking for a passage inward, "It's easiest to find a stair and go up or down until you see something you recognize. In the passages you could walk ten ships' lengths in the wrong direction before you know it."

"Where is Ixion kept?" Pasmia asked sharply. Ilias suspected her hard voice masked nervousness; at least he hoped so. "Is it near here?"

"A few decks down," Giliead answered, deliberately vague.

They found the stairway down into the big chamber with the marble pillars and glass-walled rooms, the wizard lights making bright reflections behind their glass covers. There were quite a few people there now, most sitting on the cushioned couches and chairs. A large elaborately woven carpet was doing duty as a play area for several babies and small children just big enough to walk. Some of the people pointed or called "hello" as they saw the Syprians, one of the Rienish words Ilias could recognize if the speaker didn't slur it too much. Arites waved back cheerfully, and Ilias made himself smile, since Pasima and the others kept expressions of aloof contempt. Arites, Gyan and Kias were acting as if they were completely accustomed to all the exotic colors and fine wood and crystalline glass.

As they started down the big stairway, past the portrait of the woman and her husbands, he heard Pasima ask Giliead, "How do you know which ones are wizards?"

Unable to help himself, Ilias said, "First, you get born a Chosen Vessel, then—" He cut himself off there, years of experience telling him when Giliead was about to clout him in the head in exasperation.

"There aren't many wizards on board," Giliead replied dryly, and left it at that.

They arrived at the cabin and found the wizard lights still on. The walk had given Ilias time to realize he was more mad at himself than anyone else. He had let himself forget that this really didn't change anything, no matter what Karima wanted to believe. A marriage wouldn't take away the curse mark.

He dumped his pack on one of the chairs and carried the wooden bow case into the room with the big table. He opened the case to count five goathorn bows and a bundle of sinew to string them; they had never been able to bring this many weapons along on a sea voyage before, and it was a novelty to have so many to choose from. But if they had unlimited space, they might as well take advantage of it.

Giliead brought the case containing the arrows and a set of javelins. He put it down on the table, saying nothing eloquently.

"I'll apologize to her," Ilias told him, hoping his tone would cut off further discussion. He picked up one of the bows, realizing it was old, the grip well-worn, the carving teasingly familiar. "Is this Ranior's old bow?" The words were out before he could stop them, and he winced. He didn't want Giliead to think he was using the painful past as a means to change the subject.

But Giliead only shrugged slightly, leaning one hip on the table. "No point in letting it sit in the cabinet, unused."

The curse that had destroyed Ranior, Giliead's father before the god, was the first curse that Giliead had ever faced. Even though the god had chosen him years before, this was the first time Giliead had felt its gift. At the time Ilias had had no idea that Ranior's sudden violent outbursts against his family and friends were caused by a curse; he had even told Giliead that his suspicions were just wishful thinking. Ilias hadn't realized until later that it was because deep in his heart he believed that all families turned on their children eventually, that they could teach you sheep shearing one day and take you out to die the next. He had thought Giliead lucky because it hadn't happened until he was nearly grown.

Ilias closed the bow case, twisting the leather loop that held it shut.

The reality of the god's choice hadn't really sunk in before Ranior died. He knew that until then, on some level, Giliead had still thought of himself as spending his life at Andrien, taking care of the family farms for his beloved sister until he married. Ilias was damn sure that neither of them had ever thought of doing this.

Giliead ran a hand over the bow case, then straightened up. "I'm going to check on Ixion."

Ilias nodded. "I'll go with you."

Giliead gave him a long look. "Why don't you stay here and make sure the others get settled in?"

He meant, of course, stay here and stop acting like an idiot. Ilias let out his breath. "Fine."

He reluctantly followed Giliead out into the main room. Pasima's group looked wary of touching anything, though Danias was saying, "It's not as strange as—" He stopped as they entered, looking at Pasima uncertainly.

Giliead nodded to her and started for the door.

"Where are you going?" Pasima asked sharply.

Giliead stopped in the doorway to the little entrance hall. Ilias folded his arms, able to tell from the line of his friend's back that he was gathering his patience. Pasima might be doing it out of nerves, though she hid it well. But Giliead was still the Chosen Vessel, and he didn't like having his movements questioned.

Having given everyone long enough to realize he was angry, Giliead said without turning, "To make sure Ixion is still where they think he is," and walked out.

There was a brief uncomfortable silence. Pasima dropped her bag on the floor, her mouth set in a thin line. The others looked variously affronted or uncomfortable. Ilias leaned in the doorway, thinking, *Well, here we go.*

Then Kias dumped his pack and sword down in the corner and

dusted off his hands. He eyed the group thoughtfully, possibly evaluating the chances for a peaceful evening and deciding the prospects didn't look good. "I'm going up to the big hall and see what's doing."

Arites, squatting on the floor to dig through his belongings, pulled out the bag with his writing materials and got to his feet. "I'll go with you."

Danias, by far the youngest member of the party, started to speak, then hesitated, looking at Pasima. She pressed her lips together, then shook her head slightly. "Go with them, if you want. Just . . . take care."

At least she realizes she can't keep them penned in here the whole voyage, Ilias thought. Arites started for the door, preoccupied with sorting through his writing supplies, but Kias threw Ilias an ironic glance. He told Pasima, "We'll make sure he doesn't fall overboard," and waved Danias out the door ahead of him.

There was another uncomfortable silence. Cletia stepped close to one of the cabinets built into the wall, carefully touching a square of polished wood set into the door. Gyan let out a sigh, sinking down onto the couch. He nodded toward the doorway leading to the rest of the chamber. "There's rooms in the back there. The larger one, you might take that."

Cimarus and Sanior looked at Pasima as if this was a controversial suggestion and they needed her greater wisdom to properly evaluate it. Ilias rolled his eyes. Karima had never run her household as if she were the only one capable of making a rational decision; if they had looked to her for every little thing, she probably would have sent them all to go live in the woods.

Pasima nodded gravely, and the two men collected their packs. Ilias shifted out of the doorway to give them room to pass.

Cletia turned away from the cabinet. "It's true, one of these people married . . . him?" she asked suddenly, her eyes midway between Gyan and Ilias.

"It's true," Pasima answered. Her cool eyes went to Ilias. "These people, like the Chaeans, don't understand curse marks."

Ilias felt his jaw set. "Maybe you could explain it to them."

Pasima looked away, her face hardening in annoyance.

"They understand curse marks," Gyan said, deceptively mild. Probably Pasima had forgotten his wife had died of a curse. "And as many do, they think the things are just a way to punish people clever or strong enough to survive."

Pasima frowned, slightly embarrassed, and Cletia's fair skin reddened. She began to busy herself with picking up her bag and carrying it into the other room. She darted a look at Ilias as she passed.

Recovering her poise, Pasima said in a softer tone, "I look forward to meeting these people." Her eyes settled on Ilias, turning speculative. "Especially this Tremaine."

Ilias was looking forward to that too.

As the meeting broke up, Tremaine escaped out the side door, making her way through another couple of darkened lounges and corridors, then out onto the Promenade deck. Gerard caught up with her after a few steps.

The Promenade was a roofed deck, meant to be used in any weather, with a solid wooden balustrade and huge glass windows. The *Ravenna* had been moving away from Cineth for some time, out to the open ocean, and the sea was dark and empty. There were no lights lit and the moonlight was barely enough for them to make their way along, but the deck was empty, the polished wooden boards stretching out the length of the great ship.

Tremaine waited for Gerard to say something but when he did speak, he only asked, "Was it safe to mention the Valiarde connection with Morane?"

"He told me it didn't matter anymore. I don't think he would have let me know otherwise." For years Tremaine had known that Gerard was only one of the men who had been appointed as guardian of her and her father's estate; that the other was Captain of the Queen's Guard Reynard Morane had come as something of a shock. She eyed Gerard, though it was too dark to read his expression. "You knew."

"I suspected," he corrected her carefully. "I knew there were strong ties between Nicholas and Reynard Morane in the past. I didn't realize Nicholas still trusted the man to that extent." He glanced at her. "What are you going to do?"

As always, a good question. It rather surprised her that she had the answer. "I'm not going to let anyone take advantage of the Syprians." She shrugged, wishing it was that simple. "And fight the Gardier. What else is there to do?"

He said nothing for a long moment, their footsteps on the boards the only sound besides the wind and the ship's movement. Then Gerard said, "I hope you realize you can call on my assistance. As your father would."

Tremaine stopped, staring at him, but he had already turned away, going through a dark hatch back into the interior of the ship.

The cabin door was open and Tremaine wandered in, trying to look casual. Gyan sprawled comfortably on the couch and Pasima was sitting in one of the chairs. She eyed Tremaine thoughtfully, saying, "Back from your council?"

Tremaine lifted her brows. "Apparently." She couldn't tell what Pasima's attitude was from her tone, but this was Visolela's sister.

Pasima inclined her head gracefully. "Is it permitted that we know what was discussed?"

Tremaine felt herself smile blithely. This "one monarch to another" stance was going to get old rapidly. "Not much. We're still going to Capidara to drop off the refugees, then back to Parscia to try to contact what's left of our government. The Gardier are still evil. Oh, they have managed to talk to our Gardier prisoners a little and now we know they're both ignorant and evil." Her nerves were making her feel as if her head was about to explode. "If you want the longer version, you'll have to wait until tomorrow, or ask Gerard or Ander."

Pasima smiled. "I see."

Gyan seemed to see it too and sat up, smoothing his rumpled shirt, saying hastily, "Gilead's off checking on Ixion, and Ilias is back in there." He jerked his head toward the doorway into the rest of the suite.

Tremaine nodded firmly. "Right." Under Pasima's critical gaze she wasn't going to add *Wish me luck*. She wondered if the other woman's presence had driven Ilias out of the room or if he was still too mad to want company. She went through the dining room, heard unfamiliar voices in the back bedroom, and turned into the other one. Ilias was sitting on the floor near the couch, braiding the leather cords on a scabbard.

As she stopped in the doorway he looked up, shaking his hair back. Before he could say anything, Tremaine blurted, "All right, I'm sorry. I was having a . . ." *moment of self-consciousness, cowardice and anxiety,* "Some sort of brain fever. Sorry?"

"It wasn't you, it was me." His mouth twisted ruefully. "Your people don't get married like that, do you?"

"No, we don't. It's more complicated, with flowers and things." Tremaine wandered further into the room, gesturing vaguely, too relieved to go into more coherent detail.

She sat on the floor next to him as he put the scabbard aside. Looking as if he was relieved too, he said, "For us there's usually a party, depending on how prominent the families are. Nicanor's mother's family is very rich, so when he and Visolela married they gave a big festival, and most of Cineth went to it." He reached behind him, pulling an embroidered leather bag out of the pile on the couch and handing it to her. "And there's gifts. Karima sent this to you. She had to send someone back to Andrien for them, that's why we were late to the harbor."

Her brows knit, Tremaine plopped the bag into her lap. A scent puffed up from the leather, as if the contents had been stored in a place where the air was thick with incense. She undid the wooden toggle fastening and saw it seemed to be stuffed with fabric. She pulled out two shirts, one faded green and the other soft gold, and a pair of dark blue cotton pants. The hems were stamped with geometric designs and the seams reinforced with braided leather. In the bottom of the bag was a blanket, in beautifully woven blues, greens and cream, with geometric patterns meant to represent waves and Syprian galleys. She tugged it out, smoothing the fabric across her lap. "How did she know I wanted a blanket?" She noted that her voice sounded suspiciously thick.

He watched her, a faint line between his brows. "When you're born your mother is supposed to make you a blanket. You take it with you when you leave your family. When you bring someone into your family who doesn't have one, you give them one."

"Oh." She wasn't sure why this should render her completely undone, but it had.

Ilias tilted his head to get a better view of her face, then nodded to himself. "It was the right thing, then. We weren't sure."

"Why?"

He shrugged a little, smiling. "Your people are so different."

"Gifts are always good. So's this." Impulsively she put her hand in his hair and drew his head down for a kiss.

He had kissed her once before, in the Gardier base, but that had gone by too fast for her to really absorb detail. This time she could tell he tasted spicy, like Syprian wine, and his hair smelled like a cat's, clean but with a faint animal scent underneath. Tremaine had had a series of affairs in her wild tear through the theater world but had, for some reason she couldn't fathom at the moment, mentally filed that part of her life away as over. There had been the men who thought they were taking advantage of the naive young heiress only to find that she wasn't so naive, and the men who were just casual acquaintances. She had told none of them about her father's real profession or activities. None of them had been serious about her. Maybe she had drawn back from Ander not because of the gossip about the asylum but because she had sensed he was inclined to be serious.

When she pulled back Ilias suddenly demanded, "How do you say your name?"

She stared at him. "Tremaine?"

Ilias rolled his eyes. "Your family name."

"Oh. It's Valiarde."

"Val—" He let out his breath in frustration. "I can't say it."

"Well, I—" Tremaine stared at him, struck by a sudden realization, seeing Syprian marriage customs from a different angle. "You're nervous." Growing up, Ilias must have thought of bringing in a large marriage settlement as his duty to the family; now, despite the curse mark, he had been able to accomplish it, and he was anxious not to mess it up.

That got her an actual glare. "No."

Right, he's nervous. "Wait." She got up and found her carpetbag on the console table on the far side of the room. Clawing through it, she thought, *There has to be something.* She had pared her life down to the bone, but surely— In the tangle of costume jewelry at the bottom of the bag she found a ring and pulled it out, turning back to Ilias. "Here. It's a ring my father gave me for my twelfth birthday. It's white gold, with 'Valiarde' inscribed on it. Well, it's in this script that's impossible to read, because my father didn't believe in wearing things that could be used to identify you, but that is what it says." It occurred to her that that was just as well; if worse came to worst and the Gardier captured Ilias, at least the ring couldn't be readily identified as coming from Ile-Rien.

He took it tentatively, and she realized she couldn't recall if the Syprians wore rings or not; earrings, armbands, necklaces yes, but perhaps not rings. With her luck, finger rings probably represented some terrific social insult, not that it would fit him, anyway. "You could wear it around your neck. On a cord, I mean."

Ilias quirked a brow at her, then gave her that warm smile. He didn't look nervous anymore. *Yes,* she thought, feeling the butterflies in her stomach give way to a different kind of flutter, *that was the right thing.*

She realized she could hear music, someone picking out a tune on a stringed instrument in the other bedroom. It reminded her that Pasima and the others were still there, liable to barge or wander in at any moment. "Let's get out of here."

They went up the stairs past the painting of the Matriarch to the main hall. It was quieter now, but Ilias got the idea that Tremaine didn't want to draw the attention of the few people still sitting on the couches at the center. She pulled out a bunch of keys she had tucked under her belt, looked thoughtful, then started away. "I've got an idea. This way." His initial anxiety gone, Ilias was more than willing to follow her wherever she wanted to go. He thought she was heading for the enclosed deck on this level, but she took the narrow stairwell in the side wall.

The wizard lights weren't on inside it, making it very dark indeed and impossible to see the figured metal trail signs, but Tremaine seemed to know where they were going. After they climbed up for a time she chose a door, fumbling for the handle in the dark, and Ilias helped her push it open.

"Aha, the Sun Deck," she said as they stepped out into moonlight and a cool salt-laden breeze.

Ilias whistled in admiration of the view and stepped to the railing, surveying the dark sea stretching out to infinity. The clouds had broken up and the moon was high in the vault of stars. They were nearly at the top of the ship here, with only one more deck above them. It was hard to get used to being so high above the surface of the water, hard to believe something so tall could ride the waves without toppling over. Tremaine tugged his arm and he followed her along, still looking out at the limitless sea.

The moonlight reflecting off the polished boards was almost enough to see by, but he was glad for the metal railings. Tremaine asked suddenly, "Can Pasima tell you what to do? Give you orders?"

He threw her a look though it was too dark to read expressions. He had noticed before that she thought of people in terms of tactics, like a warleader gauging an enemy force. Not a bad way of thinking during a battle, but he had had the feeling for a long time that Tremaine had been at war before the Gardier ever appeared. But if they had to deal with Pasima, that could be helpful. "Not now that you're here," he told her with a shrug. "Otherwise, she could try, since she's related to the Andrien by marriage."

Tremaine was looking down at the deck, her face in shadow. "Nicanor's marriage to Visolela?"

"Yes."

Tremaine nodded. "Who here can Pasima order around? Besides the people she brought with her."

Ilias cocked his head, thinking it over. "Nobody, really. Gyan's been married once, so he's on his own. Arites doesn't have a family, but he's more or less attached to Andrien, so he wouldn't have to obey her." He tried to think of a way to describe Arites' method of cheerfully agreeing with someone like Pasima but somehow never really aligning himself with her. "He might anyway, but not if it interfered with something he really wanted to do. Besides, he likes you better."

"He does?" Apparently surprised, Tremaine considered that. "What about Kias?"

"Kias is Ranior's sister's son." At her blank silence, he added, "He's your cousin now."

"Oh." Tremaine sounded a little overcome.

"What's your family like?" Ilias winced, hoping the question didn't sound as wary aloud as it had in his head. Considering what Tremaine had said of her father, that she had a wizard for a foster father, and that the god that lived in the sphere now had been her uncle, it was a tricky question. The only remotely normal one in the bunch seemed to be the canny old man they had met just before leaving the Rienish city, and he had been some kind of warleader.

But Tremaine just shrugged. "There aren't any more Villers, and the Denares—that was my mother's family—all lived out in the country around Lodun, and we never had much to do with them. Except my great-grandmother, but she died a long time before I was born. The Valiardes did sort of start speaking to me for a while there, but Nicholas chased them off when he found out. They never came to Vienne much, anyway."

They reached the end of the deck, where a terraced balcony looked down on the two open sections of deck below and the stern. The ocean seemed bigger here, without the bulk of the ship at their side. Ilias wandered across the open space, fascinated by the perspective. The churning white of the wake was visible on the dark water, a wide trail that stretched across the sea back toward Cineth. He couldn't believe how far they had come already. Shaking off the entrancing effect, he turned to see Tremaine standing on the open porch of a rounded structure projecting out onto the deck. Narrow windows lined the walls, and Ilias went to one, trying to peer inside, but the dark was impenetrable. "What is it?" he asked.

He saw her enigmatic smile in the moonlight. "A surprise." After fumbling with the keys for a time she got the door open. Ilias followed her, standing just inside and waiting for his eyes to adjust to the darkened room.

Moonlight poured in the myriad of windows that faced the stern and stretched back along the port and starboard. It gradually revealed silver-banded walls and glass etched with strange designs that seemed to float in a pool of night. "What . . . is it?" Ilias repeated, a little cautious.

Tremaine shut the door, further sealing them in darkness. "It's called the Veranda. It's just another place for eating, really. And dancing. It's a little hard to tell with the tables and chairs missing. The musicians would sit on the upper level." She moved forward, and he realized the glass bars sectioned off a raised dais across the back of the room. The dark pool below was just an effect of the deep black of the floor covering. He took a careful step forward, surprised that it felt soft underfoot. A deep carpet, not wood.

Squinting, he could see the pale light from the windows touch painted figures between the broad bands of silver on the wall, all of them leaping and dancing. Tremaine trailed a hand along the silver-and-glass banister. "There was a silver grand piano there once, but it's gone now, probably in storage somewhere. If the warehouses survived the bombing. And the invasion."

"Oh." He heard the note in her voice that meant she was thinking too much about her home, about what the Gardier were doing to it. He stepped up behind her, sliding his arms around her waist and rubbing his cheek against her hair. Just from the brief walk along the deck, her scent was blended with the sea air. "You people like to eat in fancy rooms a lot, don't you. There must be a hundred of them on this ship."

"Not that many, but yes." She turned in the circle of his arms and slid her hands into his hair. "Oh, by the way, I'm terrible at relationships, but this part I can do."

Chapter 8

I was told you lost contact with our launch base on the western coast," Adram said, his brow creased with worry as he shut the door behind him. The quarters of Benin, the chief Scientist, were plain, though the wood furniture was of good quality and the work-table well lit. It was warmer than the passage outside, which was lined with masonry and always held the dampness from the often rainy weather.

"Not all contact, fortunately." His brief smile at Adram's entrance fading, Benin took another glass out of the cabinet and poured a share of amber liquor into it. It was like drinking raw grain alcohol, with a whiff of fuel oil, but Adram accepted it anyway. "We know what happened."

"You do?" Adram lifted his brows, inviting further explanation. Benin was the chief of the Scientists in Maton-devara, and there were few here he could speak to as an equal.

These people had once called themselves the Aelin, but they seldom used the word anymore. It was a thing of their past, like the small villages that had once dotted the land and the careful craftsmanship that had constructed this city. Their future was in the airships and their other stolen bits of knowledge. Part of that future was the strict divisions of Scientist, Command and Service, which allowed no casual contact between the castes, and the hierarchies within each were equally strict. Adram, as a nocaste, appreciated Benin's patronage as much as he knew Benin appreciated the company. "I hate to think they would escape after wreaking such destruction."

Benin's face was serious. "It was a terrible thing. An entire stronghold wiped out, as far as we can tell, and the patrol ship that arrived soon after." He took a seat in the single armchair, grunting as he stretched his right leg to ease the pain of an old injury. "But we managed to place a presence aboard their ship."

Adram frowned, taking the other chair. He absently swirled the liquor in his glass despite its lack of bouquet. His command of the language was excellent, but he didn't understand why Benin had used the word *presence* rather than *agent*. He knew Benin would explain if he was permitted to, and the fact that he hadn't indicated the information was important indeed. "One of the native ships you spoke of? Surely they were too primitive to be of much use, even to the Rien."

"No. A Rien ship. Not a warship, some sort of converted transport craft. It's odd to think of so much resource wasted on a ship just for pleasure travel, but— But I don't have to explain it to you." Benin smiled ruefully. "Sorry, I'm too used to using small words and simple diagrams to try to impart these concepts to the Service officers. Not to mention the Command."

Adram's mouth twisted slightly in amusement as he acknowledged the truth of that. "The Rien are trying to reach Parscia by traveling through the staging world?"

"It's hard to get information at the moment. I should know more when I get the report from the gate." Benin's expression sobered. "No matter how well the advance through Rien territory is proceeding, we can't let this group evade us."

Adram let his breath out. "Yes. I can tell you, these people can be tenacious. And vicious." He shook his head slowly, letting his eyes go dark as if with painful memory. He added, almost absently, "Do they still have the device you told me about?"

"Yes." Benin leaned forward, intent. "You understand—it's only conjecture—but if we could discover how it works, and add such a device to the prototype, it would be—" He looked away, suddenly self-conscious. "But I won't burden you with my hopes."

Adram gestured, palm open. There were still many questions about the Aelin's power that he didn't understand, that Benin and others simply refused to explain, and every scrap of information was important. "It's no burden—"

The door opened without a knock or a word to announce the visitor, as was their custom. Adram saw it was Disar, the head of their Command division, and got to his feet, quickly schooling his features from annoyance at the interruption to blandness. Benin's rank allowed him to show his annoyance, though he obviously knew it would be pointless to say they had been speaking privately or that he was off duty.

Disar fixed his cold gray eyes on Benin. He had been a young man when Adram had first met him more than three years ago, with well-cut features and dark hair. He had prematurely aged, the flesh of his cheeks lined and sagging slightly, his cropped hair sprinkled with gray. The cause of the change was visible in his left temple, where an irregular lump of rock crystal an inch across protruded. The scarred flesh around it was tinged with green, and Adram didn't think the man would last much longer in his position as Command Liaison. Disar said to Benin, "Your attention is required in council."

Benin nodded grimly, glancing at Adram. "Perhaps this is the report I've been waiting for." He pushed to his feet. "I'm on my way."

Disar's eyes went blank as, message delivered, the force living inside the crystal released him. Disar blinked, threw a stony glance of contempt at Adram, then pointedly stepped to the door, holding it open for Benin. The chief Scientist finished his drink and set the glass on his worktable. "We'll speak later," he said to Adram.

Adram nodded, following them out of the room and into the dimly lit stone passage. He pulled the door shut behind him as Benin strode down the hall. As he turned to go the other way, a grip on his collar spun him around, pinning him against the wall. The punch caught him in the cheekbone, snapping his head back against the stone. He tasted blood, and the dim corridor light went black for an instant; he let himself sag bonelessly. Disar dragged him up and Adram opened his eyes to see the Command officer glaring into his face. Adram kept his eyes away from the crystal, though it was like being forced to confront a suppurated boil or an open plague sore. "You take up his time," Disar said through gritted teeth.

"I'm working with him. It's my duty." Adram kept his voice even, though the heady desire nearly overcame him to smash Disar's face in and pound his head into the floor until the crystal popped loose from his skull in fragments.

"The Rien who destroyed the launch base will be found by Command," Disar said thickly, eyes narrowed with rage. "They'll die or be processed as avatars or go to the labor pens, and the credit will be ours, not yours."

Adram dropped his eyes, to hide the bitter smile that threatened to twist his bloody lips. "I do my duty," he said softly. "As do we all."

Disar released him with a shove, turning away to follow Benin. Adram pushed off the wall, lifting a hand to his throbbing jaw. *We'll see who finds them,* he thought, watching Disar's back, this time letting the small cold smile reach his eyes. *And we'll see if he still wants the credit then.*

Chapter 9

Tremaine woke when Ilias nuzzled her temple, his beard stubble rough against her skin and his breath warm in her hair. He said quietly, "Someone's here."

"Hmm?" She yawned and blinked vaguely as Ilias rolled off the couch, shaking his hair out and grabbing for his pants. Dawnlight flooded the Veranda, and she had a good view of the two long strips of scar tissue that ran down his back. They stretched from the inside of his shoulder blades to just below the base of his spine. Ilias hadn't said how it had happened, but she suspected it was a souvenir of his and Giliead's last deadly encounter with Ixion. Ilias hadn't said much about that either, except that Ixion had used a transformation curse on him and that Giliead had thought he would have to kill Ilias. *We are going to have to do something about Ixion,* she thought, eyes narrowing in speculation. *Something permanently fatal, preferably.* She shook her head, putting it aside for later.

They had spent the night on the long black couch built against the bandstand's balustrade, facing the windows that looked out over the stern. In the moonlight the Veranda might have been some pocket of the fayre world, but it was a nightclub after all and the silver-banded walls, etched-glass balustrades and the matte black carpet should have looked tawdry in the dawn. Blinking as she gazed around, Tremaine saw that it had obviously been designed to be beautiful all the time. The early graying light cast the black and silver in shadow and picked out the bright dabs of color in the mural of entertainers. The leaping figures were all risqúely garbed ballet, opera and music hall performers, with Parscian scarf dancers and Aderassi tumblers mixed in.

Tremaine sat up, scratching her head and fondly watching Ilias struggle into his pants. Last night, thinking of the silver piano's fate had sparked a poetic image of the *Ravenna* as carrying away the last vestige of Ile-Rien, the last living remnant of a way of life and a history and a people. But it was a remnant trapped in time like an insect in amber, never to change. It had been much easier to think about something else. Pulling his shirt over his head, Ilias eyed her thoughtfully. "You didn't hear what I said, did you?"

"What?" Then Tremaine realized she could hear someone fumbling with keys in the door to the right of the bandstand, the one that led to an inside corridor. Cursing violently, she snatched her shirt up off the floor. Ilias threw her a grin.

He was leaning against the balustrade regarding the door suspiciously when it opened. Giaren, Niles's secretary and assistant in the Viller Institute, stepped inside. He was a slightly younger version of Niles, with the same sleek tailoring, though as far as Tremaine knew the two men weren't related. He spotted Ilias first and stopped, uncertain, saying, "Is Miss Valiarde here?"

"Yes." Still barefoot but having managed to get her pants on too, Tremaine waved to him over the glass rail behind the couch. "What is it?"

Giaren advanced into the room, taking in the situation with a slightly embarrassed frown. "Gerard sent me to find you. He needs to speak with you immediately." He cleared his throat, and couldn't help adding in exasperation, "You couldn't go back to your cabin?"

"My in-laws live in my cabin. How did Gerard know where—Wait." Tremaine picked up her boots, examining them suspiciously. One of the brass grommets was missing from the right one. "Damm it."

"What?" Ilias demanded, glancing back at her.

She explained in Syrnaic, "That locator spell Gerard used to follow us around the boat when we were searching for Ixion. He took a piece off my boot so he could do it at any time." Sometimes having sorcerers for friends and relations was damned inconvenient. She switched back to Rienish to ask Giaren, "What does Gerard want?"

"There's some sort of problem with the Gardier prisoners."

The Isolation Ward where the prisoners were kept was just a few levels below the Veranda on the A deck. It wasn't accessible from the interior corridors and to reach it, one had to go out on deck and then down a set of steps to a little well that sheltered the entrance from weather and the view of strolling passengers. Now a brisk morning breeze made the well cold despite the bright sunlight. The metal door, which had been in pristine condition when Tremaine had passed through it yesterday, now looked as if it had been hit by a battering ram. *Except there's no room to get one down here,* she thought, studying the situation critically and with some alarm. *This is . . . going to be a problem.* Whatever had struck the door had driven in a dent several inches deep, and the edges of the impact were blackened with what seemed to be soot. Ilias sat on his heels to examine it more closely, shaking his head at the depth of the damage.

Gerard eyed the door grimly. He had changed into a tweed jacket and trousers and white shirt, though he hadn't bothered with a tie. His clothes were slightly rumpled, but he had shaved. With his face sallow from exhaustion, he looked like a man who had just recovered from a three-day drunken debauch that he had not particularly enjoyed. He said, "The guard detachment heard absolutely nothing."

Ilias snorted. "Lucky for them."

Gerard grimaced. "Yes, I don't like to think what would have happened if one of them had opened the door. But they had no idea anything was wrong until their relief arrived at dawn."

Giliead nodded slowly, contemplating the damage with folded arms and a thoughtful expression. "It was stopped by a curse? I can't feel one on the door."

On the open deck above them, Tremaine heard Colonel Averi shouting orders at someone. The outside of each deck had been patrolled regularly last night, but the guards had apparently seen nothing unusual. From the sound of it, Averi was not happy with that report.

"A ward," Gerard corrected. "The ship is riddled with old protective wards, cast when she was first launched. To guard against theft, fire, to strengthen seals around watertight doors, to strengthen the hull. It's common practice on Rienish ships. Or it was, when we had ships." He absently cleaned his spectacles, using them to gesture toward the door. "This was a ward meant to prevent forcible entry. I'm not sure if it was specifically intended to guard the Isolation Ward, or if it was cast on all doors to crew areas. It wasn't meant to harm anyone attempting to force the door, just to keep the locked door sealed until it was unlocked from the inside."

"But there's a backlash, right?" Tremaine prompted. Nicholas had made an extensive study of forcible entrance wards, and had always said there were ways around those that weren't perfectly cast. But that involved tricking the ward into reacting the wrong way, not just applying more brute force. "If something hits a ward like that too hard, it bounces back."

"Correct." Gerard stepped forward, stooping to run his hand over the lower section of the abused metal. A silvery metallic substance came off on his fingers and Ilias and Giliead both leaned in to look more closely. "This is incinerated ether. Whatever struck this door caused the ward to respond so violently it destroyed itself in the process." He straightened up, dusting his hand off. "Fortunately, the ward must have wounded its adversary in the process and the . . . entity retreated, without trying to enter or harm anyone inside."

Giliead's face set. "I'll try to pick up a trail." He turned away, pacing slowly toward the stairs up to the deck.

Deciding to get out of the way, Tremaine went through the door into the office area, Ilias following her. Niles and Florian were already in the bare whitewashed room, both red-eyed from lack of sleep, and Dr. Divies was leaning on a file cabinet, his dark face drawn with exhaustion. The guards were in the other room, talking over the situation in worried mutters.

On the desk was one of the ship's large elegant silver coffee services, with a plate of buns. Tremaine seized the coffeepot, relieved to find it still warm and more than half-full. "So, any idea what could do this?" she asked, pouring a cup and resting one hip on the desk. She had to admit, the idea that something could attack that violently in total silence was making her nerves jump. Ilias settled next to her, taking one of the buns and breaking it open to sniff suspiciously at the jam filling.

Niles shook his head, pacing the room. "Offhand, I'd say it looks like the work of an elemental, but it would be impossible for a creature of the fay to be aboard a ship composed mostly of iron."

"And an elemental would make noise," Florian pointed out. "And besides, aren't they fairly harmless?"

Ilias reached for another bun, his bare arm warm against Tremaine's shoulder in the cool morning air, distracting her from Niles's answer. The conversation was in Rienish since most of the people in the room didn't speak Syrnaic, but she could tell he was trying to follow it. And if her hyperawareness of his presence didn't abate soon, she wasn't going to be worth anything. She shook herself. "It could be something that sneaked aboard from the island," she admitted. It was a sobering thought, especially since she and Ilias had been only a few decks up from this spot, protected by nothing but the Veranda's lighter unwarded door.

Florian nodded, looking as if the idea didn't appeal much to her either. "I told Niles about some of the things we saw there."

Tremaine nudged Ilias with an elbow, saying in Syrnaic, "Did you ever see anything on the island that could do this?"

"Sure. Ixion." Ilias wiped his fingers on his pants and studied the tray of buns for the next victim.

Florian shook her head, thoughtful. "Niles said the barrier around him hasn't been penetrated."

Leaning against the wooden filing cabinet, Divies stirred, saying, "Miss Valiarde, I wanted to ask the Syprians if there was any chance that the Gardier were put under some spell by this Ixion while still on the island?"

Tremaine passed the question on to Ilias, who turned to the Parscian doctor, and said in careful Rienish, "I do not know. Why?"

Tremaine blinked, surprised he could speak that much Rienish. She was also surprised at how erotic she found it. Divies shifted to face him, explaining, "We asked one of the Gardier what he did before he became a soldier, just to keep him talking. He seemed startled and frightened, as if it was a question of great importance, and refused to answer. Considering the man had just told us where some of the prisoners who were acting as slave labor had been taken from, and how many had died en route to the island, it seemed nonsensical. We tried the question with all the others, and they behaved in the same way. They refused to tell us anything about a childhood, a home, growing up."

"That's . . . very strange." Tremaine stared at the smudged linoleum floor, thinking it over.

Ilias had listened carefully but obviously hadn't gotten all the words. Divies waited for Florian to finish translating before the doctor commented, "Strange indeed." He nodded to Niles. "Niles suspected it was some sort of spell affecting their memories, but I'm not sure I agree. And I wonder why this information is so important. If I was captured by the Gardier, and they discovered I was born in the Bisheni Valley of Parscia, came to Ile-Rien with my family when I was a child and grew up in the Marches, what possible use could that be to them?"

Niles folded his arms, lips pursed. "But they obviously think it would be of use to us."

"Or they believe that forcing their men to forswear any past civilian life makes for a better soldier," Divies added with a thoughtful frown. "A man undistracted by thoughts of home or family. I suppose they judge the efficacy of it by their results, but I can't believe they could make all their people conform."

"I don't know." Niles took a deep breath. "Gerard and I are going to attempt to get the sphere to teach one of us the Gardier language. It should have . . . ingested it the way it did Syrnaic, and it should be able to impart it to us in the same way. Perhaps being able to communicate in their own language without the translator crystals will help us understand them."

Giliead walked into the office, followed by Gerard and Colonel Averi. Obviously ready for action, Ilias dropped the last bun back on the tray and hopped down off the desk. "You've got it?"

Giliead shook his head. "I can't see a trail." He tapped his fingers on his belt thoughtfully, then glanced at Gerard. "But if it wasn't a curse on the door, but a curseling hitting the door with its body, there might be no trail to see."

Gerard didn't look surprised. "I was afraid of that."

"That was useless," Averi growled, taking the desk chair and sitting down with a thump. "We don't have time to waste on native superstitions."

He had spoken of course in Rienish, and Giliead and Ilias both looked to Tremaine for a translation. She obliged with, "He said, 'It didn't work, blah blah blah, my ulcers make me difficult.'" Florian winced.

From their expressions she might as well have told them exactly what Averi had said. Ilias snorted derisively, and Giliead lifted a brow, eyeing the colonel coolly. He said, "I could find all the wizards on the ship. That ought to narrow it down for him."

Gerard passed this along to Averi before Tremaine could. The colonel sat up straight, regarding Giliead with sudden alertness. "He can do that?"

"That's what they do," Florian interposed, again before Tremaine could open her mouth. She hopped down off the desk, saying briskly, "What do we need? A map, keys for all the rooms?"

Armed with the ship's map booklet and the set of master keys, Tremaine trailed after Florian, Giliead and Ilias. The *Ravenna* had passenger accommodation on six decks, some of it running nearly the length of the ship, from Third Class in the bow to the Second Class area toward the stern. In assigning rooms the First Class space in the center of the ship had been filled up first. Those rooms were larger and more comfortable and also closer to the First Class dining room, lounges and the main hall, where most of the ship's community activity was centered.

Now they were moving down a corridor on C deck. The cabin doors were set back in little vestibules, two or three doors opening into each, meant to reduce noise and give a little more privacy. It struck Tremaine how dramatic the change had been since she, Florian and Ilias had first set foot on the dark quiet ship in Port Rel. The *Ravenna* had been a thing of arrested power then, occupied by ghosts and dust, with the feel, and the odor, of a disused hotel.

Now freed prisoners who had been chained in the dark for endless months kept their cabin doors open and all the lights on—even the Maiutans, most of whom would have lived in little clapboard houses not that much different from Syprian dwellings. Military wives, the families of Viller Institute workers, and the smattering of refugees from Rel and Chaire who had chosen to take the risk had come accompanied with children and pets; they kept their doors open too and hung their laundry to dry in the corridor. Tremaine could hear the tinny music of a gramophone record playing somewhere. The ship's loudspeaker system underlined the contrast by suddenly announcing, "All passengers please take heed: When on deck, stand clear of the funnels. Funnels may vent sooty water without warning."

As the announcement was repeated in Parscian, Giliead glanced inquiringly back at Florian. She translated, "It was 'beware of funnels' again." The loudspeaker also delivered exhortations concerning keeping the dead-lights on the portholes, closing outer hatches and staying off the open decks unless it was absolutely necessary. Tremaine couldn't tell if they chose them randomly or by whatever the inexperienced crew was most paranoid about at that moment.

Their passage didn't go unremarked as all the Syprians were minor celebrities on the ship, with Ilias and Giliead being the most recognized by the prisoners released from the Gardier base. People stepped out of their cabins to watch them pass, or stopped in the corridor to give them room to get by. The fact that both Syprians were wearing swords strapped across their backs probably helped attract attention as well.

It was less easy now to tell the freed slaves from the refugees, since they had gotten rid of their filthy Gardier coveralls and were all dressed in a hodgepodge of borrowed clothing: navy and army fatigues with the sleeves and pant legs rolled up or mismatched blouses, skirts and trousers donated by the other passengers. Shoes must have been in short supply because most of them seemed to be in socks or barefoot.

Giliead stopped in the corridor, turning into one of the vestibules. "There's something here. Just a trace." He hesitated, touching the dark-paneled wall lightly.

The door he had chosen stood open, and Tremaine could hear Rienish voices inside. She stepped past him and knocked on the open door. "Hello? Could we have a word?"

"Yes? Oh, hello." It was a young girl in a jumper, two little boys playing with wooden blocks on the floor at her feet. There was an old woman sitting on the couch, humming to herself and working on a stretch of cloth with thread and needle. She didn't stop working, but her cloudy blue eyes lifted to study Tremaine, then Florian and the two Syprians.

"Hello." Florian glanced at Tremaine, correctly interpreted her blank expression, and managed, "We're just . . . oh, taking a survey. Who's staying in your cabin, and where are they now, and that sort of thing."

"Oh." The girl managed to tear her eyes off the exotic sight of Giliead and Ilias in her doorway and gestured to the old woman. "It's just me and Grandmother and the boys. Lady Aviler came asking for volunteers, and my mother went."

"In the laundry?" Tremaine asked, eyeing the grandmother. According to the patrols, most of the civilian activity aboard the ship last night had centered in the hospital and the laundry. If the attempt on the Isolation Ward had been made by a sorcerer and not something that had managed to get aboard from the island, then chances were it was a refugee with a good excuse for wandering the ship at night.

The girl assured her, "No, the kitchens."

"Ah." Tremaine glanced at Giliead, asking in Syrnaic, "Is it Grandma there?"

"Yes, but . . ." He shrugged slightly, meeting the old woman's cloudy blue gaze. "She doesn't feel dangerous."

Ilias leaned against the doorframe, explaining, "When they're real old like that and not doing any harm, we usually just pretend we didn't find them."

Tremaine nodded, not sure if that said something about Syprians in general or Ilias and Giliead in particular. She turned to the young girl again and mentally switched back to Rienish. "Ah . . ." *Might as well be direct.* "Is your grandmother a sorceress or a witch by any chance?"

Either the girl was an excellent actress or was genuinely surprised at the question. "Oh, no, madam."

"So she can't cast?" Florian clarified, glancing at the imperturbable old woman.

"Oh, she can cast and heal, but she can't fly or anything." The girl made an extravagant gesture, apparently indicating Great Spells, major wards and raising fayre islands.

"I see." Tremaine bit her lip in thought. "Has she been in the laundry lately?"

The girl seemed bewildered by Tremaine's fixation on the laundry. "No, do they need help there?"

"I'll mention her to Dr. Divies," Florian put in hastily, taking Tremaine's arm to steer her out of the room. "If she can heal, they might need her down in the hospital."

"Oh, she'd like that."

As they returned to the corridor, Tremaine explained in Syrnaic, "Anybody with any real magical talent got recruited for something like the army or the Institute or trapped behind the barrier at Lodun. The ones who are left are going to be either a hundred years old like that woman or completely untrained children."

Giliead looked down the corridor with a preoccupied expression, not seeing their curious audience. "If it's a Rienish wizard, this isn't going to be easy."

Ilias nodded, his face resigned. "And if it's a Gardier wizard, there's a lot of places to hide on this ship."

Tremaine flipped through the map book again, thinking it over. The assigned living areas had been colored in with a pencil, not that that told her much. Lady Aviler and her minions had been keeping a rough list of cabin assignments; they would have to get a look at that too. Some of Second and all of Third Class should be uninhabited. Though, she supposed, there was nothing to keep people from taking those rooms except that they were smaller and less nicely appointed. Some of those rescued from the Gardier might very well have chosen to move there, if after months of crowded confinement underground they craved privacy and quiet more than anything else. "There's still tons of empty cabin space. We should check that first."

Giliead's brows quirked. "You mean there are more rooms?"

"Bunches." Tremaine showed him the map, pointing to a spot. "We're about here."

As they started down the corridor, Florian asked slowly, "So what if it's not a Gardier, or a creature from the island? What if it is someone trying to kill the prisoners for revenge?"

Tremaine shrugged slightly, still occupied with the map. "Then we just pretend we didn't find them."

After a time, Florian was called away to help the healers again, and Ilias, Tremaine and Giliead carried the search into the bow.

Ilias could feel the tension between himself and Tremaine but it was a good kind of tension, a new awareness of scent, voice, of every casual contact. He hadn't felt that with a woman since before the curse mark. It made it harder to concentrate on the search, but he liked making the effort; it had been far too long since he had been distracted like this.

Tremaine was being Tremaine, shifting from speculating with ruthless unconcern about what kind of havoc a wizard or curseling hiding on the ship might wreak to becoming girlishly flustered when he brushed against her in a narrow doorway, to catching his eye and making a deliberate innuendo. Giliead's quiet amusement grew through the afternoon, until Ilias figured he was probably going to have to punch him sometime before evening.

The bow area was more of a maze, with rooms branching off the blue-carpeted cross corridors connecting the two main bow-to-stern

passages. The deck started to slope upward here, and he saw
Tremaine grip the ivory-colored rail more often from the sway of the
ship. The cabin doors were set back in little cubbies in this section too,
four to each, but without the noisy occupation of the center section,
it was creepy rather than cozy.

With that faintly distracted air he always wore when he was hunt-
ing, Giliead prowled into an open room that turned out to be another
sitting area. It was a long chamber, the chairs and tables pushed back
against the wood-lined walls and covered with white drapes. There
was a painting on the far wall of a metal ship like the *Ravenna*, the hull
streaked with rust, the paint faded, limping into port apparently with
the help of two smaller craft. An odd choice of art for the ship, Ilias
decided. "Why did they put this here?" he asked Tremaine. "It's bad
luck."

"I don't know." She contemplated it a moment. "It could be a sort
of warning about what might be the *Ravenna*'s future." Then she
snorted derisively. "We should be so lucky."

And there's mood four, fatalism, Ilias thought wryly. Done prowling,
Giliead turned into the main corridor again, and Ilias asked, "Why is
this place called 'Third'?" He glanced back at Tremaine. "What's
third about it?"

"The rooms are smaller and less expensive," Tremaine explained,
grabbing for the rail again as the deck moved underfoot. "The public
rooms aren't as nice either. Before the war, Bisra had passenger ships
like this, only not nearly as big, and the class areas were horizontal,
with Third being on the bottom. They had locked gates between the
decks, and when a couple of the ships sank, nobody was able to un-
lock the gates in time and half the passengers drowned inside the
ship."

Ilias winced at the image that conjured. Giliead, his attention
caught, glanced back at her with an incredulous expression, saying,
"That's insane."

"That's Bisra." Tremaine shrugged, unconcerned.

Ilias shook his head, fighting off a vision of a ship like this going to
the bottom to become a metal tomb. He remembered that "Bisrans"
were the arrogant pair of men they had run into near the healer's area
yesterday. "They had these ships before the war, but not now?"

"The Gardier sank them all." She gestured to the open corridor.
"Anyway, it's not as uncomfortable as you'd think, considering people only stayed in these rooms for a few days at a time," she said, look-

ing around. "There must be communal bathrooms somewhere along the corridor."

Ilias hadn't thought it looked uncomfortable at all; it was palatial compared to some of the dirt-floored huts he had stayed in.

Giliead stopped suddenly, head cocked. Tensing, Ilias looked at the walls, the ceiling overhead, seeing nothing out of the ordinary. Giliead stepped to the wall, brushing his fingers against it as he followed it to the next vestibule. He stopped there, Ilias beside him, Tremaine drawing up uneasily behind them. "How many doors?" Giliead asked thoughtfully.

"Three," Ilias answered, studying the little cubby suspiciously. Tremaine leaned around him.

"The others all have four," Giliead pointed out.

"Ah." Ilias squinted hard at the blank space at the back of the narrow cubby where the fourth door should be. It might be missing because something essential to the ship occupied that spot rather than cabin space, but he really doubted it.

"Clever," Tremaine muttered, backing into the corridor to give them room.

Giliead stepped to the bare spot on the wall, running his hand over it. Then he stepped back and kicked it.

The door was there between one heartbeat and the next, banging open against the inside cabin wall.

Ilias relaxed slightly as he looked past Giliead, relieved and disappointed. It was a small cabin with the walls painted yellow, with two narrow beds stacked one atop the other, and a basin set into the wall below one of the perfect Rienish glass mirrors. The carpet was blue with tiny white and yellow flowers. There were cabinets built into the other walls, but no place to hide. *It's empty. Damm it.* It would have been good to get this over with.

They stepped inside and Tremaine followed, though there wasn't much room left. "No curse traps," Giliead reported, glancing around with a frown. "Doesn't look like he's spent much time here."

"But we know it's a wizard now, and not a curseling." Ilias started opening cabinets and drawers, finding nothing but a little dust. "A curseling wouldn't have the brains to hide this room."

"We don't know that the thing that tried to get into the Isolation Ward is the same thing—person—that hid this room," Tremaine pointed out. Then she grimaced. "But whoever's been staying here has been mixing with the refugees. That really bothers me."

Stooping to check under the bed, Giliead threw a thoughtful glance at her. "How can you tell?"

"The blanket is red, and the brocade along the hem doesn't match the carpet." She nodded toward the blanket crumpled on the lower bunk. "The mattresses are stripped to the ticking covers, and it's the only bedding in the room. And it wasn't here, because it doesn't go with the rest of the decor. It was handed out from the ship's stores."

Ilias felt a chill settle in his stomach. She was right; all the bedding and fabrics in their cabin were the same colors. Giliead picked up the blanket, running a hand over it. His face hardened.

"What?" Ilias asked, watching him worriedly.

Giliead dropped the blanket back on the bed, his mouth twisted. "I don't think this one is harmless."

As they came back up the corridor of D deck, Tremaine noted the First Class area was much quieter. Her grumbling stomach informed her that it was lunchtime; most people had probably gone to the dining area. She was about to suggest they do the same when Giliead stopped abruptly in a vestibule. "There's something here." He stepped up to one of the doors. "It's faint. Not like that other room. But it doesn't seem dangerous."

The door opened suddenly and they all three flinched back. But it was Gerard, with rumpled hair and in his shirtsleeves, regarding them with a quizzical expression. "Oh, it's you," he said in Syrnaic. "Did you find anything?"

"Just you." Disgruntled, Ilias leaned against the wall and massaged the foot Tremaine had stamped on in hasty retreat from the door.

Giliead managed to look as if he hadn't reacted at all. Tremaine fanned herself with the map to cool the rush of heat to her cheeks. "Damn, just rush out and yell 'boo' next time."

"What? Oh, sorry." Gerard disappeared inside the room. "Come in."

"Were you trying to get some sleep?" Tremaine went in after him, Ilias and Giliead following more cautiously. "I thought you gave that up."

"It's not voluntary, I assure you," Gerard replied ruefully. The cabin lights were on and several books and notebooks lay open on the bed. "Niles and I put an adjuration on each other to stay awake for the next few days."

Tremaine lifted her brows. That sounded fairly drastic. "Is that a good idea?"

"No, not particularly," he admitted. "Oh, thank you for packing my things, by the way." He absently shifted some books aside so he could sit down. "Being able to shave this morning was a great relief."

Tremaine shrugged it off. "It was an experiment with optimism." Gerard had an ordinary stateroom, with a built-in desk and dresser, and a couch and chair in the small open area. What wasn't ordinary was that on every flat surface there were bowls, of crystal, colored glass and china. Tremaine stepped over to look at the three on the little boule table in front of the couch, seeing each was half-full of water and had bits of things floating in it. She recognized carpet or curtain threads, splinters of wood and what might be paint flakes. "Keeping an eye on all of us?" she asked, a brow lifted wryly.

"Those are for different areas of the ship." Gerard pulled off his spectacles to rub his eyes. "There's also one for you, one for Niles and one for Florian."

"I thought there might be one for me this morning." Tremaine looked around the rest of the cabin. Giliead leaned in the doorway, a closed thoughtful expression on his face. Ilias had taken a step further in but looked as if he was reluctant to touch anything.

Tremaine noted that the mirror above the dresser was tightly covered by a blanket. She knew that scrying spells used mirrors or reflective surfaces to view their targets, knowledge gained because Nicholas had required everyone associated with him to become an expert in how to avoid sorcerous spying. Finding a reflective surface for a sorcerer to use wasn't a problem on the *Ravenna,* with all her glass balusters and panels. She glanced back at Gerard and saw he was thoughtfully eyeing her and Ilias. *He's wondering how things are going, marriage-wise.* And maybe trying to think of a polite way to ask. To forestall it, she nodded to the draped mirror. "Is Niles peeping at you again?"

"What?" Gerard stared at her blankly. "Oh, the mirror. With these scrying bowls active, I'd rather not take any chances." He added with an annoyed shake of his head, "Niles has other methods."

Intrigued, Giliead asked, "A wizard could spy on you through the mirror?"

"A Rienish sorcerer could," Gerard admitted. "It's one of the spells that is useless against the Gardier, as far as we can tell. And we don't know if they can use it against us." He frowned at a sudden thought.

"Though that was before we knew about the crystals and the . . . bizarre nature of their sorcery."

"We did find something," Tremaine interposed before he could launch into etheric theory. She dropped into the armchair, glad to rest her feet. "Someone's been hiding up in Third Class."

As she explained what they had found, Ilias took another cautious step into the room and sat down on the rug.

Gerard's brow furrowed. "That still doesn't tell us whether he came aboard at Rel, Chaire or with the freed prisoners from the island. I need to examine that room."

Ilias shifted uncomfortably. *But he wants to show me he's not afraid of Gerard's spells,* Tremaine realized suddenly. It was another gesture meant to show that he would do his best to fit in to her world, somehow even more affecting than when he had demanded to know how to say *Valiarde.* Giliead was standing back and letting him do it, not ruining the gesture by coming further into the room, though he must realize the spells were harmless to them. *Focus, focus,* she reminded herself. "So what does Arisilde make of this?"

Gerard's frowned deepened. "He . . . didn't seem to want to be of use."

"Oh." Tremaine took that in, a little nonplussed. "He's never done that before." She glanced around the room again. "Where is he now?"

"With Niles in the hospital. I'm about to go down and take over for him. For Niles, that is."

She nodded. When they had first used the sphere, before realizing Arisilde himself was inside it, it had taken both Tremaine's and Gerard's presence to get it to work. Since then it had progressed to operating by itself, or needing only the smallest nudge to initiate a complex spell. "You're being careful with him, right? I mean, he's been stolen once—"

Gerard's mouth twisted wryly. "I think it highly unlikely that he will be stolen again. I hate to think what would happen to anyone who tried."

Tremaine saw Ilias exchange an enigmatic look with Giliead. She pushed herself to her feet. "We'd better get on with it, then."

Gerard ran a hand through his hair, nodding absently. "I'll let Niles and Averi know about the room you found." He gathered up a couple of the volumes on the bed and one of the notebooks, then followed them out into the hall, locking the door behind him.

By handing Tremaine the books while he pulled his jacket on, he managed to detain her while Ilias and Giliead wandered on up the quiet corridor. It wasn't until he said, "Well, and how are things going?" in Rienish that she realized she had been adeptly maneuvered into the private conversation she had wanted to avoid.

Deliberately misunderstanding, Tremaine threw him a puzzled look. "What things?"

He gave her a mild glare and made the question a pointed, "Are you two getting along?"

Giving in, she shrugged wearily. "So far. It's been less than half a day, Gerard, not even I could mess it up in that short amount of time." She decided not to mention that she almost had.

He sighed, stopping at the narrow passage that connected the two main corridors. "I don't mean to pry, but—"

"Yes, you do mean to pry," Tremaine assured him.

"Yes, I do, but—" He shook his head. "I'm sorry. I just worry about you. Needlessly." He patted her on the arm. "I'll be down in the hospital with Niles."

Tremaine watched him go. She hoped he was worrying needlessly.

Lengthening her stride to catch up to Ilias and Giliead, she began, "You know, I think we should—" She stopped as she found them in a vestibule, contemplating three closed doors.

From Giliead's concentrated expression, they had found something interesting. He said, "There's been a curse here, not long ago. It's fresh and strong."

"Can you tell what it was?"

He shook his head, trailing a hand cautiously around the doorframe. "Your curses are so different."

"Right." Tremaine turned, seeing they had an attentive audience. Two young Rienish women in traveling dresses and a young Maiutan woman in oversized canvas pants and a sailor's uniform shirt were seated on stools in the vestibule across the corridor, with a china coffee service laid out on a footstool. Apparently this was the hour in upper-middle-class society where one had coffee with one's neighbors, even if one's neighbors were Maiutan ex–prisoners of war. "Excuse me, but do you know who has these rooms?"

"Bisrans." The older matron set her cup down on the tray with the air of someone who had just been waiting to be asked that question. She explained, "We were told they escaped from Adera and were being held at Chaire. They don't speak to anyone, but you know Bisrans."

"They're in one of those sects," the other Rienish woman put in. "The one where they dress so badly."

Tremaine translated this into Syrnaic, leaving out the sartorial comment. Ilias rubbed his chin thoughtfully. "Those men we saw near the healer's rooms?"

Tremaine nodded. "Exactly. I need to check with someone to make sure, but if one of the Bisrans is a sorcerer, he hasn't said so." She eyed the array of closed doors. *Now we're getting somewhere.*

Giliead took that in, considering it. "Did the women see anything odd, anything that might have been a curse?"

Tremaine passed the question along in Rienish, and the older woman shook her head regretfully. "We saw them all go off that way toward the dining room, while we were having coffee. But we haven't been out here that long. My sister is getting over a fever, so we had our lunch on a tray in our room, then came out here so she could have some quiet for a nap."

"What did the Bisran pigs do?" the Maiutan woman asked curiously.

"They're Bisran pigs, do they need to do anything?" Tremaine told her, distracted. She rubbed her hands together briskly. "Is there a telephone in your room I could use?"

# Chapter 10

Glancing around the dining room, Tremaine spotted the Bisrans first. They were seated at two tables near the corner. Their severe dark suits and archaic ruffled neckcloths would have stood out in any Rienish setting, even with the increasing shortages of dyes and materials in the last few years as factories had been destroyed and trade routes shut down. Against the *Ravenna*'s gold-toned wood and silvered glass, they looked almost absurd.

There were five men, two of whom she had seen earlier outside the hospital, three women and four children. The women wore high-necked dark-colored blouses and skirts far too long for fashion. The children were miniature copies of the adults.

The room was about half-full of refugees and off-duty crew. Dishes clattered through the propped-open serving door, and children played around the pillars. Someone had brought in some low upholstered stools and a cocktail table from one of the lounges, fashioning an impromptu Syprian dining set. Gyan, Arites, Kias, and, to Tremaine's surprise, Cimarus and Danias were seated there. Gyan was watching them with a faint worried frown, as if something in Giliead's manner broadcast a warning. But Arites got up and came over, saying, "Come and eat. They take stewed fruit and put it inside this crispy bread, and it's wonderful."

"Not just now." Giliead shifted him aside gently. He moved toward the Bisrans, his face holding the same deliberate concentration as when he had trailed Ixion through the ship. One of the Bisran women looked up as they approached, her eyes widening.

"Which one?" Ilias asked, eyeing the group speculatively.

Giliead paused, only a few steps from the table where four of the men and one woman sat. "It's one of them. I'm not sure which." His brow creased in annoyance. "They're too close together."

Trailing after them and still munching on a bread roll, Arites said, "These people are snobs. They won't talk to anyone, even the nice people who make the food. Why are they afraid to let their skin show? Is there something wrong with them?"

They had all the Bisrans' attention now. Their faces were startled, nervous or contemptuous. Tremaine said, "In a word, yes." The two men she had seen outside the hospital were at this table, watching with cold caution. She checked the page of the hastily typed passenger list. The volunteer in the steward's office had given it to her once Tremaine had impressed on the woman that the whole ship was liable to instant disaster if she didn't. *I'm not even sure I was lying about that.*

According to the list, the oldest Bisran man at the table was Justice Riand. Tremaine knew Justice was a title, not a name, and designated a position somewhat analogous to a Rienish High Magistrate. Except as a Bisran the man would be less bound by the conventions of law. The other three men must be his older son Bain, his younger son Damil, and a son-in-law called Carrister. The woman didn't look old enough to be the wife listed on the manifest, so she must be one of the daughters or daughters-in-law.

Tremaine looked up to see Giliead and Ilias watching the Bisrans with a hawklike intensity that wasn't lost on the rest of the room; everyone had fallen silent. Careful to use Syrnaic, she asked Giliead, "So we know he did a . . . curse recently." She used the generic Syrnaic word for spell, not wanting the Bisrans to have even that much of a clue what this was about. As far as she knew, Giliead's abilities were known only to the upper level of the Rienish command, and not even to all of them. "Is he doing one now?"

"No." His eyes flicked to her. "Make them talk."

"Right." Tremaine eyed him thoughtfully. Near a real quarry for the first time in too long, he was single-mindedly intent on his goal, and Ilias, pacing around to the far side of the table like a lion in a cage, looked the same. She stepped up, took the one open chair at the table and sat down.

The Bisrans all stared at her in astonished affront. Switching back to Rienish, Tremaine said with blithe confidence, "Hello. How are we all today? And which one of you is a sorcerer?"

Staring at her, his jaw set and his face darkening with rage, Justice Riand demanded, "What right do you have to ask this question?" From the dishes on the table, lunch appeared to be soup, casserole and the apple tart Arites had complimented. She saw that their religious frugality hadn't prevented the Bisrans from eating it.

Giliead had moved up to stand behind Tremaine's chair; from across the table she could see Ilias was watching his friend's face. He caught her eye and shook his head minutely.

Not Justice Riand. She steepled her fingers and smiled around the table. "What right do you have to be on this boat?"

"Your military kept us in Chaire until we had no choice," one of the younger men snapped.

The woman was averting her eyes from Ilias and Giliead. She spoke suddenly. "Why are these filthy natives staring at us?"

"They aren't filthy." That was literally true. Syprians understood plumbing and knew it wasn't magic, so didn't shun it as they did electric switches and other mechanical devices. They also much appreciated the novelty of hot water on tap. "We all share a suite, and I don't think the bathroom's been unoccupied since we left port. Also, I happen to have expert knowledge, since I'm married to one of them."

Even if she hadn't been trying to provoke a reaction, it would have been worth it to see the offended shock and disbelief on all their faces. The woman actually looked like she was going to be ill. Satisfied with her progress so far, Tremaine rattled the sheet of typescript ostentatiously. "So, you must be Justice Riand." She smiled engagingly at the older man, who looked as if he was now certain he was dealing with a madwoman. "And we have here Bain, Damil, and Carrister?"

Justice Riand eyed her narrowly. "You have not said what right you have to question us."

"Now, that would be telling."

The man sitting next to her spoke suddenly, "I am Bain Riand." He was dark and handsome in a square-jawed, broody way, if one liked that sort of thing. "What do you want of us?"

She opened her mouth to answer, but Giliead moved suddenly, grabbing Bain's arm. Giliead said grimly, "It's this one."

Bain gasped, from surprise or pain. Then his hand opened and she saw he was holding a small brown stone with some strands of hair bound around it with red string. Alarmed, Tremaine shoved her chair back, stumbling to her feet. She had no idea what it was, but she could recognize a ritual object when she saw one.

Bain snatched up the dinner knife and stabbed at Giliead's arm. With a growl, Giliead pulled Bain out of the chair, slapping the knife out of his hand. The Bisran men surged to their feet but Ilias shouted, his sword drawn. The sudden appearance of three feet of steel abruptly halted their rush to help.

A flash of light caught Tremaine's eye. An amorphous green mass formed in the air above the table, resolving into something with razor-sharp claws and several mouthfuls of teeth. People screamed and shouted, coming to their feet. Tremaine backed rapidly away as Ilias grabbed the elder Riand by the collar, yanking him back and setting the sword's edge to his throat. But his face set, Giliead kept his hold on Bain's wrist, saying, "It's not real."

"It's an illusion!" Tremaine shouted in Rienish. "Everyone calm down!"

Bain spit words into Giliead's face and Tremaine saw something darken the air between them. She had seen a great many defensive spells, but this one she didn't recognize. Whatever it was, it made Giliead's face suffuse with rage. With one swift shove he pushed the black cloud away as if it was a solid mass, then slammed Bain facedown onto the table. But he didn't slam him hard enough, for Bain still struggled, trying to speak. Giliead tightened the hold into a strangler's grip.

"Don't kill him!" Tremaine yelped, realizing he wasn't going to stop. They had covered this point, hadn't they? "We need to talk to him!" She looked at Ilias for help. He caught her eyes, startled, then looked from her to Giliead, desperately conflicted.

She realized she had no idea if the marriage meant Ilias had to obey her. *I can't ask him to get in the middle of this.* She hastily turned to Giliead. "Please don't kill him. He can tell us things we need to know. I'd say something manipulative, but I can't think of anything. I suppose I could throw myself on his body, but there's no way in hell I'm doing that, so—"

Giliead was looking at her from under lowered brows. Then he released the pressure on Bain's throat, half-lifting him to slam the sorcerer into the hardwood table again. Stunned this time, Bain went limp and slid to the floor.

Colonel Averi had Bain Riand taken to the Isolation Ward, to the same treatment room they had used for questioning the

Gardier. There were two armed guards by the door, and the place was now warded almost as strongly as Ixion's cell. In the outer room, Tremaine peered through the grille, impatiently hoping Bain would just give in and talk.

Bain sat in a straight-backed chair in the bare whitewashed room. Niles stood over him, arms folded. He was conducting the interrogation as calmly as if he was interviewing the man for a position on the Institute's staff. It made Bain's sullen expression seem childish.

Niles asked thoughtfully, "Why didn't you admit that you were a sorcerer when you first crossed into Ile-Rien's territory?"

It was a reasonable question, and Bain looked away, his dark brows now more sulky than brooding. "Talk, you idiot," Tremaine said under her breath. As a sorcerer himself, Bain would know how to resist the mild truth spells Niles and Gerard had used on the Gardier prisoners; this could take forever.

Finally, Bain said grudgingly, "I'm not a sorcerer. I am a lay priest."

Niles lifted a skeptical brow. He said mildly, "You didn't admit to that either." Bisran priests of most sects were sorcerers; it was the only practice of magic their government sanctioned. If Bain had described himself as a priest the Rienish authorities would have known exactly what that meant. "What were you doing in Room C374?"

A flicker of honest confusion crossed Bain's face. "I don't—What room?"

"It's a Third Class room in the bow."

Bain shook his head, sullen again. "I was not there. I have been in no one's quarters except my own."

Niles considered him a moment. It did look distressingly as though Bain was telling the truth. Either that or he was a better actor than Tremaine had expected. "What was the spell in your quarters for?"

Bain pressed his lips together, still refusing to answer.

Tremaine rolled her eyes. *This is going to take forever.* She turned away, nearly stepping on Ilias, who had been hovering right behind her. He moved back, his expression both guilty and defensive, as if he knew he had been in the wrong but was prepared to argue the point anyway.

Oh, right, that. Tremaine took his arm, tugging him away from the grille so their voices wouldn't carry through. "Look, it's all right," she said quietly, stopping in the doorway. The outer room was only just around the corner, and she didn't want to be overheard from there either. "I understand."

He eyed her, still troubled, obviously wanting to make sure she really meant it. "You do?"

"I think I do, yes." During the fight in the dining room his loyalty to Giliead had come before his loyalty to her, but she was fairly certain she had already known that. In her experience of the complex web of loyalties and counterloyalties that characterized both Vienne's underworld and its theatrical community, it wasn't that much of a shock.

Ilias just nodded, his expression turning warmer. Suddenly uncomfortable, Tremaine towed him on into the office.

There, his suit and neckcloth still in disarray from the fight in the dining room, Justice Riand confronted Colonel Averi. "Your hired savages attacked my family," he was saying, his face dark with fury.

Giliead leaned back against the desk, arms folded, with Florian perched next to him. He threw a careful look at Tremaine and Ilias as they entered and relaxed slightly at seeing no obvious signs of enmity. Gerard was standing beside the door to the other guardroom, eyeing Riand with dislike. "That one"—Riand pointed at Ilias, his hand trembling with anger—"held a weapon to my throat. I have every right to demand vengeance on my authority as a Bisran Church Warden—"

Tremaine lifted a brow. There was a law in Ile-Rien that a diplomatic representative on Rienish soil could invoke the laws of his own country against anyone who committed a crime against him, as long as the criminal was not a Rienish citizen. It had been meant to deter Aderassi and other foreigners who came to Ile-Rien to attack prominent Bisrans. Dissidents had known they were more likely to get a light sentence from a sympathetic Rienish Magistrate and jury and to get their grievance aired in the press.

"They aren't hired," Colonel Averi interrupted the diatribe. "They are temporarily attached to this ship by the authority of an allied nation, and their diplomatic credentials hold more weight than yours. Besides, the one that held a weapon to your son's throat is a Rienish citizen. That may mean nothing anywhere else in our world or this one at the moment, but I assure you it means a great deal on this ship." He eyed Riand with cool contempt. "And as to vengeance, frankly, I'd like to see you try."

Riand stared at him in astonished affront, then set his jaw, obviously swallowing an angry reply.

Tremaine pretended to be more interested in the state of her fingernails, smiling to herself. She had forgotten that marriage to her, if a Rienish court accepted it as legal, gave Ilias Rienish citizenship. Not that that was worth much at the moment, but it was interesting that Averi was willing to use it. "What was that about?" Ilias asked her softly.

"He wanted you both turned over to him so you could finish killing him," she explained in Syrnaic. "Averi pointed out that it was a stupid idea."

Ilias snorted, and Giliead growled something under his breath.

Riand was still matching cold stares with Averi. Considering that Averi was the cold stare champion of the ship, Tremaine didn't give much for Riand's chances. The Bisran said finally, "Let us speak in private."

"We are in private," Averi snapped. "There isn't anyone here who is not directly concerned in this investigation."

Tremaine knew Riand could have probably gotten a private conversation with Averi if he hadn't been aggressive enough to trip the Rienish "if a Bisran asks for it say no" reflex. From his expression, Riand might have realized it too. He struggled with himself for a long moment, then said stiffly, "It is true, my son is a sorcerer. But all he did was cast a ward, and that only to protect our quarters while we were gone."

Averi's frown deepened. "It wasn't terribly effective. We searched your quarters while you were in the dining room."

"The ward was not meant to bar admittance to corporeal visitors."

Gerard came alert, staring skeptically at Riand. "Corporeal visitors? What do you mean?" He threw a glance at Giliead, and Tremaine realized he was thinking of the Syprian god. Though she didn't think it would leave the vicinity of Cineth, it was the only incorporeal visitor the ship had had. *As far as we know*, she thought suddenly, uneasy.

Riand's eyes moved from Averi to Gerard. He said, "My son was approached by something that did not show itself. It came to him while he was alone in the sitting room of our quarters, last night. It offered him . . . an unspecified reward if he would assist it."

Florian translated for Giliead and Ilias, keeping her voice low. Giliead's brows drew together as he listened. Ilias met his eyes with a frown and mouthed the word, "Shades?" Giliead shook his head slightly, but more as if he wasn't sure rather than discounting the suggestion.

"Assist it in what?" Averi demanded.

Riand hesitated, then admitted, "Stopping the ship from reaching Capidara."

Gerard cleaned his spectacles on a handkerchief, his eyes never leaving Riand. "But he refused."

"We have no quarrel with the people on this ship." For a moment Riand looked human, weary and exasperated. "Should we destroy the very thing that our safety depends on? To trust ourselves to a . . . a man, if it is a man and not some fay or creature, we know nothing of? We aren't mad."

"He had no idea what the identity of this . . . being was?" Averi's face was immobile, impossible to read. "If it was human, if it was male or female?"

"No." Riand shook his head, taking out a cloth to wipe the beads of sweat from his forehead. All these admissions were costing him something, at least. "Its spells of concealment were impenetrable. He could tell nothing about it except presumably what it wished him to know."

"It didn't occur to him to play along for a time?" Gerard asked, still watching him sharply but betraying some exasperation. "To try to discover its identity or what it planned for the ship?"

Riand's expression hardened. "Our children are taught to refuse the temptations offered them by demons and devils. To 'play along' with such a creature would only endanger his soul."

Oh, please, Tremaine thought, rolling her eyes. She thought she had done well to keep her incredulity subvocal, but Riand caught her expression, and his face reddened. He looked pointedly to Averi, his temper tightly controlled. "May my son be released now?"

The colonel's expression was still inscrutable, giving Riand no credit and nothing to appeal to. "I'm afraid not."

Riand pressed his lips together, his eyes coldly angry. He turned and walked out of the office, one of the guards moving to follow him at Averi's gesture. The colonel frowned at the doorway. "He isn't telling us everything."

"He didn't want to say what it offered, or what it specifically wanted the boy to do." Gerard paced a few steps, lost in thought. He lifted his brows. "In his position, it's a wise move."

"Could that story be true?" Florian asked a little reluctantly. "If this sorcerer or whatever he is wants to destroy the ship, why does he need help from a Bisran church sorcerer? Even a saboteur with no magic could cause us a lot of trouble."

"He doesn't want to destroy the ship." Tremaine's eyes narrowed as she considered the problem. "He was just feeling Bain out, seeing how far he could go with him. If Bain would agree to sink a ship filled with refugees, including his own family, he'd agree to anything." She shrugged slightly. "It's a bit crude. It makes me think Riand is right, and the thing that approached Bain wasn't human." It might even be why Riand believed it wasn't human, but he just didn't want to discuss his reasoning with people he still thought of as enemies.

Gerard nodded grimly, but Averi gave her an oddly assessing look. It wasn't as bad as his "who the hell are you" stare, but it worried her. He turned his gaze to the sphere, saying bluntly, "There is an incorporeal being on the ship."

Everyone looked at the sphere, resting innocuously on the desk where Gerard had set it when he came in. It wasn't even spinning or clicking.

Tremaine shook her head, startled. "No. Arisilde wouldn't do that, not unless he went insane." It crossed her mind suddenly that that was a very real possibility. Arisilde's consciousness was trapped in the sphere; if anybody had a right to go mad, it was he.

Before they had left Ile-Rien on the ill-fated Pilot Boat, Tremaine had been planning to kill herself. It was only after discovering that Arisilde was in the sphere that she had realized some of those feelings of despair had come from him.

The images of the Syprians that had worked their way into her play and a few magazine stories had been his attempts to communicate with her. But she hadn't responded, and the sphere had been left alone and dusty, and Arisilde, left without hope, had unintentionally transferred his despair to her. She had been despondent and probably shell-shocked enough on her own, and that couldn't have helped him either; they must have just fed each other's melancholy. It was a pointed reminder that Arisilde might not be in total control of his powers, that he might cause things to happen without conscious volition. But she wasn't going to point that out to Averi. "If he's crazy, we're all dead, so there's no point in discussing it," she said curtly.

Averi eyed her for a thoughtful moment. "I'm going to speak to Niles. Perhaps if Bain's story doesn't match his father's, we won't have to discuss it at all."

Tremaine watched him go, eyes narrowed, then said in Syrnaic, "Did that sound like a threat to anybody else?"

"No," Gerard told her firmly. "He has to consider all possibilities.

But I don't think it's the sphere—Arisilde—either. For one thing, he wouldn't need Bain's help to disrupt activity on the ship."

Wanting off the subject, Tremaine asked Ilias, "What did you say you thought it was?"

"Shades sometimes make trouble by whispering in dreams." Ilias jerked his chin toward the sphere. "But your god there should keep the dangerous ones away from the ship."

Tremaine glanced at Gerard, frowning. "Is the ship haunted?" As if they needed that too.

Gerard lifted a brow, considering the question. "There's some natural etheric activity. There were a few accidents during the early voyages, and I'd be surprised if there weren't still lingering impressions. But I doubt we have any true entities, particularly any hostile ones." He glanced up, frowning. "It's more likely Bain Riand was tricked by another sorcerer, fooled into believing the offer came from some sort of etheric being."

Ilias shook his head with a grimace. "It's hard to believe Ixion is on this ship and he didn't do this."

Giliead had been listening in thoughtful silence. "It's always been him before," he admitted grimly. "But Gerard is right. He can't get out of that room with their god keeping him in or he'd be out of it now. And besides, it doesn't have his . . . touch about it." He pushed to his feet. "But . . ."

"But it won't hurt to make sure," Gerard finished.

Once out of the Isolation Ward and up on the open deck, Ilias stopped Tremaine with a hand on her arm. "I don't want you to go with us."

She lifted a brow at him. "What?" The afternoon sun was bright on the sea and the salt wind tore at their hair. Already across the deck, Giliead glanced back in annoyance to see what was keeping them. He took in the situation and suddenly found something intensely interesting off the starboard rail.

"He knows things. If he knows we're together—" Ilias made a complex gesture.

Ah. This was about the Andrien women Ixion had cursed to death. Giliead's older sister, a cousin of Ilias's who had followed him to Andrien, and Halian's daughter, who had come to live with her father. Tremaine bit a nail thoughtfully, and pointed out, "Florian's going."

"I don't want Florian to go either."

It was Florian's turn to glare at him. "What?" she demanded defensively. "You think I'm going to be within ten feet of him and suddenly succumb to his will?"

Ilias shook his head in exasperation. "Of course not."

Tremaine couldn't help herself. "Florian had high marks in will-withstanding at the Lodun entrance examinations."

Florian transferred the glare to her.

Ilias planted his hands on his hips, and said firmly, "He kills women. I don't want him to see more of you—either of you—than he already has."

Tremaine sighed. She supposed it didn't matter; she didn't have anything to say to the bastard anyway. And she could hear real fear under Ilias's no-nonsense tone. "Oh, fine. We'll be in the main hall."

Ilias lost some of the tension in his shoulders, and took her hand. "I'll make it up to you." He lifted it to his lips, and she thought he was going to kiss the back like a conventional Rienish gentleman. But instead he bit her gently in the knuckle and lifted his brows suggestively.

Tremaine freed her hand, patted him on the cheek, and said, "That's a start." She wasn't going to admit just how good a start it was.

Florian muttered, "Somebody could offer to make it up to me," but followed her without protest up the steps to the Promenade deck.

They went through the doors to the roofed and glassed-in portion of the deck that ran along the ship's side, but Tremaine sensed foot-dragging. "Did you really want to see Ixion that much?" she asked. "He's not that exciting."

"No," Florian admitted. "But I'm doing the work of a trained sorceress. If I'm going to have the responsibilities, I'd like to have a chance at the authority too."

They reached the doors that led into the main hall and the shopping arcade. The doors on either side of the hall opened to the Promenade deck, and the big room was airy without being exposed to the wind. The daylight reflected off the warm yellow woods and the mellow cream tiles. Tremaine chose a couch at the far end of the room from where the other refugees were gathered and dropped down on it, glad to rest her back and stretch her legs out. Her feet hurt already, but after all the walking on the island, it was probably just a reflex. "You're the only student Gerard and Niles have," she pointed out, not realizing it was true until she said it. "They may never have another. Maybe they just don't want to get you killed."

Florian shrugged an acknowledgment as she sat down on the couch. In a deliberate change of subject, she said, "Well, how is it so far?"

Tremaine lifted a brow at her. "What?"

Florian eyed her back. "Being married. To Ilias."

By which she meant, whether she realized it or not, *Tremaine, have you managed to mess it up yet?* Tremaine smiled thinly. "It hasn't been that long."

"A real answer," Florian specified.

Tremaine leaned back on the soft cushion, making herself think it over. She had become friends with Ilias almost before she had been aware of it, the shared danger and the intimacy of having to communicate without words creating a closeness that she would never have sought under normal circumstances. Frustrated because she had no idea how it was going, she said impatiently, "So far so good? It's only been a day. Really, between Ixion and this thing with the Gardier, there hasn't been any time."

Fortunately, Arites walked up then, plopping down on the floor in front of them with an annoyed sigh. Tremaine could interpret that expression with no problem. "Giliead wouldn't let you stay in the room and write down the conversation with Ixion, would he?"

Arites looked disgruntled. "My history of Ixion is missing important details." He gestured in frustration. "Somebody has to write these things down!"

As Tremaine had hoped, Florian gave up on discussing the marriage. Folding her arms and resting her head back against the gold-striped upholstery, the other girl said, "I wonder if Dr. Divies is right, and they do make the Gardier soldiers forget their past." She frowned. "If it isn't a spell like Niles thinks, then they'd have to have terrible punishments to enforce it. Could that be worth it?"

Tremaine took a deep breath. She was absently people-watching, scanning the faces of the passersby. Most of them were refugees, with a few crew members mixed in. Refugees tended to wander in groups and crewmen to trot. "You can't fault their record of success so far," she said, realizing she was echoing Divies's words.

Florian nodded glumly. "The more we learn about them, the more confusing it gets." She looked at Tremaine for a moment. "Giaren told me that the ship hasn't picked up any radio traffic since we sank the Gardier gunship."

Tremaine frowned. "That's not normal?"

"No. On a voyage to Capidara in our world, they could make ship-to-shore connections for almost the whole trip. We should be able to hear the Gardier talking to each other, or the other people advanced enough to have wireless, but there's nothing. It's like they're communicating only with sorcery, like that radio set they had in the caves on the island."

Tremaine shook her head. "That is bizarre." Why bother to use sorcery when a normal wireless would do the job most of the time? In Ile-Rien—or the Ile-Rien of the past—there had been a great many people born with some talent for magic, but the number of sorcerers who could do Great Spells, or whose talent enabled them to do more than charms and simple healing and small wards, was a bare fraction. "But it might be just empty territory all around us." She gave Arites a poke with her foot. "You'd never heard of the Gardier before this."

He nodded earnestly. "That's true. I didn't have a chance to send messages to any of the poets in Syrneth to make certain before we left, but I'm sure I would have remembered it if anyone had told a story about them before. And none of the traders from other places have ever mentioned them, as far as we know."

"So maybe they just aren't in this hemisphere except when they're attacking Ile-Rien."

"But then why are they attacking us, when there's all this land here?" Florian asked logically.

Tremaine followed that cold thought to its conclusion, picking at a stray thread in her shirt. Florian was still looking at her like she wanted an answer. Like she wanted someone to say it aloud. *Why is that always my job?* she thought wearily. "The Syprians don't have sorcerers like we do."

Florian's brows drew together, her face set and grim. "It must be the crystals. They must have put every sorcerer ever born to them in one of the things, and they're all still alive, still serving them, hundreds and thousands of them. That's what Gerard and Niles think." She hesitated, her eyes on Tremaine again, but shadowed. "If I'm caught—"

Tremaine sensed a "will you kill me" coming and nervously leapt to head it off. "Gervas didn't seem very interested in you. Maybe they don't do it to girls."

Florian glared at her, but at least that darkness lifted from her face. "You know, I was trying to be serious—"

"I know you were trying to be serious. It was really obvious. I'm not—" Tremaine's casual observation of the people passing through the room suddenly brought her up short. Two men, a sailor and a civilian, were walking with an older Parscian man between them. The sailor had a peremptory hand on the Parscian's elbow as if the man was being conducted somewhere. The civilian was a plain-looking, dark-haired man whose pale face was vaguely familiar, though she didn't recognize him as being with the Viller Institute. He must be a refugee, but his brown suit was a little too seedy to mark him as part of the Court or Ministry groups. He could be one of the people trapped at Chaire who had decided to take the risk, but . . . *Seedy. And furtive.* Now she remembered; he was the man she had seen with a crew member in the cross corridor, as if buying or selling some forbidden object. That wasn't the same crewman, but as he conducted the worried Parscian down the stairs, she saw him throw a surreptitious glance over his shoulder. "Hold it."

"What?" Florian demanded, looking around the room. "What did you see?"

"I don't know." Tremaine pushed to her feet. "Let's go find out."

Giliead wasn't looking forward to this. Gerard came with them down a deck to Ixion's chamber, stopping at the outer room to speak to the guards, and Giliead and Ilias waited outside in the metal-walled passage. Giliead folded his arms, glad Ilias had made Tremaine and Florian wait elsewhere.

Giliead knew it was only Gerard's influence that kept the Rienish from trying to turn Ixion into an ally. After spending this much time in their company, listening to Florian's explanations of their councils, he realized that wizards were their best warriors against the Gardier, and that their numbers were desperately depleted. If Gerard hadn't persuaded the others that Ixion was dangerous and deeply untrustworthy, Giliead knew they would have tried to bargain with him.

If something happened to Gerard, or if he and Niles somehow lost their status in the Rienish ranks, Giliead knew it might happen anyway.

The guards filed out to wait in the passage, throwing them curious glances, and Giliead stepped in. Gerard had taken out the other pieces of glass that fit over his eyes, the ones he said gave him the ability to see curses, and was studying the door.

"I know you're out there." Ixion's voice came from the other side of the sealed portal. "What are you doing?"

"Nothing of interest to you," Gerard replied, still studying the door.

"Come to make me another offer?"

"What?" Giliead asked, exchanging a sour glance with Ilias. "Are you tired of the deal you made for your life, and you want another?"

There was a long moment of silence. "I have done nothing to break our agreement." Ixion sounded sullen and weary.

Gerard pulled off the heavy glass pieces, replacing them with his normal ones. He looked puzzled, but not worried. "I saw some disturbance in the patterns, but I don't think he's tried to escape."

Giliead stepped closer to the door. Concentrating hard, he could just feel the currents of the Rienish protective curses in the air near the door. It was mightily disturbing. A curse this powerful he should have been able to see from any distance, let alone across the room. This was just a mild movement of air that should have been still, air that wove back in on itself instead of flowing in one direction. He couldn't sense any of Ixion's curses, just that deceptively gentle barrier. "I don't think so either."

"I keep to my word," Ixion said with particular emphasis. "I thought you better than that."

Ilias, who had kept silent until now, snorted derisively.

Gerard shook his head, stepping out of the room. Giliead, not wanting to prolong the interview, prodded Ilias out and followed him. "I don't see how he could have caused this," Gerard said softly. "Not from behind those wards. Unfortunately."

Giliead nodded grimly. "We'll keep looking."

As they followed Gerard down the corridor, Ilias said, "He sounded different. Was that a trick?"

Giliead shook his head slowly, giving it serious consideration. "I don't think so. Maybe he's just . . . He's never lost before."

"He lost his head," Ilias pointed out skeptically.

"Well, that," Giliead agreed. "But that was over fairly quickly, and he was winning up to then."

Ilias nodded grudgingly, giving in on that point. "So you think he realizes he can't fight the Rienish?"

"I think so. They know things he's never heard of before. Gerard took him down with a curse made of spit and a piece of Dyani's hair, and he says the god-sphere knows more than he does." Giliead nodded to himself, thinking it over. "Ixion's never had to give way to anybody before, much less beg and bargain for his life; that's got to have an effect on him."

Ilias lifted his brows, considering it. "Good," he said softly.

Tremaine had gotten to know this area of the ship very well over the course of the past day, so following the two men and their possibly unwilling companion wasn't hard. Intriguingly, they seemed to be heading back to the Third Class area, further aft and just a deck down from the room where the sorcerer had been hiding. But the blue-carpeted corridors were smaller here and the layout more confusing with more cross corridors, and they turned a corner to find their quarry vanished.

Tremaine swore and followed the corridor to its end, Florian and Arites hurrying behind her. They came to an open stairwell, and Tremaine stopped, startled to see a small group of refugees going up. None of them looked particularly well off, the men in worn traveling suits and the women in dresses that had seen several seasons. "Lot of traffic back here all of sudden," she muttered to Florian. She leaned over the smooth wooden stair railing, looking up and down, but she couldn't tell if the three men had gone that way.

The other girl shook her head slightly, frowning. "Maybe people are using the lounge areas. The windows down on this deck are all portholes with dead-lights and easier to cover at night than those floor-to-ceiling windows in some of the First Class lounges."

"No one was down here last night," Arites interposed. When Tremaine looked at him inquiringly, he explained, "Kias and I walked around a lot."

"Huh." Tremaine looked around thoughtfully. *Too many damn rooms.* But if the men wanted to do something in a stateroom, why pick one all the way down here? They must be making for a public room. "If they were cutting through here . . ." She crossed the stairwell to the next corridor and headed down it.

"You think they're spies?" Florian wanted to know. "Maybe paying that man for information?"

"Maybe." The *Ravenna*'s original skeleton crew and the small army detachment that had accompanied the Viller Institute must all know each other, at least by sight. But more navy and army personnel had been picked up with the civilian refugees at Chaire, and there might be enough now to make fading into the background easy.

They passed a room labeled THIRD CLASS GENTLEMEN'S HAIR-DRESSER, with a window looking into a dark space with barber chairs and glass cabinets, then came to an open door. Tremaine could hear low voices, speaking Parscian.

Tremaine motioned Arites and Florian to hang back, and carefully edged up to peer in. It was a long dark-paneled smoking room, probably a quarter the size of some of the First Class lounges, the chairs and tables pushed back against the wood-paneled walls and covered with dust sheets.

The three men were there, with the other crewman she had seen the suspicious civilian with before. Tremaine's grasp of Parscian was spotty, but better than that of the sailor who was trying to speak it to the nervous but adamant Parscian man. After a few minutes of listening to them argue she rolled her eyes in disgust and withdrew from the door.

"It's not spies, dammit," she reported to Florian and Arites in a bare whisper. "It's a stupid shakedown swindle. They're trying to get money out of him, claiming only Rienish citizens are allowed on the ship and that they'll report his family if they don't come across."

Florian stared, aghast. "The hell!" Before Tremaine could stop her, she stormed into the room.

The Parscian man was grimly handing over a battered pocket-watch, probably his last possession of any value. Florian grabbed the watch out of the startled crewman's hand as the Parscian backed hastily away. "What are you doing with this?" she demanded.

The sailor glared at her in outrage. The anger and frustration in his eyes made Tremaine rest a hand on the pistol tucked into the back of her belt. The man told Florian, "He was giving it to me, and it's none of your business." His gaze swept them, dismissing Tremaine but settling on Arites suspiciously. "I don't know what you want, but you can get the hell out of here."

Swearing, the civilian reached for the watch, but Florian jerked it away, falling back a step. "Why is he giving it to you then?"

The Parscian man asked a worried question, looking in confusion from Florian to the crewman. He looked hopefully at Tremaine for an explanation, and she shrugged helplessly. He was probably a refugee from Adera or the Low Countries who had been trapped at Chaire, unable to get any further or waiting to be joined by others who had never come.

The civilian tried an acid smile. "He's just giving it to us, little girl. Now take your native friends and get out."

Arites moved to Florian's side then, forcing Tremaine to step into the room so she could still get a clear shot if she needed to. He hadn't understood the Rienish words, but the tone must have spoken volumes. He stopped just close enough to the civilian to be threatening. His voice hard, he said, "You don't speak to her that way."

It startled Tremaine; she had been thinking of him as being somewhat like a Rienish café poet, someone who didn't get into fights, except rather mild ones with other café poets. For the first time she remembered that he went out on the *Swift* with Halian and the others and probably spent more time pulling oars than writing stories.

Not understanding Syrnaic, the crewman looked him over, his sneer probably from habit. Arites was more slightly built than Ilias or Giliead, and his wild brown hair was too wispy to stay in braids, his beard stubble as patchy as a young boy's. He didn't look that intimidating. "Just take your native boyfriend and get out."

Florian's cheeks were red. "You're stealing from these people. I'm going to report you—"

He sneered. "You got no proof. It's my word against a bunch of lying foreigners. They're probably spies anyway."

She shook the watch in his face, still angry. "How could you? Don't you realize what's happening?"

"That's enough." The civilian grabbed Florian's arm. Tremaine drew the pistol, but Arites got there first, stepping in to shove the man away from Florian. The crewman threw a punch that caught Arites in the chin, then grabbed his shirt, bracing to push him back. Arites knocked the man's arms aside and slammed a fist into his jaw with an audible crack. The crewman staggered back and slumped into the wall.

His companions surged forward, stopping short when Tremaine said sharply, "That's far enough. Put your hands up and back away."

Arites rubbed the shoulder where he had taken the Gardier bullet. "That hurt," he said, sounding like himself again.

"Thank you," Florian told him. She didn't look at all upset at the fallen crewman's obvious pain. She turned to hand the watch back to the old Parscian man, who was watching the situation in wary confusion.

Still covering the other two men, Tremaine asked the Parscian, "You speak Aderassi?"

"Yes, a little." He turned to her in relief. "What is going on here?"

"He's cheating you." Tremaine jerked her head at the crewman. "Passage on the ship is free for anyone, not just the Rienish."

He took a breath and nodded. "I thought it must be so." He gestured to the men in disgust. "But I didn't know what attitude the authorities aboard would take with such predators."

"I don't know either," Tremaine admitted, "But I suspect it will be harsh." She switched back to Rienish. "Florian, can you find a telephone and ask for someone to come down and take these idiots off our hands?"

"Yes. I'm sorry," Florian said, biting her lip. The angry color was starting to fade from her cheeks. "I could have done that better. I just . . . Stealing from people when we don't know what's happening in Ile-Rien—"

Tremaine nodded grimly. "I know." She really did understand. *It's not that we don't know what's happening back home, it's that we probably know all too well.*

Chapter 11

Karima has said to beware of Pasima's motives. She is not the woman to send on a journey of alliance, that it should have been someone older, like Deliana or Marenyi, with stronger ties to the councils in Syrneth. Halian agrees, and tells Gyan that Pasima will watch what the ally-wizards do, and try to make ill out of it.

—"Ravenna's voyage to the Unknown Eastlands,"
V. Madrais Translation

Tremaine and Florian caught up with Ilias and Giliead just in time for the loudspeaker to announce a lifeboat drill. Tremaine hoped to avoid it, but sailors were herding everyone out on deck, and pretending not to understand Rienish didn't work.

The crew had been organizing the refugees into groups and giving them a boat station to go to if the ship's alarm sounded. Tremaine thought it was more for morale than anything else; if the *Ravenna* sank in this world, there was no friendly shipping to respond to distress calls, and though the boats could travel long distances, few would make it all the way back to Cineth. Reaching Capidara would mean using either Arisilde's sphere or the one Niles had made to go through the etheric gateway, and trying to get all the scattered boats together for that in the confusion of a Gardier attack would be a nightmare. *Not like there's any friendly shipping left in our world, either,* she thought tiredly.

Fortunately or unfortunately, all the Syprians had been assigned to the same lifeboat station. Tremaine hoped to get through it quickly, but it took both Florian and the earnest young officer in charge of their boat to convince Pasima that throwing the davit's release lever to swing the boat out into position and lower it wouldn't constitute using a curse.

Tremaine considered the two Syprian women, Pasima arguing with polite vehemence with Giliead and Florian, and Cletia standing at her back, looking at the other passengers thoughtfully, the wind tugging at her bright hair. It occurred to Tremaine that if Ilias hadn't gotten the curse mark, he would have expected to marry someone either tall and darkly beautiful or small with hair the color of clover honey. She wondered how he felt about being stuck with a rather drab specimen of Ile-Rien's demimonde. She grimaced at herself. *But you got what you wanted regardless of anyone else's feelings, and that's the important thing, isn't it?*

Finally, Giliead glowered at Pasima, saying, "I'm telling you it's not a curse, that's how you know it's not a curse."

Pasima glared back, undaunted. "I have heard that you can't see some of these people's curses. What if this is one of those?"

Giliead stared at her, eyes narrowed, breathing hard. Ilias groaned under his breath and rubbed his eyes. Tremaine buried her head in her hands. The magazine stories and plays she had written had all been desperate adventures but the characters had moved through them effortlessly, unaffected. In reality what you got was tiresome arguments and exhaustion and people pulling you in a dozen different directions and demanding you stop for a godforsaken lifeboat drill when you had to stalk the spy/sorcerer/creature who had tried to get your stupid worthless prisoners.

After they escaped, Tremaine persuaded Ilias and Giliead to stop for a hasty meal, then they continued the search. They roamed the lower decks, padding down miles of carpeted corridors and metal-floor passages, looking at empty rooms, empty storage areas, and rooms filled with confusingly noisy machinery until Tremaine's feet were ready to fall off.

"It's like the caves under the island," Florian said at one point, pressing the heels of her hands over her eyes in despair. "Except with seasickness."

And they still had more to search.

At one point Giliead halted abruptly, turned, and led them through a foyer packed with stacked tables and chairs to a pair of embossed leather doors. He stopped with one hand on the bronze handles, looking down at Tremaine expectantly.

Her mouth quirked. This was the main ballroom, one of the largest chambers in the ship, and she knew what had drawn Giliead here. "The spell circle is in this room. It's harmless without the sphere to make it work." She sorted through the keys and unlocked the door.

The dark wood paneling and red velvet drapes, the unlit crystal sconces made the large space rich and shadowy, like a treasure cave. There was a stage at the far end for use when the room doubled as a musical theater, and all the tables and chairs had been stacked out in the foyer.

The circle had been permanently painted onto the marble tile, and it was much larger than the one that had been placed in the boathouse at Port Rel or the first one Tremaine had seen in the Viller Institute's old quarters. It enclosed most of the long rectangular room, leaving only a few feet of space along the walls. Little ward signs circled the enameled red support pillars to exclude them from transport when the spell was initiated for someone within the circle. Extending the spell's parameters outward was what allowed a sorcerer with a sphere to send the entire ship through the world-gate.

Florian was watching Giliead's rapt expression curiously. "What does it feel like?"

"It's waiting," he said slowly. "There's nothing in it now, but it smells of curses. The curses come into it from everywhere, they're attached to it by little lines of light." He looked down at Ilias, one brow lifted.

Ilias gave an exaggerated shudder. "I'm glad I didn't know that before. Let's go."

It was dark outside and blackout conditions were in effect in all the outer rooms of the ship when Giliead called a reluctant halt. They went back up to the deck just below the main hall, to the foyer with the four openings to the major cabin corridors. The steward's office was closed, no light showing through the etched-glass windows. There was a doorway open to a small bar lounge, but the windows were covered with thick curtains and the light in the foyer was limited to one small table lamp.

Tremaine leaned on the stair's cherrywood banister, wishing she could live without feet. "You going back to your cabin?" she asked Florian around a yawn.

"Yes, I think I can use some sleep." Florian rubbed her eyes wearily. "If I can get any. I've got two roommates. One's very beau monde, and she lost her fiancé early in the war, the other's older, but she lost her husband only a few months ago." She gave Tremaine a bleak look. "They think I'm too lucky."

Tremaine rolled her eyes. "Tragedy doesn't prevent people from being bastards, does it?"

"No." Florian snorted in helpless amusement, then had to lean against the paneled wall to steady herself. "I think we've come up with a new motto for the ship's banner."

"It's better than 'drowning's not such a bad way to go.' If you need a place to sleep, you can come to our cabin."

"You have a lot of people in there already, and I can handle this." She smiled. "But thanks."

Tremaine watched her go down the hall, and turned, yawning again, to find that Ilias and Giliead had vanished. She swore wearily. But after a moment she heard a thump and a strangled yelp.

Oh, fine. She started down the corridor cautiously, hugging the wall. *Now they find something.*

Suddenly Giliead bolted out of a room several doors down, skidded to an abrupt halt, his head cocked to listen. Then he took long strides to another door on the far side of the corridor, paused at the entrance, and slipped inside.

Swearing silently to herself, Tremaine advanced, trying to put her feet down quietly. When Ilias stepped out of the narrow cross corridor, she jumped a foot in the air.

Intent on something else, Ilias barely glanced at her. Motioning for her to follow him, he stepped silently to the doorway Giliead had vanished into.

Her heart pounding, Tremaine poked her head into the unlit room cautiously. It was a children's playroom, the walls painted with a jungle scene filled with parrots, flamingos, dancing bears and penguins and other unlikely combinations of animals, the colors dim in the shadows. The toys were long gone but the low wooden cabinets that had held them still lined the far wall.

Giliead was sitting on his heels in the middle of the tiled floor, staring into a dark corner. Ilias had moved to the opposite wall, easing down to sit back against it. Before Tremaine could ask what the hell they were doing, she saw the figure crouched in that dark corner.

Tremaine ducked her head, squinting to see. She thought it was a boy, or a very young man. She could just make out gangly legs in faded blue trousers and a bare ankle above a scuffed rubber-soled shoe, a bare wrist jutting out of a torn white shirt too small for it, the outline of a cap above the shadowed face. "Who's this?" she asked softly, for some reason feeling compelled to whisper.

"A shade," Ilias told her, his voice low but matter-of-fact.

Tremaine took that in, staring blankly at the figure in the corner. Then she stared blankly at Ilias. "A ghost?"

"Isn't that the same thing?" He glanced up at her quizzically. "A piece of someone that got left behind?"

"Uh, yes." Tremaine took a step into the room and halted abruptly. It was like stepping into a meat freezer. The cold seemed to come up from the floor, as if a yawning cavern opened beneath them instead of a dusty floor tiled with alternating black and white squares. *Oh yes, that's a ghost,* she admitted, swallowing in a dry throat. She side-stepped carefully toward Ilias, then crouched down to sit beside him. "What's Giliead doing?"

Ilias shifted nearer, his shoulder and arm startlingly warm against hers. "Talking to him."

"He was a stowaway," Giliead said suddenly, making Tremaine flinch. He turned his head toward them, his profile etched against the shadow. "What is that?"

It took Tremaine a moment to realize he was talking to her. "Someone who sneaks aboard the ship without paying." She hoped she didn't sound twitchy. The chill in the dim room, the silence that made even the movement of the ship seem muted, were working on her nerves.

Giliead nodded slightly, turning back to the silent figure in the corner.

Keeping his voice low, Ilias explained, "He told Gil he went out on one of the upper decks because he was afraid of being caught, but the wind was bad, and he fell."

Tremaine frowned. No one had mentioned a fatal accident. "Just recently? When they left Chaire?"

"No, it's been a long time."

Giliead said suddenly, "He remembers he doesn't want to leave the ship, because he thinks it's safe here."

Her skin starting to creep in earnest, Tremaine said softly to Ilias, "So, it's not dangerous?"

"Some are, some aren't." Ilias shook his head, still watching the creature carefully. "I don't think this one is."

She was willing to believe that. She didn't want the thing near her, but there was something pathetic about it. "How can Giliead understand him? This is a Rienish ghost, right?"

"The dead don't use words," Giliead answered her again.

It was mildly disconcerting that he could be so focused on the thing in the corner yet still listen to her and Ilias's conversation.

They sat there in silence, moisture from the damp chill air beading on the walls. Giliead let out his breath in a long sigh finally and got to his feet, moving stiffly. Ilias sat up, alert. The ghost stood and scuttled along the wall in the shadows, making toward the door. Tremaine couldn't hear its footsteps on the carpet as it slipped out. The cold faded almost immediately as warm dry air from the corridor drifted in.

Ilias pushed to his feet, reaching down to give Tremaine a hand up. "Can we do the rites for it?"

Giliead shook his head. He looked tired, his face a little drawn, and he stretched, rolling his shoulders as if he had spent time in some cramped space. "He didn't fall in the water, just onto the deck. They did rites when they found him." His mouth twisted ruefully. "He doesn't want to leave the ship."

Ilias looked after the ghost, frowning. Tremaine wondered, *Does that mean it just stays here forever? Even if the ship sinks?* She decided she didn't want to ask. Then Ilias glanced at Giliead, brows lifted. "So shades can cross seas." He sounded vindicated about it for some reason.

Even in the dim light, Tremaine could see an annoyed gleam replace the regret in Giliead's eyes. "This ship is different."

"So what did it say?" she put in, before the sea-crossing tangent could take them further afield. "Did it know anything about the other sorcerer?"

"It's seen something," Giliead admitted, leading the way out and turning down the corridor toward the stairwell again. "It usually stays down in the lower decks, below the waterline. I could tell it's seen your crew working down there. But whatever it saw . . . it made it want to leave there. And it couldn't tell if it was a man or a woman. It couldn't show it to me."

Tremaine didn't particularly like the sound of that. "So this is a sorcerer that a ghost can't recognize as human."

"That's just our luck," Ilias commented dryly.

A fter the ghost incident, Ilias and Giliead went down to the din-ing hall, which was about to close up for the night. Tremaine was tired enough that food was less important than a bath and headed back to the cabin.

As she pushed open the broken door, she realized the rooms smelled exotic and foreign now, of strange people and worn leather and the scent of the incense the Syprians stored their clothes in. She hesitated in the foyer, deciding the last thing she needed was a run-in with Pasima. No one was in the main room, but she could hear voices coming from one of the back bedrooms. She tiptoed through to the room where her bag was to dig out the gold shirt from Karima and clean underwear, then made a run for the bathroom and barricaded herself inside.

Later, Tremaine came out of the bathroom still toweling her hair dry to find Arites waiting to announce, "Ilias brought your dinner and went away again with Giliead."

"What?" She wandered after him into the main bedroom to find a tray from the First Class dining room on the marquetry occasional table. She lifted the domed cover to see potato pie, tomato cream soup, and a small coffee service. She sat down on the couch, her stomach rumbling from the smell of sweet onions and cheese. It didn't surprise her that Ilias knew enough Rienish by now to make someone from the kitchens understand what he wanted, but nonsensically it did embarrass her that he had done this for her. She didn't want him to think he had to act like a servant. Truthfully, she mainly didn't want anyone else to think he had to act like a servant. *That's just you being a Vienne snob again,* she told herself. Speaking of snobs, she could just imagine how Ander would comment on it. She set the cover aside on the floor. "Arites, did Ilias eat already?"

He dropped into the armchair opposite her, shrugging genially and pulling a sheaf of ragged paper out of his bag. "I don't know."

It occurred to Tremaine that she was supposed to be the head of this little family group. "What about everybody else?"

"I did. I don't know about anyone else." Arites arranged his ink bottle and pens on the smoking table.

Tremaine tasted the potato pie. Now she knew why the food at Port Rel had always been so terrible; all the good provisions must have been diverted onto the *Ravenna*. "Where are they? All the Andriens, I mean."

"I don't know where Ilias and Giliead went. Gyan is with Pasima and Ander, speaking to some of your people. I think one of them was named Avil-something." Arites considered a moment. "Avil-er."

Oh, goody, Tremaine thought dryly, pouring herself coffee. At least Gyan was there to watch out for Andrien interests, anyway.

Arites smoothed a rough sheet of thick paper. "And Kias is with his girlfriend."

Tremaine choked on her coffee. "His what?"

"He met a woman last night. I don't know her name. She's Rienish."

Of course. That's why he and Arites were roaming the ship all night. It sounded like Ilias's decision to marry a foreigner might not be as unpopular as Visolela had feared, especially with single men of poor families. "He can't speak Rienish," she pointed out.

"I know." Arites nodded earnestly. "But it didn't seem to matter."

This . . . sounds like someone else's problem. "He's a fast worker," she commented with a lifted brow, setting her cup down.

After a moment she was aware of Arites watching her thoughtfully. Finally, he asked, "How did you know those men were thieves? To me, and to Florian too, they looked no different than anyone else passing through the hall."

Tremaine hesitated, trying to think how to frame a response. She could put it down to a misspent youth in the poets and artists' cafés and the theater world, which tended to share boundaries with the older, darker and poorer areas of the city where such men were common. But that wasn't the truth. "After my mother died, my father took me on walks through the city, and then questioned me afterward on what I thought of the people we saw." At the time she had been used to Arisilde's undemanding guardianship, and it had seemed just an annoyance; later she realized that Nicholas had been showing her what danger signs to look for and how to listen to her instincts. "I didn't know it at the time, but he was teaching me how to see the difference between men like that and men who are just minding their own business."

Arites nodded slowly. "I think I see. Thank you for telling me that story."

Tremaine had almost finished her meal when Ilias returned, planting himself at her feet. "Thank you for bringing me dinner," she told him, self-consciousness returning.

He shrugged, shifting to lean comfortably against her knee and appropriating the last few scraps of potato. He was wearing her ring on a leather thong around his neck. She decided she could get used to this, and maybe it didn't matter what anyone else thought. *Maybe Ander can stuff himself.* She noted Ilias's hair was damp and he smelled like salt water. "Where did you take a bath?"

"We went to that bathing place we saw," he told her.

Tremaine frowned thoughtfully at the top of his head. "The First Class swimming pool?" They had passed through the pool room earlier today to find that Lady Aviler's group had had it opened as a way to try to keep the younger refugees occupied. The pool was filled with salt water from the ship's unlimited supply and housed in a large tiled chamber with a mother-of-pearl ceiling. Ilias and Giliead had both been impressed. Tremaine just wished somebody would open the steam bath and other special services in the rooms off the pool's gallery, but she supposed they couldn't have everything.

"That's it," he agreed. She processed the fact that his clothes were perfectly dry. Syprians didn't seem to have much in the way of nudity taboos, even in public. *I suspect I'll hear about this tomorrow.*

Giliead came into the room and flung himself down on the bed. From his disgruntled expression, she suspected he had been prowling the suite looking for a relative to start a fight with and was bitter at coming up empty. It didn't surprise her; he had been worked up all day to kill a wizard and been balked again and again. Ilias, either less bloodthirsty or just more easily distracted, poked at her dinner thoughtfully, asking, "What do you call this again?"

"The white part is potato, the red part is tomato." The Syprians found most Rienish food palatable, if strange. The only thing they had refused to eat that she knew of was the cranberry pie the kitchens had produced for breakfast that morning, on the grounds that cranberries were reserved for offerings to the dead.

Peering hopefully into the near-empty coffeepot, Tremaine heard Pasima's voice out in the sitting room. "Oh goody, she's back," she sighed.

Giliead pushed up off the bed, his face set in grim lines, headed for the door. *And the ring keeper strikes the bell for round two,* Tremaine thought, eyeing his expression. Arites was still engrossed in his writing, but she saw him wince in anticipation. Hopefully it would cut up Pasima's peace as much as it would everyone else's. Obviously thinking the same thing, Ilias watched his progress, his brows drawn together in concern. Then as Giliead strode past he stretched out a foot and tripped him.

Giliead stumbled forward and slammed his shoulder into the doorframe, barely catching himself. He glared down at Ilias incredulously. Ilias grinned up at him. "Got you."

Giliead grabbed for him, but Ilias was already shoulder-rolling away, Arites having quick-wittedly snatched his feet out of his path.

After a brief struggle Giliead had his friend in a headlock, and Tremaine was watching wryly, wondering if Ilias had developed that instinct for deflecting possible family arguments before or after he had come to Andrien. Then behind her, someone cleared his throat. Tremaine twisted around to find herself looking at Captain Marais, standing in the doorway. "Miss Valiarde," he greeted her calmly. "The cabin door was open."

"Oh, yes. It got broken." She sat up hastily, putting her cup aside and gesturing to a chair. "Captain Marais, won't you sit down?" *And why in God's name are you here?* She wasn't aware he ever left the wheelhouse, and if he wanted to talk to any of them, he could have had them summoned there.

Giliead released Ilias and both eyed the male interloper in their territory with wary cordiality. Businesslike, Marais nodded to them, as if finding them rolling around on the floor like oversized puppies was an everyday occurrence. He took the straight-backed chair at the desk, turning it around and taking a seat. Giliead dropped down onto the bed again, but Ilias stayed sprawled on the floor, propping himself up on an elbow. Arites shifted around to face Marais, attentively prepared to take notes. Marais glanced at their Syprian stenographer with mild curiosity, and explained to Tremaine, "I wanted to ask your friends some questions."

"Ah." She managed not to look immediately suspicious and defensive. "About what?"

He lifted a brow at her, and she wasn't sure she had succeeded. But he said only, "Just a possible problem with our course." He sat forward, frowning and pressing his fingers together. "You may know that the *Ravenna* was fitted with a wireless detection system before the war." He saw her blank look and elaborated, "It's an experimental system to detect icebergs in the path of ships by sending out a wireless signal. If the signal strikes a large solid mass, it bounces back and is picked up by the detection device. It was under study at Lodun before the war started."

Ilias sat up, demanding impatiently, "What's he saying?" Giliead was regarding her with lifted brows and Arites had his pen poised impatiently.

"I don't know yet, just wait," she told them in Syrnaic. Gesturing for Marais to continue, she switched to Rienish to say, "Sorry, just try to ignore them."

The captain cleared his throat and forged ahead. "We've been using the device throughout the voyage. This morning it returned a signal to us."

Tremaine frowned. "So we're nearing land? But it's not Capidara?"

"No, not yet."

"Huh. I'll ask them, but you know they don't sail too far from the coast of the Syrnai." She paraphrased Marais's account in Syrnaic.

It took a while to get them past the explanation of the wireless detection system, but once there, Ilias scratched his chin thoughtfully and said, "It could be the Walls."

"The Walls?" Tremaine repeated, having to hold on to her patience. "And that would be?"

"The Walls of the World," Arites elaborated eagerly. "You don't have that where you come from? It's mountains that stick up out of the sea. Like islands, but they're all connected. And there are old cities there, like the ones on the Isle of Storms. I hope that's what it is. It'll make a wonderful story."

"Damn." Worried now, Tremaine tried to visualize the scene Arites described. "That could pose a problem. To put it mildly."

She translated for Marais. The lines in the captain's brow deepened, and he looked very much as if this information was not what he had been hoping for. Controlling his frustration well, he said finally, "If they knew this was here, why didn't they mention it?"

"He says that a word of warning might have been helpful," Tremaine translated.

"We didn't know it was really here." Giliead sat up, propping his folded arms on his knees. The fight and the discussion had distracted him, and he seemed in a better mood. "We don't know where here is, except east and more ship's lengths from Cineth than anyone can count. And I've never talked to anybody who ever saw it, except Hisians."

"They lie a lot," Ilias clarified.

Tremaine absorbed that for a moment. "Not about this, evidently." Hopefully, she asked, "When you say 'Walls of the World,' you don't mean all the way across?"

Giliead and Ilias exchanged one of those looks. Giliead said, "The stories say there are ways through, but I don't know whether we should go north or south to find one."

Tremaine passed this along to Marais. He reflected on it for a moment, staring absently at nothing, then got to his feet. "Please thank them for me, Miss Valiarde."

Ilias watched him leave, frowning, then glanced up Tremaine. "We're not going to get to Capidara in three days, are we?"

She rubbed her face wearily. "I wouldn't bet on it."

Tremaine had trouble sleeping. The ship's roll seemed worse than it had at any point in the voyage so far, and dim thoughts of storms and sinking kept her out of deep sleep and in a half-conscious doze. Once she was certain she felt the ship sway over and back upright, as if it was making one of its high-speed turns. She finally woke to Pasima standing over her, shadowed by the light from the open door. "What?" she managed to croak.

After one last sweep of the interior crew areas, they had ended up in the maid's room of the cabin. Ilias was a warm presence against Tremaine's side, sleeping on his stomach, arms wrapped around a pillow. Despite the mane of tousled hair, she could see one open eye regarding their visitor with hostility. Tremaine wished she could share wholeheartedly in the hostility, but she felt Pasima would rather have stabbed herself with a hot poker than come in here unless it was an emergency. Pasima confirmed this by saying, "A man is here for you. I don't understand what he wants, but it seems important."

Tremaine heaved up on one elbow, by habit fumbling for the bedside lamp. As she pressed the switch and the red-shaded light came to life, everybody flinched, and Ilias vanished under the blanket. "What the hell . . ." she muttered. The rumpled shape on the floor was Kias, sleeping between the beds in a nest of pillows and bedding. "Sorry." She switched the lamp off again. She had seen enough to know that Giliead was in the other bed, now accompanied by Arites. She vaguely recalled Arites coming in late in the evening and a minor scuffle as he had climbed over Giliead. She remembered Ilias saying something about Syprians not liking to sleep alone, especially in strange places. *God, they must not have wanted to sleep in the other rooms with Pasima's little band.* Either Gyan was being a diplomat again, or there just hadn't been room for him.

Tremaine clambered out of bed, managing not to step on Kias, glad she had elected to sleep in her cotton nightgown. She didn't mind the half-naked and entirely naked Syprians wandering the cabin at night, but she saw no reason to join the parade, especially if they were going to have visitors this early in the morning. She recovered her dressing gown from the floor and pulled it on, stumbling after Pasima as the other woman led the way out and into the main room.

Everyone else seemed to be awake and dressed. Cletia, Gyan and Danias were sitting in the main room, watching their visitor curiously. It was a naval officer, his uniform cap tucked correctly under his arm, though his tie was rumpled and there was a coffee stain on his shirt. He took in her appearance and winced sympathetically. "Sorry to disturb you, madam."

"Right. I mean, that's all right." Tremaine pushed her hair back, trying to see past the bleary film that seemed to be clouding her eyes. She found herself listing to the right. She grabbed the doorframe for balance, realizing it wasn't because she was drunk or hungover but because the boat was leaning. "What's wrong?" she demanded, suddenly more awake. She recalled the earlier turn clearly now; it hadn't been a dream.

The officer just shifted his balance to accommodate the new angle of the deck, as did Pasima. "We're coming about, madam. The captain requests your presence in the wheelhouse, along with any of the Syprians who might be able to advise him on our course." He added uncertainly, "We tried to ring you, but no one answered."

"It must not have woken me. No one else will touch the telephone," Tremaine answered, distracted. *He didn't say that nothing was wrong, he just said that we were turning.*

"Oh, I see." She couldn't tell if he did see or if he was just being well-bred. "Can you be there soon, madam?"

"Yes, I won't be long." He nodded and turned for the door. The deck was already moving back toward the horizontal, and Tremaine asked, "It's the Walls, isn't it? We found the Walls?"

The officer hesitated, then decided it was obviously no secret. "Yes, madam." Another hesitation, then he shook his head, adding gravely, "It's one hell of a wall, all right."

The dawn view was best from the open walkway that jutted off both ends of the bridge, designed so a crewman could look down the side of the ship and warn the captain that he was about to shear off the end of a dock. The sight that filled the vista from sea to sky was enough to drive the lingering cotton fuzz from Tremaine's sleep-dulled brain.

The jagged ridge of mountains rose out of the sea some distance off the ship's port side. The upper slopes were green where small tropical forests clung to the rock, spilling over sharp cliffs in curtains of vine. Beaches clung to their feet in little coves created by folds of rock. Sheltered places were formed by offshore reefs and pillars of stone that thrust up from the waves. Approaching it by boat, anywhere, would be treacherous.

Giant clefts and crevices broke through the rock at frequent intervals, waves crashing through them. Leaning on the rail, Tremaine stared in fascination as they passed a giant tear in the mountain that went all the way through to the other side, big enough for several locomotives to travel abreast in.

None of these openings was even vaguely suitable for the *Ravenna*, though one of her launches might make it through a cleft without being smashed to pieces. If the pilot was skilled and lucky.

Gyan and a couple of ship's officers, with Ander to translate, were standing on the deck behind her having a consultation about navigation. Gyan had a long wooden pole, marked with a cross brace, which he was using to peer at one of the fading stars in the gradually lightening sky.

Tremaine went back into the wheelhouse, where the helmsman and his mate stared worriedly at various monitors and dials. From overheard conversations she gathered that something called the boiler feed pumps were causing the intense interest, and if they failed all the turbogenerators would go down like a house of cards. Not that they needed anything else to worry about at the moment. *Great, they've got Gyan out there with a stick trying to figure out where in hell we are, and the boilers might fail.* She went back to the chartroom where the Gardier maps were spread out on the big table with Captain Marais,

Colonel Averi, Ilias, Giliead, Pasima, Count Delphane and several of the ship's officers gathered around. Fortunately, Florian was there to translate, leaving Tremaine free to wander around and scavenge from the room's large supply of coffee and rolls. It amused her grimly to see Pasima's suspicion, as if the Syprian woman thought they had conjured the Walls as a trick.

Tremaine wasn't sure of nautical miles and distances, but the *Ravenna* covered a lot of water at 30 knots, and she had been paralleling the Walls for some hours without any sign of a break. The ship had come about late last evening when it became obvious that she was going too far out of her way for no reason.

"What about taking the ship back through the etheric world-gate now, instead of waiting until we're closer to Capidara?" Count Delphane asked, studying the map with a frown. In the bright electrics of the chartroom he looked aged and exhausted, his gray hair thinning and his face sallow and drawn. He looked almost as bad as Colonel Averi. *They know more about what's happening at home than they've told us,* Tremaine thought dryly, eyeing them as she poured herself another cup of coffee. If that was what the knowledge did to you, perhaps it was better they kept it to themselves. She sure wasn't going to ask for it.

His arms folded, Colonel Averi shook his head. "The navigator's calculations show that in our world we're crossing through the Maiutan archipelago. It's a hotbed of Gardier activity, and the sorcerers say opening a large gate for the ship could draw them straight to us. We will if we have to, of course, but it would be best to find the break in the range the Syprians believe is out there."

Delphane's frown deepened, and he rubbed his eyes. On impulse, Tremaine handed him the cup of coffee, and he took it with a muttered thanks.

Ilias saw she was back and came over to report, "The Walls weren't marked on the Gardier map, but it does show something to the south. They thought it was an island, and they came this way to avoid it. Gyan's trying to figure out now if it's in the same place as the stories say the Wall Port is."

Tremaine frowned. "What's a Wall Port?"

"A break in a Wall, with a trading port. None of us have ever been to one, but the stories say the breaks are big, big enough for this ship."

"And the Gardier have something planted right in the middle of it. That makes sense." Tremaine nodded, unsurprised. "Horrible inevitable sense."

The ship's telephone rang, making Pasima flinch. Ilias saw it and snorted derisively. "She should be up here when they blow the big horn," he said, low-voiced.

Tremaine lifted a brow. "Perhaps I can arrange that."

The lieutenant who answered the telephone was saying, "Yes, she's here. Yes, I believe they're all here." He held the receiver up, motioning to Tremaine. "Madam, it's for you."

Tremaine handed her cup to Ilias. "It has to be Gerard."

As she took the receiver, the ship's operator said, "Hold for the hospital, please."

In another moment, Gerard's voice said, "Tremaine? Come down here at once and bring Giliead with you. The Gardier prisoners are dead."

An early-morning hush hung over the ship's hospital, where many of the patients had been moved off into the Second Class cabins on the same deck. Tremaine perched on the desk, Niles paced the office area and an exhausted Florian sat next to a distraught nurse. Giliead and Ilias were with Gerard in the Isolation Ward, looking at the secure rooms where the Gardier prisoners had been held. Dr. Divies was currently with the army surgeon in the operating theater, examining the corpses.

All but one of the Gardier had died in the night, apparently victims of a virulent poison. The only surviving prisoner was the woman, who now lay in one of the smaller wards in the hospital, with one armed guard at the door and two more inside.

"I suppose someone's warned the kitchen staff?" Tremaine said, swinging her feet against the desk.

"This is insupportable," Niles fumed, not really answering her question. His tie was knotted incorrectly, for him a sign of great agitation.

Florian looked up, wearily pushing her hair back. She didn't appear as if she had gotten much sleep. "Niles did reveal charms on all the food stores as soon as he realized what had happened."

Tremaine frowned. Despite that, she wasn't much in the mood for breakfast. "The poison wasn't in the food then?"

"Only the soup," the nurse answered her, sounding sick at the thought. "It was the only part of the meal that the hospital staff didn't eat too." She gestured helplessly. "The first day most of the Gardier didn't eat it and the ones who did were ill. I thought it might be the spices, so I asked the kitchens to make a batch without so much."

"Did the kitchen staff know it was for the Gardier?" Tremaine asked.

The nurse looked up, frowning. She was young though there were already touches of gray in her dark hair. "Yes, I said it was for the prisoners. The patients' food was separate, and the guards on the Isolation Ward were in shifts, so they could go to dinner. Some of the patients still can't keep much down and—" Realization hit and she added uncertainly, "Oh, you don't think . . ."

Tremaine shrugged. The kitchen staff were probably all Rienish and Aderassi with perhaps a few other nationalities mixed in. Poison was a weapon of choice for Rienish domestic murderers; her perusals of *Medical Jurisprudence* had told her that much. "Are we sure it was actually a sorcerous poison and not just something somebody sprinkled in on impulse when they realized who the soup was for?"

"It worked so fast," Florian protested. "Surely something you could find in a kitchen wouldn't be so . . . virulent."

Tremaine tapped her lower lip, lost in thought. "I bet I could put together something, if I had time to really look." She turned to Niles to ask a question and saw he was giving her that look again. "What?" she demanded.

Niles shook his head in annoyance. "Dr. Divies has already explored that possibility, but a cleaning agent or anything else readily available in the kitchens would have had more specific symptoms."

Ilias and Giliead walked in with Gerard. "Anything?" Tremaine asked hopefully.

Giliead shook his head. "No trail. But a curse on the food wouldn't leave one."

"In a way, this changes nothing," Gerard said grimly. He hadn't had a chance to shave yet, and it gave him a faintly disreputable air. "We just have to keep looking."

By the end of the day, Ilias thought he and Giliead and Tremaine had been over almost every pace of the ship, with no sign of their quarry. They had even gone down into the *Ravenna*'s mysterious innards, where the curses that drove her lived.

A sailor had guided them through those dark noisy spaces, down alleyways crammed with metal and pipes in indescribable combinations, or across little bridges over vast spaces of growling labyrinthine shapes, all of it making an indescribable din. The stink was worse than the flying whale or the Rienish wagons without horses, and there were many of the Rienish trail signs that meant danger. He knew if Pasima or any of the others knew all this was down here, they would never have set foot on the ship.

One of the sailors who worked there, a big dark-skinned man whose duty, as far as Ilias could tell, was to keep all these metal guts working, had looked both him and Giliead over skeptically, then gestured to the red markings and the levers near them, speaking with serious emphasis. Tremaine translated, "He says not to touch anything, especially the releases for the watertight doors."

"Can't argue with that," Giliead agreed with a wary glance around. They were in one of those crowded alleys between rows of boxy metal shapes and pipes. Even the wizard lamps made more shadows than light, and the air was foul.

Ilias gave the man a grim nod, wishing they didn't have to come down here at all. "What's a watertight door?" he asked carefully, having a sudden vision of doors below the water level in the hull, perilously keeping out the sea.

Tremaine translated the question, and the man stepped back to pat the thick frame of the doorway behind him. Tremaine listened, frowning, then translated, "Hatches that close off the compartments if the hull is breached. They can all be shut from the bridge in moments. He says on the first voyage a man was killed in one during a drill." She paused, obviously thinking it over. "I don't think I wanted to know that."

Ilias leaned forward, eyeing the heavy slab of metal. It was at least a handspan thick. He exchanged a look with Giliead.

Gerard had told them the only curses that were supposed to be down there were protective, meant to stop rust and fire and other things that might damage the ship's insides; Giliead had been unable to sense most of them but then they were beginning to believe that there were some Rienish curses he just couldn't see.

After that nerve-shattering experience they had fled to the upper decks, to the topmost one. Here the covered hulls of the ships' boats were cradled just below the railing, and there was an open space outside between the first and second of the giant chimneys. It was floored with polished wood, and Tremaine explained that it was meant for some kind of game. It was a good place to lie in the salt-laden breeze and watch the sunset and the distant outline of the Walls.

Tremaine had found a wooden contraption something like a couch and dragged it onto the open area near where Ilias and Giliead sprawled on the sun-warmed boards. Propping up one end and sitting in it, she surveyed the view, saying, "So. If this sorcerer who spoke to Bain is a Gardier, why hasn't he done the mechanical disruption spell and sunk us yet?"

They had been discussing this off and on all day. Ilias sat up, propping himself on his hands. His headache from going so far belowdecks had finally started to fade. It was another world up here, impossibly high above the water, all sky and air and sea forever. You could easily forget the troubled waters they sailed. "Your god won't let him use his curses, except on the other Gardier."

Tremaine gave him a sour eye. "He is not a god. Just call him Arisilde."

Ilias was fairly sure he didn't want to be on such intimate terms with a foreign wizard god, no matter how much he liked Tremaine and the other Rienish. It had taken him a year or so just to get used to knowing their own god personally. He caught Giliead's amused eye. His friend was lying on his stomach with his head propped on his folded arms, and Ilias could tell he was thinking the same thing and laughing at him. He thumped him in the ribs with his bootheel. Giliead grunted and changed the subject, saying, "We're too far out. If he sinks the ship, he has no way to get to shore. Any shore."

"He could take one of the lifeboats," Tremaine put in thoughtfully. "They're made to travel long distances if they have to. But you're right, if he's not a good sailor, he might not like the idea much. I sure as hell wouldn't try it if I were him."

Ilias scratched his chest absently, still thinking it over. "But how did he get here? Could a Gardier really have come off the island with us?" After the improbability of being here and of surviving all these years, killing one more poisoning wizard seemed ridiculously easy; it was frustrating that they couldn't find him.

"A Gardier spy could have come aboard at Chaire, with the other refugees," Tremaine admitted. "But that was a last-minute change of plans, so he would have gotten the chance more by luck than anything else." She steepled her fingers. "I don't believe in luck."

Ilias lifted a brow at her, and Giliead snorted wryly. "What?" she demanded.

"You live on nothing but luck," Ilias told her fondly.

"It's careful planning," she insisted, apparently serious. "I am not a lucky person."

Giliead rolled over and stretched. "If it is a Gardier wizard, why not do the same as a Syprian wizard would and poison everyone on the ship?"

Ilias shrugged. "The same reason. He can't sail this ship alone, even with—what was his name?—Bain and all his family's help." The tour through the lower decks had brought home just how complex a task it would be.

"That's one reason," Giliead agreed. He sat up on his elbows, squinting against the setting sun to see Tremaine. "He must have killed the prisoners because he didn't want them to talk to you. But why try to make Bain help him?"

"He needs the help of another wizard for something else," Ilias said, not liking the idea.

Tremaine's brow furrowed. "If we can get past the stupid Walls, we'll reach Capidara in three days. In two days we should be close enough to go through the etheric gateway and finish the rest of the trip in our world, since the Gardier don't have Capidara blockaded yet. He doesn't have much time."

Giliead lifted a brow, considering. "He may try for the Gardier woman. Or if Bain hasn't told you everything, if his father lied—"

"We need to be there tonight, in the healer's rooms." Ilias met his eyes, understanding completely. It had been a frustrating day, and they were both ready to finish this off.

"Of course, he'll expect that." Tremaine sounded as if she preferred it that way.

So we're not having much luck, though I suppose we could turn up another Bain." Tremaine shrugged, sitting on the leather-clad arm of a chair. "We wanted to try a trap."

"Niles and I were considering something of the sort. It's obvious the woman will continue to be a target." Gerard polished his spectacles, the calculation in his eyes belying the absent gesture. Gerard and Niles had taken over the First Class smoking room as a work area and laboratory. Tremaine had never been there before and was unsurprised to find it as opulent as the ship's other public rooms. The high ceiling rose to a dome and the walls were paneled in dark woods framed with strips of copper banding. The overstuffed red leather club chairs stood about on an inlaid stone-tile floor, and Parscian carved screens framed the marble hearth. Now two of the blocky tables had been pulled into the center of the room and were stacked with books, papers, beakers and flasks, jars of herbs and powders and crystals. Several charts with incomprehensible figures and glyphs partly covered a surrealist seascape, and an easel had been put up in one corner to support a chalkboard. Wooden crates were stacked against the opposite wall, a few pried open to reveal more books. With no space restrictions to worry about, Niles must have brought the Viller Institute's entire research library and all the sorcerous paraphernalia there had been time to haul aboard. Gerard lifted his brows. "But of course—"

Tremaine finished the thought, "He has to know we'll be waiting for him."

"Yes. Our opponent will have to be aware of that. But he also may feel he doesn't have a choice." Gerard paced a few steps. He had the drawn look that Tremaine saw in the mirror, that everyone on the ship seemed to wear now. Considering Gerard hadn't had more than a few hours' sleep in the past three days, it was a miracle he was on his feet at all. "If we present Balin with evidence that one of her own people killed her companions, it could go a long way toward making her more forthcoming. He'll want to prevent that at all cost."

Tremaine nodded, running a distracted hand through her hair and wincing at the odor of engine oil that came away on her fingers. Ilias and Giliead had gone on to the dining room, on the grounds that setting the trap meant they would probably be up all night again and they might as well do it on full stomachs. Suddenly what Gerard had said penetrated, and she glanced up, frowning. "Wait, who's Balin?"

"The Gardier woman. That's her name." Gerard regarded her thoughtfully. "Did you not want to know?"

Tremaine gave him a thin smile. "I don't care if they all had names, children and gray-haired old mothers wasting away waiting for their return."

Gerard's expression grew sardonic, but he continued, "Of course, our opponent may not have counted on Giliead's unique abilities. Gervas did say that they were only able to detect two sorcerers on the Swift, myself and Arisilde's sphere. Unless this saboteur is somehow able to get access to our conferences, he may not realize Giliead has any special power at all."

Tremaine eyed him thoughtfully, swinging her leg against the table. "You think Giliead's a sorcerer, whether he knows it or not?"

"It's one theory. I think the Syprian gods are actually selecting potential sorcerers. The Chosen Vessels learn to use their magic with the god's help, and possibly with some assistance from other Vessels?" He glanced at her for confirmation.

Tremaine nodded slowly. "They said there were journals, left by older Vessels."

"Just so. Those who aren't Chosen either let their potential lapse or learn to perform small harmless charms, probably without realizing it, that never draw the attention of the gods or the Vessels. And others find a rogue sorcerer to learn from and turn themselves into abominations like Ixion." He stopped pacing, regarding her thoughtfully. "I wouldn't mention this theory to any of the Syprians."

Tremaine snorted. "No, really."

"But to get back to tonight." Gerard gestured with his spectacles. "The Gardier, as far as we can tell, seem to disregard the Syprians completely, so the saboteur may not regard Giliead's presence in the hospital as a deterrent."

"Speaking of deterrents . . ." Tremaine said reluctantly. "Any idea why Arisilde didn't do anything to stop this?"

Gerard frowned. "No, not yet."

She let out a worried breath. "I don't think Averi and Ander really understand what he's capable of."

"I tried to use the sphere to cast a ward around the hospital this afternoon. Niles tried with it as well. We both failed. Niles has used his own sphere, but it simply isn't as powerful as Arisilde." Gerard regarded her grimly. "I suspect Arisilde doesn't feel he should waste his strength in protecting Gardier."

"Damn it." Tremaine shook her head. "I was afraid of that. It could mean he's not as all there as we thought, in which case . . ." *We're trusting our lives to a crazy man trapped in a metal ball.* She rubbed her eyes. *Maybe I don't want to kill myself anymore not because Arisilde was trying to communicate with me from the sphere, but because I've gone insane.*

They sat there in glum silence for a moment, then Gerard shook his head. "There's not much we can do now, except try to stop this Gardier."

Tremaine chewed her lip, distracted. "We're sure we're dealing with a Gardier, then?"

Gerard frowned. "No. We're not."

Tremaine got to the dining hall in time to eat with Giliead and Ilias, then by common consent they headed back to the cabin. Tremaine was hoping to be able to grab a nap, since it was going to be a long night.

But when they reached the cabin Tremaine saw Pasima and Cletia were occupying two of the chairs in the main room, with Sanior sitting at their feet. She groaned mentally and heard Ilias mutter, "Oh, good." Giliead just set his face in a stony expression.

The three Syprians must have been having a conversation, but the talk stopped when they saw Tremaine and the others enter the foyer. Cletia and Sanior looked uncomfortable, but Pasima had her Ice Queen face on. Tremaine meant to plow through the room without acknowledging any of them and had almost made it to the sliding doors when Pasima said, "A word, Tremaine, if you please."

Tremaine stopped with one hand on the door, the sanctuary of the back area of the cabin teasingly within sight. *Oh, why not.* "I can think of a few choice ones," she said, turning around. "That lifeboat drill was being conducted by an officer of this ship. Would you behave that way to one of your own captains?"

Everyone looked startled except Ilias, who leaned against the wall as if making himself comfortable for a long siege, and Pasima, who looked annoyed. She snapped, "I didn't want to risk exposing myself to your curses."

Giliead, who had planted himself in the middle of the room with his arms folded, still stone-faced, told her, "If the ship sinks, you can congratulate yourself on your purity on the bottom of the ocean."

Pasima's lip curled. "Cursed ships don't sink, more's the pity."

"All our others have," Tremaine retorted.

"So you've told us." Pasima eyed her. "No one has seen evidence of this."

"Evidence?" Ilias broke in with a derisive laugh. "Are we supposed to take you to the sea bottom to look for it?"

Pasima stood, her lips tightening. "The only one who has seen this land you come from is him." She jerked her head at Ilias as if pointing at him or saying his name would contaminate her. "A man with a curse mark who coincidentally is taken in marriage by you—"

"So Pella of the Cineth council is on our side? Because that's not the impression I got," Tremaine interrupted, her anger rising with dangerous speed. She had the feeling she was seeing Pasima's real face here, the one that Ilias and the others had seen all along. "And if you're suggesting the Rienish government chose me to bribe Ilias to silence, then I have to say they don't share your taste in courtesans." About 90 percent of that was an insult to herself, but never mind. "If you think we're lying to you, why did you come on the damn trip in the first place?"

Pasima drew breath to reply and stopped suddenly, the words unsaid, flicking a wary glance at Giliead.

Tremaine stared at her for a long moment. *Ah. I understand why they're here now. Why she's here.* Pasima meant to prove Giliead wrong, to show that the Rienish sorcerers were as dangerous to the Syprians as their own wizards. Her voice tight, she said, "So we bribed Ilias with me, what did we bribe Giliead with? And the god? It didn't strike me as being big on material possessions." Pasima didn't answer. "Well?"

Studying Pasima thoughtfully, Giliead said, "That's what she's here to find out."

"I see. It was brave of you to admit it," Tremaine assured her. "Wait, you didn't, did you?" She turned for the door, knowing if she stayed any longer, she would be hurling objects at Pasima's head. "Let's go."

She would have felt fairly stupid if nobody followed her, but Ilias and Giliead both did. Once they were out in the corridor, she snapped, "How long have you known that?"

Ilias looked at Giliead, who shrugged, saying, "Since she was chosen to come. Gyan, Karima and Halian all knew it too."

"Great." Tremaine put both hands in her hair, a symbolic gesture to keep the top of her head from exploding. "And you didn't think to mention it?" Being an ambassador, even a lousy ambassador, was a lot harder than she had thought.

Ilias again looked at Giliead, who lifted a brow, shifting the conversational burden back. Ilias thought about it a moment, then said with apparently honest curiosity, "What could you have done about it?"

Tremaine let out her breath and gave up. "Good question."

Chapter 12

They ended up back in the main hall, Tremaine curled in a corner of the couch with Ilias sprawled next to her and Giliead on the floor in front of them. The large room was nearly empty except for a small group of refugees seated on the other cluster of couches and a couple of weary-looking young officers near the corridor down to the Observation bar. The crystal-covered lights were turned low, though the entrances to the Promenade deck on either side of the chamber had been closed off with curtained doors. To Tremaine the place had a late-night, much-used feel, like a theater after the show was over. All that was missing was the scent of stale smoke and wine.

Avoiding the subject of Pasima, Tremaine had told them about her hopes for Arisilde. "So I think it makes sense. Arisilde needs a body, Ixion knows how to make bodies."

"He won't give you the curse, not willingly," Giliead said, eyeing her thoughtfully.

"*Willingly* is the key word." Tremaine shrugged, well aware it wasn't going to be easy but not ready to admit it. "He's a sorcerer who treated with the Gardier. We execute enemy sorcerers. Or we would, if we could catch any. When we get to the government-in-exile, they're going to need a reason to keep wasting someone's time warding a prison for him."

Giliead lifted a brow. "It won't do any good to kill him if he just goes back to another body hidden on the island somewhere."

"That's the part where it gets tricky," Tremaine admitted.

Ilias frowned. "How is the god going to get out of the sphere and into the body?"

"He's not a god." Tremaine gestured, frustrated. "And I don't know that part yet. It's just an idea."

"We never bargain with wizards," Ilias told her firmly. "It's a good way to get your insides boiled."

Giliead contemplated the scuffed tile floor. "You think your friend would want that?"

Tremaine knew he wasn't talking about getting their insides boiled. She rubbed at a worn spot on the upholstery, avoiding his eyes. "After he's got a body, he can tell me."

"Who's this?" Ilias asked, looking at something above her head.

"What?" Tremaine stared. After a moment she realized Giliead was looking expectantly in the same direction. She twisted awkwardly around. A young girl was standing behind the couch, smiling tentatively. She had long reddish brown hair braided neatly back, and her plain blue coat and skirt, white stockings and sensible shoes all spoke of a boarding school.

She said, "Hello. I'm Olympe Fontainon."

"Oh. *Oh.*" Tremaine blinked, staring up at her as the light dawned. There were two men in dark tweed suits standing a short distance away regarding the refugees, the officers, the Syprians and Tremaine with equal suspicion. They had to be Queen's Guards, members of the traditional personal bodyguard for the queens of Ile-Rien.

The Princess Olympe sat down on the marble-topped cocktail table next to the couch, crossing her legs neatly and looking even more like a child. Tremaine, who had never followed the court much, tried to remember how old she was and failed. "I wanted to see them," the girl explained to Tremaine, looking at Ilias and Giliead again. "I've heard so much."

"Right." Tremaine ran a hand through her hair, trying to gather her thoughts. Ilias nudged her impatiently with a foot, and she said in Syrnaic, "This is Olympe, the . . ." she fumbled for the right words, "the Matriarch's first daughter, one of her heirs." She turned back to Olympe, switching to Rienish, "This is Ilias of Andrien and Giliead of Andrien, the god's Chosen Vessel." *My husband and my brother-in-law. Right.* That one was still taking some getting used to.

"I heard you have a criminal sorcerer locked up somewhere below," Olympe said matter-of-factly, as if she discussed such things every day. Considering who her mother was, she just might.

"Not me personally, but yes," Tremaine agreed.

"But he's not a Gardier?"

"No."

"I've never seen a Gardier." She sounded somewhat glum about it. *I hope you never do,* Tremaine thought, not wanting to imagine the circumstances under which that meeting would occur. Before she could reply, Olympe added, "I wanted to go ashore and see the native city, but of course no one would let me."

Tremaine opened her mouth to say something placating about after the war, but met the girl's direct gaze. "Well, if you learn Syrnaic, they can tell you all about it." Inspiration struck, and she added, "One thing you could do. You could ask to meet and speak with Pasima, the head of the delegation the Syprians are sending to your mother's government. Florian or I could translate for you." Yes, she wanted to turn an adolescent Fontainon princess loose on Pasima. Yes, indeed.

"I could do that. I could do *something*." Olympe looked at Tremaine, her head cocked to one side. "You're Tremaine Valiarde. Was your father Nicholas Valiarde?"

Tremaine hesitated warily. This was always a problematic question. "Yes."

"My mother knew him. She cried when they said he was dead, then she said he was probably only pretending again," the princess informed her earnestly.

Tremaine became aware her mouth was open. She had been about to say that her father couldn't possibly have known the Queen, but the bit about "only pretending" had rather put paid to that. *She knew him, all right,* she thought grimly. Knew things nobody should know, just like Reynard Morane did.

Olympe looked away, her young face turning shadowed. "Everyone thought she sent me here because she didn't love me, because she thought the ship would sink. But she sent her two cats with me, and her favorite maid Amiase, and a copy of the Royal Charter that's three hundred years old and the crown that King Fulstan wore at his coronation. The cats are in my room with Amiase, and Count Delphane tried to put the Charter and the crown in the ship's safe, but the cases were too big so they're under Captain Marais's bed."

Trying to make sense of the rapid flow of words, Tremaine abruptly put two and two together. "She let Reynard Morane stay behind in the city." The man who had been Captain of the Queen's Guard for years, who must be a trusted advisor. Her stomach felt tight from tension. *The Queen doesn't think she'll make it to Parscia.* Olympe wasn't here as part of a chancy contingency plan, she was the only plan, the only hope. The Queen and the rest of the royal family were acting as decoys for the party aboard the *Ravenna.*

"Yes. There were others. She sent them ahead, or to other places." Olympe stared at her, blinking suddenly brimming eyes. "She looked at me and she looked at my brother and she picked me. I don't know how I feel about that."

"Don't count your older brother out yet," Tremaine said with grim wryness. "Trains can make unscheduled stops." It wasn't an idle hope. In the long history of Ile-Rien, its monarchs had either been useless victims or clever manipulators who carried themselves grandly through disaster. That last look might not have been a choice between which child the Queen loved best, but between which child would fare better on a cross-country hike.

"You think so?" Olympe wiped at her eyes.

Tremaine hovered between reassurance and raw truth, and had to go with truth. "I don't know. But it wasn't your choice."

One of the men came forward, stooping to touch Olympe's sleeve, saying with a combination of diffidence and parental authority, "My lady, it's late. You should go back to your cabin now."

Obediently getting to her feet, Olympe asked Tremaine, "Are you going back to your cabin?"

"Uh, no. We have something to do later."

Giliead had suggested faking a fight in a public room, preferably the main hall, and that Ilias could pretend to stab him. Not to be outdone, Ilias had offered to actually stab Giliead for verisimilitude. Tremaine had rejected both embellishments to the plan, knowing they were only making fun of her for offering them some fake blood, a concept they found hilarious, from her stage makeup box.

She had to admit that pretending a fall and a minor knee injury was easier and more suitable to their needs. It was just serious enough to warrant going to the hospital but not urgent enough to require Niles or Gerard for immediate sorcerous healing. So Giliead obligingly tumbled down a narrow stair in the Second Class area, and Ilias helped him to the hospital, Tremaine trailing along behind.

The guards Averi had posted at the entrance let them pass, and Giliead limped down the green metal passage to the office area. A tall gaunt man glanced up from the clipboard he was studying. Tremaine recognized him vaguely as the army surgeon. "We think it's his knee," she explained. There were two soldiers there as well, stationed by the door to the wardroom occupied by the last Gardier prisoner.

No one but Dr. Divies had been told there would be extra patients tonight who wouldn't necessarily need medical services. The surgeon handed the clipboard off to a tired-looking nurse, telling her, "Get him to a bed, please, Miss Calere." Then he reached for the telephone. "Niles is still watching the kitchens? I'll call Gerard then."

Only emergency cases, crew members and military personnel were supposed to get their injuries tended by Niles or Gerard; Tremaine should have realized the military doctor would include the Syprians in the last category. "Oh, no, the Syprians really don't like sorcerous healing," she said hurriedly, trying not to wince at how fatuous she sounded. "It's against their religious beliefs. If you could just get Dr. Divies to look at it?"

The surgeon hesitated, frowning and probably thinking she was insane. Then he reluctantly set the receiver back on the cradle. "Very well."

Ilias and Giliead had heard him say the sorcerers' names, and both hesitated, watching Tremaine, despite the nurse's attempts to get them to move. Gerard and Niles were supposed to stay out of the hospital tonight to avoid frightening away their quarry. Tremaine nodded to show it was all right and gestured for them to follow the nurse.

She led them into the wardroom next door to the one where the Gardier woman was installed. There were six metal-framed beds, three on each wall, and a couple of sideboard cabinets for holding extra supplies. The room was empty except for a very pale Rienish woman stretched out on one of the beds with a compress over her eyes. A younger woman with a little boy sat anxiously beside her. Startled, she looked up at the new arrivals.

Ilias dumped Giliead into the bed the nurse indicated and jerked his head toward the women. "It would be better to get them out of here."

Tremaine nodded absently. She knew the presence of other patients would keep this from looking too much like a trap, but she didn't suppose anyone else would see it that way. "They may not be able to move them tonight," she pointed out, trying not to sound too hopeful.

Not understanding the Syrnaic conversation but probably catching Ilias's worried tone, the nurse hesitated. "Is this all right?"

"Oh yes," Tremaine assured her hurriedly. "We were just talking about something else."

The nurse went out, and Tremaine pulled up a stool to sit next to the bed. Ilias perched next to Giliead, appropriating one of the pillows to lean against the headboard. "Remember not to move your leg."

"I know that." Giliead threw him an annoyed look, struggling to find a comfortable position on the narrow bed and still look wounded.

Tremaine used the polished steel panel over the ventilator grille to watch the other patients. It seemed an unlikely group for their rogue sorcerer to hide in, but the man—or woman—must be an accomplished master of disguise or misdirection to make it as far as he had. The woman in the bed was gray-haired, old pain lines etched in her face. It might be a chronic illness, something that had flared up with the stress of the evacuation perhaps. The younger woman wore a plain gray suit and could be daughter or companion, the boy, a grandson or another relative orphaned by the war. They were both staring at Ilias and Giliead, who was still grumpily shifting around on the bed. Then the younger woman seemed to realize it and looked away, a flush reddening her cheeks as she pulled the little boy into her lap. He still stared, his thumb tucked securely into his mouth.

Dr. Divies arrived in a rush, nodding briskly to the women but heading immediately to Giliead's bedside. "Gentlemen, Miss Valiarde." He pretended to study notes on a clipboard.

"We think it's his knee," Tremaine prompted helpfully.

Divies nodded, pulling up another stool and sitting beside her. "It's a quiet night," he said, apparently just making conversation. "We only have about twelve patients here."

"That's good," Tremaine said, distracted as Divies scribbled on his notepad, holding it so she could read: *three are Averi's men.* "I see," she muttered. *He's horning in on our plan. Bastard.*

Divies eyed her sharply, saw she understood and got to his feet. Nodding to Giliead and Ilias, he went over to the woman in the other bed.

Watching him worriedly, Giliead asked, "What did he tell you?"

"Averi has three men here disguised—probably badly—as patients," Tremaine explained grimly. Their opponent, if it was human, would surely find it odd that three soldiers had all suddenly acquired indeterminate and not very disabling wounds that required them to lie about in the hospital instead of patrolling the boat. And she hoped this sorcerer really was a Gardier. If he was Syprian and had been listening in on their supposedly confidential Syrnaic conversations, they were the ones who were going to look like idiots.

Ilias made a derisive noise. "Your plan was better."

As Divies gave instructions to the younger woman, the little boy, temporarily unattended, made a beeline for the two Syprians, regarding them with fascinated curiosity. Ilias absently ruffled his hair, rather with the attitude of someone acknowledging a friendly dog. Tremaine thought in sudden alarm, *Children. Gah!* Did Ilias want children? Hopefully not. Surely not if he meant to continue his career killing wizards. *Oh, come on,* she told herself then, *none of us are going to live that long.*

The woman called the boy back with an apologetic smile, and she and Divies helped the older woman to stand. Giliead told Tremaine, "You'd better leave too."

Tremaine lifted her brows. They had discussed this. Too many people hanging around would be suspicious, and if the spy knew about the sphere, he might think Tremaine would have it with her. Still, she eyed them both long enough for Ilias to look wary and Giliead defensive, then stood briskly. "Right, I'll see you two later then."

"Where are you going?" Ilias demanded.

Tremaine snorted. It seemed as if marrying a man from a matriarchy did not eliminate peremptory demands as to where one was going. "Back to the cabin—eventually."

A nurse had been detailed to help the two women and the little boy, and Tremaine followed them out, pausing in the corridor to consult the more detailed crew map she had now.

On one side of the hospital, past a locked door separating crew from passenger areas, was a complex maze of food storage rooms, including cold rooms for meat and milk. They had been searched earlier in the day, and some were actually in use and filled with provisions. Others, like the room meant specifically for linen drying and not much use for anything else, were empty. The other end of the corridor was also blocked by a door but not locked, as it led to the printer's and carpenter's workrooms and eventually to the crew messes and quarters. Again, all those areas had had a search by Ander and Averi's men and a walk-through by Giliead, and some were in use by the crew and the small army detachment. Directly across from the hospital, past the stairwell and the paneled walls that concealed boiler hatches, was a another long corridor for Second Class bedrooms, presumably mostly empty. Closer toward the bow was the locked and empty Second Class swimming pool. *Two swimming pools and a room specifically for the use of ripening fruit, plus several hundred sitting areas of indeterminate purpose, all with confusingly similar names,* she thought in frustration.

Tremaine rubbed her temple, wishing she had thought to ask for a headache powder from the dispensary. The problem was that all this space was expected to be used, the storage areas full to bursting, the passenger rooms happily occupied, the crews' quarters and workrooms bustling with activity day and night. With the ship barely half-full of either crew or passengers, someone could not only remain concealed simply by moving around, he could run a wine bar and a floating baccarat table and never be found unless it was by pure luck.

She consulted the map again, heading absently toward the stairwell between corridors. The map showed what appeared to be another smaller stairwell in the storage area immediately adjacent to the hospital. *Huh, that's odd.* Flipping through the map booklet, she found the corresponding area on the deck just above. *Aha,* Tremaine thought, stopping as she bumped into the smooth wooden stair rail. Just overhead were vegetable-preparing rooms, the china pantry, the liquor storage, all tucked in right next to the kitchens, the private dining rooms and the First Class dining area. Of course, all those rooms would need quick access to the food storage. Hurrying up the carpeted stairs, she wondered what else they needed quick access to up there.

D o you think she's really going back to the cabin?" Giliead asked, craning his neck to make sure Tremaine was out of earshot.

"No." Ilias snorted derision at the naive question. "I just wanted to see if she'd tell me."

Giliead acknowledged that with an ironic twist of his lips. "I'm not worried about her ruining the trap, it's these others."

Ilias nodded grimly. "I thought this was our idea. Why is everybody else shoving aboard?"

Giliead settled back, eyeing him thoughtfully. "So what is it like being married?"

"I don't know, it's only been a day." Considering Giliead's youthful penchant for disastrous women, he was probably expecting something more dramatic. "No, wait. It's been a whole two days."

"It's been a long two days." Giliead slumped further down in the bed and grumbled, "I want to kill this damn wizard. It's bad enough having Ixion on board."

Ilias had to agree with him there.

The tall thin healer came into the room then, glanced around, and moved to stand over them, eyeing Giliead. Ilias watched him warily. "What if he wants to look at your leg?"

"Ah, I'll . . . act hurt," Giliead said, doubtful.

Neither of them knew what the Rienish healers—the ones who weren't wizards—were capable of. Ilias wondered if the man could tell there was nothing wrong with Gil just by looking at him. "Maybe I should have stabbed you."

Giliead glared at him. "Oh, thanks."

"Not in the gut or anything," Ilias amended absently.

The dark-skinned healer, Divay or some other impossible to pronounce Rienish name, came in then and called the other healer away. Giliead sank a little lower in the bed, maybe hoping to avoid more notice, and Ilias breathed in relief. It was going to be a long wait.

Tremaine prowled through the maze of kitchens and their attendant service areas, avoiding the room where a group of sleepy volunteers, men and women, some Rienish and some Aderassi, sat around a table with a coffeepot and a bottle of brandy. Niles was with them, still on guard against sorcerous interference with the food supplies. He was holding a sphere, absently rolling it back and forth on the table as he listened to one of the chefs speak. Tremaine hesitated, but saw it was the smaller sphere Niles had made for the Institute, not Arisilde. She wasn't using sorcery, so she passed unnoticed.

She found the small stairwell behind the room that held the kitchen's giant grill and went down it to the locked door at the bottom. Fumbling with her keys, she got it open to find herself confronted by a darkened utilitarian corridor, the metal walls painted yellow, lit only by infrequent emergency lights. It was blocked by another door perhaps forty feet along, but a number of doors and a side corridor opened off it. It smelled empty and faintly of dust, but she found herself standing still and listening intently. It was quiet except for the muted thrum of machinery and the whisper of air through the vents, ever present this far down in the ship. *Oh, boy,* she thought dryly, telling her nerves to stop jumping. It reminded her too much of the stories that had long formed a part of Ile-Rien's popular literature, where some innocent but hapless person ventured into the dark depths of a cellar or crypt or ravine and was eaten headfirst by some fay horror. She hated those stories.

The door immediately to her right had a plaque that read GRO-CERY. She fumbled for keys and opened it, flashing her torch around to see an L-shaped room lined with empty shelves and metal bins. Warily following the room around the corner, she breathed, "There you are," as she spotted the closed door with a transom over it.

There were several headboards for hospital beds leaning against the wall and a couple of plain wooden chairs with padded leather seats stacked next to them. Carrying a chair over, she stood on it and peered carefully through the transom to find herself looking down into a small half-lit room lined with cabinets and counters: the hospital's dispensary.

She climbed down from the chair, pleased with herself. The map had implied this door existed, and it only made sense; though this area had ended up being used for dry goods, the ship's designers had probably also intended it to double as storage for medical supplies.

She unlocked the door and eased carefully into the dispensary, shutting it behind her and turning the key again, not liking to have that empty darkened room at her back. She checked the dispensary door, unlocked it and opened it just a hair to peer out. All she could see was the closed door to a wardroom at the end of the short passage. The office area with the wardrooms housing Ilias, Giliead and the Gardier prisoner were on the far side of this warren of rooms. *Well, here I am.*

She amused herself for a while by searching the dispensary shelves for interesting items that might be useful at some future date, but the drug cabinets had secure locks that none of the keys on her ring matched. Flattening her hand against the glass, she felt a tingle start in her fingertips. Wards, intended to drive off prospective thieves by that warning tingle that promised so much worse if the cabinets were actually tampered with. That meant picking the locks was out of the question. The wards had probably been set back when the ship was commissioned, by sorcerers long dead in the war. Regretfully, she pulled her hand away, shaking it to get the blood flowing again. *Dammit. Laudanum would have been nice.* Rolls of gauze and medical alcohol she could do without. Hearing movement out in the hospital passage, she hastily retreated back into the storage room, pulling the door to but not locking it.

Looking around, she pulled the chair back over and took a seat. She might be in for a long wait.

The night wore on. Leaning back against the pillows at the head of the bed, Ilias shoved his hair back and forced himself not to twitch. Giliead had his eyes closed and was resting his head against Ilias's shoulder, pretending to sleep, but Ilias knew he was listening for curses. Through the open doorway, Ilias had watched people come and go for a time, but now all was quiet.

Giliead opened his eyes, and said softly, "Take a look around."

Ilias slipped off the bed without question and went to the doorway. No one was in the outer area except the two guards at the door of the Gardier woman's room. The bright light of the curse lamps made the shadows sharp as steel, and the place seemed artificial and strange now that it was nearly empty of people. Ilias scanned it, alert for any telltale signs of curses. He didn't have Giliead's sense for them, but he knew to look for blind spots in his vision, surreptitious movement, changes in the air. Ilias walked past the guards, exchanging a glance of mutual suspicion, and turned down the passage to the other rooms.

The lights were softer here and most of the doors were closed. He paused beside an open one to see the healer—not the dark-skinned man that knew their plan, but the other one, the tall thin man with sparse gray hair—sitting at a table writing. Near his hand was one of the small flat healing stones.

Ilias walked the rest of the passage, up to the second door out to the ship's corridor and the two guards posted there, then returned to Giliead. "The other healer has one of those rocks," he reported, dropping down next to him on the bed again. Gerard had explained about healing stones, rocks with curses cast on them that made injuries and illnesses heal more quickly.

"That must be what I felt." Giliead shifted with a wince; he had been lying still so long the pretend pain in his leg was probably real by now. "I think I can hear more of the Rienish curses now, the ones I haven't been able to tell were there. They're quieter than our wizards' curses, I just have to listen harder. And it helps that there's so few people around."

"Good." Ilias had to admit it was a relief. He trusted the Rienish— or most of them anyway, but it had made him uneasy that they had curses that Giliead couldn't see. And it would be good to be there when Giliead told Pasima that, too.

Ilias looked around the empty room again, the neat little beds, the shadows cast by the dimmed curse lights. "Maybe we should have just patrolled the ship tonight. If he's somewhere else while we're stuck here . . ."

"I know." Giliead grimaced, shifting uncomfortably again. "But this is a good plan."

Ilias let out a breath. "Waiting just makes me—" He halted abruptly at Giliead's sudden startled expression. "That isn't a rock."

"Not a rock," Giliead agreed, clambering out of the bed as Ilias leapt to his feet. He reached the doorway a pace before Giliead, only to halt in his tracks. The floor of the outer room was nearly covered with a thin layer of pearlescent mist, curling up against the walls, licking the legs of the chair and the table.

It had touched the feet of the men guarding the prisoner's door; Ilias shouted harshly, "Hey, don't you see that?"

The men didn't respond, both staring straight ahead, their faces still as stone. Giliead swore and pulled Ilias back as a tendril of mist reached for them. He bent down, brushing his hand through the upper level of the mist. "All right?" Ilias asked tensely. If this curse worked on Giliead, he didn't know what they were going to do.

Giliead nodded and stepped out cautiously, the pearly mist clinging to his boots. He took one step, then another, having to force his way through the smoky substance as if it was heavy bog mud. Ilias saw the mist creep over the threshold and knew that unless he wanted to wait this out standing uselessly on one of the beds, he needed to move now. He stepped up onto the seat of a chair near the door, then jumped to catch the ridge around the doorframe. From there he swung his legs, just reaching the first of the heavy cabinets against the outer wall. Giliead leaned in to give him a push from behind, and Ilias scrambled to a precarious perch atop the cabinet, crouching to keep from banging his head into the ceiling.

The tall Rienish healer appeared in the opposite doorway, staring in astonishment. "Stay back! Don't let it touch you!" Giliead motioned urgently, and the man halted. Even though he couldn't understand the Syrnaic words, his startled eyes took in the strange mist, Ilias working his way along the line of cabinets, and the guards' dead faces and empty eyes. The man spoke sharply in Rienish and vanished back down the passageway.

"I hope that meant 'hold on, I'll go for help,' " Ilias said under his breath. He had the feeling they were going to need it.

A t first the darkened storage area had been unnervingly quiet and isolated, giving Tremaine the feel of being locked away in the bowels of the ship. But after the first hour familiarity had bred contempt, and now it was not only unnerving but deadly boring.

She was slumped down in the chair, her head propped on the back. Then she realized she must be asleep and dreaming, because Arisilde was crouched on the floor next to her.

He was sitting on his heels on the dusty tile, looking much like the last time she had seen him. His white hair stood out in wisps around his face, and his violet eyes were shadowed in the dark room. He was wearing a ragged sweater and battered canvas trousers, and he looked as disordered and wild as a flower fay. Only the fine lines of laughter and pain around his eyes and mouth marked him as human. He smiled sadly, and said, "Your father never liked to show his hand. He went on and on about it. Very important. Can't do it, you see."

"Can't do what?" Tremaine straightened up a little, blinking, falling back into the habit of marshaling the patience and wit it took to get sense out of Uncle Ari at times like these. When she was very young her mother had explained to her that Arisilde's mind worked in several different planes at once; not like a train jumping from track to track, but like five trains going in all directions, some of them straight up or down in relation to the tracks. That only made sense to someone who knew Arisilde. And Tremaine's mother.

"These goings-on, here. You and those young men have to deal with it. I can't show my hand in it, just now."

Tremaine rubbed her eyes and found herself saying in confusion, "Uncle Ari, you don't have any hands anymore."

Arisilde laughed delightedly. "That's right!" Bemused, he looked down at his fingers and wiggled them thoughtfully. "I'd forgotten. But all the same, I can't show them. Not obviously, you know." His voice changed in tone, sharpening, growing darker. "Not taking someone's nasty spell and shoving it back down his throat until he chokes on it." He glanced up suddenly, blinking. "Oh, sorry. Having a moment, there. Interfering at this point would be dangerous to someone else, you see. I can't see my way clear to it."

"You can't help," Tremaine translated suddenly. *Someone's nasty spell . . .*

"Sorry, but you know I—" Arisilde cocked his head, his eyes growing even more distant. "You need to wake up now."

"What?" It was damn hard to think while asleep. She was surprised she had never realized that before.

His voice sharpened. "Tremaine, wake up!"

Her head jerked and she was awake, alone in the deserted storage area. She sat up, scrubbing her face and shivering, partly from nerves, partly from cold. In the dim light that fell from the transom, she could see her breath misting in air that had been a little too warm when she had dozed off. She dug out her torch and switched it on, flashing it over the dusty floor. *Dammit.* Her own ramblings had scuffed it up so much she couldn't tell if anyone else's footprints were there.

A noise from the other side of the wall made her twitch. *A door banging?* She stared. *People don't bang doors in a hospital, not this late at night.*

She shot to her feet, opening the door to the dispensary. Her fingers made damp prints on the metal, but the arcane cold was already fading, vanishing in the warm air of the hospital. Another bang greeted her as she stepped through the little room and put her ear to the door. She unlocked it hastily, certain she heard muffled voices speaking Syrnaic.

The lights were still on in the hospital passage, the wardroom door at the end still closed. She hurried down it cautiously, cursing a squeaking boot. She peered around the corner, but the passage ahead was clear, the doors along it all closed but one.

Frowning, she tiptoed to the open door and peeked in. A small office, lit by a single desk lamp, its walls lined with bookshelves and glass-fronted cabinets. The army surgeon was slumped over the small desk, the books and papers and the telephone toppled to the floor, the receiver lying just out of reach of his limp fingers. *Oh no.* The man must have been attacked by an intruder, but—

Something moved, a shadow blurred, a dark but transparent form stooped over the unconscious man. It was just straightening up, just turning toward her. Tremaine shoved away from the door, ran full out down the passage, careening into the wall as she rounded the corner. She reached the dispensary door and swung inside, slamming it behind her and putting her shoulder to it as she frantically twisted the lock. The thump as the thing hit the door sent her scrambling away from it.

The next thump nearly slammed the door off its hinges, but she was already out the back way into the storage area, bolting through it and back toward the corridor. She didn't remember to shout for help until she reached the stairs.

Ilias reached the end of the row of cabinets, glad they were sturdy and attached to the wall. Standing like statues, the guards still hadn't reacted, and Ilias hoped the men weren't dead. He couldn't see from this angle if the mist had crept under the closed door to the prisoner's room yet or not.

Grimly plowing his way through the thickening mist, Giliead reached the doorway. He pulled the unconscious men away from the door, dumping both across the table and lifting their legs up out of the mist. Their bodies went limp, but neither man stirred.

As Ilias perched on the edge of the cabinet, Giliead pushed at the door. It opened a few handspans and stopped, blocked by something just inside. Giliead set his shoulder against it and shoved. It gave way abruptly and something fell inside; as Giliead swung the door open Ilias saw it was the other Rienish guard, now sprawled across the nearest bed. He must have been standing just inside the door.

Ilias craned his neck and saw the Gardier woman, dressed in a blue robe and sitting on a bed across the room, her legs drawn up. She was still alive and aware, her pale face tense with fear, but the mist was licking at the edges of the blankets, creeping up onto the bed. Her eyes flicked from them to the mist, as if she wasn't certain which was the greater threat.

Giliead started toward her, grunting with the effort it took to move his feet. "It's getting thicker, like it knows we're here," he said, using the doorframe to drag himself along.

"Wonderful," Ilias muttered, uneasily studying the stuff as it billowed upward near the center of the room. He couldn't see the doorway out into the corridor, as the passage curved away. If the healer had gone to summon help, the other Rienish should be here by now, but he couldn't hear anything from the corridor but a distant banging. He looked to see how Giliead was faring, then his gaze snapped back to the center of the room. The mist wasn't just billowing up, it was melding into a form, something a man's height, with recognizable arms and a head. "Gil—"

"What?" Several laborious steps into the room, Giliead looked back and saw the shape. "Damn," he snarled. He turned back, grabbing a chair and shoving it into the doorway so Ilias could reach it.

Ilias grabbed the doorframe for balance and stepped down onto the seat. The mist was higher now and one tendril curled over the polished wood, just brushing the toe of his boot. The blood pounded in his head and blackness rose up at the edges of his vision. Wavering, he managed a clumsy leap to the bed, half-collapsing against the wall.

He shook his head to clear it, blinking, as Giliead demanded, "Are you all right?"

"Fine." Ilias pushed away from the wall but kept one hand on it to steady himself. Fortunately, the bed was a little higher than the chair seat, but that slim margin of safety wouldn't last long. Now he knew why the guards hadn't made a sound. "What's it doing out there?"

Giliead reached the doorway again. "Guess," he said grimly, grabbing the back of the chair and slinging it at the growing creature.

Ilias leaned out to catch a glimpse of the misty body re-forming as if the wood had never passed through it. It glided toward the door even as Giliead forced it shut. Ilias leapt to the next bed, then the next, just opposite the one the Gardier woman was crouched on. She scuttled away from him as far as she could, clutching the metal rail of the footboard, glaring at him and spitting something in her own harsh tongue. Ilias rolled his eyes in annoyance and jumped to the head of her bed. *I hate these people.* "Believe me, I'd rather not," he told her sincerely.

The mist was creeping over the edge of the bedcovers now and Ilias had his eye on the waist-high cabinet against the far wall. He lunged forward, grabbing the Gardier woman around the waist and dragging her to her feet. She shouted, pounded on him and tried to claw at his eyes. It went through his head to dip her into the mist just a little to slow her down, but if it killed her, this would all be for nothing. He managed to get an arm around her to pin her arms to her sides, steadied himself with one hand on the wall, then took the long step over to the cabinet.

Her struggles made him lose his balance, and he slammed both of them into the green-painted metal wall, sliding down it into a half crouch before he could catch himself. The woman's bare feet went off the cabinet and dangled only a few handspans above the curse mist. With a gasp she went still, and Ilias dragged her up, setting her feet on the cabinet. "That was harder than it had to be," he said, breathing hard.

Giliead was braced against the door, watching them, his expression aghast. "I hope the Rienish appreciate this," he said through gritted teeth.

Ilias braced himself with one hand against the ceiling. The Gardier woman had decided to stop being stupid and was actually holding on to him now, which helped, but the mist was still rising. "Speaking of that, where the fuck are—" he began, then the words caught in his throat as something struck the door, nearly slamming the solid barrier off its hinges.

Giliead swore, shoving away from it. The door banged open and the mist figure flowed in. With no weapon and no chance to reach for any, Giliead flung himself at it.

Ilias yelled in pure reaction, thinking he was about to see Giliead torn apart. But the thing grappled with him, tried to throw him aside and failed. Ilias bit his lip until he tasted blood to keep silent, not wanting to distract Giliead. From here it looked like his friend was struggling with a disturbing figure of transparent shadow, mist billowing out of it like smoke. It had to be Giliead's resistance to curses helping him; the thing had battered through that strong door easily enough, he knew it could kill a man.

It might not have been able to shove Giliead aside easily, but it forced him backward, step by step. It was bent on reaching the Gardier woman, frozen in fear at Ilias's side, and he looked frantically around for a way to retreat. The mist had risen to cover the nearest bed, cutting off that avenue, and there was nothing else in reach.

A voice somewhere out in the other room, speaking in a tongue that didn't sound like Rienish, startled him, and he reflexively tightened his hold on the Gardier woman. *It's Niles,* he realized suddenly. Not speaking; shouting, declaiming, his voice strained with effort. He realized the Rienish wizard was trying to drive away the curse mist, that the words he spoke were a curse in themselves; it made the skin creep on the back of his neck. Niles sounded like Gerard had on the *Swift,* when he had killed Ixion's sea-curseling. Like he was doing battle, like he had to fight to get the words out.

The mist-figure shoved Giliead back another step and another. Giliead's head was turned to the side, but Ilias could see the sweat beading on his temple, staining his shirt. The Gardier woman whimpered in terror. "Hold on," Ilias said through gritted teeth, talking to Giliead and not the Gardier. "Just a little longer." Then Ilias heard Gerard's voice join Niles's and the mist curling up over the edge of the cabinet flattened down, as if pushed by a stiff breeze. Ilias scanned the room, saw it was happening everywhere.

He edged along the cabinet, pulling the woman with him. The mist had dropped at least a handspan, nearly below the level of the beds. As it slid down from the blankets, he shoved off from the wall and leapt with her. She helped him this time, slamming a hand out against the wall to steady them as they landed. Relieved she was going to cooperate, he released her waist and grabbed her hand instead, making the long steps to the next bed and the next.

They were at the one nearest the door when the mist-figure tore away from Giliead, trailing wisps of vapor and shadow. Giliead stumbled back, recovered and lunged after it, but the receding mist caught at his boots and he fell, careening over into a cabinet.

The shadow-creature surged toward Ilias, stretching out a long arm for him. He ducked and shoved the Gardier woman behind him, scrambling back, but they were trapped at the head of the bed.

He crouched, braced to move, the figure looming over him, mist still weaving through the shadowy form. Then between one heartbeat and another it was gone.

Ilias slumped down on the bed, shoving his hair back, his heart pounding. Giliead got to his feet, still looking wildly around. The Gardier woman sprang up off the bed and ran out the door, only to appear an instant later, propelled back into the room by Gerard. Other Rienish pushed in after him, Niles, guards, Averi. Everyone was talking and yelling in Rienish.

Giliead came over and sat down heavily next to Ilias. He rubbed his eyes, his hand still shaking a little, probably from muscle strain. Gerard, white-faced and grim, deposited the Gardier woman on another bed. He and Niles both looked as if they had fought a battle, their faces drawn and exhausted, the white shirts under their jackets sweat-stained. Niles leaned over the Rienish guard who had been inside the room, one of the men the mist had made into living statues. He patted the man's face, peeled back his eyelids, and Ilias saw the man stir. *That's a relief,* he thought, nudging Giliead with an elbow to make sure he saw.

Giliead nodded, some of the tension leaving his body. "They all live?" he asked Gerard. "It didn't kill anyone?"

Gerard glanced at him, his face still set. "We found two men dead, the soldiers posted at the outer door. They were in contact with the substance the longest."

Giliead winced.

In the doorway someone stumbled, and Tremaine shoved in past him. Her eyes fell on them first, and Ilias saw the tightness in her face ease. He smiled faintly.

She came further in to stand next to them, resting one hand on Ilias's shoulder. Her skin felt cold, and he had the urge to rub his cheek against her hand, but he didn't think she would like that in front of strangers.

She snapped a question at Gerard, and he answered, shaking his head. She looked at Ilias and demanded in Syrnaic, "There were two of them?"

He shook his head, startled. "No."

Giliead looked up, frowning. "We only saw one."

This provoked another argument in Rienish as Gerard translated their answers to the others, then Niles and some of the guards hurriedly left the room. "What is it?" Ilias asked Tremaine worriedly.

She shook her head slightly, her brows drawn together. "I saw one too, on the other side of the hospital."

"You may have seen the same one, before it came after her." Gerard glanced at the Gardier woman, still huddled on the bed and watching them warily. "It was focused entirely on her?"

Giliead nodded. "It looked that way."

Gerard eyed her speculatively. "You saved her life. Perhaps she'll speak more readily now."

They all looked at the Gardier woman. She couldn't understand the Syrnaic or Rienish conversations but she obviously didn't like the steady gaze of so many eyes. She spit at them.

Giliead snorted and looked away, but Ilias's gaze went to Tremaine. She regarded the woman for a moment, apparently calm, but Ilias saw her eyes go flat. He lurched forward in time to catch her as she lunged for the Gardier. He got a hard elbow in the ear before Tremaine abruptly subsided. Ilias let her go, tense in case it was a ruse. The Gardier had at least had the sense to flinch, flattening herself back against the wall.

"Fine." Tremaine straightened her sleeves, still watching the woman with a deadly calm. "Let's get out of here."

Chapter 13

Like Elea's voyage to Thrice Cumae, we arrive at the Walls of the World. I never thought to live to see such a sight, and only hope to carry word of it home again.

—*"Ravenna's voyage to the Unknown Eastlands,"*
Abignon Translation

Tremaine led Ilias and Giliead to her hiding spot in the storeroom where Arisilde had appeared to her, to see if Giliead could tell if anything had really been there or not.

By the light of the open dispensary door, Ilias crouched down on the floor to examine the minute traces left in the dust. Giliead just shook his head. "If he was here, he didn't leave anything behind him. But gods don't volunteer information for no reason. If he told you he couldn't help us in this, he meant it."

He's not a god. I don't think. Tremaine rubbed her gritty eyes. She was far too weary to have a philosophical debate just now. "How do I know it wasn't just a dream?"

"If it was a dream," Giliead told her firmly, "you'd know."

Now, sitting at a scrubbed wooden table in the kitchen's First Class cold pantry and coffee service room, surrounded by cabinets and counters of stainless steel and nickel-chromium, it seemed very much like a dream. Tremaine propped her head in her hands, wishing the hard questions would all go away.

The kitchen volunteers were still around and she realized the threat of sorcerously poisoned food must have both offended and deeply worried the ones who had been chefs or restaurant workers in Ile-Rien. A group of them were in the next room now, discussing their original plan to serve some of the ship's store of carefully hoarded beef tomorrow and if that was still a good idea. Tremaine had been living on coffee to the extent that the lingering odor of it from the giant urns along the wall had made her ill, so when one of the Aderassi volunteers had come in and wordlessly opened a couple of bottles of wine for them, she had almost been ready to kiss the man's feet.

"Why didn't it just spread that mist through the whole ship?" Ilias asked, cautiously taking another sip. It was different enough from the musty Syprian vintages that he had almost spit out his first mouthful, causing Tremaine to yelp with dismay and badly startling the kitchen staff in the next room.

Tremaine considered the question, massaging her temples. "I think it was afraid of Gerard and Niles and the sphere. It couldn't fight all three of them. Maybe that's why it wanted Bain Riand's help, to take them on while it was finishing the Gardier off." She shrugged, turning her glass around. "Gerard thinks it wasn't a human sorcerer. That Riand was right, that it was some sort of construct or creature, with only limited abilities. Maybe it did get aboard at Chaire as a spy, but when it realized we had Gardier prisoners it broke cover to kill them." And those prisoners must have known something important, even if they hadn't realized it. As their best interrogator, using a combination of persistence and mild charms, Niles was going to continue to work on the Gardier woman tonight. Whatever she knew, they had to find it out.

Giliead, warned by Ilias's choking fit, had been more cautious with the wine at first but was now putting away as much as Tremaine. He poured another glass, pausing to curiously examine what was to his eyes the enigmatic writing on the label. "Are we sure it's dead?"

"I saw it disappear." Ilias shrugged doubtfully. He admitted, "A body would have been nice. And you thought you saw another one?"

Tremaine nodded, gesturing helplessly. "I may have seen it just before it appeared to you. I'm not sure. Arisilde sounded like he was only talking about one person. He said 'someone's nasty spell.' " She recaptured the bottle for one last glass.

"But if this was a Gardier creature, I thought your curses wouldn't work on it." Giliead lifted his brows.

"Well, there's that. But Arisilde's spells do work, and he must have been helping with the banishing." Tremaine swirled her glass, watching as the wine ran down the sides. Some hotel or Great House in Chaire must have decided that the contents of its cellar were better off going to the bottom on the *Ravenna* than being left for the Gardier. She wasn't familiar with this winery, but the stuff had legs like a cabaret dancer and left a taste in her mouth like spring in the Marches and newly cut hay. Too bad the people who owned and worked the vineyards would die or flee, and the grapes would rot on the vine this summer. Only the headiness of the vintage made the poignant sting of that thought bearable. "I think—" She tried unsuccessfully to swallow a yawn. And she couldn't remember what she had been about to say. "I think I can't think anymore."

They had left the kitchens and were in the C deck corridor when the general alarm blared from the ship's loudspeaker.

Gerard heard the alarm sound as he and Niles reached the wheelhouse; Arisilde's sphere had warned them minutes earlier. The steering cabin was dimly lit, so the helmsman could see out and the illumination wouldn't betray the ship. Through the large array of windows the moon lit the sky and turned the sea to a rolling gray plane; for a moment Gerard couldn't see what was wrong. Then an officer standing at the front of the room gestured hastily to the side door. "Out there, gentlemen."

Captain Marais and two of the other officers were out on the starboard side wing, Marais watching something through field glasses. As Gerard stepped out the door with Niles at his heels, he saw the airship.

Instincts gained from living through far too many bombings in Vienne halted him in his tracks; it took a surprising effort to force himself from the illusory shelter of the wheelhouse and out onto the windswept wing.

"Yes," Niles said ruefully from behind him, keeping his voice low. "That's all we need tonight."

The airship was still some distance away, a black shape outlined against the star-filled sky. The distinctive jagged fins and tail gave it a predatory appearance, especially in the dark; it was no wonder the

Syprians had thought the things were giant avian beasts. The angle of the fins told Gerard it was pointed away from the ship and toward the distant rocky shadow of the Walls; any other detail was impossible to make out.

"The lookout spotted it a few moments ago," one of the officers explained, glancing back at them as they approached. "It changed course at nearly the same moment, so it must have detected us."

Gerard nodded grim assent. They knew the overhead concealment wards weren't as effective when the ship was moving.

"It looks as if it's turning away," Niles pointed out with annoying calm. He had the sphere tucked under his arm, and Gerard could hear it still clicking angrily. The airship must be out of its immediate range; he didn't think Arisilde would have waited for instructions to attack.

"It must have got some warning that we're not an easy target." Marais lowered the field glasses. "Where's Colonel Averi?"

"Still down in the hospital." Gerard knew Ilias and Giliead had destroyed an airship on the Gardier's island base a few days before he and Tremaine and the others had arrived on the Pilot Boat. The sphere had destroyed another during an attack on the Andrien village and a third that had tried to escape the assault on the base. If this airship had received any communication from the island or from the Gardier who had escaped by boat, its crew had every reason to be cautious.

Niles shifted the rattling sphere to his other arm, saying thoughtfully, "It's a pity we can't capture it intact. But we can't chance letting it escape."

Gerard looked at him, startled. For years they had fled in terror from Gardier airships. Now . . . "Yes." He smiled thinly. "We can't let it escape."

Captain Marais glanced back at them, the dark obscuring his expression, but the tone in his voice was approving. "I agree. But it's too far ahead of us. We're faster, but to avoid us all it need do is fly across the Walls. If it doesn't, we can't trust that it isn't leading us into an ambush."

"But if it thinks we're running from it, it may turn back toward us," the second officer pointed out, sounding intrigued.

Marais shook his head reluctantly. "We'd have to drop to half speed to let it catch us. I don't want to take that risk."

Count Delphane had commented that Marais thought he was in

command of a battleship rather than an oversized excursion ferry, and Gerard was glad to see this evidence of caution. But he said slowly, "Unless they see us use an etheric gateway, and they turn back to try to detect our etheric signature."

"Or to try to get close enough to attempt to use our spell circle to follow us." Niles smiled to himself. "I like that."

The second officer was nodding. "We've had to turn west far enough that we should be out of the Maiutans. And we won't be there long enough for a Gardier patrol to find us."

"Check our course," Marais told him sharply. "Verify our position in relation to our world." He lifted the field glasses again, adding dryly, "I'd rather not materialize in the middle of an island."

Tremaine stopped to listen to the loudspeaker again. They had reached the main hall to find it deserted. The earlier announcement ordering everyone to leave the open decks and seal all outer doors and that the watertight doors belowdecks were closing was worrying, but there was no one to pry information out of.

"What does it say?" Ilias demanded in frustration. "It always talks too fast."

"We're making a gate," she translated. "It—he said we're going to gate back to our world, change course, then gate back here again. That means—"

"We're setting a trap," Giliead finished. "We must have come up on a Gardier ship. Or a flying whale."

That's it, I've got to see what's going on, Tremaine thought, determined. "This way." She headed for the side doors, pushing through them and stepping onto the Promenade deck. The enclosed deck had a panoramic view of the sea and night sky through its large windows, stretching most of the length of the ship. Ilias and Giliead reached the windows first, looking for the airship, both nearly bonking their heads on the glass trying to see straight up.

No one else was on the Promenade; Tremaine thought they were not technically violating the order to stay inside, since the deck was enclosed, but she pushed the heavy door shut just in case, making sure the latches clicked. She went to join the men at the railing, studying the clear and for the moment empty moonlit sky. "The damn thing must be behind us." She tapped her fingers on the railing, impatient and anxious. "So what the hell are we—"

Giliead stepped back, swearing and clasping a hand to his head as if something had struck him. Then between one blink and the next the deck was brilliant with daylight, the sea outside choppy under a cloud-streaked blue sky. The ship's expansion joints creaked, a massive bass groan of complaint thrumming up through her metallic bones as the deck rolled violently; Tremaine bounced off the glass and banged into Ilias.

Holding the rail to keep her and himself upright, Ilias asked Giliead uneasily, "Are you all right? Was it the curse?"

"Yes." Giliead caught the rail as the ship swayed back over, then began to roll into a turn. He was grimacing from the pain. "It caught me by surprise," he said through gritted teeth.

"So you can feel an etheric gate open," Tremaine said, holding on to Ilias and nervously watching the sea draw nearer as the ship leaned into its turn. "That might come in handy. If we live through the next five minutes," she added tightly.

The deck tilted more sharply under their feet as the turn continued and Tremaine spared one hand for the rail, her palm sweaty on the polished wood, and Ilias tightened his hold around her waist. Her stomach informed her that she really should have had more dinner, or something besides wine to settle it.

The *Ravenna* swayed upright as the ship came about, strained metal emitting another heartfelt groan, the ship's own voice protesting this abrupt handling. Ilias hissed between his teeth. Pressed against him, Tremaine could feel his heart pound. His hair brushed her cheek as he turned his head to say to Giliead, "That's taking an awful chance. Remember when—"

"We capsized Agis's fishing boat," Giliead finished, sounding a little unnerved. "Vividly."

"I don't think that would happen," Tremaine muttered, but her imagination had already taken flight. *At least you closed that door.* All those outer doors on the passenger decks were heavy and thick, functioning as watertight hatches. But even if Gerard and Niles and Arisilde somehow managed to right a capsized *Ravenna* with sorcery before the ship sank, she didn't think the Promenade's windows would survive that first deadly roll. Ilias's thoughts must have been along the same lines; he squeezed her waist and kissed her on the back of the head in a combination of reassurance and relief.

Tremaine forced her brain past the image of imminent disaster. The ship was steaming through the daylit sea now, roughly back the way they had come. *We're home,* she thought, realizing it with surprise. *Sort of.* They were back in the ocean that lay between Ile-Rien and Capidara and not the strange foreign seas the Syprians sailed. "I wonder how long it will take—" The loudspeaker interrupted her with a brief warning. She translated it as, "Here we go again." Giliead swore succinctly.

Tremaine felt the ship jerk and roll, as if the entire weight of it had skipped sideways. The Promenade was suddenly plunged into darkness. They were back in the Syprians' world.

Giliead had a hand pressed against his temple, wincing. Ilias said grimly, "There it is."

Tremaine followed his gaze, blinking as her eyes adjusted. A short distance off their bow the airship was outlined in sharp black silhouette against the moonlit sky. Giliead took a sharp breath. "Your god is about to—"

Red and orange blossomed under the black shape of the balloon. Tremaine heard the distant rattle of machine-gun fire, as the airship reacted to their sudden appearance, but it was too little and too late. She felt a certain savage satisfaction; she wished the Gardier woman locked up in the hospital or the Isolation Ward or wherever she was now could have seen it. *So it's too late for us to win, but we can hurt you. We can hurt you almost as bad as you've hurt us.* "That's another one down," she said, mostly to herself. "How many to go?"

The fire encompassed the airship's shape and it rolled, fragments of the undercarriage tumbling down toward the water.

Despite heavy limbs and a fuzzy brain, Tremaine had trouble sleeping. She was half-expecting Arisilde to appear again, but if he did, she didn't remember it. She woke, groggily, to Arites leaning over her, saying, "The ringing thing is trying to speak to you."

"What?" she demanded blearily, glad she hadn't bothered to undress. They had ended up in the maid's room again, Ilias curled up next to her, Giliead sprawled in the other bed. At some point Ilias had shifted over, flung an arm around her waist and pillowed his head on her shoulder; she was so exhausted it hadn't even woken her.

"It speaks only in Rienish, and very fast," Arites explained apologetically. "I can't understand anything it says except your name."

Neither Ilias nor Giliead had moved, probably the result of wine that contained considerably more alcohol than they were used to.

"You mean the telephone?" Tremaine elbowed Ilias until he groaned and rolled over so she could sit up and struggle free of the sheet. Standing barefoot on the carpet, she was unprepared for the roll of the ship, and it nearly pitched her on her face. It seemed even worse than usual; she wondered if they had hit bad weather following the Walls.

She recovered, gripping the bedpost, and made it across the room. Kias wasn't on the floor this time. Either he had gotten up early or had set up housekeeping with his new girlfriend. "You actually answered the telephone?"

Arites was already at the door. In the light from the other room he looked chagrined. "The noise it made was piercing. And it wouldn't stop. And," he added a little defensively as she followed him out into the main room, "I don't see how listening to a speaking curse box speak is any different from using the light from curse lights to see."

No one else seemed to be in the suite, possibly due to the piercing noise of the speaking curse box. "It's not, except they aren't curses." Luckily, he had left the receiver off the cradle, and she picked it up, yawning. "Yes?"

The connection crackled, and a male voice, sounding annoyed and relieved, said, "This is the ship's operator speaking. Is that Miss Valiarde?"

"Yes." Tremaine massaged her forehead. She had expected to have time this morning for a leisurely bath; she had the feeling that just wasn't going to happen. "This is me—she."

"Colonel Averi needs to speak to you immediately."

It was a meeting again, in the Third Class drawing room with the wall-sized mural of Parscian fishing boats, and Tremaine was obviously late for it. Gerard, Ander, Colonel Averi, Captain Marais, Count Delphane and Lady Aviler, and some of the navy and army officers were present. Everyone seemed to be in various intense conversations, except for Averi, grimly standing sentinel at the front of the room, and Captain Marais, seated with his arms folded and his face resigned. One of the Gardier maps had been tacked up to a carved wooden screen above the marble hearth.

Tremaine slid into the back of the room where Gerard was standing and eased up to his side. She had changed her shirt hurriedly and splashed water on her face; she felt bleary and barely awake, and everyone else looked as if they had been up for hours and had access to coffee and breakfast and a bath. Even Gerard looked less drawn and exhausted. "Did you and Niles release each other from that no-sleep adjuration?" she asked around a yawn.

"Yes, last night, after we destroyed the airship," he admitted, sounding relieved. "In fact, Niles is still asleep. He was so confused when Giaren woke him this morning we decided to let him rest." He added ruefully, "Of course, he's going to need it."

"Why? What is this?" she asked, frowning. She had assumed this was about their little Walls problem or the attack on the airship. Either that or Averi had summoned her to give an in-person account of what had happened in the hospital.

Gerard's expression of consternation didn't enlighten her. "There have been some developments—"

At the front of the room, Averi abruptly took the floor, slamming his hand down on the writing desk. "Gentlemen, quiet! We've spoken about this all morning, and the best option we have is to destroy the Gardier outpost."

"The what?" Tremaine blurted.

Sometime later, Tremaine followed Arites's directions and found Ilias and Giliead in the First Class swimming pool, deep in the interior of the ship on D deck. She walked down the tiled stairs into the large chamber, all tiled in cream and green, the splashing and yelling in Syrnaic telling her she was in the right spot. A gallery running all along the top of the room had doors that led into steam and massage rooms, now locked, and the vaulted mother-of-pearl ceiling stretched up through the deck above to make a gentle arch. The pool was filled with salt water, accessed from tanks that were topped off from the unlimited supply outside, like the saltwater plumbing available in all the bathrooms.

There were a few people sitting on deck chairs down at the far end, an older woman and two men, all well dressed and chatting comfortably despite the two naked Syprians trying to drown each other.

Tremaine walked along the side to the far end, past the two piles of clothes and boots. The tiled walls threw back distorting echoes, and she couldn't hear the spectators' conversation, so she knew it should be safe to talk here. She knelt at the edge of the water, and called, "Hey!"

Ilias, who had just shoved Giliead under with a seal-like leaping tackle, surfaced and shook the hair out of his eyes. He spotted her and swam over, grabbing one of the handrails to pull himself up to the curved tile edge. He grinned up at her, his hair streaming water. "Come on in."

"No, no, I don't think so." Tremaine eased back out of arm's reach. "I need to talk to you two."

Giliead swam up, looking a little abashed to be caught having a good time. He asked, "Did you find out why we've stopped?"

Tremaine hadn't realized that the ship's roll felt odd because it had stopped moving forward until Averi had mentioned it at the meeting. She took a deep breath. "Partly. Last night, after they destroyed the airship, they figured out that we were fairly close to the place where Gyan thought the Wall Port might be. So they stopped to send out a boat to find it. The boat had illusion charms to keep it from being seen, which was a good thing, since the Gardier are definitely there."

She paused, pushing her hair out of her eyes. Both men were watching her gravely now. "The boat came back a little while ago. They found the port at a big break in the Walls. The break is large enough for the *Ravenna* to get through, and the launch couldn't find any sign of rocks or reefs. But the problem is that the Gardier have some kind of outpost above the port, with a scaffold tower that another airship was docked at. The one we took out must have been heading for the same place. Anyway, the boat couldn't go too far into the harbor, but it looked like the people who live there were going crazy, with a lot of the native ships leaving. They—meaning Averi, Captain Marais and Count Delphane—want to destroy the Gardier outpost and capture the airship." It had surprised her at first that Count Delphane had been in favor of an attack, but maybe their success against the gunship at Cineth and the airship last night had convinced him.

Ilias was nodding, and Giliead said, "It only makes sense. If this is the closest break in the Walls—and the only one we can find that the ship can fit through—you need to secure it."

"That's what they said." Tremaine hesitated. "And the thing is, they want your help. Our help. To scout the native port."

Ilias had to admit to an excitement that had nothing to do with the prospect of battle with the Gardier. He had heard tales of the Walls for years, and seeing them from the *Ravenna*'s deck had been wonderful enough. Actually setting foot on them and visiting a Wall Port was incredible.

In the second bedroom of their cabin, Tremaine went through her belongings, storing away a number of items in the bag Karima had given her, including the set of metal instruments she used to open locked doors and the small shooting weapon she had taken to carrying with her. "I need a different pair of boots," she told him, looking genuinely worried about it. "It would be all I need for someone to see through my Syprian disguise because like an idiot I'm wearing rubber-soled boots made in Vienne."

Ilias, repairing a broken thong on Giliead's baldric while Giliead sharpened their swords, looked up with a frown. "You could ask Cletia," he said doubtfully. "She might loan you hers."

Giliead snorted. "But that would be helpful on her part."

Tremaine put her bag down on the table with a thump. "Let's throw caution to the winds and ask her."

As she went into the main room, Ilias followed out of curiosity. He was surprised to see Cletia seated in one of the chairs, sharpening her sword. Cimarus and Danias were crouched on the floor in front of the couch, sorting through a provision pack. Gyan stood with arms folded, surveying the scene critically. "What's this?" Ilias demanded, fearing the worst.

Gyan cocked a brow at him. "Pasima has told the Rienish that Cletia and Cimarus are going with you."

Ilias stared at him, then pressed his lips together to keep in the first comment that came to mind. He looked helplessly at Tremaine, who folded her arms, and said, "Oh, joy."

Cletia's shoulders hunched stubbornly, but she ignored them. Giliead stepped into the doorway behind him, and Ilias didn't need to look at him to know what his expression was. In a tight voice, Giliead pointed out, "This is a scouting mission for a war party. The more people we send, the more likely it is the Gardier will notice us."

Cimarus bristled at the implied insult, and Cletia began, "Pasima has said—"

Pasima stepped into the room with Sanior trailing her. "Pasima can speak for herself," she said, smiling a little, as if she meant to settle an argument between quarrelsome children. "What's wrong?"

Ilias exchanged a sour look with Giliead. They both knew that Pasima was just making sure her bed cushions were feathered on both sides. If she could prove the Rienish false, her side of the family would have the credit for it; but if the Rienish proved to be valuable allies, she wanted to make sure they were beholden to her as well as to Giliead. It wasn't worth the argument.

Tremaine evidently thought so too. She eyed Pasima for a long moment with that disconcertingly direct and calculating stare she was capable of. Then she said, "Fine. Now give me your boots."

The Rienish preparations for battle took longer than Ilias had expected. He and Giliead had debated over which weapons to take, assembled some provisions and were ready to go. Since their duty for the war party would be to scout the Gardier post from within the Wall Port, it was more than enough. But the Rienish took longer to assemble their men and weapons and still seemed to be running around collecting things. And having curses put on themselves by god-spheres. "I don't understand why you have to do this," he told Tremaine as they walked down the passage to Gerard's quarters.

"Yes, you do, you're just being difficult," Tremaine replied.

Since grumbling "I am not" would tend to prove her point, he rolled his eyes and said nothing.

Gerard's door stood open, and Tremaine knocked on it and stepped inside. She didn't halt suddenly, but Ilias registered the tightening of her shoulders. He followed her in, spotting the cause almost immediately. Ander was sitting in the armchair across the room.

Gerard, standing at the desk paging through one of the Rienish flat books, glanced up. "There you are. Ready for the spell? Ander's just had it." The god-sphere sat on the little table in front of the couch; as Tremaine walked in, it clicked loudly at her. There were still curse bowls filled with water cluttering up every available surface.

"Of course." Tremaine favored Ander with a smile so sharp it could have cut leather.

Ander got to his feet, saying something to Tremaine in Rienish that Ilias wasn't meant to understand, except that he caught the words "how" and "husband" and guessed the rest. "I'm fine, thank you for asking," he replied in Syrnaic, leaning his shoulder against the wall and folding his arms.

Ander inclined his head, acknowledging the hit. He wore the same gray garments that the other Rienish soldiers did when they fought. "So you don't mind Tremaine having a curse put on her?"

Ilias eyed him acerbically. Of course he did. Gerard had convinced the god-sphere to teach Niles the Gardier language so they could better question their one remaining prisoner. But the Rienish had decided that some members of the war party should learn it too, in case they got the opportunity to overhear or question any Gardier in the Wall Port. It made sense in a way, as the Gardier seemed never to bother learning the languages of the people they fought, and this was one of the few things the Rienish could do that the Gardier couldn't. Tremaine had immediately volunteered.

Ilias knew she had had the curse put on her before; it was how she, Gerard, Florian and Ander had all learned Syrnaic. But the idea still made him uncomfortable. Tremaine had her back to him, poking at one of Gerard's curse bowls on the cabinet across the room. Ander was still regarding him with that expression of pleasant inquiry that was somehow adding up to an aggressive challenge in Ilias's head. Repressing the urge to just hit him, Ilias said pointedly, "No, I don't mind."

"Really." Ander nodded pleasantly to him and to Tremaine's unresponsive back, sketched a gesture of farewell at Gerard, and left the room. Gerard shook his head with a sour expression.

"That was fun." Tremaine rubbed her palms together briskly. "Let's get this over with, shall we?"

It was afternoon by the time everyone was ready to go. The bright sun threw long shadows, which would help the concealment charms Gerard had put on the *Ravenna*'s launches.

Tremaine waited with Gerard on the boat deck, impatient to go now that everything was ready. Their boat was being lowered in its davit, bringing it level with the gate in the railing so they could step aboard. There would be four boats in all. The first would leave with the Syprians, Ander, Florian and a few of Ander's men, including Basimi, an engineer named Molin and an army sergeant named Dubos whom Tremaine hadn't met before. The others would follow an hour later, giving them time to find a spot for the troops to conceal themselves and to start scouting the port and the Gardier outpost. Gerard and the sphere would be coming with the troops. "You will be careful," he said now. The sphere tucked under his arm clucked metallically at her, as if echoing the sentiment.

"Of course." Ilias, Giliead, Cimarus, Cletia, Arites and Kias were waiting nearby. Ilias was pacing impatiently, Giliead looked stolid, Arites appeared to be telling Kias the history of everything the Syprians knew about the Walls, and Cimarus and Cletia managed to look both defensive and aloof. Tremaine suspected Arites and Kias had been a last-minute addition to make sure Cimarus and Cletia were outnumbered.

All the Syprians wore the loose wraps that could double as ground cloths or blankets in an emergency, and Tremaine was glad she had borrowed one of those from Pasima too. The colors were all dull browns or grays that faded into the rocks and dirt better than the brighter colors of their clothing. Pasima's boots mostly fit her, but the soft leather had no arch support whatsoever. She was also the only one who didn't have a sword slung across her back, but though Ilias and Giliead had brought extra blades, she saw no reason to carry a weapon she couldn't use. What she did have was a visible sheath knife borrowed from Gyan and a holstered revolver attached to the back of her belt and hidden under her shirt and wrap.

" 'Of course,' " Gerard mimicked her unexpectedly. He continued in exasperation, "Tremaine, we've come a long way—"

"Don't wreck it now?" she finished, taken aback by his vehemence. Taken aback and hurt. She had thought Gerard at least believed her to be a little bit competent.

He let out a frustrated breath. "That is not what I meant."

They stood there in silence a moment, Tremaine watching him carefully, trying to decide if he thought she was that unreliable or if it was just the situation. *He's worried. He's always worried, but we've come so far, and we're so close.* She said, "I know it's hard to tell, but I'm serious about being careful. Really. Besides, we're not doing that much, just scouting."

Gerard rubbed his eyes, rueful and tired. "I seem to remember our excursions on the Pilot Boat were officially designated a scouting mission."

Tremaine cocked a brow at him. *Not exactly engendering my confidence, Gerard.* But the boat had clunked into position, and the sailors were opening the gate in the railing, and it was time to leave.

Ilias perched up in the bow of the boat to guide the Rienish helmsman through the treacherous waters, watching for the darker shapes of rocks just under the waves. Giliead was posted on the starboard for the same reason and Kias aft. Tremaine, Arites, Cletia and Cimarus sat near the bow, with Florian, Ander and the other three Rienish toward the stern. Other boats with the rest of the war party would be following throughout the day.

Past the barrier islands, which were just long spits of sand and sea wrack, were giant stone pillars, thrusting up out of the water all along the base of the Walls, some as big as two or three ship's lengths across, the tops sprouting small jungles of deep green vegetation. The barrier islands were enough to shield these inner coves from the constant movement of the waves, but Ilias thought that during a storm it would be suicide to be caught here.

"Slow, slow, and over that way!" Catching sight of a dark lump under the surface, he motioned hastily, using a pidgin mix of Rienish and Syrnaic for the instructions.

Muttering to himself, the sailor adjusted their course slightly, using the wheel and the levers that apparently controlled the speed of the boat. Past the obstacle safely, Ilias saw the edge of a little cove formed out of the base of this Wall. There wasn't much beach, just large flat rocks, washed by the low waves. But the stone in the cliffs above them was honeycombed with passages, forming steep rough trails leading up. "Here." Ilias pointed. "Let's try here."

The helmsman squinted to see the cove in the dusky shadows under the cliff, then nodded, turning the wheel to adjust the course.

"There?" Tremaine stepped up beside the helmsman, grabbing the railing to steady herself.

Ander was beside her before Ilias could explain his choice, saying emphatically, "We're still too far from the port."

"We're too close." Ilias rounded on him impatiently. "If they have gleaners, they'll work out from the port at least this far down. And there could be settlements up in the cliffs. If somebody asks us why our ship isn't where we said she was, I don't want to answer that question, do you?"

Ander stared at the cove, stone-faced, then spoke to the helmsman in Rienish too rapid for Ilias to catch any words. The helmsman, ignoring the tension, nodded. After exchanging more rapid speech, the helmsman guided the boat toward the cove.

Ander moved to the stern without another word. Tremaine rolled her eyes and followed him. The helmsman saw Ilias's sour expression and slanted a sympathetic look at him.

Giliead stepped up beside Ilias, leaning his hip on the railing. He watched Ander's retreat grimly, saying in a low voice, "He wanted you to ask him first if we could try that cove, instead of just telling the crewman."

Ilias snorted. Good warleaders let everyone do their jobs instead of finding excuses to prove they were in charge. "That's going to be fun."

Giliead nodded, annoyed. "It must be just us. He's not up here telling this man how to steer the boat."

Ilias eyed the wheel, the levers and knobs set into the wood beneath it. "Maybe he just doesn't know how."

Tremaine moved back between the row of benches and caught Ander in the stern. "Excuse me."

"Look." He rounded on her angrily. "I'm in command of—"

Tremaine switched to Syrnaic, keeping her voice low. "That was not a challenge to your authority. Syprians work in tight little family groups and make decisions by committee." She noticed that Basimi and the other two Rienish in the group were looking away with studied interest in the scenery. Florian, the only one who could understand Syrnaic besides Ander, had hastily shifted forward to sit with Arites, out of earshot. "God knows how it works, but apparently it does. If you push one of them, you push all of them, and Ilias may be willing to take your obvious contempt and lump it for a while, but Giliead won't."

Ander glared at her, taking two deep breaths, then looked over her shoulder. She knew he was looking at Giliead, whose eyes she could feel boring into them across the length of the boat. They were coming into the cove, the wet gray stones rising up around them, the boat slowing as the engine cut out. Everyone was moving to the front to see or to help moor the boat. She heard a splash as someone went into the water to tie it off. She hoped she didn't have to point out to Ander that Cineth and thereby the rest of the Syrnai's recognition of Ile-Rien as an ally had hinged on, and continued to hinge on, Giliead's opinion as Chosen Vessel. That it was on that opinion alone that the Syprians' fragile acceptance of Rienish sorcerers rested.

Ander's eyes came back to her. His expression was still stony, but she thought the flush might be from awareness of a tactical mistake rather than anger. He said curtly, "Thank you for bringing that to my attention."

"You're welcome." Tremaine turned, but a hand on her sleeve stopped her.

"Tremaine . . ." he began.

She just looked at him, waiting, one brow cocked. It was then that she realized that what Ander thought of her didn't matter at the moment. That perhaps it didn't just signal the end of an ill-considered infatuation on both their parts, but the end of any friendship between them.

Maybe he realized it too. After a moment he let her go, and she walked back to the front of the boat.

They had been walking and climbing a torturous path along the cliff top for a couple of hours, with Tremaine cursing Syprian footgear the whole way. The waves below washed the narrow sandy strips of the barrier islands and the towering rocks; above them the jagged gray peaks of the mountain loomed. The pockets of terrain that had been in shadow all day were almost cold.

Kias had gone ahead to scout, leaving trail signs scratched on the stone for them to follow. They had been bypassing small settlements of people Ilias said were gleaners, who lived by fishing and picking through the remnants of wrecks and whatever flotsam the sea washed up. They wanted to avoid these little communities to keep anyone from getting too close a look at the Rienish members of the party.

They turned away from the cliff face and through a narrow tunnel in the rock. It opened up into an only slightly wider gorge that wound down through the mountain, a trickling stream playing over mossy rocks down its middle. *Oh, that's going to be fun to walk on,* Tremaine thought, contemplating sliding the whole way on her bottom. At the head of the gorge, Giliead stopped, consulting a scratched marking on the stone. "He's found a place where the war party can gather."

Tremaine leaned against the wall and pushed her hair back. "So we're close to the port?"

Ilias pointed across the jutting crags. "It's right there, past that bluff."

Tremaine nodded, knowing the trail sign had somehow pinpointed the place's location exactly for him. She was going to have to learn a rudimentary version of the trail signs, just for safety's sake. The complexity of the designs had certainly explained why Ilias and Giliead had managed to memorize so many of the *Ravenna*'s directional signs in so little time.

She passed this information along as Florian, Arites and the others caught up with them, resisting the impulse to add loudly, *That all right with you, Ander?*

He seemed to have taken what might have been a badly judged rebuke well enough, and Giliead hadn't exploded. She flatly refused to believe Ander was resentful of Ilias out of jealousy for her; it was more likely some leftover impulse of the playboy and noble scion he had once been, thwarted at getting his way. But that didn't sound right either. *Oh hell, I don't know,* she thought wearily. It was strange to be the peacemaker. All in all, she thought being the troublemaker was a more advantageous position, and less stressful. *I can't think why I gave it up.*

"We're walking." Florian prodded her from behind, and she realized Giliead and Ilias were already halfway down the gorge, leaping from rock to rock with the ease and unconcern of mountain goats. Wearily, Tremaine pushed off the wall.

Chapter 14

All the Rienish members of the party except Tremaine left the group to take cover in the sheltered overhang Kias had found. There was enough room there for the strike force to gather, and Kias had gone back to the landing point to wait for the other boats to arrive and to lead them back to it. Tremaine fully expected to have to listen to instructions all over again, but Ander only eyed her grimly and said, "We'll be waiting."

As she and the Syprians continued on, Tremaine started to see the signs of occupation that Ilias and Giliead, walking a little way ahead, must have spotted long ago. In the rocks above the trail a faded red tarp blocked off a cave; someone's home, probably. Shards of broken pottery had trickled down a small gully further on and far above it dun-colored fragments of cloth hung on a rope stretched from one cliff to another.

Abruptly the trail turned, the rock faces falling away to reveal a city in a vast terraced bowl, the buildings perched on ledges of varied heights thrusting out like a giant staircase. Most of the structures were lean-tos or shanties, constructed of gray storm-wracked wood, but they were clustered around solid buildings of a smooth butter-colored stone with small round towers and curved walls. *It's like the underground city,* Tremaine realized, frowning. The stone buildings were constructed differently, but many had been ruined a long time, and halfway down the tiers two awkwardly shaped pillars stuck up at an odd angle, the tops of both raw jagged stone. *Not just like, but . . .* But someone else had built this place, and the current inhabitants were just squatting on it.

The city led down to a harbor sheltered by the cliffs, the entrance guarded by more of those rock pillars jutting up from the blue water, the tops covered with a tangle of jungle growth. The place was alive with people and the harbor crowded with small craft and larger ships, much less orderly than Cineth's docks. Tremaine didn't see any Syprian galleys at first glance or, for that matter, Gardier vessels. Most of the ships seemed to be leaving. As she watched, a big two-masted one lifted anchor, its oars taking it out of port while the crew scrambled to raise the sails.

Everyone was standing and staring. "I can't believe we're here," Ilias murmured. Cimarus pointed out something to Cletia, who nodded excitedly.

Arites was poking Tremaine repeatedly in the ribs. "Look at the statue."

"The what?" He pointed down toward the big awkwardly shaped pillars. She peered more closely at the base and realized they weren't pillars, they were legs, their bare feet planted firmly on a stone plinth. It was the lower part of a giant statue, broken off just above the knees. At its full height it must have been tall enough to pat the very top of the dome of Vienne's Grand Opera. "Oh, that," she agreed, impressed.

She stepped up beside Ilias and Giliead, who had stopped on the edge of the trail to survey the scene. "I can't see the airship from here."

Giliead jerked his chin toward the red cliff jutting out on the far side of the city's bowl. "It's just past there, hanging out over the water."

The wind shifted, and the smell hit her with the force of a slap: dead fish, woodsmoke and too many people. A flock of large gray gulls wheeled and shrieked overhead, adding to the din. Tremaine rubbed the back of her neck. She was sweating from a mix of stage fright nerves and the damp air and was suddenly ready to have this over and done with. And they couldn't all stand here like lumps without drawing the wrong kind of attention. "Damn. Well, come on."

Giliead took the lead as they made their way down the trail, past the cleared rubble from an old rockfall, and onto the first ledge. From there a broad stairway of chipped stone led the way down. The buildings loomed up around them, cutting off the view. Most of the people seemed to be engaged in moving out of their homes, carrying goods down the stairways. Casks, bundles, bags, bales, large painted clay jars were crammed everywhere, filling the ruined buildings, or being dragged or trundled down the broad stairs. Tremaine began to see why the inhabitants were forced to live in lean-tos and tattered tents: the older permanent structures were all used for cargo storage.

The Wall people themselves were a mixed bag, some dark-haired and dark-skinned in various shades of coffee color, others big in stature, with sallow skin and brown or red hair. Ilias and Cletia's bright blond heads tended to stand out, and most of the Wall men kept their hair cropped short. They stared at the newcomers or watched them warily, but no one offered a challenge. Tremaine suspected they were too busy leaving. Only the youngest babies were carried; everyone who could walk was helping shift a box or a bag. Tremaine heard talk in a babble of languages, none of which she understood.

They crossed another ledge, coming to a stairway down to an open plaza where some trading still seemed to be taking place. At least, people were standing around arguing rather than carrying their belongings to the harbor. The plaza had a circular fountain in the center and bright-colored awnings to shield sitting areas with rugs and stools.

With so much to look at, Tremaine didn't see the enormous round faces carved into the walls overlooking the plaza until she was halfway down into it. Craning her neck to look, she stumbled on the stairs. She bit her tongue to hold in a Rienish curse, and Arites caught her shoulder to steady her. Waiting below, Ilias looked back up at her, frowning, and she waved him on, saying, "I'm fine, I'm fine."

She glanced up again as she reached the bottom, shielding her eyes against the sun. The carved faces were rounded, softened by time and wind, their expressions uniformly serene.

The others gathered around Giliead, who jerked his head to indicate a group of men and women at the other end of the plaza, talking intently to one of the Wall Port traders. They were tall, dark-skinned people, dressed in loose bright-colored trousers, sashes and coats. "Those are Chaean traders. The one with the topknot is a shipmaster," he told Tremaine.

She nodded. She knew the Chaeans were a people the Syprians

had regular contact with, even though they didn't always get along with them. "We could talk to them, find out what happened when the Gardier arrived."

Giliead lifted a brow. "They'll think it's odd if we just walk up to them." He considered the problem a moment. "But if we wait a little, they may come over to us."

Ilias was nodding like this was a perfectly normal situation. Cletia and Cimarus didn't seem to find it unusual either. Tremaine blew out a breath, deciding not to argue. "Ah . . . All right. So we just stand here?"

Arites leaned in to say, "This is a place where ships buy provisions. We can act as if we're waiting to talk to one of the traders."

Giliead nodded, looking around. He chose one of the awnings where a group of people were arguing vociferously, stepping into its shade and planting himself there solidly. The others just stood where they were. Tremaine tried it for a few moments, then gave up. She couldn't just stand there feeling self-conscious. She strolled casually over to the next awning, where there was another trader and another angry discussion, pretending to be checking out its prospects.

After a moment she glanced back to see the Chaean traders approaching the Syprians cautiously, looking as if they wanted to be friendly but weren't sure how it would be received. Arites had taken a seat on the ground near their awning, making notes on parchment scraps, his bag propped in his lap as a makeshift desk. One of the younger Chaeans was lucky enough to pick him to speak to first, making a gesture toward the parchment and commenting on it. Arites looked up at him with a grin as he replied, waving an arm to indicate the whole of the Wall Port.

Fascinated, Tremaine watched the attitude shift in all the Syprians, as if Arites's action had somehow committed them to diplomacy rather than hostility. She had always thought of the Syprians as gregarious people; now she wondered how much of that had been simply luck at meeting the right Syprians first, under the right circumstances.

Cimarus let himself be drawn into conversation with two other Chaean men, and the shipmaster stepped up to the awning to speak to Giliead and Cletia. Ilias was the only one who hadn't unbent. He was leaning against the outer pole of the awning, arms folded, not openly hostile, but his expression was closed and not encouraging. None of the Chaeans attempted to approach him.

She saw Giliead, listening as Cletia spoke with polite gravity to the Chaean shipmaster, flick a worried look at him. *Chaeans know what curse marks are,* she realized abruptly. She was pretty sure they didn't follow the custom the way the Syprians did, but they would know what it meant. She bit her lip, trying to think if ignoring the situation would be better than saying something to Ilias about it. Then someone behind her said, "Greeting."

Tremaine turned and found herself facing two Chaean women. One was older, her curly dark hair streaked with gray, and the other possibly her daughter. They had the same long straight noses and high cheekbones. They wore embroidered open coats over brief singlets and loose billowy trousers. It was a style of dress Tremaine felt she could have gotten to like as much as she did Syprian clothing. Realizing they were waiting for a response, she said, "Ah, hello."

"Where's your ship?" the older woman asked in careful Syrnaic.

"We went aground down the coast, came up here to buy supplies while the others are working on her." Tremaine managed to suppress a wince. *Could you have blurted your cover story out in a more transparently false way? I think not.* She just hoped the others had remembered it.

That out of the way, the younger woman shifted forward and asked confidentially, "Is it true that Syrnai women can have more than one man? Bonded to her, I mean."

"Oh, sure." *So did everyone know that but me?* But it explained why the two women had approached her. It was curiosity, not suspicion. Tremaine felt the biting tension ease in her shoulders. "For a first marriage anyway. If you can afford it."

The older woman looked across at the Syprians, brows lifted speculatively. "How many of those men are yours?"

Tremaine suppressed the sudden urge to say *All of them.* "The blond one." *What the hell.* "My other two are with the ship."

Both women eyed Ilias speculatively. Neither commented on the curse mark, which could be politeness or just that they hadn't noticed it, and Tremaine, Ilias and Giliead were all being wildly oversensitive. Realizing she was missing an opportunity here, she asked with what she hoped was innocent curiosity, "What is that big black thing in the cliffs above the harbor? It looks . . . different from everything else."

"Newcomers brought it," the older woman answered, her expression sobering as she shifted to face Tremaine again. "You won't believe this, but it's a ship that flies through the air."

"Through the air?" Tremaine made a snap decision on how much surprise to show; it would be easier for all of them to admit they had some knowledge of the airships than to have to fake astonishment and disbelief. She felt fairly sure Ilias, Giliead and Arites could have pulled it off in their various ways, but Cimarus and Cletia were unknown quantities. She nodded, frowning worriedly. "We've heard stories about that. Are they dangerous?"

The woman nodded a grim assent. "They've killed a lot of people here, apparently. We were told they slew a number of traders in the upper part of the city with wizardry—" She threw a quick look at Tremaine, as if suddenly recalling her audience. Seeing no immediate reaction, she continued, "Some traders groups got together and tried to drive them off, but that just made it worse."

"How long have they been here?"

"Not long. Our factor said they first saw the flying ships nearly three season turns ago, coming out of the east. It was only late this season that they came to the port and claimed the promontory for their own. Now everyone is leaving." She gestured in resignation. "We would have been gone already, but because of all this turmoil, our provisioning took forever. We'll leave on the evening tide."

"I think we'll leave as soon as we can, too," Tremaine agreed, still looking in Ilias's direction. He was studying the crowd and she saw the moment when he tensed and shifted from defensive wariness to aggressive challenge. Frowning, she followed his gaze. A new group of travelers were coming up the stairs of the lower level entrance to the plaza, but they didn't look that different to her eyes than the men already here. They were big, light-skinned but tanned dark from the sea. Most had shaved heads or dark hair pulled back into a shoulder-length tail. They wore clothes of rough colorful fabrics and leather, but their only jewelry was on their weapons: gold and polished stones decorated the hilts of short swords, knives and a curving sharp thing that looked like a small scythe some had strapped across their backs.

The two Chaeans had spotted the newcomers as well. "Oh, this will be interesting," the younger woman said, low-voiced.

Obviously this was something that as a Syprian Tremaine would be familiar with. She managed to paste on an expression of generic concern, hoping no one had noticed her stupidly blank face. The Chaean men were fading into the background, watchful caution etched on their faces. The shipmaster came to collect the two women.

The leader of the new arrivals strode toward Giliead and Cletia's spot under the awning as if planning to claim it for his own. Without seeming to hurry, Giliead rose and met him several paces from it.

They confronted each other for a long moment. Then the leader grudgingly stepped back and Giliead casually moved past him. He went toward the lower-level exit, the other Syprians following without hesitation. Tremaine shook her head, falling in with them. She should have known the Syprians would pick the largest and most heavily armed group in the Wall Port to start a fight with. *Hell, they decided to ally with us against the Gardier. Of course they're insane.*

"What was that about?" Tremaine asked Ilias as they went down the steps out of the plaza.

He threw her a quizzical look. "They don't like us."

"Why? Did you kill all their wizards?"

He snorted. "They don't have wizards. They're Raiders."

Tremaine lifted a brow. "Are they really raiders? Do they actually raid?"

"Of course."

"And they don't like you because?" Tremaine persisted.

"We sink their ships," he admitted.

"What, and leave them to drown?"

"Of course not." He threw her an annoyed look. "They're all dead by then."

They came out of the stone city's warren just above the port. Ilias paused at the top of the last cracked set of stairs to take it in. This place had been just a story for so long; he would never have expected to actually set eyes on it.

It made Cineth's harbor look like a child's toy. Embraced in the curve of the cliffs, hundreds of stone docks jutted out from the rocky terrace, sheltering dozens and dozens of ships of every size and shape. Among the oared galleys and small mixed-rig merchant ships, he saw at least two big Merokian three-masted carracks, ships that were almost legends in Cineth. As the Chaeans had said, many ships were leaving, or preparing to leave. People moved everywhere, hauling cargo, bargaining, arguing as flights of white and gray gulls wheeled and shrieked overhead. The masts were like a forest, the sails every color imaginable.

In the distance he could see several pillars of stone, their tops covered in green carpets of tangled jungle, marching out from the mouth of the harbor. They were placed too conveniently as a breakwater to be an act of nature. He whistled softly, awed at the idea.

Giliead had stopped beside him and, obviously sharing the same thought, said, "Imagine driving all those pilings in deep water."

Ilias shook his head in amazement. Automatically scanning the docks, he spotted the war prow of the Raider vessel and nudged Giliead to make sure he saw it. It was too bad they didn't have the time to take on the Raiders while they were here; he would have given a lot to see them react to the *Ravenna* bearing down on their ship.

Behind them, Cimarus said, "They must have used curses to build this harbor." Ilias might have been imagining it, but he didn't sound as if he was entirely condemning the idea.

"Not necessarily." Tremaine came to stand next to Ilias. He glanced back to see Cletia regarding her warily, but Tremaine didn't notice. Or at least appeared not to notice. She continued, "They might have just been good builders. Are there any stories about who first lived here?"

Ilias shook his head, shrugging. "People from long ago, like the ones who built the city on the island."

"Look at that!" Arites pointed, sounding as excited as a kid at a festival. "Look how long that dock is."

Ilias stood on his tiptoes to follow Arites's pointing finger and see past the jumble of masts. He spotted the long stone projection extending out from the far side of the harbor. It stood higher in the water than the docks on this side and looked half again as wide as well. He started to protest that it was an inner breakwater, but then he thought of the docks he had seen in Ile-Rien.

Echoing his thought, Tremaine said, "The *Ravenna* could pull up to that with no problem." She glanced thoughtfully at Ilias. "The one she was at in Port Rel was too short because it wasn't built for her. The big ships all leave—left—from the ocean docks at Chaire."

He wished she wouldn't be so careful to speak of her land in the past tense; there was a chance they could still win it free. It was why they were out here after all. But he just looked at the stone dock, estimating distances. "I don't think it's big enough for her, but yes, it's not meant for these ships."

Giliead nodded slowly. "The Chaeans have barges maybe half the size of the *Ravenna*, but they're river craft."

"What does this mean?" Arites demanded. "That the Wall Port has a dock for such large ships?"

"That the long-ago people who built the Wall Port had some damn big ships." Tremaine turned to start down the steps.

"Why do you care about that?" Cletia asked, pausing to look out over the harbor now that the rest of them were out of the way. She had been too proud to elbow her way to the front before.

"Normal human curiosity," Tremaine tossed dryly over her shoulder without pausing. "Some humans have it."

Ilias followed her, throwing Cletia a sour look. He had thought her less annoying than Pasima, but with the older woman absent, she obviously thought it was her job to act suspicious.

The steps curved down to a wide platform just above the docks. Ilias saw there were matching steps curving in the opposite direction, maybe a hundred or so paces along the harbor front. He realized it was meant to be viewed from the water, by ships coming to port, and wondered what the effect would be if they could see it from the right direction. There were peddlers all along the walkway, some with just blankets to spread their wares and others with little awnings, selling everything from grilled fish to bolts of cloth. All of them seemed to be overwhelmed with commerce as people tried to buy provisions before leaving the port.

As the others caught up Tremaine halted, turning back to say in a low voice, "All right, this is what we're going to do. You three"—she pointed to Cletia, Cimarus and Arites—"stay down here. We're supposed to be buying supplies for our wrecked boat, so look at things, ask prices, bargain, just don't commit to anything."

Cimarus gestured around. "The traders are all too busy with the people leaving. We won't even be able to talk to one."

"That's the point." Tremaine's assumed air of patience had an edge to it. "We don't want people remembering us as the funny Syprians who disappeared suddenly without picking up their goods. Got it?"

Arites had already turned to study the merchants' cubbies along the upper level, but Cimarus looked at Cletia, whose face was a study in conflict. Ilias could see as if it were written there in trail signs that Cletia had been told by Pasima to keep a close eye on Tremaine, but that she thought this a good plan. She nodded grudgingly. "It's well. This place is big enough that each merchant will think we went to someone else."

As usual, Tremaine's face gave nothing away, but Ilias knew she hadn't asked for Cletia's approval and probably resented it. She only said, "We'll meet back here in about—" She gestured in frustration. "Oh, dammit."

The Rienish measured time in a way Ilias couldn't make any sense of. He supplied, "At twilight."

"Right," Tremaine confirmed, turning to head briskly up the harbor front. Ilias caught up with her in a few strides, Giliead following unhurriedly. She leaned toward him to ask softly, "Where is this goddamn airship? Am I going in the wrong direction?"

Ilias looked over her head, his eyes sorting out the curving shapes of the Wall buildings. A rising outcrop blocked all view of the flying whale from the port. He jerked his chin at it. "It's past there, probably perched in the rocks past those towers. We need to follow this curve around, then maybe do some climbing to get up near it."

"Oh." She shaded her eyes to look. "That's a relief."

A s they wound their way up the broken stairs toward the flying whale's promontory, Ilias saw more and more signs of the Gardier's occupation.

All the city terraces on this side had already been abandoned, though some of the inhabitants were still here, huddled in bloody stinking heaps in doorways or sprawled in the dirt-covered paths. Big sandflies hummed in clouds over the corpses, and the smell hanging in the damp air made his stomach want to turn.

"I can't believe the rest of the city hasn't left already," Tremaine said, low-voiced. Her face had a pained, pinched look. Ilias wanted to ask her if she was all right, but instinct told him it would not be well received. Besides, the only way to avoid the sight and smell was to turn back, and they needed her to look at the Gardier's camp, to report to the others the things he and Giliead wouldn't recognize.

"It's not a city," Giliead answered her, glancing up to make sure their approach wasn't overlooked from this angle. He had already found and led them around three curse traps, probably meant to alert the Gardier if anyone passed by. The traps were small fragments of crystal, placed on paving blocks or atop walls. Giliead had told them he could see the curse spread out around them like giant spiderwebs. It would be nearly impossible for the Rienish soldiers to move through here without tripping them, and destroying them would surely alert the Gardier. "It's just a lot of people who decided to live here because of the harbor and the trade. There was no one to get them to act together on anything."

"The rich merchants probably didn't want to leave, at first. The poor ones probably can't," Ilias added.

Tremaine nodded grimly, stumbling a little on the uneven path. "That's typical."

The old buildings of smooth stone became fewer and smaller, their backs buried in the rocky cliffs. They took to creeping through the rocks and scattered brush, still winding their way up. Finally, Giliead stopped, crouching low behind a stony ridge and gesturing for Ilias to come up and take the lead. Ilias slipped past Tremaine and forged on up the scrubby slope. He pulled a fold of his wrap up over his hair, so the muted browns and grays of its weaving would help conceal him.

As he neared the top he caught a glimpse of the flying whale.

It took all his attention first, blotting out the sky, its shadow falling across the outcrop. The huge oblong shape was black as night and the body was narrow at the front, the middle swelling out until it narrowed again at the rear. A jagged ridge ran the length of its back to the cluster of long sharp-edged fins in the tail. Even though he knew now that it wasn't alive and didn't eat people, the looming presence still made his flesh creep.

Ilias reached the top of the slope and peered cautiously over the edge. Below the flying whale the flat ground of the promontory supported a skeletal metal tower. It was pyramidal in shape, ladders reaching up to a flat platform at the top, about a ship's length and a half off the ground, just below the squarish compartments hung at the bottom of the flying whale's swollen belly. A ramp bridged the distance between the whale and the tower's platform.

There was a Gardier on watch at the base of the tower, his brown clothing nearly the same color as the dirt. To the left of the tower there were roughly carved stone steps, leading down to a lower level of the promontory and a flat paved platform that must have been built by the same ancients who had constructed the Wall Port itself. Stairs led down from it to the now deserted portion of the city, and he could see another Gardier patrolling there.

On the other side of the tower, partly sheltered by the cliff face, a scatter of metal huts stood, their walls streaked with rust. A pair of Gardier walked on the packed dirt between them, talking. Big round wizard lights were mounted atop the flat roofs, their glass surfaces glinting in the sunlight. The doorways had squiggly marks painted on them in black; the Gardier never decorated anything, so Ilias assumed it was writing.

Behind one of the huts he could see big fat metal tanks, like the ones they had found in the Gardier stronghold on the island. He noted the Gardier were building another tower toward the far end of the promontory, its skeletal frame half-constructed. Ilias sunk back below the lip of the slope and crept along it until he found a rockfall that would provide an observation post with good cover. Then he went back for Giliead and Tremaine.

As he drew near he heard Giliead say, "He's smaller and harder to see."

Tremaine replied impatiently, "I understand that, but how do you know who does what when? That Kias should be the one to scout the trail, that Ilias should go first to look for cover, that you should lead the way through the town. How do you decide without talking about it?"

"Sometimes we don't, sometimes we argue. But most of the time everyone knows what they do best," Giliead explained, easing to his feet to follow Ilias. He added dryly, "Why does Ander act as if he leads your family when he has no part in it, when your father left his rights to Gerard?"

Good question, Ilias thought, turning to lead the way back to the rocks, his ears pricking for the answer.

"He's not— Giving orders is how it works, in our world." Tremaine climbed carefully after them, swinging her bag around to carry in front of her. "Most of the time. Ander is a captain in the military."

"But you're not on his crew, you don't take orders from him," Ilias pointed out as they neared the rocks, crouching to stay out of sight. He stretched out on the gravelly ground, finding a clump of grass to peer through.

"Yes, well, it's a talent." Tremaine scrambled up next to him and pulled the Rienish seeing glass out of her bag. It was an odd-looking device, with two short tubes instead of a single long one. "This isn't much of an outpost. I was really expecting something more impressive," she said under her breath.

Ilias thought it was more than enough, since its presence was keeping them from passing through the strait. "I don't think we could handle anything more impressive."

Giliead's expression had gone distant. "There's something in that big building, something powerful. It smells like . . . the thing on the

Ravenna, the thing that lets you go to other places, but not quite the same."

"Oh ho," Tremaine muttered thoughtfully. "That sounds like a spell circle."

Dusk had darkened the shadows and turned the sky to a rich purple as Tremaine climbed a rocky slope in Ilias's wake, the other Syprians following along behind. She glanced up in time to see a big dark form emerge from behind a boulder. Ilias greeted it with a nod, so she assumed it was Kias. Grabbing the tufts of dry grass for handholds, she struggled the last few feet and stood next to Ilias on a narrow flat just below the mouth of a large cleft of rock. As she rubbed her aching back, two Rienish soldiers in gray fatigues stood up from the cover of the rocks, one of them ducking back into the cleft. "Any trouble?" Ilias asked Kias softly as Cletia and Arites scrambled up onto the ledge behind them.

Kias shook his head and added a shrug. Tremaine couldn't see his expression in the dim light, just the fuzzy outline of his fraying braids, and decided he was trying to convey that there hadn't been any trouble from intruders, just impatience from their own party. This was confirmed when Ander strode out of the shadow of the cleft, demanding in Rienish, "Well? What the hell took so long?"

"We have plenty of time," Tremaine answered in Syrnaic. Behind her Cimarus arrived, dusting his hands off and moving to stand next to Cletia. Giliead walked up the slope surefootedly and stood next to them. They had spent the afternoon watching the movements of the Gardier around the tower, making sure there wouldn't be any surprises. At one point Ilias had gone back for Arites, so he could sketch a map of the compound. Tremaine didn't mean to wreck this. She could have said as much to Ander, but her tension and tiredness made her long for a fight. "Did the plan change to a daring daylight raid while we were away?"

Before Ander could answer, Gerard stepped out of the shadows behind him, asking, "Everything all right?"

Disappointingly, Ander failed to fall for the bait, saying roughly in Syrnaic, "Tell us what you found."

Ilias and Giliead both looked at Tremaine, which she took to mean that she had the floor. With a silent groan, she followed Ander and Gerard back into the shelter of the rocks.

She blinked as she stepped through the entrance, suddenly finding herself in firelight. There was a sight-masking charm across the opening, keeping the light from being seen past the overhang of the cliff. Ilias flinched as he stepped through, throwing a worried look back at Giliead. Giliead did one of his eyebrow dip things that evidently told Ilias it was all right. Kias seemed used to the effect by now, but Arites stopped to look around, startled, and Cimarus and Cletia abruptly froze.

There was a fire in the center of the sheltered space and a few carbide lamps strewn around. The cleft was now crowded with Rienish soldiers in gray fatigues, most of them checking their rifles or the small crossbows that were immune to the Gardier's mechanical disruption spell. The murmur of quiet conversation died away as the assembled men eyed the scouting party, knowing that this meant the time for the attack was near.

Florian made her way toward them. She was carrying the sphere in its familiar leather pouch. "That's a relief," she said. "We were getting worried."

"We just wanted to make sure we got a good idea of how the place was laid out, how they guard it," Tremaine replied absently, watching Cimarus and Cletia out of the corner of her eye. Giliead was having a staring contest with Cletia.

Low and angry, Cletia said, "You could have warned us." Walking through the sight-masking charm had unnerved her, and she wanted to blame someone for it.

"I won't warn you unless it's something to worry about," Giliead replied with what was probably meant to be annoying calm.

The younger woman turned away stiffly, leading Cimarus over to the cave wall, as far away from the Rienish as they could get.

Florian took the situation in with a wince. "Sorry," she murmured.

Tremaine shook her head. "Don't be," she said in Rienish. "It just encourages her." She took the squares of rough-cut parchment that Arites had been trying to hand her for the past minute and knelt to flatten them out on the rough stone. "Here's a diagram of the area around the tower." She brushed her hair out of her eyes with a grimace. A day away from coffee might have been expected to do her good, but she felt like a benzine addict coming down from a bender.

Gerard knelt beside her, and Ander sat down to look at the rough diagram, all business. A Rienish officer she didn't know came to join the group as well. After Tremaine finished interpreting her notes,

Giliead and Ilias took turns describing the terrain. Finally, Ander nodded slowly. "It's what we expected. They haven't had long to establish a foothold here."

"Our priority has always been the airship," Gerard said quietly. "But the possible presence of a spell circle changes the situation. If we can't secure the airship, then it can't be allowed to escape."

"We can take the flying whale. It'll be easy," Ilias said suddenly. He was speaking Syrnaic, but Tremaine knew "airship" was one of the Rienish words he knew, and he must have understood at least part of what Gerard had said.

"Easy?" Ander lifted his brows. "To get inside."

"Inside," Ilias repeated in Rienish, mimicking Ander's upper class Vienne accent exactly.

Gerard ignored them, looking thoughtful. "You think a small group should go in first to take the airship?" he asked in Syrnaic.

Giliead was nodding. "As soon as your men hit those curse traps, the Gardier will know we're coming. But I could lead a few of us past just the way I did today and be in their camp before they knew it."

Ander was listening intently, frowning. "We could send Basimi, Dubos and Molin in with them to get aboard the airship, take it out of its mooring so the Gardier don't have any chance to use it against us."

"I'll have to go in as well," Gerard pointed out. "If there's a crystal in the control cabin, the sphere may have to destroy it. It would be better to capture it intact, but there should be another crystal on the base powering the spell circle itself—"

"We can't risk that," Ander interrupted. "I want you with the sphere at a distance, taking out the lights and counteracting any spells they throw at us."

They had slipped back into speaking Rienish. Tremaine said in Syrnaic, "Giliead could handle the crystal. If there is one aboard."

Ander eyed her, then eyed Giliead. "Could you?"

Giliead's expression was cryptic. He consulted Ilias with a lifted brow. Ilias tilted his head slightly, an answer Tremaine couldn't interpret. Giliead looked at Ander. "We'll find out," he said evenly.

J ust remember, this was your idea," Ilias whispered.

Giliead nudged him impatiently. "Get up there."

Ilias ghosted up the slope, staying low to the ground. Everything was quiet except for the sea crashing into the rocks below and the rush of the wind. The wizard lights blazed over the dirt and tufted grass of the compound. In front of the flying whale's tower, a Gardier still kept solitary watch, his shooting stick slung over one shoulder, pacing back and forth, scuffing his boots in the dirt in boredom. The other guard was still there on the lower level, where the path up from the Wall dwellings ended, though Ilias couldn't see him from here. He knew the man was pacing on the paved stone flat, the wizard lights striking sparks off the crystal devices at his belt. The one guarding the flying whale had no devices, at least not that they had seen through the Rienish distance glasses.

Ilias crept closer, clinging to the shadows at the base of the rocks. The flying whale's silent presence made the back of his neck itch. It hovered over the compound like a thundercloud. As he looked up at it the metal ramp to the tower creaked, as if it swayed a little, pulling against its mooring ropes; he told himself it was just the wind. *What are they waiting for?*

There was a crackle and a faint pop, then the wizard lights pointing toward the whale tower and the approach from the city were extinguished, leaving only the cluster of metal huts lit. The glow emanating from the open doors of the flying whale gave only enough illumination to make out shapes and forms on this half of the compound.

The guard on the far side of the huts trotted into view, calling anxiously to the others. The flying whale guard answered him, sounding annoyed. The door in the largest hut opened and more Gardier came out. They moved around, some standing and talking, some going off to investigate the lights. They sounded irritated or curious, not alarmed. The flying whale guard stayed at his post in the darkness, watching the others across the compound. Ilias scrambled over the lip of the slope and started forward.

One of the Gardier appeared at the top of a hut and turned the still-working wizard light there, making it sweep the dark half of the promontory. It flashed across the packed earth, a white circle blazing a path over the dirt and tufted grass, then swept out to play over the water. *Damn, didn't plan on that,* Ilias thought with a grimace.

On the level below there was a faint scuffle, a sound that might have been a choked-off cry. It startled the flying whale guard, who turned toward it, pulling his shooting stick off his shoulder. Before he could call out Ilias slammed into him from behind, his forearm wrap-

ping around the man's throat to silence him. Ilias on top of him, the
guard went down, desperately clawing at his arm. Ilias held on grimly,
planting a knee in the guard's back when he started to weaken, keeping his hold taut until the body under him collapsed.

Ilias turned the Gardier over, prying his eyelids up to make sure he
wasn't faking. Giliead arrived in silence with a rope and a makeshift
gag, and they rapidly got the man trussed. As Giliead rolled him into
the shadows, Ilias saw the light sweeping toward them and slapped
his friend on the back to warn him. Giliead shoved the Gardier into
concealment and hastily crouched against the rock, Ilias huddling
next to him.

The light rushed toward them and Ilias buried his face in his arm
to save his eyes. There was another crackle and the moving light went
out. A Gardier called out, more worried this time. Ilias came to his
feet and Giliead scrambled past him to grab the tower's ladder, starting up.

Dim shapes that he knew were Basimi, the two other Rienish, and
Cimarus burst out of concealment below the slope, racing across the
compound. Basimi reached for the tower's ladder and Ilias grabbed
his shoulder to halt him. Basimi stopped immediately, earning Ilias's
approval. He looked up at the top of the tower; after a moment
Giliead leaned briefly over the side, signaling that it was safe. Ilias let
Basimi go, nodding for the others to follow him.

Almost there, Ilias thought. He watched them climb, then started
after.

"Good," Tremaine breathed as the searchlight winked out. She
and Cletia were watching from the darkness and relative safety
of the slope where Ilias had spied on the outpost earlier. Hugging the
stone surface to keep from being seen, Tremaine was sweating and
her stomach was knotted with anxiety. Gerard was back behind the
Gardier's perimeter wards, at a vantage point in one of the old city
towers, with Ander and the rest of the strike force waiting. Giliead had
been hard-pressed to keep the few of them from setting off the alarm
wards in the dark as they had crept up here; Tremaine was glad Ander
had agreed to keep the others back until the airship was secure. Kias,
Arites, Florian and another couple of Rienish soldiers were at the
platform on the lower level; it had been Kias and Arites's job to take
out the guard there.

Cletia stirred restlessly beside her. Wanting to be out killing some-body, Tremaine supposed. Then Cletia said, low-voiced, "You must not be a woman of much importance to your people, if they send you out to fight."

"I'm planning to let you do the fighting," Tremaine told her dryly. "Pasima must have lots of minions. I didn't think she'd miss one."

"I am not—" Cletia began in a furious whisper. Then she turned her head sharply. "Wait, I heard something."

"What?" It was too dark to read expressions; Tremaine could barely see the outline of the other woman's head. "Where?"

More Gardier suddenly boiled out of the larger structure, one shouting an alarm. Tremaine caught the words, and it badly startled her, until she belatedly remembered the sphere's new language spell. "What? They're saying someone's coming, someone tripped the alarms." She started to stand, but a hard shove to her back knocked her down into the gravel.

Cursing, Tremaine twisted around to see Cletia standing, ducking under a sword swipe from a tall figure. *Where in hell did he come from?* she thought, shocked. She shoved to her feet and flung herself for-ward, tackling the dimly seen shape around the knees.

He went down with a strangled yell and Tremaine got a face full of stinking leather. Cletia sprang on him, nearly stepping on Tremaine's head, and Tremaine saw the sword slash down. Cletia stepped back and Tremaine struggled up off the still-twitching body. "It's a Raider," Cletia said, aghast. "Why would he attack the Gardier—"

Tremaine pushed to her feet, sick with dread. "Are they mercenaries?"

Cletia nodded tightly. "The merchants must have hired them."

"Oh, shit," Tremaine whispered.

Ilias slipped through the doorway in the belly of the whale. It was re-assuringly like the other flying whale they had entered back on the Isle of Storms: this first chamber, starkly lit by a few small white curse lights hanging from the ceiling, was long and low and meant for cargo, though now it was nearly empty. It was all ribbed metal, less startling now that he had seen the *Ravenna*'s lower decks. The floor was covered with a soft corklike matting, muffling sound. He wrin-kled his nose against the bitter acrid odors. There were similar taints in the air aboard the *Ravenna,* as there had been in the Rienish city he had visited briefly, but there they were softened with the more normal scents of cooking and wood and leather, and the exotic fragrances so many of the Rienish wore on their bodies.

Cimarus stood watch at the inner door, his sword drawn. In the harsh light Ilias could see he was white around the eyes and sweating. No way to help that, and Cimarus wouldn't accept reassurance from him if he offered it. He stepped past him into the whale's main passage.

The corridor was low and narrow, lit by more curse lights dangling from the ceiling. It was all crew quarters through here, small gray rooms with cold narrow beds that were practically shelves attached to the walls. No color, no decoration, no belongings except one of the brown coats left lying on a bed. Giliead or one of the others had opened all the doors, to make sure no Gardier remained behind.

Ilias reached the end of the corridor and the dark chamber lined with metal vats, pipes leading up from their tops into the ribbed ceiling. Molin, the Rienish who was supposed to make the whale's guts work for them, was there examining the handles on the pipes. Ilias whistled to tell the man he was there so he didn't get accidentally stabbed in the gut. Molin looked up, nodded and waved him on. Ilias passed hurriedly through the shadowy chamber. The acrid odor was far worse here, and he knew now it was from the liquid in the vats, the stuff that made the flying whale's insides work just like it did the *Ravenna*'s boats and the city's horseless wagons.

He heard a yell and a sudden scuffle ahead and plunged forward, nearly tripping over a dead Gardier on the threshold. It was a large room with bright curse lights and a few wooden tables and chairs, lined with metal cabinets. Giliead stood near the opening into the forward part of the whale, just pulling his sword out of a Gardier. The man fell to his knees, then collapsed, dropping the crystal device he held. Giliead turned to crunch it under his bootheel just as another Gardier dropped out of a trapdoor overhead.

Ilias drew his sword, lunging in as the man landed, taking off the arm that held the crystal with the first stroke. The Gardier fell back with an agonized cry, and Ilias stepped in for the finishing blow.

He freed his sword with a jerk and stepped back away from the spreading pool of blood, keeping a wary eye on that trapdoor. It led up into the flying whale's top portion. "Where's the others?"

Giliead kicked the other crystal free of the dead Gardier's arm and grimly crushed it to fragments. He jerked his head toward the other door. "Up front. They found—"

Ilias heard muffled popping sounds. *Not good.* "That was a shooting weapon."

Startled, Giliead headed for the door. "It was outside."

The floor tilted, staggering them both sideways.

Shouting Raiders streamed up the steps from the city, stormed across the compound, right into the Gardier guns. Some of them carried torches and Tremaine caught glimpses of wild-eyed men, shaven-headed, waving swords and the small scythelike weapons. A fusillade of shots went off as the Gardier fired on them. "Dammit," Tremaine snarled, ducking down behind the rocks. The damn Raiders were ruining everything. *And they must have run right over Florian, Arites and the others down there.* Where the hell was the Rienish troop?

More yelling figures burst out of the rocks behind them and Tremaine and Cletia bolted up the slope without having to discuss it, suddenly finding themselves on the open ground of the promontory. Cletia spun around, sword lifted, but Tremaine dragged at her arm. The airship provided the only possible shelter. "Come on!"

They dodged across the compound in the confused dark, avoiding the charging Raiders by luck more than anything else. Tremaine pulled the pistol out of her belt. Most of the Raiders hadn't made it to the Gardier buildings; their bodies were strewn at the edge of the light, and Tremaine could smell burning flesh. They had run into a spell trap; she hadn't heard enough shots to account for all those dead.

They were almost to the tower when a Raider rounded on them, lifting his sword. Tremaine shot him before Cletia could turn around. Another one fell heavily at her feet, an indistinct shape with Syprian braids pulling a sword out of his back.

Tremaine fell back a step, banging into the metal leg of the tower. She didn't see it was Arites until he straightened up. "What happened to Florian and the others?" she demanded.

"I don't know," he gasped, gesturing to the confusion. "They were on us, and we scattered."

No help for it, she thought in frustration. They had to keep moving. Shots echoed off the rock and several Raiders spun and fell in mid-charge. The Gardier were starting forward to clean up. "Right. Get up the ladder, hurry." Tremaine prodded Cletia and the other woman grabbed the ladder and started to climb. Tremaine followed as soon as Cletia's feet were out of the way. She felt the structure shake as Arites started up after her and she clung hard to it despite the sweat making her hands slick. Cletia reached the top and scrambled up onto the platform.

Tremaine dragged herself over the edge, terrified of falling. She crawled to the center of the platform and pushed to her feet, getting a view of the dark confusion on the promontory below. The sea and most of the sky were blotted out by the giant black curve of the airship overhead. Cletia was hesitating at the head of the ramp and Tremaine waved at her to go on. "Get in there!"

She heard another flurry of shots and something struck her in the back, staggering her forward. Tremaine ran into the handrail, the impact with the metal like a punch in the stomach. She realized Arites had knocked into her as he staggered and fell. She heard more shots from below and had the sense to drop to a crouch. Sucking in a breath to ease the pain in her midsection, she looked around and saw Arites sprawled in a jumble on the platform behind her.

Oh, no. She scrambled toward him and tried to roll him over. She felt moisture and lifted her hand to see it black with blood.

"Cletia, come here!" Tremaine snapped. She grabbed his arm, dug her fingers into his belt, and managed to drag him onto the ramp. Cletia landed on her knees beside him, her hands hovering above his bloody shirt as if she was afraid to touch it. "Help me," Tremaine snarled through gritted teeth, dragging him up. Cletia grabbed his other arm and they lurched forward, hauling him up the ramp and into the dubious shelter of the airship.

Tremaine got a confused impression of a big dimly lit room as they stumbled onto a cork-matted floor. Cimarus was suddenly there, helping ease Arites down, demanding, "What happened?"

Tremaine crouched beside Arites. The electric light was muted but it was enough to show her the wash of blood down the front of his cotton shirt. She pulled the matted fabric aside and saw the angry wound in his chest where the bullet had left his body. *No,* she thought, torn between blank shock and rage. *Just no.* Cletia was telling Cimarus, "Raiders spoiled the trap—"

The floor tilted abruptly, throwing Tremaine forward over Arites. She landed hard, skidding on the deck. Cletia staggered into her brother and they both went down in a heap. "Dammit, what now?" Tremaine snarled, struggling to sit up. The lights flickered and the wrenching screech of strained metal tore the air. Her stomach lurching with vertigo, Tremaine pushed herself up, uncomprehending, and looked out the hatch.

The ramp was gone, the tower was gone, and the dark shape of the mountain was rapidly receding.

Chapter 15

Tremaine started to stand, but a sudden stabbing sensation in her back caught her in a crouch, breathless with pain. She thought for an instant that someone, possibly Cletia, had actually stabbed her. But as she gingerly eased herself down again she realized she had hurt a muscle in her back picking up Arites. *No, don't think about that.*

They were in the airship's cargo hold, ribbed metal struts supporting the sides and roof. A few bare round electric bulbs suspended overhead threw puddles of glaring light down on a cork-covered deck and a small collection of crates stacked in the corner and secured with rope webbing. The open outer hatch framed a dark sweep of sky and the black shapes of the mountains the airship was inexorably rising past. Cimarus was nearest it, staring out in transfixed horror. Clutching her back and trying to ease to her feet, Tremaine said urgently, "Cimarus, close the door. Close the door before someone falls out." It seemed enormously important.

Cimarus didn't move. "Goddamn it." Tremaine cautiously rolled to her knees. If she had wrenched something, surely she wouldn't be able to move even this much. Her mind tried to relive the moment when Arites had staggered into her, knocking her into the railing, and she ruthlessly suppressed it. "Do I have to fucking do everything?" She glared at Cletia. The other woman stared back at her, then blinked, shook herself a little, and pushed to her feet.

"How do I close it?" she asked uncertainly as she moved toward the hatch.

"What do you mean how do you—" Tremaine looked at the door and saw it was some sort of sliding panel. "All right, fair question. Go to the wall there and try to push it from the side."

As Cletia stepped past Cimarus he flinched as if she had woken him from a trance. She leaned on the sliding panel, moving it a few sluggish inches. "Help me," she commanded Cimarus impatiently. Still moving like a sleepwalker, he stepped forward and put his weight against the door.

As it started to rumble closed, Ilias bolted out of the interior doorway and slid to an abrupt halt, staring at the night sky still visible through the hatch.

"Yes, it's what you think it is." Tremaine got her feet under her and stood cautiously, like an old washerwoman; the stabbing sensation was less painful. Ilias moved to her side, catching her arm. She realized she was shaking and hoped he wouldn't notice. He was looking down at Arites, shocked and stricken, but she didn't want to think about that right now. She told him, "We have to turn this thing around, find a place to land."

Cletia got the door shut, Cimarus holding it in place while she fumbled with the unfamiliar handle, finally getting the lock to catch. With effort, Ilias looked away from the fallen man, telling Tremaine, "We found some Gardier on board. There might be more."

Tremaine nodded. *So we'll kill them.* But it was good of him to tell her. Cletia came away from the door, going to her knees next to Arites, and Tremaine knew she had to get out of here now.

"Is he all right?" Cimarus asked, moving to her side.

Cletia shook her head, saying thickly, "He's dead."

"Don't—" Tremaine stopped, lowered her voice to a normal conversational tone and continued deliberately, "Don't any of you say that."

Cletia looked stricken, like a child who had been shouted at, but she nodded obediently. Cimarus looked at the floor, his face white. Maybe Tremaine's tone of voice wasn't as normal as she thought, but it had done the trick.

Ilias was tugging her arm, and she thought, *right, landing.* She followed him up a passage that ran through the airship, passing doors, then an engineering room with fuel vats. Everything was poorly lit by the bare bulbs, now swinging a little with the ship's movement and sending leaping shadows up the walls. They passed Dubos, leaning out of a trapdoor overhead, demanding, "What the hell happened?"

"We lost our mooring," Tremaine answered vaguely, waving him back to what he was doing. "We're working on it!" Past a room littered with blood-soaked dead Gardier, they found Giliead and Basimi at the end of another passage. There were more doors here, all of them opening into small rooms crammed with equipment or storage cabinets. The outer walls of those little rooms had broad slanted windows, looking out into the night sky. The only closed door was the one at the end of the passage, the one that must lead into the airship's control cabin. "I think he's saying we need to get into here," Ilias reported, his voice tense.

Presumably Basimi was the "he." "What happened out there?" he demanded, sounding almost angry. Giliead was looking at Ilias, and somehow must have read the answer to his own questions there. His face set, and he looked away.

Tremaine touched the door. It was thick metal, which was presumably why they hadn't broken it down yet. It was more like one of the *Ravenna*'s watertight hatches than the light flimsy doors in the rest of the airship. But there was a key lock in it. *I can pick that.* Basimi kept asking questions she couldn't bother with right now. "Is there a wireless room we can get to?" she asked, cutting him off.

He stared at her, as if she was the one not making sense, then jerked his head back toward one of the open doors. "Yes, there."

"Send a message to the *Ravenna*, tell them what happened. They're listening to the main Gardier frequency, they should hear it."

"I should be able to tune it to our frequency—" He hesitated. Realizing that if he obeyed this order it would be that much harder to question the next, and the next. Perhaps calculating that with the Syprians present his options for refusing were limited. It didn't tell her what Molin and Dubos would do.

Tremaine turned to face him. "You heard rumors that I'm crazy."

She kept her voice level and even, but something in her eyes made Basimi's expression go wary and still. "Some."

"They're true. But I'm not in the army, and neither are the Syprians, and they think I'm in charge. What do you think?"

He wet his lips, his eyes flicking to Giliead, then Ilias. He said evenly, "I think you're in charge, ma'am."

"Good. Now go send a message."

He nodded shortly and moved past them toward the wireless room.

"Right." Tremaine turned briskly to Ilias. "Do you know where my pack is?"

He stared at her a moment. Then, his face carefully neutral, he lifted the strap on her shoulder. "You mean this?"

Tremaine swore at herself, pulling the leather bag around, fumbling in it for her lockpicks. At least Basimi hadn't been there for that little moment. Even in Syrnaic she would have looked like a fool. "Now let's get this open." Ilias stirred restlessly, not quite jogging her arm, but it jogged her memory. "Oh, the Gardier. You two go look for them."

Giliead touched her shoulder. It was a gesture of shared pain, not sympathy, and that she could take, though she couldn't risk looking up at him. He went down the passage in long strides, ducking his head under the lightbulbs.

"Take Cimarus with you," Ilias called softly after him. "I'll stay with her."

Tremaine found the picks, shaking them free of her handkerchief. "No, you won't, you'll go with him."

Ilias turned back with a protest, but she cut him off ruthlessly. "I don't want him killed because Cimarus was too busy wetting himself in fear at the fact that we're a couple hundred feet in the air. Now go."

Ilias hovered, obviously torn between annoyance and alarm that she was right. After a moment he swore in frustration and followed Giliead.

Tremaine planted a hand on the wall to catch herself if her back tried to give out again and eased down to her knees, eye level with the lock. She pressed her hands together for a long moment, willing the trembling to stop, then carefully inserted a pick into the lock. Investigating the tumblers by feel, focused entirely on that, she didn't look up until she heard a soft step behind her. But it was only Cletia, advancing cautiously up the passage, stopping to look into the room where Basimi worked at the wireless. Cletia saw her glance, and explained, "I'll watch for Gardier while you do that."

Even in her current state, Tremaine had to admit it made sense. Cletia drew her belt knife and stationed herself in the passage, and Tremaine went back to the lock.

Time stopped until Tremaine felt the tumblers click over. The door popped open with a hiss of released air, and she awkwardly pushed to her feet. Cletia turned, drawing Tremaine back hastily, and it belatedly occurred to her that the door might have been locked because someone was inside. She had somehow just assumed the airship had accidentally come loose from its mooring and was drifting.

But Cletia gave the door a careful push and it swung open to reveal a small empty cabin, the front wall of which was all windows, framed by the girders that supported the gondola's structure. The control panel itself was narrow, with a small ship's wheel attached below a box with a few circular dials. There were boxes suspended from the ceiling with more dials, rather like barometers to Tremaine's untrained eye. But sitting in a metal mount above the control panel, glittering malignantly in the yellow cabin light, was one of the large crystals.

Tremaine eyed it warily. That wasn't one of the Gardier's small crystal devices that could perform one or two limited spells; that was one of the "avatars," just like the one Gervas had threatened her with on the island. And if their theories were correct, there was a sorcerer's soul imprisoned in it. A Gardier sorcerer, dangerous and probably angry at being stolen.

"Nothing but stars," Cletia said under her breath. She was looking out the port and the limitless view of the night sky above the dark sea.

Tremaine stepped carefully into the cabin, wondering if she should just grab the crystal and smash it. But if they could take it intact, it might make the disaster of this mission a little more worthwhile. "We're just going straight up. Probably a good thing, or we would have hit the mountain. But we can't do that for long." *Stop babbling,* she reminded herself.

Cletia took a cautious step after her, studying the array of unfamiliar devices in consternation. Then she jerked her chin toward the wheel. "Can it be sailed like a ship? We could guide it back to the Wall Port, or to the *Ravenna.*"

It was the first time Tremaine had heard one of Pasima's contingent lower themselves to say the ship's name. But if Cletia was going to attempt to take an intelligent interest in the problem, she wasn't going to discourage her by pointing that out. "It's sort of like a ship. We have to figure out how to make it go back down." She moved forward, eyeing the various panels dubiously. "A big lever with an arrow on it would be nice—" She caught a movement among the dials, too quick for her to see exactly which one. "What was—"

Tremaine felt a slight jolt underfoot, like a train bumping over a switch. Then a shock of familiar vertigo went straight to her stomach.

Following Giliead, Ilias climbed up the ladder from the vat chamber onto a long narrow catwalk of flat metal bars. It was lined with walls of a slick brown fabric that felt like dead skin to the touch and was lit by curse lights that reflected a dim orange glow. He knew the whole of the upper part of the flying whale was like this, with ladders leading up to yet more catwalks. The other two Rienish had gone to search the rest of the lower part, and this was the only other place stray Gardier could be hiding. There had been one lurking up here in the first flying whale they had encountered, so searching was a necessity. But even knowing the whale wasn't alive, the place still made his skin creep.

Ilias glanced back as Cimarus followed him up the ladder; the boy was trying to look brave, but the color had leached from his skin and he mostly looked sick. Ilias wasn't feeling too great himself as the upward motion of the whale did unpleasant things to both his stomach and his ears, but Tremaine had been right that Cimarus was too distracted and jumpy to be worth much. Ilias exchanged a look with Giliead, who shook his head with a resigned grimace. Giliead told the boy quietly, "See those black ropes connecting the curse lamps? Don't touch them."

Cimarus looked uncertainly up at the thin black rope suspending the globe of wizard light. "If you're dying, on your last breath, don't touch the black ropes," Ilias added more forcefully. Then he remembered that Arites lay dead in the cargo hold below them and wished he hadn't.

When Ilias had first come back from Cineth with the curse mark burned into his cheek, Halian and Karima had pretended not to see it. But he had run into Arites on the path to the sea, and the poet had stopped him with a hand on his shoulder, leaned close to peer at the mark, and said, "Damn, that must have hurt." It had been the first normal conversation Ilias had had in days.

He put the memories aside as they searched the area rapidly but carefully, working their way up catwalk by catwalk. The places where the curse lights weren't lit were the worst, preventing them from checking whole stretches of the catwalk and the lengths of the ladders at once. The delay made Ilias grit his teeth; he was anxious to get back to Tremaine. He knew she was badly upset by Arites's death and that she would hide her grief like she did everything else, packing it all away until it ate her from the inside out.

They found no Gardier by the time they reached the top level, and Giliead turned for the ladder, saying, "There's nobody up here. We need to go back down and . . ." He trailed off, probably because he had no idea how to finish the sentence. Ilias sure didn't.

"Can we get back down?" Cimarus interrupted, his voice rough. "Can the Rien make it go down?"

"Maybe, if nobody asks them stupid questions," Ilias told him.

"What do you know about it?" Cimarus shot back. "You're the ones who brought us here. Visolela said this was mad—"

Giliead, one hand on the ladder, turned suddenly and caught the boy by the shirt, yanking him forward. "Listen to me." Giliead's voice was still quiet, but a muscle jumped above his jaw.

Ilias let out his breath, shaking his head in frustration. When Giliead lost his temper it tended to be all at once, with no warning, at least to the people who didn't know him well. Cimarus was stupid to push old grievances at a time like this.

Giliead said deliberately, "What brought you here is Pasima's distrust of anything that she can't give orders to. That's not my problem. Now keep your mouth shut, or—"

Ilias felt the jolt through the metal underfoot and grabbed one of the support bars. *Falling,* his gut said in panic, but it was over before he could draw breath to yell. Giliead dropped Cimarus and staggered back, shaking his head as if he had taken a blow. Ilias lurched forward and caught his arm, steadying him before he stumbled into the ladder's opening. "What happened?" he demanded, dreading the answer.

Giliead shook his head unsteadily. "We just went somewhere."

Tremaine made a faint noise of protest that froze in her throat. A cloudy gray sky now filled the port in front of her. She flinched back in pure shock. "I didn't do that!"

"Do what?" Cletia stared from her to the port and back again. "It's day. How is it day?"

"Oh. Oh. Oh, damn," Tremaine said weakly. Cletia and the other Syprians would have been in the cabin when the *Ravenna* had moved between worlds to trap the other airship; she wouldn't have seen. . . .

Sick realization set in, and Tremaine wished she was lying next to Arites in the cargo hold. *The sphere is on the* Ravenna. *We don't have a sphere, any sphere. We have a dead Gardier wizard in a crystal who hates us.* "Oh, this did not happen—"

"Stop that!" Cletia snapped, a shrill edge in her voice. "It doesn't help when you say that!"

"Sorry." Tremaine took a deep breath and rubbed her eyes, hoping maybe it would just go away. She looked again. No such luck.

"What is it?" Cletia demanded, strained. "What happened?"

"We—it made a portal. It went through an etheric world-gate." Cletia shook her head, confused, and Tremaine forced herself to explain, "It's how we travel from world to world. How we took the *Ravenna* from Ile-Rien to your world, how the Gardier go from your world to Ile-Rien. Except there are more than two worlds." She had sent Gervas to another world with Arisilde's help, stranding the Gardier in a hellish landscape. *Oh, so this is how poetic justice feels.*

"But you can make it go back," Cletia protested. "If that's how your people travel—"

Tremaine shook her head, pointing at the crystal, glinting dully now in the daylight. Perched in the metal holder, the yellowish tint and dull patches on its facets made it look more like a malignant growth than a piece of rock. "It took us, and it's Gardier. It's not going to listen to me. Oh, wait!" Tremaine grabbed Cletia's arm, staring at the sky. It was gray, too thick with clouds to really see any color. The sky of the world she had sent Gervas to had been red. "Maybe— Maybe it took us back to Ile-Rien. Not Ile-Rien, the distance is all wrong. But our world. In which case, we'd be a few days sail from Capidara." She stepped to the panel and tried to look down to the ground below, something she had been reluctant to do so far. As if seeing what was below them would make it real and put the final nail in the coffin.

But what lay below wasn't that revealing. Tremaine could see only more clouds, as if they were traveling over puffy bundles of cotton wool. *I'm looking down on clouds,* she thought, distracted. How many people now except for Gardier got to see what clouds looked like from above?

Behind her, Cletia said slowly, "Capidara is the land we were going to on the ship."

"Yes. We were going to get near where it would be in your world, then go through a portal to get to it," Tremaine told her impatiently.

"I know, Pasima told us. I meant why would an enemy take us somewhere we were going in the first place?"

"Uh." Tremaine felt a headache coming on. She eased back from the control panel. "Good question." She looked over the dials and other things again, her brows knit. They weren't going up anymore, she realized. The airship was moving forward. *That's not good.*

She heard a noise behind her and turned to see Basimi, his expression aghast, staring past Cletia out the port. "What the hell—"

For some reason his shock galvanized Tremaine. Maybe because she didn't trust him. "We gated," she told him succinctly, eyes narrowing. "Maybe to Ile-Rien. Probably not. Can you or Molin fly this thing?"

His aghast stare switched to her. "Are you—" she had the feeling he was veering away from the word "crazy." "Serious?"

Tremaine lifted her brows, saying acidly, "Does the situation look serious?"

He moved past Cletia as the other woman looked worriedly from him to Tremaine, unable to understand the Rienish conversation. He studied the controls a moment, his face fixed in a grimace. He pointed to one of the boxes suspended from the support girder, one that had a round dial with a pointer surrounded by squiggly Gardier characters. "I bet that's a compass, though I don't know if that symbol at the top is north or not." He looked hopefully at Tremaine.

She shook her head, chewing her lip. "They were studying this stuff at the Viller Institute. Some of them would probably know." Too bad they weren't here. She glanced up at him. "Did you send the message?"

He nodded. "I got an acknowledgment from the *Ravenna,* then it was cut off. That's when I realized the window in the wireless room was showing daylight." He said helplessly, "Ma'am, at most, I was supposed to fly this thing to the *Ravenna.* This is a little beyond me. Before the war I was a shipping clerk for Martine-Viendo. I don't know—"

"Just try, that's all we can do. Look, why is it flying by itself? Is it the crystal? I know you don't know, I just want an opinion."

Putting it that way seemed to help him organize his thoughts. He looked over the controls again, tapped another dial cautiously, muttering, "That might be an altimeter." He shook his head finally. "My opinion is yes, it is flying by itself. Look at the wheel there." He pointed and Cletia, whose face said she was desperately trying to follow the conversation whether she understood a word of Rienish or not, leaned around him to look. "It's moving by itself, correcting our course against the wind. I don't see what else could be doing that but some kind of spell."

Tremaine peered at the wheel. After a moment she spotted the slight motion as the wheel turned to the right, then back. Her stomach clenched. "Oh, great," she said under her breath, glaring at the crystal. *Where are you taking us, you little bastard?* And had it formed the portal on its own, with the spell circle on the outpost, or had it somehow been called back by the Gardier in this world?

"Let me try this—" Basimi touched the wheel gingerly, then with one hand tried to turn it. After a moment, he gripped it with the other hand, shifting his weight to get better leverage. Heart sinking even further, Tremaine watched him apply his full strength to it, until his face reddened and he grunted with effort. He gave up with a gasp, stepping back. "No good." He shook his head, gesturing helplessly toward the wheel. "It's like it wasn't meant to move at all. But I can see that thing steering it."

She heard Ilias's voice in the passage. Cletia turned, ducking out the doorway with a rapid Syrnaic explanation.

Basimi was still looking at her. Tremaine wet her lips, weighing precipitate action versus the chance of making the situation even worse. Picking the lock and the appearance of strangers in the control cabin might have caused the crystal to form the portal.

All right, think. The clouds prevented any view of the ground now below them, but if the airship had been called back to a Gardier base that was occupying the same space in this world that the Wall Port had in the other, surely the airship would be landing at it by now. So the airship was probably traveling toward another Gardier stronghold. "We can try to stop it by taking the crystal out of that holder. Then we'd have control over the airship, at least."

Basimi nodded. "That's about it, ma'am."

"Right." Tremaine stepped to the doorway. She nearly ran into Molin and Dubos, who must have heard everything she and Basimi had said; both men looked grim. Giliead and Ilias were in the passage just behind them, listening to Cletia. Giliead's expression was incredulous, but Ilias just looked dismayed. He was the only Syprian who had been to Ile-Rien and back, with a brief unscheduled stop in Hell when Florian had tried to change the parameters of the reverse adjuration. In the open doorway of one of the side cabins, Cimarus stared horrified toward the window. "And we don't know if we're in the Rien place or not," Cletia was saying nervously. "And—"

"There's a big sorcerer crystal in here and it made the portal and is now flying the airship all by itself," Tremaine interrupted hurriedly in Syrnaic. "I've touched one before, and it didn't hurt me, but I want Giliead to see if he thinks it's booby-trapped."

He was already moving forward, pushing between Molin and Dubos. As he stepped through the doorway he halted abruptly, his eyes caught by the view through the port.

"We're not at that other place, are we?" Ilias asked, coming in behind him. He sidled up to the port as if worried he might fall out through the glass, looking warily down at the clouds below. "The red sky place?"

"No. No, I'm sure . . . not." Tremaine saw Giliead looked a little green. Being suspended in midair had to be a startling experience for the Syprians; she had been in hot-air balloons before, at summer fêtes before the war. Though certainly none of those had ever gone this high. She suddenly didn't want Giliead to exhibit any weakness in front of Basimi, and to distract him said hastily, "Did you feel it happen like before? When we went through the portal?"

He shook himself a little, glancing down at her, and she knew there was no way in hell he was going to show weakness in front of anybody at the moment. "Yes, it felt like— Being pulled through a weir. But fast." He focused on the crystal, taking a step toward it. "I can't tell if there's a curse trap or not. I can tell there are curses on it, or inside it. It's not like your god-sphere, it can't hide itself when it wants to."

"Right." She took a deep breath. "Take it out of the holder."

Giliead brushed the back of his hand against the crystal's milky facets first; Tremaine was reminded of an electrician testing a possibly faulty switch. Then he gripped it carefully and lifted it out of its metal cage.

Basimi slipped past him, sharply eyeing the wheel. He gripped it, leaning on it again with all his strength. He let go, swearing. "Didn't work."

Tremaine squeezed the bridge of her nose. It had been a forlorn hope, anyway. She turned to Ilias and Giliead, saying in Syrnaic, "I need you to look for something. A bucket or container we can fill with water."

Giliead nodded understanding, carefully setting the crystal back into its holder. "You want to put the crystal in water, like you did with the god-sphere?"

"That's it." They had stored Arisilde's sphere in a bucket of water at one point, trying to keep the Gardier from tracing it through the etheric vibrations it emitted.

"Didn't Gerard say that didn't work?" Ilias pointed out, sounding dubious.

Tremaine pushed her hair out of her eyes. "Because we put the Gardier crystals in there with it. And probably because the sphere was touching the side of the bucket. The idea is to insulate it, so we'll have to suspend the crystal inside it somehow."

Ilias lifted his brows. "Without letting it touch anything but water."

"Right." Tremaine was aware she was starting to look desperate.

Ilias threw a worried glance at Giliead, but promised her, "We'll work on it."

Ilias didn't quite shove Cletia and Cimarus down the passage in front of him, but he wanted to. They reached the big room with the wall cabinets and the tables and chairs. "We need to search this thing again, this time looking for water, and something that will hold it, about this big," Giliead told them, holding his hands about a foot apart.

"They must have water and containers for it where they keep their provisions," Cletia suggested.

Giliead nodded, gesturing around the main room. "They have places to sleep aboard this thing, they must have food and water, probably in one of these cabinets somewhere. But before anything else happens—" He glanced down at Ilias, his brows knit with concern. "We need to do the rites for Arites."

Ilias took a sharp breath, looking away briefly. "You're right."

"But should we do it now?" Cletia said, frowning. "We don't know if this is the Rien place, but we know we aren't . . . where we're supposed to be. If we release his soul here, will it be able to find the right place?"

Ilias stared blankly at her, startled, then looked hopefully up at Giliead. "Do you know?"

Giliead frowned slowly, staring into space. "When did he die? I know it was before the daylight came."

Cimarus nodded, glancing at Cletia for confirmation. "I think he died before the flying whale came off the ground."

A brief look of relief crossed Giliead's face. "Then it shouldn't matter. His shade will be back where he died. We can always do the rites again once we get back, just in case, but . . ."

Ilias didn't need to hear that thought aloud. *If we don't get back, we need to do the rites now.* "I'll see if Tremaine can be the third."

Giliead nodded agreement, resting his hand on Ilias's shoulder. "Try to persuade her. I think she needs it."

Cletia half reached toward him, as if she had meant to touch his arm and reconsidered. "She didn't . . . take his death well. I don't think we should—"

"I don't care what you think," Ilias interrupted sharply.

Giliead just eyed her coolly, then jerked his head at Ilias. "We need to get Arites ready."

Cimarus bristled but didn't quite dare to react as Ilias deliberately thumped him with his shoulder as he pushed past.

M a'am, there's a problem."
Tremaine glanced up, blinking. She had stepped out into the passage to rest her aching head against the metal wall for a moment. She thought the headache might be from the altitude, but it could also be from her brain trying to climb out of her skull through sheer terror. Dubos and Molin were talking quietly in the map room, but the steady thrum of the airship's engine made the words unintelligible no matter how close to the open door she edged. She had wanted to sit down, but Arites's presence in the cargo hold had made her allergic to the entire back half of the airship. She pushed off from the wall, following Basimi back into the control cabin. "You can call me Tremaine," she pointed out.

"If you're going to be in charge, I'd rather call you ma'am," he told her, stepping into the cabin. He didn't need to point out what the problem was. They had left the clouds behind.

She moved closer to the streaky glass of the port. The late-afternoon sun shone out of a reassuringly blue sky smudged with gray rain clouds, but it wasn't the brilliant azure of the Syrnai or the winter blue of Ile-Rien and Capidara.

Some distance below the airship, patchy sunlight glinted off water. Shallow water, tinged brown with sand or dirt, with wavelets washing up on small irregular patches of land crested with grass. *A tidal flat?* she wondered. In the distance was the darker outline of more solid land, but much of it was obscured by a bank of mist and rain. It fit in with her theory of a nearby Gardier base terribly well. *With the accent on terrible.* She wet her lips. "It still might be—"

"Look up." Basimi leaned passed her to point, the sleeve of his fatigues smelling of grease and fear sweat. "There."

She looked. In a patch of open sky she could see the outline of the moon, faded as it always looked in a daylit summer sky. Basimi showed her a smudged scrap of paper where he had worked out dates and the phases of the moon. "It's full. It was waning when we were at the Wall Port, and I worked out that it should be half-full at home." He met her eyes, his face bleak. "We aren't home, and we aren't in the Syprians' world."

Tremaine rubbed her forehead. *I think I'm going to be sick.* "Shit." *We need a sorcerer.* What they had was a Chosen Vessel.

"And that thing is taking us straight to the Gardier," Basimi added, glaring at the crystal.

That at least she could do something about now. "I know how we can get that thing to let go of the controls."

He stared at her worriedly. "Without breaking it? We need it to get back."

"Without breaking it. The others are looking for the things we need. I'll go see if they've found them yet."

"Ma'am, there's another problem." Basimi stopped her before she could step out the door.

How soon I grow to hate those words. She reluctantly turned back to him. "What?"

"I was pretty sure this was a fuel gauge, and it looked like it was showing empty." Basimi tapped one of the dials. "I sent Molin back to bang on the tanks, and they sounded hollow. It means the Gardier didn't refuel at the Walls. They must have meant to do it in the morning."

"Great," Tremaine said under her breath. The Gardier didn't seem to have very good fire prevention methods in place inside their airships. All their wards seemed to be meant to protect the things from outside attack. Not letting a fueled airship sit around at its mooring tower was at least a sensible precaution. *But it's killing us.* If they could get the crystal's cooperation, they needed a vehicle to take them back to the point where they had passed through the etheric gateway, so they would be close enough to the Wall Port spell circle. But an airship with no fuel was useless. "Check. Find fuel."

She started down the passage, but found Dubos and Molin waiting for her outside the map room. Dubos gave her a fatherly smile, or what she supposed was a fatherly smile, since Nicholas had certainly never looked at her in such a fatuous way. He said, "We need to talk sense, Miss. Now we both know you can't be giving orders to us in a matter of life and death. If you want to be in charge of your native friends there, that's fine, but . . ." He shook his head, his expression of benevolent kindness inviting her understanding.

Tremaine thought it over, absently rubbing her jaw. As she saw it the problem with telling people you were going to kill them was that sometimes they believed you, then you had to do it before they could counterattack. And she had acquired a loose tooth sometime in the past hour. *I'm just so tired.* She nodded slowly. *And Arites is dead, and he was funny and nice and I liked him, and he liked me.* "How many times have you opened an etheric world-gate?"

Dubos's benevolence faltered just a little. Molin's eyes flicked to him and away. *Right. I know whose idea this was. It's always the polite ones you have to watch out for; at least the bastards are being honest about their feelings.* She continued idly, "I've forgotten how many times I've opened gates with Gerard. I did it once by myself with the sphere. When I say once, I mean just there and back. Which makes me the closest thing to a sorcerer we've got, and we're going to need one to make the crystal take us home." She jerked her head toward the control cabin. "Oh, I don't know if you've noticed, but we're not in our world, and we're not in the Syprians' world. I think I know how we can take control of the airship back from the crystal without destroying it—since it's our only way back, that might be a bad idea—and I was going to get Giliead— that's my brother-in-law—to help me, but you're right, I should just bow out now, before I make a mistake." She shrugged. "So. Basimi's waiting." She gestured helpfully toward the control cabin. "Have at it."

She could feel their eyes on her back as she went down the passage. She stopped in the main room, threading both hands through her hair and swearing in frustration. She needed to settle Dubos and Molin quickly. But the ability to cut off the crystal's control of the airship was her only advantage at the moment. She sure as hell wasn't going to tell them that the only person on board with any chance at all of communicating with the crystal was Giliead. Ilias came into the room, his face grave and tired. She asked, "Did you find a bucket?"

He looked at her for a moment, his brow creasing. "The others are looking. But there's something you and I and Gil have to do first."

"What?"

"We need to do the rites for Arites. So he won't be a shade."

Tremaine stared over his shoulder a moment, then shook herself a little. The image of the dead stowaway boy Giliead had found came to her, haunting the empty children's playroom. "Yes, I see. I have to be there?"

"You need to learn how to do it," he told her firmly. "So you can do it for us if you have to."

Tremaine clapped a hand over her eyes. She wished he hadn't put it quite that way, but it made it impossible for her to refuse, which was probably his intention. "All right."

Ilias led her back down the narrow passage to the crew cabins. Giliead was waiting for them in the open doorway of the cabin nearest the cargo hold, his expression sober.

She looked inside to see Arites laid out on the bunk. His face was relaxed, but the bloody wound in his chest allowed for no sentimental illusions; it had been a violent and painful death.

Tremaine had seen more dead bodies than she could count in the Siege Aid Society and the bombings of Vienne, and she had caused a few deaths herself, from the one in the mental asylum to the Gardier attempting to escape the Isle of Storms by airship. This was the first one that felt like a kick in the gut.

Giliead stepped into the cabin, and Ilias gave Tremaine a gentle push to get her to follow him, saying, "If someone dies at home, you scatter three handfuls of earth on the body. If they die elsewhere, or at sea, or if you find a stranger's body, you use three locks of hair. It's usual to get three people, but if you're alone, you just use three locks from your own head."

Tremaine nodded. "Is that all? What do you do . . . afterward. With the body."

"A pyre, or a burial, or give it to the sea." Ilias shook his head slightly, as if it truly didn't matter. "If we can get him back with us, we'll do that. But if we can't, it's all right, as long as we do the rites."

Giliead took out a horn-handled belt knife, found a braid that had come loose and cut an inch of hair from the end. Then he took a handful of Ilias's hair and did the same. Ilias was still looking at Arites and didn't react to the tug and snip.

Giliead handed Tremaine the knife, and she realized this was a truncated version of the actual ceremony. There was obviously a specific order in who cut whose hair, but it wasn't important she learn it. If one of the others was with her, she would have someone to show her the order; if she was alone, it wouldn't matter. She cut a lock from under her ear and gave it to Giliead.

Chapter 16

Adram was out on the broad third-floor balcony, looking over Maton-devara. He had taken in this view often, but it never failed to strike him anew. It had once been an elegantly designed city, with spacious stone buildings looking down on a thriving port. It was still a thriving port, but the temporary structures housing the labor and the Service workers crowded the streets until it resembled a hive more than a place of human occupation. It was teeming with people in the ubiquitous brown uniforms or the drably colored clothes of the civilians, and the cool morning air was heavy with the odor of diesel fumes. He lifted an ironic brow, leaning his forearms on the carved scrollwork of the railing. He had seen slums that were more attractive.

"Adram, there you are." It was Benin, and even though the chief Scientist was the closest thing he had to a friend here, Adram made sure his sardonic expression had changed to a noncommittal smile before he turned. It was wasted on Benin, who was too excited to notice. "Adram, we are about to capture a Rien raiding party."

"What?" he demanded, badly startled. "Where?"

"Here!" Benin drew him away from the balcony, into the wide arch of the doorway, as if he feared someone passing below might overhear. "We've had contact with our presence aboard the Rien ship, but it had no way to convey their exact location until they reached the

Barrier post. It wasn't able to warn us of the attack the Rien made on the compound—"

"An attack on the post?" Adram frowned. "How can that be?"

"They were able to destroy the airship on patrol, then infiltrate the native city without our watchers noticing." Benin's expression was sour. "I'd like to blame the inadequacies of Command's defenses, but it's more likely they used that device. They were already in the compound, aboard the airship docked there, before there was a hint of anything wrong, apparently. At least, that's what I understand from our presence. None of the men at the post escaped." He gestured excitedly. "But the avatar aboard the airship gated back here, and it must have a party of Rien aboard. This is our opportunity. They must have one of the devices with them, or they couldn't have infiltrated the post's perimeter without warning."

Adram nodded, thinking hard. "Yes, this is a fantastic opportunity," he said slowly. Fantastic for him. "Can you get me assigned to the search group?" At Benin's startled expression he hastily amended, "I know Command is to be trusted, but I know you want to be sure the device is brought to you. . . ."

Benin smiled knowingly. "I was hoping you would volunteer. Frankly, I trust no one else. Command can order the Service not to destroy it, but I don't trust them to obey such orders in the heat of battle." He clapped Adram on the shoulder, a rare gesture from a member of the Aelin's high rank.

Adram nodded in relief. "You won't be disappointed in me. Though . . . what if the Rien have already destroyed the device? They may do so to keep it out of our hands."

Benin looked grave. "It's a possibility that concerns me. But you must make sure at least some of them are captured alive, so they can tell us all they know of it." He snorted wryly. "With that, at least, Command should have no difficulty. Questioning recalcitrant prisoners is the favorite duty of men like Disar. I suppose it's the only pleasure left to him." This remark was treading uncomfortably close to treason, and Benin threw a penetrating look at Adram.

Adram kept his face sober. "You can trust me."

Benin nodded, clapping him on the shoulder again. "I know I can. Come on, I'll get you assigned to the search."

Chapter 17

Florian's first indication that things had gone horribly wrong was when Kias grabbed her arm.

They were crouched in the rock below the lower-level approach to the Gardier's camp. Florian was keeping one eye on the slim form of Birouq, the young soldier who had taken the place of the Gardier sentry, and the other on the dark outline of the airship's mooring tower. After Kias and Arites had killed the Gardier and dragged him away, Birouq had stepped into the man's place, so any observer above wouldn't notice the missing sentry. It was too dark to see much, but Kias was at her side, and Arites had moved off to cover the other half of the approach from the city below them.

She had bit her tongue in anxiety when the searchlight had started to sweep the compound and swore in relief when the sphere burned it out a moment later. *I just wish they'd let me use the sphere,* she thought, shifting uncomfortably as she knelt in the gravel. *It likes me; they didn't need to risk Gerard on this.* He was the most powerful sorcerer they had left; he might be the most powerful sorcerer all of Ile-Rien had left, if the Gardier had destroyed the people trapped behind the barrier in Lodun. It should be her job to take the risks in the field, leaving Niles and Gerard to protect the ship. But she was all too bitterly aware that no one would risk sending her as the sorcerer unless they thought it was a suicide mission, just as the rescue party to the Isle of Storms had been. *How does Tremaine do it?* she thought in frustration. *Being half-mad helps, but she's made them realize she can do the job.*

Kias stirred beside her, and she felt him brush her shoulder as he turned back toward the steps down into the deserted Wall buildings. "What is it?" she whispered. She didn't know him as well, but like all the Syprian men she had met, he treated her with a combination of chivalry and casual acceptance that made him easy to be around.

"Somebody's moving down there." He stood up suddenly and she heard his sword clear leather. She looked worriedly toward the post on the rise above them, afraid the Gardier would see the abrupt movement. Then something whistled past her head just as Kias yanked her out of the way. The darkness was suddenly populated with shouting shadows; she staggered as someone slammed past her. *Gardier,* she thought in shock, scrambling to retreat and finding her back against the rock. Then she heard the clash of metal and saw the outline of an upraised sword.

Kias struggled with one of those shadows and suddenly went down. Florian leapt forward, throwing herself down on him and gasping out her concealment charm. She looked up, her throat tight with terror, to see two tall figures standing over them. She couldn't see their faces in the dark; there was nothing to tell her what they were except the odors of sweat, blood and filthy leather. More figures, dozens more, streamed up the stairs from the upper section of the city. It had been completely deserted earlier as she and the others had crept up it, she was sure of that.

The moment stretched, then one of the men muttered something in a language she didn't understand, and they joined the yelling mob heading up toward the post. Florian let her breath out with a shudder.

In the dark and confusion the charm worked better than it ever had for her before; people veered around them without even pausing. In the heavy dark she couldn't see Arites or Birouq and with Kias unconscious she was afraid to call for them and break the charm. Kneeling beside Kias, she touched his head gently, feeling wetness on her fingers in the tangle of his braids, and groped for a handkerchief to press against the wound. He stirred, groaning, and she whispered hastily, "Don't move!" She started to tell him about the concealment charm, then bit her lip, realizing he might think of it as a curse. *Better not,* she thought.

He lay still. She heard shots and screams from the post above and swore under her breath. *What happened?* She couldn't believe it had gone so wrong.

Then she heard voices calling in Rienish and more gunfire. The men who had burst through here like a hurricane were suddenly fleeing back down into the city in ones and twos. This was rapidly followed by the most welcome sound in the world, the whoosh-thump of an electrical generator exploding.

"Thank God," Florian breathed.

"What was that?" Kias demanded, sitting up.

"The sphere—it's destroying the post." The gunfire had stopped as well. The sphere must have turned the Gardier's own mechanical disruption spell against them again.

"We need to get up there." Kias struggled to his feet, and she gripped his arm to keep him upright, dispersing the charm with a gesture. He staggered, clutching his head.

"Who's down there? Birouq?" Someone called from above in Rienish.

"It's us," Florian called back. "What happened?" An electric torch flashed and Kias winced away from it, but Florian saw men in Rienish gray fatigues. She helped Kias sit down on the rocks, then blundered after the soldiers.

"What happened?" she asked again.

The one with the torch shook his head, answering, "Natives from the port attacked the place before we moved in, set off those spell wards."

"And I think we lost the damn airship," someone with an Aderassi accent said.

"Lost it?" Florian repeated, startled. She peered up past the outcrop. There was just enough reflected light for her to make out the top of the pyramidal mooring tower; the giant dark shape that had been attached to it was simply gone. *Oh, no.* "Where's Tremaine and the others?"

"I don't know, ma'am. Just stay down here until they say the area is secure."

One of them tossed her an electric torch; switching it on, she found Birouq's body on the paved flat. The light revealed the bleak sight of a dark stain on his chest; she thought it must be a stab wound. She searched, increasingly worried, but couldn't find Arites anywhere.

Stepping into the passage again, breathed in relief, mostly that it was over. She doubted the little ceremony would bring her any peace, but maybe it was too soon to tell.

Ilias shook out his hair, looking relieved himself. "Should we go try to put the wizard crystal in water now?"

"Oh." She rubbed the bridge of her nose to cover her expression. "Not yet."

"Not yet?" Ilias repeated, puzzled.

Giliead eyed her with one brow lifted. Tremaine couldn't stand that steady regard, considering what she was going to have to ask him to do at some point. She stepped into the cargo hold, gesturing at the crates in the corner. "Let's see what's in these." She grabbed the net that held them in place, trying to pull it off.

Still looking thoughtful, Giliead moved her out of the way and started to unhook the webbing. Ilias glanced around the hold, then picked up a leather bag that lay near the wall, saying, "This belonged to Arites. He'd want you to take care of it for him. It's got his writings in it, the ones he didn't leave on the ship."

Tremaine backed away from his attempt to hand it to her. "Why would he want me to take care of it?" From what she had understood of Ilias's explanation of Andrien family relations, Arites had been a free agent.

"Because you're a poet too," Ilias pointed out patiently.

She accepted the bag reluctantly and Ilias went to help Giliead, heaving the first loose crate down from the stack. *Poet*, Tremaine thought. It was another slight mistranslation of Syrnaic, since it was what the Syprians called anyone who wrote. Her plays and magazine writing had been a part of her life left behind when the war started. But she found herself taking a seat on the deck and opening the bag.

Inside was a roll of the rough Syprian paper, tied with leather string. Pushing it aside she saw there were a few sheets of the ship's stationery in the bottom, with Arites's wooden pens and a little carved stone bottle of ink with a cork stopper. There was also a collection of trinkets: copper earrings incised with Syrnaic characters, smooth bone counters painted with primitive little figures of animals and people, woven strips of cloth in a range of warm colors. She pulled out a handful, wondering.

"He brought those to trade for Rienish things," Ilias explained, glancing up from the crate he was prying open. "There should be some in there. He has lots more back on the ship."

She dug further, finding the cache of souvenirs. There were buttons, a box of matches, a watch crystal, a wine label and a few battered sepia postcards, one showing the Queen Ravenna Memorial, another the Opera House at Givarney, a third the Summer Palace in Parscia. He had gotten a good deal for the postcards she decided, tucking them back into the bag. The places they depicted might not exist much longer. She unrolled the scroll to find it covered in messy Syrnaic handwriting. "He was writing a chronicle of all this, wasn't he? What happened on the island, the trip to Capidara."

Giliead was looking into the open crate with an air of dissatisfaction. Ilias came over to peer at the script, running a finger along one of the lines of text. "That's just what happened since we reached the Walls. He probably left the rest back with his other things."

Tremaine pulled out a page that had two columns of words on it. "What's this?" It was more neatly lettered than the other sections, but she thought it was the same handwriting.

"Those are words in Syrnaic." Ilias pointed to one column, then the other. "And those are the same words spelled out the way they sound in Rienish, or as close as he could come."

Tremaine stared at the neat columns, flabbergasted. "He was making a Syrnaic-Rienish dictionary?"

Ilias frowned. "What's a dictionary?"

"It's a list of words, and what they mean." *He was making a Syrnaic-Rienish dictionary and he didn't know what a dictionary was.* And Arites had been a young man; if he had lived, what else would he have contributed to Syrnaic letters? For some reason this thought made tears sting.

Then someone coughed in the doorway, and Tremaine looked up, hastily wiping her eyes. Cimarus stood there, holding a small metal crate. He offered diffidently, "I've found something that will hold water."

Tremaine rolled the pages up hurriedly, tucking them back into the bag and setting it aside. "Let's see it."

He carried the crate over, depositing it on the deck with a grunt. "It's heavy, but it's the right size." He opened the lid. The sides were of some heavy dull-colored metal and the inside was padded and lined with a slick brown cloth. Tremaine thought it looked rather like a case for a delicate philosophical instrument. Or a delicate sorcerous instrument. *Oh-ho.*

Ilias leaned in to inspect it, lifting his brows. "It's exactly the right size."

"It smells like the crystal." Giliead came over to crouch next to them, examining the box carefully. He glanced at Cimarus. "Where did you find it?"

"In the bow, the third little room to the right, in a cabinet." Cimarus eyed the box dubiously. "It's a curse box?"

Giliead exchanged a thoughtful look with Ilias. "In the flying whale we found on the Isle of Storms, there was a crystal in that room. It wasn't in a case like this."

"That's where we found the maps," Ilias elaborated.

"Maybe they use the crystals for navigation." Tremaine nodded to herself. The Gardier used crystals for their wireless; they might rely on spells instead of navigational instruments as well. She gave Cimarus a rather twisted smile. "Good job. This is exactly what we need."

Cimarus was looking at them all as if he suspected their sanity. He said carefully, "I don't understand. If the crystal is in water, it can't make curses?"

"Etheric vibrations—curses—can't travel through water," Tremaine told him.

"So why don't they drown wizards?" Cimarus wanted to know.

Giliead made a faint derisive snort. Ilias rolled his eyes, and said, "Because they have plenty of time to kill you."

"And in Ile-Rien it's murder and somewhat illegal, but the point is"—Tremaine dragged the conversation back to the topic—"etheric vibrations also can't travel through certain metals, like iron. Like this box is made of." Feeling a lecture coming on about how something as simple as the laying of train tracks had relegated the fay, once a major threat in Ile-Rien, to a mere nuisance, she sat back. "So it's perfect."

Cimarus accepted that with a nod, getting to his feet. "I'll tell Cletia to stop looking."

Tremaine agreed absently, tapping her fingers on the box. Ilias nudged her. "Let's go try it."

She bit her lip, considering. "No. Not yet."

Giliead frowned. "Why not?"

Before Tremaine could think of an answer, she heard a slight scuffle in the passage as Cimarus met someone coming this way, and they must have had to squeeze around in the narrow space to get past each other. This gave Tremaine a chance to shut the lid of the box, scramble up and assume a demure seat on it with Arites's bag in her lap by the time Molin stepped into the room. He glanced guardedly at Ilias and Giliead, who were both watching him with nearly identical suspicious expressions. He told Tremaine, "Basimi wants you to come up and show him how to stop that crystal without breaking it."

Tremaine looked up at him quizzically. "I imagine he does." She added with a shrug, "Do you happen to know how close we have to be to an etheric spell circle to make the gate open?"

Molin, unexpectedly, buried his face in his hands. "We don't have time for this."

"Funny, that's what I was thinking," Tremaine agreed sincerely.

He shook his head wearily. "I'll go talk to them."

Ilias watched him go, frowning. "What was that about?"

Tremaine let out her breath, trying to think of a way to explain it that wouldn't get anybody killed. "Dubos wants to take over."

"Take over?" Ilias stared, affronted. "Take over us? Like Ander?"

"Not like Ander. Ander has qualifications for the job." Ander, personal conflicts aside, she would have trusted. He knew enough about the spheres and the Gardier crystals to listen to her, and he was experienced with etheric gateways. He might be an ass at times, but he was an ass who got his men out of tight situations mostly alive. Whether Giliead would have seen it that way or not, she couldn't tell. "But, yes."

Ilias's face went still and he consulted Giliead with a glance and a lifted brow. Giliead thought for a moment, eyes narrowing. Then they both started to stand.

"Hold it," Tremaine said sharply. "Not yet."

Ilias stared pointedly at her. Tremaine stared pointedly back. Then Ilias muttered something in exasperation and threw his arms in the air. Giliead made an annoyed huffing noise and returned to the box he had been digging through.

Tremaine rubbed her eyes. Maybe she shouldn't have pushed it to this point. Maybe she should have just stood aside and offered advice in a loud voice until somebody listened to her. But if Giliead thought another man, any man other than Ilias or maybe Halian, was behind the idea to get him to speak to the crystal, there was no way he would entertain it for an instant.

It wouldn't work with an ordinary sphere, like the one Niles had made. But the Gardier crystals, the large ones anyway, had to store a sorcerer's consciousness the same way the Damal sphere had somehow come to store Arisilde's. That was the theory, at least. An ordinary sphere needed a sorcerer who knew the etheric gateway spell in order to make it work. Arisilde's sphere already knew the spell; it just needed access to the spell circle and to be asked nicely, the way Tremaine had asked it when she had dumped Gervas in another world. The Gardier crystals had to work the same way, considering she and Cletia had seen this one make a gate for the airship with no assistance whatsoever. She just had to hope that the crystal could hear and respond to Giliead, the way Arisilde could. And that it could be bribed. The bribe wasn't a problem; Tremaine was fairly sure a Gardier sorcerer crystal that decided to switch sides could write its own ticket once they returned to the *Ravenna*. Up to and including the spell for one of Ixion's makeshift bodies, no matter what they had to do to Ixion to get it.

If this bit of blackmail with Dubos didn't work . . . She hoped that maybe she would only have to kill him. She found, amazingly enough, that she didn't want to kill anybody. She propped her chin on her hand, looking at Ilias. "So you'd throw someone off this thing if I asked you to?"

Prying open another crate, Ilias paused to consider this, staring thoughtfully into the distance. "I don't know. Do you have any of those chocolates with you?"

Tremaine felt herself smiling. There was no word for "chocolate" in Syrnaic and Ilias had used the Rienish word, slurring his way through the pronunciation. "Yes, but I was saving those to bribe you for sex."

"Oh." Ilias gave her a crooked smile, apparently liking the implication that he could be had for a handful of pastilles. If she persuaded Giliead to make the crystal work for them and it somehow changed what Giliead was, or how he thought of himself, Ilias would hate her.

Wrestling down another crate, Giliead paused to give them both a withering look from under lowered brows, but Tremaine saw amusement there too. Surely it wouldn't be too hard to talk him into it. Surely he would see reason. Watching his faintly disgusted expression at finding the crate packed with pistols, she felt a distinct sinking sensation. And then there was Ilias.

Pulling out brown parcels that looked like folded Gardier coveralls from his crate, Ilias asked seriously, "Do you really have some?"

"No, unfortunately." Tremaine heard someone coming down the corridor and pretended to be engrossed in searching through Arites's bag again, only looking up with an inquiring expression when Dubos stood over her. Grim-faced, he said, "We're nearing land." Ilias and Giliead had both gone still, watching him with concentrated intensity.

"Then you better do something about it, hadn't you?" Tremaine shouted at him, suddenly fed up. She dropped the bag and surged to her feet, ignoring the warning twinge from her back. "This thing is taking us straight to the Gardier and I could stop it, but I can't do it with you lot that can't tell an etheric gateway from your own assholes second-guessing and arguing with me. I'll listen to you about explosives and whatever else it is you do, but this is what I do, and you can damn well listen to me!"

Dubos stared at her, breathing hard. Tremaine was peripherally aware that Ilias had come up on the balls of his feet, near enough for comfort but not close enough to take Dubos's attention off her. The man said angrily, "We're dead if you're not right."

Tremaine rolled her eyes. "Oh please, we're dead now. We died the moment that crystal gated us. You want me to do something about it?" She met his hard gaze, adding persuasively, "You can always kill me if I mess it up."

Dubos swore, scrubbed the sheen of sweat from his forehead with a sleeve. "God help us, you are crazy. You're in charge."

Tremaine gave him an ironic nod. "Thank you." She told Ilias in Syrnaic, "We win. Grab the box."

She managed to stride purposefully rather than run toward the control cabin, Ilias behind her with the metal box, Giliead following him and a desperate Dubos bringing up the rear. She wished she hadn't told Dubos that he could kill her if she failed. His eyes hadn't even flicked to Ilias or Giliead looming behind her, which meant that getting rid of her that way hadn't crossed his mind the way it had more than crossed hers. And if that was the case, then maybe he was just trying to do what he thought was best, and she didn't want to know that.

They passed Cletia and Cimarus in the main room, both looking up from prying open a recalcitrant cabinet. They had bundled the Gardier corpses out of the way, and apparently wrenched open every locked container in the room. An assortment of ration packages and canteens were piled on the floor.

"I'm a wireless operator, I don't know how the hell I got elected to drive this damn thing—" a sweating Basimi was saying as she reached the control cabin. He broke off, staring hopefully from Tremaine to Dubos as they all crowded in. "Did you work it out?"

"You were right," Dubos told him grimly, gesturing to Tremaine.

She was too busy staring out the port to mind the byplay. The sky was still misty and patchy gray with clouds, but the airship seemed much lower now and a wide stretch of beach, dotted with clumps of seaweed and driftwood, lay beneath them.

Ilias put the box on the floor, opening the lid. He looked up at Tremaine, tossing his hair out of his eyes. "Ready?"

Tremaine nodded tensely, looking at Giliead. "Let's try it."

Giliead gazed firmly at the crystal as if challenging it. Then he pressed his lips together and seized it, lifting it out of the holder. *God, I think he can hear it,* Tremaine thought, her stomach clenching. And if putting it in the container didn't work . . .

Giliead placed it carefully in the nest of padding and Ilias closed the lid, pressing it down until the catch snapped into place. Everyone looked to Basimi, who rubbed his hands off on his pants and took hold of the wheel. He yelped, "That's it!"

The relieved swearing and enthusiastic back-patting from Dubos and Molin made translation into Syrnaic unnecessary. Giliead picked up the container, saying, "I'll put this somewhere out of the way."

"Wait." She took a deep breath. Time to broach the idea of communicating with the crystal to Giliead. "The next thing we need to do—"

"The hell—" Molin stared out the port, his face aghast. "Airships! Two of them!"

Tremaine stepped to the port, bile rising in her throat. *No. Not now.* A dark shape dropped out of the clouds, the jagged fins etched against the sky, some distance off this airship's bow. She didn't see the second one, but Basimi pointed, and there it was, angling up toward them from inland.

"They're firing!" Dubos yelled, starting back. "Get down!"

Either Ilias and Giliead understood that much Rienish or the man's body language told them all they needed to know. Ilias stretched, grabbed Tremaine's arm, and yanked her back through the doorway. She heard the distant crackle of machine-gun fire as Giliead ducked through after her and the other men hit the floor.

Heart pounding, Tremaine flattened herself against the metal wall, Ilias tense beside her, and Giliead crouched in the hatch. There was no crash of breaking glass.

Cautiously, Tremaine peered back inside the control cabin. "Nothing happened."

"They shot into the balloon." Crouched on the floor, Basimi stared upward as if he could see through all the layers of duralumin and membrane. "Must have pierced some of the cells." He sat up enough to see the controls, tapped one of the dials. "We're losing altitude." He added grimly, "They want us alive."

"Don't these things have wards?" Molin demanded, kneeling on the floor.

"Not anymore." Tremaine grimaced. "They're all tied in to the crystal. We got rid of them when we shut it up."

Everyone was staring at her. Angrily, Dubos said, "So it's put it back and lose control, or try to run for it with no fuel and a holed balloon and get shot down?"

"We can't run," Basimi said urgently. "Some of the hydrogen cells might already be on fire."

"Don't we have guns?" Molin protested. "I found the bomb bay and it was empty but—"

"I don't know where the controls are." Basimi gestured helplessly. "There's nothing here— maybe in one of the other rooms— I don't know if they're even loaded—"

Tremaine stared at the dark shapes outside the port. One was hanging off, the other coming rapidly closer. Giliead and Ilias were both watching her worriedly, Ilias glancing from her to the port. No time, and they were miles away from the spot where they had first gated, miles out of range of the Wall Port's spell circle. She could feel the airship losing altitude, feel the deck sinking under her feet. The Gardier airship would be right on top of them as they went down. *Yes. Yes, it will.* "Can we blow this thing up?" she interrupted. "Set the fuel on fire, or something?"

Dubos turned to her, his expression intrigued. "Of course. Without wards, these things are flying bombs."

She nodded to herself. "Then we let them force us down, then blow this thing up. If we're lucky, we can take out one of them too." The Gardier craft were warded, but wards might not hold against a burning airship slamming into them.

"Uh." Basimi stared at her. "With us on it?"

"No, we're jumping off." She turned to tell Ilias and Giliead, saying in Syrnaic, "We're going to get close to the ground and jump out, and we won't be able to use the airship again because we're setting it on fire. Tell everybody to get any supplies we need to the cargo hold, but only what we can carry. Oh, and that Gardier clothing you found. And the crystal in the box is the most important, that goes before anything else."

Ilias tore down the passage, Giliead pausing to grab the crystal's box before striding after him. The others were still staring at her. "Well?" she demanded. "Are we blowing this thing up or not?"

Dubos drew a hand over his face, then suddenly grinned. "I guess we're blowing this thing up." He shoved to his feet and pushed out past her.

Basimi waved Molin after him. "Get the maps and their code-books!" Still in a crouch, he turned the airship's wheel, aiming it further inland.

Am I forgetting anything? Tremaine wanted to pace as she racked her brain, but there was no room for it, and she was still leery of gun-fire through the port. Outside she could see they were moving over dunes tufted with long yellow grass, the detail growing sharper as the airship sank lower. "You're doing that, right?" she demanded.

Basimi nodded sharply. He was gripping the wheel tightly, guiding the airship closer to the ground in a tightening spiral. "I'm forcing it down, making us look like we're dropping faster than we really are. When I leave the controls, it'll drift back up a bit. Hopefully right into the Gardier."

Guns crackled again, somewhere behind them. Tremaine flinched but didn't hear any kind of an impact; just a warning. Then she saw the roof of a wooden structure pass below them. Suddenly she and Basimi had a good view of steeply pitched roofs, battered by wind and storms, with round stone chimneys, then they were out of sight.

Tremaine found herself meeting Basimi's eyes. He licked his lips, brow furrowed, and said, "People. More Gardier."

She said coolly, "Those didn't look like military buildings. If it's a civilian town, that will just make it easier to find a boat to get back within range of the Wall Port spell circle." *It's amazing how I sound like I know what I'm doing.* It was better than sounding terrified.

It convinced Basimi, at least. He nodded more firmly and turned his attention back to the controls. He was guiding the airship into another turn, bringing it further down toward the dunes below. "You'd better get back there. I'll try to bring it to a stop and we can jump then."

Tremaine started for the door, then hesitated. "Don't wait too long," she told him, suddenly worried he might mean to sacrifice himself. She didn't know if Basimi had the martyr temperament or not.

"Don't worry about me," he assured her fervently. "I can't wait to get rid of this damn thing."

Reassured on that score, Tremaine headed down the passage at a trot, wincing as it jarred her sore back. She found Dubos in the fuel room. He had his pack on the floor beside him and was attaching something with a long fuse to one of the machines there. "We're nearly down," she told him. He nodded and waved her on.

She passed down the row of crew quarters, hesitating outside the room where Arites's body lay. Ilias had said a pyre would do, that the method didn't matter as long as the rites had been done. She shook herself and went on.

The others were in the cargo hold and Tremaine did a rapid head count, making sure they were all there. The door was open and Ilias and Giliead had taken the cargo netting off the crates and were rigging it up as a rope ladder, tieing it off to the hooks near the hatch with Cimarus and Molin's help. "Brilliant," Tremaine muttered to herself. She sure wouldn't have thought of it. Fresh air heavy with damp and the salty-foul scent of marshland streamed in through the opening.

An anxious Cletia waited with their packs in the center of the room; someone had wrapped a rope around the box with the sorcerer crystal, tieing it up like a parcel with a loop to sling over a shoulder. Tremaine grabbed her pack out of the pile, opening it to see Arites's bag tucked inside. She made sure her pistol and the remaining cartridges were still there, then grabbed a couple of Gardier pistols from an open crate and scooped in extra ammunition for them. She closed the flap, fastening it down tightly, and slung it over her neck and arm.

"Arites?" Cletia asked her. She threw a glance at Ilias and Giliead. Ilias tested the knots attaching the net to the floor hooks, and Giliead leaned dangerously out of the hatch, studying the ground below. "We leave him?"

"We're going to burn the airship once we're off," Tremaine told her. Ilias didn't comment but she saw him lift his head and knew he had heard her.

"Oh, that's all right then." Cletia looked away in relief.

Tremaine heard the low buzz of the engine cough and sputter, then catch again. Giliead shouted roughly, "Come on, we're low enough!"

Cletia grimaced and grabbed a couple of pack straps, heading for the hatch. Tremaine caught hold of the ropes attached to the crystal's box and hauled it after her. Giliead took it away from her as she got it to the hatch, pushing it out and using the rope to lower it.

Tremaine blinked out at the gray sky, seeing the dunes below and the tufts of yellow grass much closer than they had looked from the control cabin. Ilias and Cimarus were already on their way down, swarming down the wildly swaying net like the born sailors they were. Reaching the end of the net, they dropped to the soft sand below, rolling to absorb the impact. Giliead, bracing his back against the side of the hatch as he lowered the heavy box, advised her, "Try to go limp when you drop, let yourself fall and roll."

"Oh sure, that's likely," Tremaine snapped. Taking a deep breath, she crouched, took a firm hold on the net and swung down.

She climbed clumsily, the heavy knotted cords scraping her hands, cursing Ilias and Cimarus both for making it look easy. Above, Cletia was flinging out their packs. The hard part came at the end, when her reaching foot found empty air. Gritting her teeth, afraid to look down, Tremaine freed her other foot and let go.

The ground was nearer than she thought and she hit sand and tumbled down the side of a dune. Winded, she rolled over, feeling her back twinge in complaint. She sat up gingerly, managing to spit out some sand. Cletia was just dropping to the top of the dune above her, the dark bulk of the airship blotting out most of the sky overhead. Tremaine couldn't see the first Gardier airship, the one that was just above their airship, but the other was circling in, still some distance off. She saw with relief that Giliead had lowered the crystal's box and that Molin was starting his climb down. The rise of the dune blocked her view of Ilias and the others. Her back throbbed in earnest as she flailed to her feet and stumbled through the soft sand.

She managed to get around the dune to where Ilias was waiting, glaring up at the airship. He spared her a glance, calling, "You all right?"

"Fine." Cletia and Cimarus were scrambling around picking up the packs and Molin had the bags with the Gardier wireless books and maps. Tremaine spotted the crystal's box sitting heavily in the sand. She reached it, standing protectively over it as she gazed up at the airship. She could see Giliead still in the hatchway, but no sign of Dubos or Basimi. *They can't talk to Giliead,* she thought. *Dammit, I should have stayed up there to translate.* Ilias started swearing, using some words the translation spell hadn't included.

"I can't hear the engine," Tremaine said under her breath. She couldn't remember if the low buzz had been absent before she had fallen into the dune, or if it had just now ceased.

Their airship started to drift upward, the wind pushing it a little away from them. The nose of the Gardier airship bearing down on it appeared just past the dark bulk. Tremaine's stomach clenched and she heard Ilias make a helpless noise in his throat. She drew breath to yell, to tell Giliead not to wait for the others, to get out now.

Then Giliead swung out on the net and Dubos and Basimi appeared in the hatch above him. Ilias bounced in pure relief, punching the air. Tremaine wanted to sit down on the box and put her head between her knees, but there wasn't time. "Come on," she shouted, dragging at the box. "It's going to blow up! The damn things fall when they blow up!"

"Go!" Ilias waved the others on and grabbed up the box. Tremaine ran with him, the sand dragging at her feet, stumbling as she looked back over her shoulder at the two airships. Giliead and the other men were on the ground now, rapidly catching up with them. With no one at the controls the airship rose, closer and closer to the Gardier ship, which suddenly began to angle away from it. Gunfire sounded, and bullets peppered the sand only a few feet away.

Then the gray daylight went yellow. Tremaine stumbled, looking back up to see their airship's balloon suffused with red and orange, burning from the inside out. It drifted sideways, brushing against the Gardier airship, which was turning sharply to escape.

Basimi arrived at her side, panting, his forehead streaked with sand and sweat. "The wards," he muttered. Clouds of black smoke belched from tears in the membrane of their craft, blocking their view of the second airship still some way off.

Tremaine just watched. The Gardier wards might be like the ones on the *Ravenna;* she was thinking of the door to the Isolation Ward, which had given way in a burst of etheric energy when it was hit by a force too strong for it to resist. The gondola of their airship was burning furiously now and it abruptly came loose, crashing to the ground in the marsh. Relieved of that weight and with so many of the individual hydrogen cells torn open, the enormous balloon rolled sideways, enveloping the other airship. "That's got to do it," Tremaine murmured.

The explosion staggered her back; she winced away from the burst of flame and the wash of heat.

Ilias pulled at her arm. Giliead had taken the crystal's box away from him and stood at his side. Cletia, Cimarus and the others were staring up at the fiery spectacle.

Tremaine nodded, turning away from the burning airships. The other Gardier airship would come, but hopefully they would think everyone aboard their quarry had died in the fire. She felt stretched nearly to the limit, as if her endurance and sanity would just snap at any moment. But they had a long way to go.

I t was still dark when another soldier finally arrived to tell them the outpost was secure. With her borrowed electric torch and Kias at her side, Florian climbed up the sloping path to the promontory.

It was lit by carbide lamps now, the stark light revealing the bodies of the Raider mercenaries sprawled everywhere, in twisted heaps. Florian's stomach roiled at the smell of charred flesh in the cool damp air. The men had been hit with fire, with choking clouds and other Gardier attack spells; they had been helpless against them. Rienish soldiers moved among the bodies, looking for survivors, but there didn't seem to be many. "This would have happened to us without your god," Kias said softly, finding a path through the carnage for them.

Florian just nodded, not bothering to correct him about Arisilde Damal's godhood. She had been awake so long the scene was beginning to take on an air of unreality. She made it to the first metal building without throwing up and saw several dead Gardier lying beside the doorway, killed by Rienish gunfire when the sphere had stripped away the post's defensive spells. There were men inside, searching cabinets and poking through the debris with electric torches. She asked about Gerard and was directed to a large structure at the rear of the camp.

Kias looked around as they made their way between buildings, but with the confusion of lanterns and flashing torches and Rienish moving everywhere it was hard to make sense out of the chaos. "I can't see Giliead or Ilias," he told her, sounding worried. "They're usually easy to find."

"I expect they're with Gerard." But she kept expecting Tremaine to appear. And she was concerned about Arites.

The ruined generator was still belching black smoke into the air and they detoured around it. They found the large building with its double doors standing open, lit by several powerful carbide lamps. Florian grimaced at the sight inside. "Giliead was right, it was a spell circle. *Was* being the word."

The circle was about twenty feet across, neatly painted in white on wood panels laid out on the dirt floor. But about halfway around the familiar symbols were singed and the wood scarred, as if something powerful had burned the circle away. *Something powerful did just that,* Florian thought soberly. Gerard knelt near the edge of the circle, writing in a tattered pocket notebook, the sphere sitting on the floor beside him. She could hear it clicking and spinning even from the doorway.

She stepped cautiously inside. The metal tripod in the circle's center, where the Gardier placed the sorcerer crystal that powered both the circle and the etheric gateway spell, was just a lump of melted metal and glass shards, still steaming in the cool air. "Gerard?"

"Florian." Gerard glanced up briefly. "Sergeant Mastime told me he'd located you and Kias, and that poor Birouq didn't make it."

"Yes, the Raiders— We didn't see them coming, he didn't have a chance." She looked for Kias and saw he had remained prudently in the doorway. He was eyeing the circle suspiciously. "But Arites was with us, and we can't find him. And where are Tremaine and Ilias and the others? I thought they would be with you."

Gerard scribbled another note. "They were on the airship."

Florian halted. "What?" she said sharply.

"The *Ravenna* received a wireless message just before the airship vanished through the etheric gateway. The boarding party was attempting to enter the locked control room door. Tremaine was with them." He lifted his head finally, and his face was bleak, the lines around his eyes and mouth accentuated by the stark light and his exhaustion. "That's the last we know."

Florian looked at the burned symbols, sick. "They can't come back through this circle. But the *Ravenna*'s circle—" She blinked in horrified realization. "They don't have a sorcerer. Gerard, they don't have a *sphere*."

On the floor the sphere spit angry blue sparks. Gerard got to his feet, moving like a weary old man. "They have nothing," he said bitterly.

Chapter 18

Tremaine wiped sweat from her brow, nervously scanning the sky again. From the still-rising clouds of black smoke, the burning airships had drifted further away and crashed in the marshy flat.

They were slogging through the dunes in the direction of the houses she and Basimi had seen from the control cabin. The sky seemed even more heavily overcast and the air was cool and damp, the light breeze carrying a salty tinge. Ilias had found some driftwood, and he and Cimarus dragged it along behind, using it to obliterate their tracks. Tremaine hadn't thought of that and was glad they had. Not far ahead, as the dunes flattened out into grassland, lay the cover of a spreading forest. The trees were short and scrubby with light gray bark and tiny sprays of leaves.

It seemed a little crazy, even to Tremaine, to go toward where the Gardier had to be, but they needed transportation. They had to find something at least capable of allowing them to return to the vicinity of the Wall Port so they could use the spell circle. If the *Ravenna* had left by then . . . *Then we'll be stuck there,* she thought in annoyance. Her speculations on possibly making a deal with the Chaeans or some other traders for passage close enough to Capidara to make an etheric gateway were interrupted when she realized that wouldn't work. Capidara didn't have a spell circle, at least not yet. The way the *Ravenna* traveled with her own spell circle gave the ship maximum mobility in creating world-gates; they no longer had that advantage. *And I have to convince Giliead to make the crystal work for us. And he has to convince it to take us where we want to go and not kill us.* One thing at a time, she reminded herself with a mental groan. Right now they had to worry about not getting caught.

Molin said sharply, "The other airship."

Swearing, Tremaine looked wildly around until she spotted it. It was just cutting through the lower level of clouds, pointing away from them, heading toward the column of smoke still rising darkly from the marsh. The others were already running for the forest and she bolted after them.

Reaching the shelter of the green canopy was a profound relief. "I don't think it saw us," Dubos said quietly, as they moved further in over a carpet of dead leaves, their steps crunching quietly. Tremaine thought they would know soon enough.

They were well into the woods when Giliead halted abruptly. Tremaine held up a hand to tell the others to stop. She realized she had used the same gesture Ander did and felt absurdly self-conscious. But it worked as Dubos and the others jolted to a halt.

Giliead looked back, collected Ilias by eye, then told Tremaine, "We're nearly to that village. We need to scout ahead." Ilias jogged up to join them as Giliead set the crystal's box down. Ilias touched Tremaine's arm lightly, as if making sure she was still there.

"Right. We'll wait here." Tremaine used her sleeve to wipe sandy sweat off her face. Giliead had had plenty of time to get the lay of the land while leaning out the airship's hatch, but she had the suspicion that everybody knew more about what was going on than she did.

Tremaine watched them dodge through the trees until she lost sight of them. Dubos and Basimi moved to her side, Basimi asking, "They're scouting ahead?"

"Yes." Tremaine nodded, losing a little of her tension. She had thought they would object. Cimarus was hanging back, watchfully studying the terrain behind them for signs of pursuit. She suspected he would be more use now they were on the ground, in a situation he was more familiar with. Basimi just stood there, drawn and exhausted, but Dubos and Molin kept their eyes moving, wary and tense. Cletia was pacing back and forth, moving up through the trees a little to look after Ilias and Giliead, then restlessly returning to the others. She wore her sword slung over her shoulder as the Syprian men did. Cletia had a brain to go with her attitude, Tremaine decided. She hadn't frozen up aboard the airship.

Tremaine worried a fingernail until she bit it to the quick and tasted blood. Time passed at an unendurably slow crawl. "They got them," Molin muttered.

"No," Tremaine snapped. Ilias and Giliead had spied on the Gardier for days in the base in the Isle of Storms' caves. She didn't think they would be caught. And it was too quiet. *If the town is that close, why can't we hear anything?* Why weren't the people running out to watch the airships burn?

Everyone heard Ilias coming back before she did. She watched him running lightly toward them. Giliead wasn't with him, but he didn't look too worried. He came to a halt in front of her, reporting quietly, "The village looks empty. There's no sign of anyone."

She hadn't been expecting that. "What do you mean, empty? You mean they went to the airship wreck?" Cletia was at her elbow, listening intently, and Tremaine shifted to make her back up a step.

Ilias rubbed his arm across his forehead, leaving a streak of sand and soot. "No, it's deserted. Grass is growing between the stones in the street. And the houses we looked into were empty."

Tremaine bit her lip. "A ruin?" She was thinking of the underground city on the Isle of Storms, and the remnants at the Wall Port. Did the Gardier have some odd habit of choosing long-deserted dwellings to establish their bases? But how long could wooden houses last on a seacoast with no one to take care of them?

He shook his head. "Gone a few years, maybe more."

She nodded slowly. *That's odd. But if they left boats . . .* "Show me."

The others reluctantly agreed to stay behind and Tremaine followed Ilias to the edge of the woods where Giliead waited. There was an old dirt road there that turned to cobbles as it entered the little town.

Tremaine saw it had been the only street, that the houses spreading out from it were linked by dirt or gravel paths. All the pathways were littered with dead leaves and fallen branches.

The houses were built of some kind of gold-veined wood, with round chimneys of the same small gray stones that formed the cobbled street surface. The windows were round as well and the tops of the doors curved to match, and the sills seemed to be molded of clay. Unlike Syprian dwellings, there were remnants of glass in the windows.

"The Gardier must have driven these people away when they built their stronghold here," Giliead said softly, as they picked their way down the street. Broken glass crunched under the litter of leaves and dirt. "Or killed them all."

"Or took them for slaves." Ilias gave the ruined town a dark look. "How many people can they war against at once?"

"More than we thought, apparently." Tremaine stepped close to a wall, picking at the metallic glitter buried in the board, thinking it was gilding. But it was part of the wood, another texture woven in with the grain.

It was all so picturesque that Tremaine wondered for a moment if it was fake, not really meant to be lived in. In Ile-Rien before the war, romantic little villages were often temporarily constructed in the Palace park and the Deval Forest, as part of the winter and summer festivals. But this was too big, there were too many houses. She peered through a shattered window to see broken bits of furniture, rotted drapes of faded fabric clinging to the walls. The wind had covered the floor with a carpet of sand and dirt and some animal had carried in bones and what looked like cracked crab shells. She shook her head, making herself focus on the problem at hand. "No sign of a harbor?"

"I don't think there is one, just the beach and the marsh," Giliead told her, his brow creased.

"We should go that way and look for boat sheds." Ilias jerked his chin toward the end of town. "But if their boats were just drawn up on the beach, they'd be washed away in the first storm after the place was abandoned."

"Right." Tremaine grimaced. She had assumed that a seaside town automatically meant a harbor, but with this marshy coastline there might not be any deep-water boats at all. Her stomach clenched. *Just a little boat, just enough to get back to where the Walls would be and make a gate to get to them. That's all we need.* "How far is it? Should we get the others or leave them in hiding until we find something?"

Ilias looked up at Giliead, consulting him, and Giliead shook his head, saying, "Let them stay there for now. Until we went up in that thing, I never realized how much they can see from above. It's better if fewer of us are moving around."

He was right. Tremaine groaned under her breath. "Come on."

Ilias slipped ahead of her, leading the way between the houses, staying close to the gold-veined walls. The ground here was uneven, covered with weeds and high yellow grass, and Tremaine tripped over half-buried stones that might have marked the borders of garden plots, and once a battered iron pot. The houses here had fared worse; some roofs had given way, and one or two whole structures swayed over in the midst of complete collapse. Then the houses stopped at another wide cobbled walkway with nothing beyond it but the dunes tumbling down to the edge of the wide beach. Ilias threw a grim glance back at her. "I think we found their harbor."

"Shit," Tremaine said succinctly. Sometime in the past a channel had been dug from the beach up through the sand to the cobbled walkway, which must have served as a dock. Now the channel was empty of water and silted up nearly to the level of the houses. It would have been harder to tell what it was, if there hadn't been several sailboats all bigger than the *Ravenna*'s launches and the even larger shape of a barge half-buried in the silt.

Tremaine rubbed her eyes, remaining on the walkway as Ilias and Giliead jumped down to investigate. Chunks of driftwood, dried seaweed and a few bright orange crabs bore witness that the sea must still fill the silted channel during high tides. The buried boats must have been inundated every day, and their sails were just ghostly tatters, the hulls battered gray wood. Digging the channel had been an enormous job; it was all such a lot of work to go to waste.

Ilias looked into one sailboat, kicked the broken hull of the other and came back to scramble up onto the walkway beside Tremaine. He didn't say anything, just threw her a worried look. *Yes,* Tremaine thought, suppressing a groan, *we're dead.* Now the only source of transportation they knew of was the Gardier stronghold their airship had been heading for. Wherever it was.

Ilias reached over and took her hand, squeezing it reassuringly. He was still watching Giliead, who had climbed up into the wrecked barge and was poking around inside. "We just have to keep moving. Gil and I have been in worse places."

"Where?" Tremaine started to ask, but Giliead jumped down from the barge and ran back across the channel.

"What is it?" Ilias demanded as Giliead boosted himself up onto the walkway.

Giliead drew them both back into the shelter of a battered wooden awning. "That was a Gardier ship," he said grimly.

Tremaine looked at the dark hull, intrigued. "How can you tell?"

"It was metal, and it had the same kind of moving thing your boats have down inside it."

"An engine? Did it look usable? By us?" *By people who don't know what they're doing?* was what she meant. Though Molin was an engineer, maybe he could . . .

He shook his head. "It was full of sand. It's been here at least as long as the others."

"Maybe we could—" Dig it out, conjure spare parts to fix the engine, drag it out to the water, borrow fuel oil from the Gardier. "Never mind." She clapped a hand over her eyes. "Let's go back to the others, figure out where to look next." *Tell them I don't know what the hell I'm doing.*

Taking a careful look up at the sky, Giliead started back through the town. "We'll find something," he said over his shoulder. "That's not enough fishing boats for a village this size. There's got to be more somewhere. There might be better anchorage on the far side of the marsh."

Following, Tremaine knew that wasn't necessarily true. She looked back at the barge, cursing it for being useless. "The Gardier must have left that here when they attacked. Does that make sense?"

"No." Ilias glanced back at her, frowning thoughtfully. "Why not take it away to fix it?"

She had to agree there. It was the losers who left wrecks behind, not the winners. Not when they had bothered to build an outpost on the captured territory.

Giliead stopped abruptly, head tilted to look up. "Flying whale."

Tremaine saw the dark predatory shape dropping out of the clouds and swore. Ilias must have been keeping an eye out for likely places to hide; he caught Tremaine's arm and they bolted for a shadowed doorway in the next house.

Inside the door Tremaine stumbled on the debris-covered floor, feeling something mushy and soft through the thinner soles of Pasima's boots. Grimacing, she placed her feet gingerly. This house had a number of large windows and the broken glass was mixed with the softer rubble. "Did they see us?" she demanded.

"I doubt it, not from that angle." Giliead remained by the door, flattening himself to the wall to see out.

Ilias leaned around him. "I think they're going back toward the flying whale fire."

Wanting to distract herself from a situation she could do nothing about, Tremaine looked around, squinting to see. Even with all the windows, the cloudy sky wasn't allowing much light in. The one windowless wall was lined with shelves built into little cubbies. Some of the little cubbies were still stuffed with objects that she couldn't quite make out in the dimness.

She moved cautiously toward it, hearing glass crunch underfoot. At closer inspection, the contents of the cubbies looked like rolled-up sheaths of leather. *So this was a shoemaker's shop?* she wondered. She poked at one, shook it by the end to frighten away a score or so of large beetles, then pulled it out. It wasn't until she unrolled it that she realized it was a book.

It was wide, the leather cover soft enough to be able to roll up or fold. The paper bound into it with heavy cord was thick and soft, more like cloth than parchment. The characters were too regular to be handwritten, the lines too rigidly formal. The pages had been printed in a press. She stared at those characters, trying to think why they looked familiar. She realized she still had her pack, with Arites's bag tucked inside it. Ignoring the bugs and the mushy debris, she crouched down on the floor to fish it out, thinking, *this was a library.* The stuff underfoot was composed of pages that had fallen or been washed out of the shelves and soaked in water. It turned her cold to imagine the Albaran Library at Lodun or the city libraries in Vienne reduced to this state.

She found the last page of Arites's chronicle and twisted around to let the dim light from the window fall on it. She saw at first glance the Syprian characters were completely different, but as her eyes drifted down the page . . . "Well. That's a kick in the ass for you," she said under her breath.

"What?" Ilias asked.

She looked up to find him and Giliead leaning over her, trying to see what she was so intent on. "The flying whale is gone," Giliead explained. "What's that?"

"This is Arites's writing." She flattened it on her knee so they could see, and Ilias knelt at her side for a better look. "This is where he copied the markings on the Gardier buildings when he drew a map of the outpost. Now look at the printing in this book."

Ilias leaned closer. "It's the same. This squiggle here, and all those. It's Gardier writing?"

Giliead pulled another one from the shelves, flipping it open.

Tremaine shied away from the rain of beetles and got to her feet. "I think they're all filled with Gardier writing," she told them, pulling another book out at random.

Ilias watched for a moment, then threw a worried glance at the door. "We need to keep moving."

He was right, they couldn't spare the time for this. Tremaine tucked away Arites's page, then on impulse shoved in three of the Gardier books, bending them to make them fit. "Let's go."

She followed both men outside, casting a nervous glance up at the now empty sky. Giliead picked the path again, finding a winding way through the houses, taking advantage of all the cover the overhanging roofs offered. "These people have the same language as the Gardier? Or they attacked their own people?" Ilias asked her over his shoulder. "Why?"

"I don't know why, but I think they did." Tremaine looked at the houses they passed, seeing them with different eyes. She had assumed this was a society as primitive as those in the Syrnai or the Wall Port. But the glass windows, the printed books and the dredged canal all painted a different picture. The barge marooned there must have belonged to the town like the sailboats, not the town's conquerors. If this town had been conquered at all, and not simply abandoned for some reason.

Taking quick looks through each open door they passed, she spotted something on a wall and stepped in to look. It was a carved wooden box with a glass dial in the center marked with the Gardier characters. It had five hands, but it looked a lot like a clock face. Tremaine brushed dust off the carving. It was delicate work, the fine lines incised into the wood, then somehow filled with pigment. The design was of various hot-air balloons, some far more elaborate than it seemed possible to construct. One looked like a Gardier airship, but in this depiction the spiked fins seemed fanciful rather than intimidating. "That's what I thought," she said to herself.

"Will you come on?" Ilias hissed at her from the doorway.

As they reached the edge of town, Tremaine could tell Ilias and Giliead were relieved to return to the relative security of the trees. That light green canopy looked delicate, but it was just enough to mask them from any view from above. She followed them without really seeing where they were going, too lost in thought to pay attention.

Then Ilias stopped suddenly and Tremaine walked right into him. Feeling lucky that his sword hilt hadn't given her a black eye, she saw he was studying the ground. Whatever it was, Giliead's attention was caught by it too. He turned, circled wide through the brush, then came back to the same spot. Giving in, Tremaine asked impatiently, "What is it?"

"Someone crossed our path," Ilias reported, pacing to the side, eyes still on the ground. "Not one of our people. The feet are too small and the boot print is wrong."

"Not a Gardier, then. At least not—" Tremaine didn't hear anything, but she caught the way Ilias's face went still and the sudden look he threw at Giliead. Giliead didn't acknowledge it but turned away, moving with apparent idleness toward a thicker stand of trees obscured by brush and reeds. Ilias started casually in that direction too, his eyes still on the ground. But something about the way he held himself told Tremaine that his attention was elsewhere. Scratching her head and looking anywhere but at the brush, she continued randomly, "At least not so that we could tell, since really, just the feet. But—"

Whatever was in hiding abruptly woke to the fact that it was being stalked. It burst from cover on the far side of the stand of trees. As it ran further into the woods, Tremaine caught a glimpse of a small figure, possibly a boy, dressed in dark clothes. Both men bolted after him and Tremaine bolted after them.

Running full out, she could just keep Ilias in sight as he dodged through the trees. Then he stopped abruptly and darted in another direction. Stumbling to a halt and listening hard, Tremaine thought he had stopped running. Picking her way cautiously, she spotted him standing back against a tree trunk, watching something through a screen of brush. Trying to make her steps silent, she carefully edged up to his side. He took her arm, showing her the gap in the leaves to look through.

Their prey had led them to the edge of a nearly dry riverbed that cut through the forest, its wide sandy banks sloping gently down to a shallow stream of water that trickled over rocks and gravel down the center. As she watched, the boy trotted up to a small camp under the overhanging trees near the bank. A little fire smoldered and a woman was kneeling next to it, using a rock to scrape the skin off a grubby yellow root vegetable. The boy was apparently telling her about his encounter, pointing back toward the woods. Three younger children gathered around, wide-eyed. A jury-rigged tent had been made from a gray blanket and a rope stretched between two saplings; a couple of battered canvas bags seemed to be their only possessions. "He tried to double back on us, but he led us right to them," Ilias commented in a whisper. "How stupid was that?"

"Suicidally stupid," Tremaine agreed softly. But maybe the boy wasn't used to being tracked by Syprians. The boy, the woman and the children were all dark-haired, pale-skinned, lean and bony, though that might be from lack of food. Their clothes were grubby gray or brown, pants and loose shirts, all the same except the woman seemed to be wearing a tabard over hers.

Ilias looked around as Giliead ghosted up through the trees. Ducking to stay out of sight of the camp, Giliead whispered, "There's no one else nearby."

Ilias nodded. "Well?" he asked Tremaine.

She bit her lip, considering it carefully. It was a chance to get some information. These people didn't exactly look like a Gardier patrol, but if they raised an alarm . . . *We'd have to kill them. I'd have to kill them.* She was suddenly very aware of the weight of the pistol tucked into the back of her belt. *Well, probably not the kids.* They looked too young to give coherent reports. But the woman and the older boy. She let out her breath. Oddly enough, it was harder risking other people's lives than it was to risk your own. "I'll go talk to them. You two stay back."

"Wait." Ilias stopped her as Giliead cut back through the trees again and Tremaine realized he was working his way around behind the little camp. She adjusted the set of the pistol, making sure the tail of her shirt hid it. Ilias nodded at some invisible signal, though Tremaine couldn't see Giliead at all now. "Careful," he told her.

"Right." Tremaine couldn't look at him when she needed to concentrate. With one hand behind her back resting on the pistol's grip, she stepped out of the brush.

The woman stared at her, then scrambled to her feet. The boy pointed, saying urgently, "I told you!"

He spoke in Gardier, though his accent was thick and different from the prisoners aboard the *Ravenna*. Again, it was disorienting to hear the language without the translator. The woman snapped a word at him Tremaine didn't catch, then glared at her suspiciously. "Who are you?" Her face was set in hard lines but her voice trembled just a little. The other children, so young and dressed in such baggy clothes they might have been boys or girls, stared too, the youngest one sucking on a finger.

At least she hadn't started screaming about Rienish invaders.

Tremaine had to focus a moment to make sure she spoke Gardier and not Rienish or Syrnaic. She had spoken it to Ander and Gerard for practice, but this was different. "I'm a traveler." The woman's frown deepened. Tremaine restrained herself from shouting "Where's a damn boat?" It would be better to work up to that. "Do you live in the town?" she asked.

The boy stared past her, obviously trying to see if Ilias or Giliead were with her. He said, "No, the *Domileh* don't let anyone live there."

"The *Domileh*?" Tremaine inquired cautiously.

"We don't use that word anymore," the woman said hastily. "He means the Command."

Scientist, Command and Service were the classes or ranks the Gardier were organized into. *So far, so good.* "Why don't they want anyone to live in the town?"

"They said it was dangerous, too vulnerable."

The woman was staring at her as if she was insane. Tremaine wasn't sure if that was because her questions were strange or the woman was just uncannily perceptive. "Too vulnerable to what?"

"To attack."

This was beginning to resemble the interrogation of their late un-lamented prisoners. Nothing but short vague annoying answers. "Attack by who?" she persisted.

"Is this a trick?" the woman demanded suddenly. "We follow the rules, we don't go there."

Tremaine pressed her lips together. *I'm inclining toward violence again.* "Look. We don't come from here." Belated inspiration struck, and she added, "We've been traveling a long way, we don't know the rules for this area. Could you tell us what they are?"

The woman's expression hovered between suspicious and dubious. "I didn't know there were places with different rules, not anymore."

Tremaine spread her hands helplessly, trying to look innocuous rather than dangerously annoyed. "Neither did I."

"Why aren't those men with you in the Service?" the boy asked suddenly. "They didn't look like Labor."

That was the word Gardier used for slaves. The woman threw him a quelling glare. Making a hasty change of subject, she said quickly, "The rules say we can't live in Devara, or any of the other old places."

"Devara is the town? The only town nearby?"

"Yes." She hesitated. "It's the only one before the Maton."

Tremaine nodded, trying to think of a way to ask what the hell a

Maton was without arousing their suspicions. She decided to just assume it was a place to live. "Does the Maton have a harbor?"

"Yes, it was built where the port was." The woman looked honestly
curious for a moment. "You really come from somewhere else?"

"Yes. Uh . . . how is the war going?"

She shook her head wearily. "I don't know. They used to announce
about it in the Maton, but since we left . . ." She made a throwaway
gesture.

Right, Tremaine seethed inwardly. *Who cares? We destroy so many
places.* But this woman didn't exactly look like she was reaping the
benefits of a conquering army. "Which way is the Maton again?"

Giliead stepped out of the brush suddenly. The children scattered
in terror and the woman backed away in alarm. The boy turned to her
triumphantly. "I told you I saw—"

"Gardier are coming down the streambed, eight, maybe more,"
Giliead said urgently.

"Boring conversation anyway," Tremaine said under her breath,
turning to run. Just as she reached the brush she heard a man shout
in Gardier. She looked back to see the woman's face twist with fear
and anger. She shoved the boy away. "You led them down on us!"
Calling to the other children to follow her, she grabbed the youngest
and ran away down the sandy bank of the stream.

"Wait—" Tremaine started automatically, then snarled, "Oh, forget
it." Ilias caught her arm, propelling her toward the woods and she
took the hint and ran.

A scatter of shots sounded behind her and Tremaine staggered into
a tree, looking back. She saw Ilias only a few steps from the safety of
the trees, staring out at the creek bed. The woman had made it across
the shallow stream but lay sprawled in the mud just beyond it. The
three children were huddled in confusion beside the body.

Tremaine saw Ilias take a step toward them and drew breath to yell
at him. Then brown uniforms appeared through the screen of leaves
and she heard men running down the bank, splashing in the water.
Ilias ducked into cover and Tremaine turned and ran.

Ducking low branches and stumbling over the rough uneven
ground, Tremaine suddenly realized the boy was running with her.
They came out into a small clearing and the boy looked around
wildly and started to bolt to the left. Tremaine lunged and caught his
hand, jerking him to a halt. "Not that way!" she snapped, then had
to repeat it in Gardier when he stared at her blankly. Running wildly,

he would lead the patrol right down on them like that stupid woman probably had.

Tremaine pulled him with her, taking as straight a path as possible away from the streambed at a rapid walk. If Ilias and Giliead didn't catch up with her soon . . . The boy, unexpectedly, kept a tight grip on her hand. *So he's not as feral as all that,* she thought cynically. "Just keep moving," she told him, keeping her voice quiet.

She heard branches stir behind them and spun around, free hand on her pistol grip. It was Giliead, pushing quietly through the brush to join them, his face set in grim lines. "Where's Ilias?" she demanded.

"He's covering our trail." He glanced at the boy. "The woman was dead. They took the other children away."

She looked at the boy too. He was staring wide-eyed at Giliead. And he had a bag of rough cloth slung over his shoulder. She said in Gardier, "Give me the bag." If he had a weapon in it, she didn't want to get stabbed in the back.

He glared at her. "I didn't steal it. I was going to follow her, until I saw—"

Tremaine felt a surge of cold rage that had nothing to do with the boy's refusal. *Stupid woman ran into them and got herself killed right in front of me.* The Gardier patrol must have assumed she was a fleeing Rienish spy. *Instead of me.* And left the children to be picked up by the soldiers. She didn't suppose that Gardier foundling houses would be any better than their slave camps. She repeated, "Give me the bag."

He met her eyes, his glare wavering, and handed over the bag.

She slung it over her own shoulder and started away. Giliead gave the boy a gentle push to get him moving again. She said in Gardier, "The patrol killed that woman. Was she your mother?"

He shook his head. "My mother died in the Labor pens in the Maton. That was Besta."

"Why were you with her?"

"Someone told the Proctors about things my mother said and they put her in Labor, and gave me to Besta. Besta's man died in Service and she was going to have to go into the Labor if she couldn't find another place. So she left the Maton, and I went with her."

Tremaine frowned. "And they shoot people who leave the Maton?"

He hesitated, throwing a wary look at her. "She stole from the town, Devara, the one we're not supposed to go into. She thought they might come after her."

Ilias caught up with them before they reached the others. The boy flinched at his appearance, then carefully peered around Tremaine to stare at him. "They lost our trail and went back to the stream," Ilias reported. "We need to get out of here." He glanced at the boy, concerned. "Did you tell him about the woman?"

"Yes." Tremaine asked the boy, "Do you know the way to the Maton?"

He looked wary again. "Yes."

Cimarus or Cletia must have heard them returning; they entered the clearing to find the others already on their feet and collecting their belongings. Giliead moved immediately to pick up the crystal's box. "We heard the shots," Basimi told her. Frowning in confusion, he nodded to the boy. "Who the hell is that?"

Tremaine grabbed one of the supply bags Cletia had packed, slinging it over her shoulder. "That's our native guide."

When it was nearly too dark to see, Cimarus appeared next to Tremaine to say, "Ilias says we should stop now."

Tremaine halted, leaning against a sapling, and wiped the sweat from her brow. They had walked for the past few hours, finding their way along the edge of the salt marsh. There were thick stands of trees and boggy patches of mud, and ponds choked with reeds and water lilies with unexpectedly beautiful purple and white flowers. The Gardier boy knew the general direction of the Maton, but he admitted that he had always traveled on the roads. It was the Syprians who were finding the way and keeping them moving through the dense woods at close to a run.

Tremaine had a stitch in her side and wet feet, so she said, "Oh, so we're saying his name now, are we?"

Cimarus shifted uncomfortably. He had always been carefully polite to her, either out of Syprian respect for women in authority or fear of reprisals from Ilias and Giliead. But it hadn't escaped her that he tried his best to treat Ilias as a nonperson. Tremaine rubbed at her sore foot through the damp leather of her boot, letting him stew for a moment, then said, "We'll stop now."

Basimi, Dubos and Molin weren't far behind her, burdened with the packs from the airship. "What are we doing?" Molin asked as they came to a squelching halt in the muddy grass.

"Stopping for the night," Tremaine reported, starting to pick her way in the direction she thought Cimarus had taken.

"Good, can't see a damn thing." Basimi sounded weary.

After a few moments of picking their way through the damp darkness under the trees, Giliead's voice said quietly, "In here."

"Here" turned out to be a stand of larger trees with denser canopies, set up on a little island of dry ground. It was choked with vines and saplings and Tremaine had to fight her way through until she stumbled into a cleared space, lit by a small fire half-buried behind a bank of dirt. Ilias was crouched next to it, carefully feeding it twigs. The fallen branches had been used to make a second canopy, shielding the fire's light from above. Cletia and Cimarus were sorting through the contents of a pack, and the Gardier boy sat nearby, hugging his knees and staring at the fire. The crystal's box was planted in the middle of the makeshift camp.

Tremaine let her bag fall and wearily eased herself to the ground. The place didn't look easy to stumble on and the fire's light was invisible from any distance away. No one would spot this as a campsite. Except for the fire, it didn't look like a campsite even when you were sitting in it. In Ile-Rien, this was the kind of country where you carried a pocketful of old iron nails in case you stumbled on a hungry fay. Tremaine just hoped that if this world had the equivalent, their pistols would discourage it.

Dubos, Molin and Basimi dropped their packs and sat down, Dubos nodding approval of the camp's concealment. "They'd have to land right on top of us to find us."

Molin shook his head wearily. "Don't give fate any ideas."

Giliead appeared with an armload of wood for the fire, depositing it and shouldering Ilias aside. Ilias gave way, shifting over to sit next to Tremaine, then lying down to rest his head in her lap. She ruffled the warm weight of his hair. His queue was loose again and he had leaves stuck in the tangles. Cletia threw a look at them but dropped her eyes rather than get into a staring contest with Tremaine, who was in no mood to lose. Basimi had gotten out one of the maps from the airship and was trying to read it by the dim firelight, Molin already seemed to be asleep and Dubos was repairing a broken muddy bootlace.

"Any problem with junior there?" Tremaine asked Ilias, idly rubbing the back of his neck. The Gardier boy was still glaring sullenly at the fire, but there was just enough light to see his eyes flicking around restlessly. She had gone through the bag earlier, finding it contained spare clothes, some for Besta and some that must be for the children, stale bread and some printed papers that looked like identity documents. There were also a number of trinkets, like nails with gilded heads and a tarnished metal plate with decorative etching that might have been pried off a clock like the one Tremaine had found in the town.

"He ran away twice," Ilias said around a yawn. "Fell in a pond. Twisted his ankle in a hole."

"Three times," Giliead amended, a wry smile in his voice. "The last time we ignored him and he came back on his own."

Tremaine sighed. *I'm glad I didn't know about that.* She was also glad she had left him to their care; she would have shot him by now. Questioning this afternoon had allowed her to figure out that Matons were communities of workers built up around mines, farms, factories and any other necessary places. The Maton they were heading for was built around a port and a major airship landing field, and was one of the most important in this region. Or so the boy thought, anyway.

Cletia took a small metal pot out of her pack and moved over to the fire. Giliead made way for her, cautioning, "Nothing that anyone will be able to smell."

Cletia rolled her eyes. "I know that." She poured water from a canteen into the pot and put it at the edge of the fire to heat. With Cimarus to hand her things, she got out another bowl and began to put together the contents of various leather bags and packets.

Tremaine watched this process, puzzled. "You brought your own rations?"

Cletia shrugged slightly. "You people eat cranberries. Pasima was worried."

It was Tremaine's turn to roll her eyes. She knew she was just distracting herself from what she had to do. *Maybe later, after we eat.* Dubos stirred himself and dug something out of his pack. "Is she making dinner? Here's something to go with it." He tossed over a package of bread wafers. Cletia picked it up, examined it cautiously, then nodded her thanks to him.

"Why do they keep calling me *thala*?" the Gardier boy demanded suddenly. "What does that mean?"

Tremaine had to think a moment, massaging her temple, the other hand still tangled in Ilias's hair. Speaking Gardier was giving her a headache, and mentally translating Gardier mispronunciations of Syrnaic into Rienish and back didn't help. "*Talae*. It's Syrnaic for *boy*."

"Oh." He still looked disgruntled, as if displeased it wasn't an insult. "What's Syrnaic?"

Tremaine closed her eyes briefly. *I don't need this.* "It's the name of the language they speak."

His brow furrowed as he tried to digest what was apparently an entirely new concept. "Speaking other languages lowers us."

Tremaine lifted a brow at him. "Lowers us to where?"

He eyed her warily, failing to fall for the bait. *Yes, I'm so good with children.* Any moment, someone was going to use the word *Rien* and he would probably start screaming. But she needed a guide for the damn Maton. "If you told them your name, they could call you that."

The boy didn't reply.

Deciding she might as well try to get some more information out of him, Tremaine asked, "Besta said someone attacked. Who attacked?"

He shook his head, shrugging. "It was before I was born. They used *arcana* and killed a lot of people."

"*Arcana* is magic?" The sphere hadn't known that word, or some of the words the woman had used. It had gotten its vocabulary from a Gardier translator crystal and they had assumed it was complete, but the Gardier might not have bothered to include old outmoded terms.

The boy shrugged again. Tremaine thought that she was going to get very tired of that shrug before this was over. Then he added, "Everyone says now it was the Rien."

She scratched her nose to hide her expression, giving the idea serious consideration. Before he was born would be twelve or thirteen years ago. If the government and Crown of Ile-Rien had been carrying out a war of aggression on a foreign power in another world, they had managed to keep it a tight secret. With the political scandals that seemed to hit every few years, that seemed unlikely. Plus the fact that the sphere's ability to open etheric gateways had come as a complete shock to the military men involved in the Viller Institute's project. She just didn't think Colonel Averi was that good an actor.

The boy added unexpectedly, "But my mother said they didn't start to say that until a few years ago. She also said she thought the attack didn't happen like they said it did, that it was a lie." He shook his head. "I don't know. But afterward they said we were in danger, we had to be prepared, so it didn't happen again. We have to attack the Rien before they attack us, we have to protect ourselves. And everybody who is able has to go into the Service."

Tremaine absently extracted another leaf from Ilias's hair. She noticed peripherally that everyone else was quiet; though the Syprians couldn't understand the conversation, they were well aware the boy could be telling her what they needed to know to survive. Basimi and Dubos were holding themselves in an uncomfortable stillness, and Molin's eyes were open though he didn't sit up. Cimarus was an unmoving lump near the fire, Cletia was leaning so far over her work that her hair came near to trailing in it. Giliead looked abstractly off into the night and she could feel Ilias's tension through her hands. "Just the Service? How do they decide who gets to be in Command or the Scientists?"

He shrugged again. "I don't know. Maybe my mother did."

Tremaine let out her breath. It sounded like the mother had been something of a rebel. *It's too bad she's not the one sitting here now.*

Cletia caught her eye, and Tremaine realized she was telling her the food was ready. Tremaine nodded to her and gave Ilias's shoulder a shake. He sat up and everyone seemed to stir a little in relief at the broken tension. Cletia began handing out pieces of the wafer bread with a lumpy mixture piled on it. Tremaine accepted hers reluctantly. Cletia was true to her word: It didn't smell like anything. Giliead stepped over to drop one into the boy's hands. The boy looked blank with surprise, as if no one had ever handed him food before in his life. He looked around at the others, saw they were eating it, then wolfed it down.

Tremaine took a cautious bite. It tasted like very grainy porridge, with sweet spices mixed in, but it was warm and more filling than the dry rations.

"My name is Calit," the boy said suddenly.

It was much later, when most of the others had gone to sleep, that Dubos said quietly, "This world, this is the one the Gardier come from, isn't it? Not the one where the Syprians live, and not our world."

Tremaine shifted a little. Ilias and Giliead were off in the dark, taking the first watch, and Dubos had taken over keeping an eye on the fire to make sure it didn't burn too brightly. Cletia and Cimarus slept close to each other a little distance from where Molin and Basimi had collapsed. She said, "I think it must be."

He nodded slowly. Apparently neither of them had to say how important it was to carry this information back to the *Ravenna*. He nodded to Calit, where the boy was curled up near the fire. "You think we can trust him?"

She snorted derisively. "Do you?"

He shrugged, surprising her. "Might be." At her incredulous stare he smiled faintly. "I've read quite a bit about our wars with Bisra. Back in the early ones, a couple of hundred years ago, their Priest-Sorcerers used to make a big point to the peasant foot soldiers that if they didn't fight to the death, God and the church and their family and everyone else would spit on them and they'd go straight to hell. But many of those who were captured alive or surrendered were cooperative. They talked about their commanders and what they knew of the troop movements, they helped dig trenches and build barricades. The thing was, they believed their Priests, and since they weren't dead, they figured they weren't Bisran anymore and they should join Ile-Rien, Church, Old Faith, and all."

Tremaine turned that over thoughtfully. "Those were Bisran peasants." Only an artificial border drawn arbitrarily on the map had kept them from being Rienish peasants anyway.

He shook his head a little. "People are people. They need something to belong to."

Tremaine suddenly didn't want to talk about it anymore. She didn't want the Gardier to be people; it was easier to kill them when they were just faceless enemies. She straightened her legs, stretching. "What were you before the war?"

Dubos poked at the fire. "I was an inspector in the Prefecture."

"Oh." Startled, Tremaine let the silence draw out. He looked old enough to have been a young constable when her father's alter ego Donatien had been operating in Vienne. "I'm going to go check on the others."

Vines clung to her and little bugs whined in her ears as Tremaine made her way through the dark toward the outer edge of the island. Mud squished unpleasantly underfoot. "Hey, I need to talk to you two," she whispered softly, knowing they were out here somewhere.

"Here," Ilias whispered back. "To your right."

She fumbled toward his voice, tripping on a tree root. There was more light here at the edge of the trees, but not much. She could only see vague lumps in the dark. "Is that both of you?"

Something large shifted near the base of a tree. She assumed it was Giliead. Ilias said, "Yes. What's the matter?"

She sat down cautiously, finding a mostly dry seat on a matted clump of grass. She hesitated, but it was suddenly harder to wait and wonder than to just get it out in the open. She said, "Giliead . . . Do you know how the sphere works?"

"No." Giliead sounded puzzled at the question.

"Arisilde is inside it, and a sorcerer—or any person with enough magic—talks to him, and asks him to do the spell to open the gate and take us through." She hesitated, then added, "It works like a Gardier crystal."

Giliead was quiet for a moment. "Why are you telling me this?"

He knows, Tremaine thought. She could hear it in his voice. She could feel Ilias staring at her, could sense his confusion. Her voice came out harder than she intended. "I think you know why. We need someone to make the crystal take us back to your world."

"I'm a Chosen Vessel." Giliead's voice sounded stony. "I talk to gods, not—" He cut it off abruptly.

She heard Ilias swear under his breath. *Now he knows too,* Tremaine thought. She couldn't stop now, not for anything, even if she was making a horrible mess of it. She persisted, "You used a spell Gerard gave you to get away from Ixion."

"I wasn't the one who made it work," Giliead said deliberately. "All I did was hand it to Ixion."

"You won't be doing a spell this time either. You can't do a spell you don't know, even if you have magic. You'd just be asking the crystal to do it for us, the way I asked Arisilde to do it for me that time."

Giliead snorted derisively. "That's a god."

"That's my uncle." Tremaine took a sharp breath. "He's as much of a god as the person who's trapped inside that crystal."

Giliead got up abruptly and walked away a few paces. Tremaine froze at his sudden movement, startled, then made herself relax, shifting a little to ease the ache in her back. Ilias didn't move and she was afraid to look at him, even though she couldn't see his face in the dark.

Giliead came back and she could feel him looming over her. Then he said quietly, "It's different."

She hadn't expected that. "How is it different?" she demanded.

He sat on his heels in front of her. She still couldn't see his face, just smell his musky sweat and feel his body heat. "Because I'm

Syprian." He suddenly sounded desperate. "What if that's the difference? What if that's why your wizards can heal you and defend you and protect you, and ours go mad and kill for the sake of killing?"

Tremaine turned that over, aghast. "I don't think that's it. Gerard didn't either. Think so, I mean. He thinks it's the way they're taught. He thinks you do have good wizards, they just don't know they're wizards, or they stay in hiding."

Giliead took a deep breath. "Ilias—"

"Don't ask me," Ilias said roughly. "Don't ask me this."

Giliead hesitated. "Why not?"

"Because if I say you should do it and I'm wrong—" He couldn't finish.

Tremaine took a deep breath, pushing her hair back wearily. *This is going just as well as I thought it would.* "Just think about it. There's nothing we can do now, anyway. In your world we're in the middle of the ocean, miles away from the Walls. We need a boat before we can do anything. So just . . . think about it." She got up, feeling her way through the tangle of trees back to the fire.

Ilias waited for Giliead to speak but his friend just sat there in a silence broken only by the hum of insects. He knew he was being a coward, but he didn't want anything like this to be his decision. Ilias had thought for a while that Syprian wizards might be corrupting the same curses that the Rienish used for good; that the Rienish way was how it was meant to be and the Syprian wizards turned it into a foul distortion. But Giliead had followed that thought further, and Ilias was afraid he might be right. Finally, Giliead stirred, saying, "Go tell Cimarus it's his watch."

Ilias didn't move. After a moment, Giliead caught him by the back of the neck and dragged him into a brief one-armed hug, pulling him off-balance. Then Giliead stood up, dumping him onto the damp ground.

Ilias didn't argue, getting to his feet and weaving a path through the trees.

The Rienish Dubos still sat by the fire, keeping his own watch. On the edge of the camp, away from the others, Tremaine had found a relatively dry spot in the leaves and lay with her head pillowed on her arm. Ilias kicked Cimarus in the ribs, stepped back as he woke in a startled flurry, and jerked his head toward the trees. Cimarus took the hint, getting to his feet with a glare at Ilias but going to join Giliead anyway.

Ilias picked his way quietly toward Tremaine and lay down next to her, snuggling up behind her and burying his face in her hair. He felt tension go out of her body suddenly and knew she hadn't been asleep.

Chapter 19

Florian and Kias searched for Arites among the dead and wounded until morning before admitting that he wasn't there to be found. The few Raiders who had escaped the Gardier's defenses had taken no prisoners. The sphere, which had been helpful in tracking down several Gardier wounded who had crawled off into the rocks, couldn't or wouldn't find Arites. Finally, they had to face the fact that somehow Arites must have ended up aboard the airship with the others.

Florian kept hoping against hope that the airship would reappear, but when dawn broke over the peaks of the Walls she felt hope begin to die. She picked her way back through the ruined compound and found Gerard, Ander and Kias with several Rienish soldiers gathered around a man sitting on the ground. As she reached them she saw it was one of the Raiders. His hands were tied, his shaved skull streaked with blood and dirt. The soldiers were watching him warily. He glared at Kias, defiant and angry, and spit words in a language she didn't understand.

Kias let his breath out and rubbed his forehead wearily. He told Gerard and Ander, "They were hired as mercenaries by a group of the traders in the port to clean this place out. Shitheads," he added, aiming a halfhearted kick at the prisoner, who snarled at him.

Gerard's face was bleak. "Then it was a coincidence."

Ander swore under his breath and looked away. "Bad luck."

Bad luck, Florian thought. *There has to be a better word for it than that.* "Gerard, do you want me to help question prisoners?" They had a new group of Gardier prisoners now. More officers, and more of the little belt devices with the crystal shards. But the large crystal, the one that had powered the spell circle, was a shattered mass of half-melted fragments, destroyed in the battle with the sphere.

It took Gerard a moment to come back from his own thoughts and focus on her. He shook his head. "Why don't you go back to the ship? It's been a long night."

She opened her mouth to argue, then realized it really didn't matter. She had been no help here to anyone, and there was no point in staying. "All right."

The *Ravenna* had steamed cautiously into the mouth of the harbor, and now apparently half the port was in hiding and the other half was down there staring at her. The Syprian eye shapes hastily painted onto the bow seemed to be reassuring to some of them, perhaps as a sign that this set of strange newcomers were actually open to alliances. Florian knew Averi and Count Delphane wanted to make an agreement with the Wall Port people similar to the one with the Syprians. Before she left, Kias had been hauled off to meet with a group of merchants from the port who had rather bravely come up to the outpost to find out what had happened.

On the launch, halfway back to the ship, Florian realized no one had told Gyan about Ilias, Giliead and Arites, or Pasima and the others about Cletia and Cimarus.

They met her on the boat deck with Sanior and Danias, anxious for news. No one who could translate Syrnaic had returned to the ship yet, but they must have realized something had gone badly wrong from the way everyone was behaving. When she told them what had happened, Pasima turned away with a drawn face, put her arm around Sanior and walked away, Danias trailing after. Gyan had just stared off at the port, nodding. Then he hugged her tightly and followed the others.

After that, Florian didn't want to go back to her cabin. Her two roommates, both of whom had lost loved ones in the war, had implied before this that she was undeservedly lucky. She didn't feel like facing their condemnation or belated sympathy at the loss of her friends.

She ended up staying on the boat deck, walking along the rail around and around, the sun warming her back and the wind pulling at her hair as if nothing was wrong. When someone hailed her she stopped, blinking, not sure how long she had been pacing.

It was a very young man in army uniform who trotted up to her, saying urgently, "Miss, the sorcerer prisoner has been asking for one of the natives, Giliead. At least I think he's been asking for him. We can't understand what he's saying. I can't find Colonel Averi or Captain Destan or the sorcerers, and this is the first time he's spoken to us, and I thought it might be important."

Florian nodded. "They're still at the port." She tried to make herself think straight. *It could be a trick, but— I don't know, at least I can find out what he wants.* "I'll come."

They hadn't traveled long the next day when they reached the road. Tremaine had tramped along through the forest in silence, lost in thought, and the others were too worried to talk or too occupied with keeping up and not losing their footing on the muddy ground. She hadn't tried to reopen the crystal discussion with Ilias and Gilicad, and they hadn't raised the subject.

He'll do it. I know he'll do it, she thought. For one thing, Giliead had been brought up to self-sacrifice. What was making her stomach churn was the possibility that he might be right. But if Gerard's theory was correct, Giliead and every other Vessel before him had been using magic all along, whether they knew it or not. None of them had gone mad yet. As far as she knew.

When she wasn't worrying about that, Tremaine was evolving a plan that was probably completely insane, but she couldn't think of anything else. "Do I look like one of your people?" she asked Calit.

The boy, trudging along beside her, gave her a startled sideways glance. "What else would you be?"

She shrugged. Since it was his answer to most questions, she could hardly complain. But as unintentionally unhelpful as the boy was, he was giving her a picture of the Gardier, or the Aelin as they called themselves. A small civilian population was totally given over to supporting the war effort. Only the families of the higher-ranking Command or Scientists traveled or had luxuries; those in the Service class spent all their time working and knew little or nothing about what went on in the other Matons. "You said Ilias and Giliead didn't look like Labor. What made you say that?"

The boy's brow furrowed as if he had never been required to think analytically before. The Gardier didn't waste education on people destined for Service or Labor, which fit in with what their prisoners had told them. "They have too much hair. And him, Ilias and that woman, their hair is a funny color. They just look funny."

Tremaine nodded. The Gardier prisoners and the ones attached to the island base all seemed to have black or brown hair and to be pale-skinned. The paleness undoubtedly came from spending so much time underground on the island, but the hair color seemed to be a general trait. She, Dubos, Molin and Basimi could pass for Gardier well enough, especially with the uniforms they had taken from the airship; there was no way the Syprians could, no matter what they wore.

Shortly after that Ilias had dropped back to report finding the road.

Cautiously emerging from the cover of the trees, they saw a road about twenty feet wide, made of gravel packed into dirt, cutting a path through the thick marshy woods on either side. "This is the way to the Maton," Calit said defiantly, as if used to being argued with. "I told you it was here."

"And we believed you," Tremaine couldn't help adding, though she tried to keep her voice noncommittal. She had the idea Besta had not encouraged the boy to offer his opinion much. She also refrained from pointing out that Calit's sense of direction was if anything worse than his sense of fashion. The Syprians had actually found the road by scouting ahead and somehow managing to interpret Tremaine's translation of Calit's vague descriptions of the terrain.

"Something's coming." Staring uneasily down the road, Ilias motioned everyone to get back into concealment. "It sounds like one of your wagons."

"My wagons?" Tremaine repeated blankly, heading hurriedly for the bushes. They could all hear it now, a low rumbling coming from around the bend in the road. Ducking under the low branches, she suddenly got it. "You mean an automobile?"

"One of those," Ilias agreed, tugging her into cover.

Everyone crept back through the woods, burying themselves in the tangle of heavy green brush a short distance from the road. Crouching, Tremaine heard Basimi mutter, "It's a truck. I think."

She looked cautiously. Rattling slowly down the gravel road was something that looked like a truck as designed by someone who had only heard one badly described. It was mostly a big wooden crate on a metal chassis with a large engine in front of it, and it had six metal-rimmed wheels instead of four. Judging by its current speed, these defects caused it to move slowly at best. There was also no windscreen, and the steering column sported a wheel the size of a millstone that the driver peered over the top of.

Watching it trundle slowly past, Ilias said, low-voiced, "I just realized what seemed strange about that town."

Giliead nodded. "No stables, no cowsheds."

Ilias stared at him in exasperation. "If you knew, why didn't you say it?"

Giliead looked at him as if he was insane. "You didn't tell me you wanted to know."

"Never mind," Tremaine interposed. Both men had been on edge all morning, and she was grimly certain of being responsible for it. "I know what you mean. The streets weren't big enough for wagons or motorcars." Maybe they didn't have draft animals, like the Maiutan islands back home. "I think they relied on boats and hot-air balloons and airships, until . . . something happened. They had to change the way they lived, or something made them change it."

"That attack you said the boy talked about?" Ilias prompted.

"Maybe." She eased to her feet as the truck rattled past, leaving foul diesel exhaust in its wake. "Whatever attacked them, it wasn't us."

They followed the road, staying in the cover of the forest, until they saw more trucks; Tremaine began to feel that Calit was right, that they were close to the city. Ilias and Giliead led them deeper into the woods then, at an angle to the road, though how they knew they were heading toward the sea again Tremaine had no idea.

But after a short difficult walk through the thick brush and the heavy cover of the trees, Ilias reappeared, telling Tremaine, "You've got to see this."

"I'm not so sure about that," she said to herself, tripping on vines and roots as she trudged up a low hill in his wake.

The brush thinned out and suddenly through the trees she had a clear view of the gray cloud-streaked sky, and below it the immense expanse of an airship landing field.

It was a vast empty plateau of flat ground, with two black airships tethered in open areas between four giant arched barnlike structures that stood some distance apart. The buildings were larger than the airships, and the human figures moving in and out of them looked tiny by comparison. Made of ribbed metal and wood, each must easily be half the size of the *Ravenna*. Tremaine was baffled for a moment, fumbling for the field glasses in her bag.

Standing by a tree, Giliead asked softly, "What are those?"

Tremaine finally saw the familiar shape of an airship's bow poking out of one giant doorway, and it suddenly made sense. "They're hangars. Sheds for the airships."

Giliead nodded slightly and beside her Ilias relaxed. She realized he had been worried about giants. Considering their brief experience in the world Florian had accidentally taken them to when using the sphere for the first time, she wasn't surprised. *Small mercies. We're drowning in Gardier, but no giants,* she thought bitterly.

Dead leaves crunched behind her as the others caught up, Basimi whistling softly as he caught sight of the airfield. Cimarus murmured in awe and she heard the others making various startled comments.

Tremaine ignored them all, studying the distant line of buildings on the far side of the landing area through the field glasses. The terrain sloped down and in contrast to the hangars, the structures there seemed to be all shoddy temporary buildings crowded together. Past that she could see larger structures rising above them. They looked as though they might be stone towers, perhaps three or four stories tall at most. According to Calit, that was the old city that the Maton had grown around. The harbor would be at its feet.

"What about an airship?" Dubos said suddenly.

Tremaine lowered the glasses, staring at him. "What about one?"

His pack over his shoulder, the sheen of sweat and dirt on his forehead, he was studying the landing field intently. "Instead of a boat. Our mission was to get one, after all. Might be nice if we came back with one."

She considered it dubiously, peering at the nearest shed through the field glasses. "I don't know. I was thinking of stealing somebody's fishing boat, not making off with a military craft."

"They don't have any artillery emplacements around the field," Basimi pointed out. "Doesn't make much sense with what the boy said about an invasion that they fought off."

"No, but that invasion sounds like a political invention." Molin frowned. "It means if we could take off, they'd have to launch another ship to go after us."

Basimi snorted. "There's nothing to stop them from doing that."

Dubos shook his head. "I'm saying it's a thought, I'm not saying I think we should do it."

Ilias was nudging Tremaine in the arm. "They think we should steal a flying whale?" he asked, obviously intrigued. Giliead stepped closer, interested.

"It's not a good idea," Tremaine told Ilias firmly. He would know just enough Rienish to pick up on that. And she sensed that he and Giliead would welcome the distraction from the problem of the crystal.

"Why not?" he demanded.

"Because—" She hesitated. *There's something obvious about it. Somewhere there's a Gardier saying, "They ended up here because they were after one of our airships, they lost the one they had and they'll go after another."* "Because my gut says it's not a good idea."

Ilias considered it, then nodded slowly. "All right."

Tremaine let out a breath. She told the others in Rienish, "Basimi's right, they shot us down once, there's nothing to stop them doing it again. And the airships will have more guards than a boat. We need a quiet escape, with no shooting."

"You're right," Dubos admitted, sounding more reluctant than grudging. "I just hate going back empty-handed."

I'm surrounded by optimists again, Tremaine thought, rolling her eyes as she stuffed the glasses back in her pack. Empty-handed, full-handed, any kind of handed, they would be lucky to get back at all.

Florian stood in the room belowdecks confronting the locked door. She wasn't alone; the guards were in the corridor behind her, but the air was clammy and warm down here no matter how hard the vents worked, and there seemed to be shadows in every corner despite the overhead electrics.

She cleared her throat. "Hello," she said cautiously in Syrnaic. "They said you were asking for Giliead."

She heard movement on the other side of the door. "I was, my flower. Where is he?"

His flower. Florian pressed her lips together. *As if I need that right now.* "He isn't here just at the moment. Did you want something?"

There was a silence. "What about Ilias? Or is he refusing to speak to me?"

"He's not here either."

"I see. Can you perhaps take a message to them?"

"No, I can't. Look, if you aren't—"

"You are not, I think, the young woman I spoke to before?"

"We've never met." She shook her hair back impatiently. "And if you just wanted someone to chat with, I've got things to do, so good-bye."

"Don't be hasty." There was a slight hesitation. "You have some power yourself, I smell it through the door."

Florian's lips twisted in disgust. *I could've done without knowing that.* "Yes," she admitted reluctantly. For all the good it did her or any-one else.

"You know I have sworn to use my skills for your people."

"That's not quite how I heard it." *That's enough. Ilias was right about him, he's just trying to get a reaction out of me.* She turned for the door.

"That aside . . . Another wizard on this ship has been trying to con-trol me."

Florian stopped, facing away from the door, feeling a cold prickle of unease climb up her spine and settle in her stomach. "What do you mean?"

"He comes to the door, or sometimes to one of the walls, and whis-pers his curses to me. They have had no effect so far . . . that I know of. He came again last night."

She turned slowly, staring at the unrevealing door. "Are you seri-ous?" *He—it—whatever that thing was in the hospital is supposed to be dead. It was a construct, it disappeared when Gerard and Niles did the banishing adjuration.* But Tremaine had said she had seen it in the sur-geon's office at the same time she thought Giliead was fighting it in the wardroom, that there might be two of them. When nothing fur-ther had happened that night, they had thought she was wrong, that she had seen it just before it had gone to the wardroom.

"Does it worry you? I admit, it worries me." Ixion continued in a conversational tone, "I thought at first it was some plot of yours—not yours personally, you understand. I thought I was being toyed with. But then yesterday he came to the door, and I realized that my guards spoke to one another during his curse, as if they were unaware of his presence. And why should one of your wizards hide from his own men?"

Florian wet her dry lips. If this was true . . . Then Gerard and Niles had banished a construct, but the sorcerer who created it was still on the ship. "Did he say anything, tell you his name, who he was?"

"No. But it occurs to me that when he comes again I might engage him in conversation."

She nodded slowly. "Yes, you might do that."

Walking along the dusty road toward the Maton, Tremaine's stomach was eaten up with anxiety, and it was taking more of her willpower not to hit Calit or to tell Basimi to shut up about the damn stinging bugs. At least he had obeyed her injunction to only complain in Gardier, even when no one else was near.

The Gardier civilian clothes she wore were coarse and itchy and would have been unbearable if the day hadn't been overcast and fairly cool. Hers had come from Besta's bag and the uniform coveralls Basimi, Dubos and Molin wore were from the airship. There wasn't much traffic on the road, only the occasional truck and a few small groups of people plodding along like themselves. The presence of all the foot traffic was what had made Tremaine agree to this plan.

They had decided to split into three groups. Tremaine, with Calit as a guide, would use Besta's identity papers to get into the Maton and search the harbor for a boat to steal. Calit had explained that the papers just certified that the bearer's name was Besta and that she had charge of a boy named Calit and three other children and their rank was Service. According to him, Besta was not an uncommon name. Tremaine figured the Gardier would not have been able to identify the woman they had accidentally shot yesterday yet anyway, especially without her papers. She also figured she had about a 30 percent chance that Calit would attempt to betray her and that she would have to kill him.

Basimi, Dubos and Molin would poke around in the outlying areas of the Maton, where identification papers weren't required, trying to find out where to steal supplies for the trip. The Syprians, who could neither speak Gardier nor pass for Gardier, were going to scout the coast to look for a spot near here that the boat could put in to pick up the rest of the party. Once the boat was stolen.

That is, most of the Syprians would be scouting the coast. Giliead would be staying behind to try to communicate with the Gardier crystal.

Earlier, while the others were still changing into their Gardier clothes, Tremaine had said uneasily to Ilias, "If we're going to steal a ship tonight . . ."

Ilias had nodded, wiping his nose. "He'll do it. Or, at least, he'll try."

She let her breath out in relief, looking over to where Giliead and Cletia were crouched on the ground going through their supplies. "Is he mad at me?" she asked, feeling like an idiot.

Ilias's expression said he agreed with that assessment. He snorted. "No."

"All right, all right." She eyed him worriedly. "Just be careful."

"Me?" Ilias grimaced, giving her a rueful look. "You're the one going into the leviathan's den."

Leviathan's den fit it well enough. *I feel overwhelmed*, Tremaine thought, sick to her stomach. They were passing between buildings now, metal-walled and metal-roofed, starting to rust at the joins. She saw more figures, men and women both, in the plain brown uniforms such as Basimi and the others wore, but most of these people were civilians. They were dressed as poorly as she and Calit, and many were occupied with unloading handcarts into the larger round storage buildings.

There was no sign of the color and whimsy that had given the ruined village so much character, but despite the work going on it wasn't all grim silence. They passed a small lot with plank tables and chairs that seemed to be an open-air eating establishment. Some of the buildings seemed to be divided up into apartments or family dwellings; she saw small children playing inside doorways, smelled food cooking, heard laughter, saw women or older children hurrying about on errands. But according to Calit, this was where the Service families lived. She thought the Labor pens wouldn't be quite so homey.

Calit tugged on her arm. "Up there, that's where they ask for papers."

Tremaine threw a look at Basimi, making sure he heard. He nodded, said, "See you later," in Gardier, and took the next turn, Molin and Dubos following.

She and Calit rounded a corner and reached an earthwork wall, where a metal gate stood open and a short line of people were waiting to get their identification papers checked so they could pass through. Tremaine's stomach tried to crawl up into her throat as she joined the line.

Looking around to try to distract herself, she saw that in the maze of temporary buildings there were signs of attempts to build more permanent structures. Down one of the byways was a half-constructed two-story building with heavy timbers set into the ground to form supports for the walls and a foundation of quarried stone. But it was roofless, and no one was working on it. "Why did they stop?" she asked Calit. "Don't shrug."

He arrested it in midmotion, shoulders lifted, throwing her a startled look. He turned it into a wriggle, saying, "Got sent off to the war, probably."

They reached the front of the line, where a tired-looking older man in Gardier military uniform looked over their documents. Tremaine kept one eye on Calit, but the boy just chewed a fingernail, radiating adolescent boredom. The guard passed them through the gate without comment.

Her sweat turning cold in the breeze, Tremaine took Calit's hand and went into the Maton.

The path curved, leading down a rough hillside where steps were gouged out of the dirt and the temporary buildings dropped away. Tremaine got a view of the heart of the Maton and stopped to stare.

It had been a city once, with rambling buildings and four-story towers of quarried stone connected by winding cobbled paths. They had the same round windows and curved doorframes as the village. The mansard roofs had fanciful carvings under the eaves; she couldn't make out much from this distance except the impression of curves and jubilant shapes.

This hill wasn't high enough for a good view, but she could glimpse water between the buildings and knew the city must curve around the port. There were temporary metal structures here too, the round storage houses and the long low barracks, crammed into every open space and crowding the elegant stone. She was fairly sure those open spaces had been garden plots once, or parks. One of the larger towers at the far end of the curve had the great dark shape of an airship moored to its roof. She couldn't see much from here except the outline of the spiky ridge along the back and the tail fins, but it looked larger than the other airships on the field, dwarfing the top of the building.

Calit hadn't stopped, and she hurried down the rough path, catching up with him in a few long steps. "Did your mother say anything about the city that was here before the Maton?" She kept her voice low, as the path was more crowded down here.

"She used to live here, when she was young. There was more room then." He flicked a cautious look at a party in uniform making their way up the other side of the path. These men and women didn't wear just simple coveralls, but long jackets belted over pants and boots, though it was all in the same brown. Tremaine ignored them and was ignored in return, though the back of her neck prickled at their nearness. Calit lowered his voice a little. "Back then people could live anywhere they wanted."

Tremaine just nodded. She didn't want to carry on the conversation when there were so many people to overhear.

The path got a little wider, turning to cobbles as the stone buildings rose up on either side. Uniforms were everywhere now, strolling and talking, walking hurriedly, going in and out of wide rounded doorways. There were still enough civilians for her and Calit to blend in, but she noticed that some of them had much better clothing. At least, it was better material and more elaborate, though it still had the same dull colors. Calit had said, or said that his mother had said, that everyone had to give up all luxuries, or all appearance of luxuries, when the attack had happened so long ago.

Tremaine knew they were close when she could smell dead fish on the salt-scented breeze. They went around a corner, veered around another larger stone tower and went through a noisy area where round metal storage huts were being loaded or unloaded. They dodged a flotilla of handcarts and were suddenly approaching the port. It was bigger than Tremaine had realized; the angle and the height of the older city had hidden it from view until now.

Old stone walkways and new wooden piers extended out in rows where ships of all sizes were docked. Cargo barges, dark-hulled gunships like the one the *Ravenna* had destroyed, larger warships of classes she couldn't identify. Wood-framed warehouses lined the harbor front, packed with boxes.

So much variety, she thought, biting her lip as she looked over the array of boats. They needed something only a few people could sail, something not too big or complicated. There had to be simple fishing boats somewhere; surely all these people had to eat. They hadn't solved the problem yet of how Dubos, who had some experience sailing, was going to get in past the gate to help her get the thing out of the harbor and to the meeting point. *Worry about that later,* she thought a little desperately, taking Calit's hand and leading the way along the docks.

Giliead took a breath, eyeing the box that held the Gardier curse crystal. The burnished metal case looked alien and malevolent, but that might just be his imagination. "I don't want to do this."

"I don't want you to do this either," Ilias admitted.

Cimarus and Cletia were waiting on the other side of the clearing, ready to leave on the scouting foray. Giliead wasn't sure how much Ilias had told them about what he was about to do. He didn't expect it was much, but that was something he would have to worry about later. He nodded. "But I want us to stay here less." He reached for the box lid.

As he lifted it he was conscious of Ilias slipping to his feet, taking a step back as Giliead had taught him long ago. He could see the shifting haze of dark colors that clung to the dull facets and the rock the crystal grew on like a fungus. He knew the colors were the substance that Gerard called ether.

He had felt the curses coming out of these things before, but he had never had the leisure to focus on one for this long. He had expected it to feel foul, like Ixion, like the Gimora wizard, like the shades in the Sura Vale; on the whole, he decided this would have been easier if it had.

He felt the tentative mental touch of the thing. It wasn't like the god-sphere; it wasn't as in control, as aware of its surroundings or of him. He saw it start to reach a tendril outward and shot out a hand, not sure if he could block it or not. It pulled back from his touch, startled.

When it came down to it, Giliead wasn't sure he knew how to talk to it. Treating it the way he would a shade, he pushed a thought toward it: *Can you hear me?*

He felt it withdraw, startled. He wondered if the Gardier spoke to it in a different way, if it wasn't used to this method of communication. Curious, he asked it, *Do you know what you are?*

Nothing. He carefully pushed an image of himself toward it.

Time seemed to still. He waited, taking a calming breath. Then it pushed an image back to him.

It was a woman's face, fading too quickly, too unformed for him to make out many details. He reached for the image, trying to concentrate on it, and felt it retreat abruptly.

He looked up at Ilias, his expression rueful. "I think this is going to take a while. You'd better go." It wasn't a far walk to the sea—Giliead could smell salt on the wind even from here—but it was late afternoon already, and it might take a while for them to find a suitable landing.

Ilias nodded reluctantly, ruffled Giliead's hair, and went to follow Cimarus and Cletia.

Adram watched Disar pacing in front of one of the trucks, the Command officer's face set in a grimace of frustration. Adram looked away to conceal the dark amusement in his eyes. They had been searching the airship hangars and the woods at the fringes of the field all morning with no success. Now, their vehicles parked on the open field in the tall shadow of the reserve hangar, their Service men sitting around idle, Disar was running out of options.

Disar's second, a young man named Etrim, had spread the map out on the truck's tailgate, marking their route. Sweat was beginning to roll down his brow despite the cool breeze and the omnipresent clouds of the season. Adram didn't know what the Command personnel had been threatened with if they failed to capture the Rien, but he suspected it wasn't pleasant. It was yet another reminder of how lucky he had been to be able to talk his way into the Science branch.

Disar stopped to look over Etrim's shoulder at the map, muttering, "I was certain they would be after an airship."

Adram had been afraid that they were. But the Maton, while it was the only source of transportation in this area, had more to offer than airships.

Etrim shook his head with a grimace. "Perhaps they still are, sir." He tapped the map. "We may have missed them in these cuts and valleys through the woods there. . . ."

"No, our sweep was thorough." Talking to his young assistant, Disar sounded almost human. He touched the crystal embedded in his forehead thoughtfully. "The report said there are at least nine of them. I should have been able to detect that many people, especially since one of them must be using etheric—" Disar's face went still. His eyes looked into that distance, his face taking on that air of distraction that meant he was listening to the voices that controlled him.

"We're looking in the wrong place," he said softly. He turned, his cold dead eyes falling on Adram. "Take your men and head for the west side of the Maton. Wait for further instructions there."

Adram inclined his head in acquiescence and headed for his own vehicle. The Rien must have used magic, allowing the Avatars to sense their location. *Damn.*

Chapter 20

It was coming on toward evening, the overcast sky just beginning to darken, by the time Ilias started back through the woods with Cimarus and Cletia. It had gone as well as a scouting foray by three people who were barely speaking to each other could go. He hadn't had much to say to either of them even before the curse mark, as Visolela's family had never mixed much with the Andrien, so the silence had been awkward rather than companionable. Worry about Tremaine in the city and Giliead with the crystal was eating away at him; he would even have welcomed the distraction of an argument.

The coast was rockier here, the beaches more shallow and the land plunging down sharply in cliffs rather than stretching out into marsh. They found two inlets Ilias judged as marginal and, finally, one that would do nicely; it was sheltered by outthrust fingers of rock, and not easily spied on from the crumbling cliffs above. There was a narrow strip of beach where they could land a boat with a shallow draft or swim out to one that needed the deeper water. Ilias had scuffed one boot in the wet sand. "This'll do," he said aloud, forgetting for a moment that he wasn't talking to himself.

Cletia nodded, hooking her thumbs in her belt. "It's a good choice. If we can just get the boat."

Cimarus came back to them from the water's edge, wondering, "How are we going to do it? One of us should go into the city with them to steal it, so we can guide them here, but how can we do that when they only let certain people in?"

Ilias had been wondering that himself. He could describe this place to Basimi or one of the others, but he knew the way the Rienish measured distances was wildly different from the way the Syprians did, and it was going to be problematic. Both Cletia and Cimarus were looking at him. Apparently he was only supposed to talk when they wanted answers, so he shrugged and ignored them.

It was still early yet for the others to return, so they stopped there to scrub some of the swamp mud off their clothes and skin in the surf before heading back. Ilias moved down the beach away from Cimarus and Cletia, aware the two were talking quietly but letting the wind and surf-sound cover it. He heard enough to know they were speculating on what Giliead was doing with the crystal; he didn't care to hear more, knowing it would just make him angry.

Now they walked back through the twilight forest with the short gray-barked trees, the spreading canopies of tightly bundled leaves more than enough to shield them from flying whales. Ilias was turning over ideas about how to get to a boat without getting killed, but not with much success; he just hoped Tremaine had thought of something clever and not too crazy.

Ilias stopped abruptly, not certain what had alerted him. Behind him Cimarus and Cletia halted and he could tell from their startled silence they felt it too. He scanned the woods, seeing nothing but narrow trunks, shadowy in the dusk, yellow grass and dusty brush clinging to the gentle rise and fall of the land. Sniffing the air, he couldn't catch a hint of anything but salt from the sea and the omnipresent stink of smoke from the Gardier city.

But something was wrong. He motioned to the others, starting to back away. *We covered our tracks, we covered the Rienish's tracks, we left no hint of a camp.* It was just Giliead and the crystal left here, and the Gardier would have to step right on top of him to find him.

Maybe they didn't find him; maybe they're waiting to find someone else. It wasn't worth the chance; they could fade back and approach from another direction. He made a throwing-away gesture, telling the others to split up. Cletia clicked her tongue in acknowledgment, and Ilias veered back and to the left, breaking into a run.

A scatter of sharp reports from a shooting weapon told him he had guessed right. Grimacing in dismay, Ilias ducked, weaving through the trees, heading for the deeper woods. A man shouted but it wasn't

Cimarus; he knew if either he or Cletia had been hit, the other would have stopped and he would hear them.

Something shot up out of the grass in front of him and he slid to a startled halt. It was a man's outline, formed of mist, dust and leaves caught in the air that shaped it. It was dismayingly like the one on the ship, the thing that had fought Giliead in the healer's rooms. He dodged sideways away from it.

Something slammed into his back, knocking him sprawling in the high grass. Ilias gasped, flailing back and reaching for his knife, convinced someone had tackled him. Then the numb heaviness in his legs struck him and he swore, pounding a fist on the ground in frustration. *It's that same fucking curse.* The Gardier had used it on him twice on the Isle of Storms. Knowing it wore off eventually didn't help.

Ilias heard bootsteps running toward him and struggled to push himself up. The mist-creature had vanished, but that wasn't much of a help at the moment. He didn't have a chance to drag the sword out of its scabbard, but he had the knife in his hand. The first Gardier reached him and he slammed it into the brown-clothed leg as high up as he could reach. The man fell back with a pain-filled yell, but the one right behind him swung the butt of his shooting weapon.

Ilias flung up an arm to shield his head. The next thing he knew he was flat on the ground, tasting blood and dirt, pain radiating through his skull. The world was alternately dark and blurry, but he knew he wasn't unconscious, just stunned. He felt it when they poked him, dragged his sword off and searched him roughly for more weapons, pulling his jerkin and shirt open. His legs were still numb from the curse but he kept trying to sit up. With each try the world went away and came back, worse each time.

He realized dimly he was being slung over somebody's shoulder; his head throbbed brutally, but the rush of blood helped clear his senses. He tried to fling himself free and realized his hands were chained behind his back, the manacles biting into his wrists. *Damn it. That's not going to help.* He blinked and squinted, getting a bleary upside-down view of an open clearing in the woods, the one near where they were to meet Giliead. It was now occupied by three Gardier wagons, all big black boxes with the beds covered by square canvas tents.

His captor dumped him on the ground abruptly and he landed with a gasp. He tried to roll over and realized his feet were chained as well; there was more slack but not enough to stand up once the curse let him. He twisted around and saw Cimarus and Cletia nearby, both chained as he was, with guards standing at their sides. *No Gil,* he thought, gritting his teeth as one of the Gardier hauled him upright. That was a relief. His legs were starting to tingle with renewed life and he was able to sit awkwardly on his knees, though keeping his balance was difficult. The pounding in his head made the world sway. He threw a glance at the others again and saw Cimarus looked as if he held back panic only by strength of will and Cletia's grim expression hid terror. Ilias could tell by the way they were hunched there that the same curse had been used on them. "It goes away," he said quickly. A Gardier shouted and kicked at him.

Another spoke sharply and Ilias looked up, squinting in pain as his head throbbed with the quick movement. Standing over him was a tall man with some kind of strange scar or growth on his temple. Then he turned and the dimming light caught his face; Ilias saw it was actually a crystal, sunk into his skull.

He had to look away, feeling his gorge rise. He couldn't think what it meant, why the man had a curse crystal embedded in his head. *He's a wizard,* he thought, sickened, *or . . . the slave of a wizard?*

The wizard stared into the trees, his face distant and pensive. Ilias knew with a sudden cold certainty that the man was looking at Giliead, that he knew exactly where he was.

The man turned back, pacing thoughtfully toward Cletia. She looked away as he drew near, her face set in rigid tension. Ilias threw his weight sideways, making his guards mutter angrily as they struggled to hold him upright. A boot struck his ribs, doubling him over, taking his breath away.

He looked up, breathing hard, and saw the painfully bought distraction hadn't worked. The wizard was still standing in front of Cletia, examining her thoughtfully. Ilias heard Cimarus struggling somewhere behind him. Then the man stepped away and she shuddered in relief. The wizard barely glanced at Cimarus, stopping instead in front of Ilias.

Ilias looked up at him, sickeningly fascinated by that crystal. From this angle he could see the skin around it was going foul, tinged with rot where it wasn't scar tissue. Then he saw the man's eyes.

They were dark, opaque, and human wizard or crystal wizard, whatever it was looked out through those eyes.

Then the gaze shifted and it was a man looking down at him. The Gardier blinked, seemed almost confused for an instant. Then his expression hardened and he drew the shooting weapon from the small sheath at his side.

This time Ilias wrenched backward out of real fear and not an attempt to distract his captors. The guards tightened their hold on him and the man stepped close, grabbing a handful of his hair to yank him upright. Ilias felt the cold weight of the shooting weapon rest against his temple.

Ow, he thought in frozen anticipation, squeezing his eyes shut in reflex. He thought it would be quick—he had seen what those weapons had done to others, to Arites—he knew what it would do to his head.

Past the pounding of his own blood he heard a shout. *Gil's voice.* The pressure of the metal on his temple dropped away and the hard grip on his hair released. Sagging backward, he opened his eyes as the wizard stepped away from him. He couldn't believe he was still alive. Then he saw Giliead standing in the high grass at the edge of the woods, three Gardier cautiously advancing on him. "No!" he shouted furiously, appalled. "Are you crazy?"

The butt of a shooting weapon struck Ilias hard on the shoulder. Giliead's grim expression didn't alter as he let the Gardier seize him.

Twisted away from the blow, Ilias snarled, "Stupid . . ." and couldn't think of a word bad enough.

The Gardier shoved Giliead forward, one of them coming around with the chains. The wizard didn't bother to watch anymore, ordering two of his men into the woods with a gesture. He had known Giliead was there, he had known Giliead would surrender if he threatened the right person. And he knew who that right person was. Ilias swore under his breath, feeling the bleak rise of despair. It was that damn crystal.

In confirmation, the men sent into the woods returned, one of them carrying the heavy metal box. The wizard moved away to meet them. As one of the men held the box, he undid the catch and lifted the lid, staring intently inside. Giliead had his hands chained behind him now and had been forced to his knees across the clearing; he was facing away, so Ilias couldn't even mouth a question to him.

Another Gardier moved toward Ilias now, looking down at him thoughtfully. Occupied with watching the wizard, Ilias threw him a contemptuous glance.

This one stepped up close to him, reaching down, and Ilias tensed against a blow, twisting his head away. He could still feel the cold spot on his temple where the open end of the weapon had rested. But the Gardier lifted the ring that hung from the thong around his neck.

Startled, Ilias watched him turn the metal circle in his fingers; the fading sunlight caught it, throwing back a silver-that-wasn't gleam. Ilias tried to keep his face blank, knowing the man was trying to read the intricately curved symbols. *He might see it's Rienish. I should have taken it off.* But if the Gardier didn't guess by now that they were the ones who had arrived on the captured flying whale, then the ring wouldn't tell them anything. It surely wouldn't tell them how many others had come with them, which was the only thing of value they had left to hide. Ilias hoped the wizard couldn't find that out as well just by looking at Giliead.

Then the Gardier's hold tightened, tugging at the thong. Ilias found himself looking up into dark eyes that gleamed with a dangerous revelation. For an instant it was as if he was facing a completely different person who had suddenly taken over the skin of the brown-clad stern-faced Gardier in front of him. After the wizard, it was more than disconcerting. Ilias pressed his lips together, unconsciously lifting his chin. Then the Gardier said, "Valiarde."

Ilias stared, nonplussed and too startled to guard his reaction. One of his guards asked a sharp question. The Gardier confronting him didn't acknowledge the interruption, his eyes still locked on Ilias. He said, "You understand me?" in Rienish. His voice was different from the others and he spoke the words with the same accent as Tremaine and Gerard. Ilias realized the man had said "Valiarde" in that way too, giving it the fluid Rienish pronunciation. His face gave him away, and the man let the ring fall back to Ilias's chest, saying, "Yes, I see that you do."

Across the clearing, the wizard shut the box lid with a snap and Ilias flinched. The Gardier stepped smoothly away from him, managing to be moving unhurriedly toward the nearest wagon by the time the wizard turned around.

Ilias stared after him, not sure what to think. He was certain that the Gardier were supposed to be unable to speak any language other than their own, or no more than a few words. *But the Rienish couldn't have hidden men among the Gardier, not here.* Tremaine and Basimi and the others hadn't even known *here* existed, and Gerard always said their real disadvantage was how little they knew of their enemy.

But the man had read the writing on the ring, which Tremaine said was deliberately difficult, even for someone familiar with the language.

The wizard shouted orders and the guards dragged Ilias to his feet. At least the curse had worn off entirely and he could move his legs again. He saw they were hauling him toward a horseless wagon and managed despite the chains to kick one in the kneecap, twisting to almost avoid the return punch in the stomach. It didn't help; they slammed him into the footboard of the wagon, flipping his legs up and dumping him inside. They threw Cimarus on top of him before he had a chance to wriggle out of the way, knocking the breath out of his lungs.

Face mashed into the foul-smelling wood of the wagon bed, pinned by Cimarus's weight, Ilias worked to get air and listened for the others. He was relieved to hear more thumps and an annoyed snarl from Cletia. The footboard banged shut and he bucked and managed to heave a groaning Cimarus off him. It was dark; the Gardier outside had pulled the cloth cover down over the back and he could hear them tying it off. "Gil?" he whispered urgently.

"Here," came from the other side of the wagon bed. His eyes adjusting, he could see Giliead struggle to turn over and heave himself into a sitting position. "Ilias, I—"

"Shut up." Wincing, Ilias rolled over and wiggled until he could sit up. "Did you see that other Gardier, the one that talked to me?"

"Yes, I didn't hear what he said."

"He spoke Rienish. He knew the—" He gasped as Cimarus kneed him in the side in his efforts to get upright. "—the word on the ring Tremaine gave me."

"What does that mean?" Cletia demanded from the corner. "What word?"

A dull roar shuddered through the wagon and Cimarus flinched violently, banging into Ilias, and he heard Cletia yelp. Then the wagon jolted into motion, throwing him into the side wall. Ilias had to lean there, the pain in his ribs making him want to curl into a ball, before he could shove himself upright again. "Gil?"

"I don't know," Giliead answered, raising his voice just enough that Ilias could hear him over the wagon's rumble. He knew Giliead was thinking it through as he had. "But it doesn't seem possible."

"What word?" Cletia asked again, sounding desperate.

"Her family name," Ilias told her impatiently. He leaned back against the wall though the rattling of it made his teeth ache. His head and shoulder throbbed and his ribs ached with every breath. It would be nothing to what would happen later, now that the Gardier knew they could use him to make Giliead do what they wanted. "You shouldn't have done it," he said bitterly. They would both be better off dead.

Light was coming in through chinks in the canvas canopy and Ilias's eyes had adjusted now. He could see Giliead working his way back to the footboard to try to see out though the flaps. "While we're alive, there's a chance," Giliead said, stubborn as stone.

Ilias shook his head, biting back an answer that wouldn't do either of them any good. He could see the outline of a Gardier against one flap, holding on to the outside of the wagon. *We could slam into him, knock him off, and— Jump off chained hand and foot?* Not exactly an improvement in their situation.

The foul smell of the wagon's innards began to fill the hot dark space and sent Cletia into a coughing fit. "A chance of what?" Cimarus asked, his voice thick.

Ilias looked at Giliead and didn't answer.

C oncealing his agitation behind a bland façade, Adram watched the prisoners being loaded into the truck. Damn Disar for returning before he could speak further to the man with the ring. In fact, damn Disar altogether. His eyes narrowed and a slight smile played about his lips. *I think it's time.* Strolling over to the Command officer, Adram told Disar, "I'll follow along behind in case you need assistance."

Disar turned a withering expression on him. Adram could tell from his eyes that the man wasn't under the control of the crystal at the moment. He knew that the crystal's control was limited to short lengths of time; finding the stolen avatar even through the shielding of its case and using it to get a sense of the feelings of the native sorcerer must have drained its resources. "I don't need your assistance."

"Nevertheless." Adram allowed himself a thin smile. *No, what you need is a few good blows to the head with the appropriate blunt instrument.* Oh yes, it was time.

The Service men had hauled the last native, the one with sorcerous ability, to the truck. Ignoring Adram, Disar watched him intently. A big man with a wild mane of braided brown hair, the native threw one last dark look at Disar before he was shoved into the back of the truck. The look promised painful death, and Adram was struck again by the intelligence and intensity in that anger. When the natives had approached the trap, Adram had only to step on a dry twig to alert the man in the lead to the danger; if Disar hadn't been so quick with his spells, they would have escaped altogether. "What do they call themselves?" he asked, forgetting to sound diffident. The soft colors of their clothing had been faded under a brighter sun than had ever shone over this land, and the copper and leather armbands and earrings and other barbaric jewelry added to the savage aspect.

"I have no idea." Disar eyed him, suspicious and perhaps a trifle disconcerted. But his gaze hardened to contempt and he said, "Too bad there were no Rienish among them. I could watch you betray your own people."

Adram's brow lifted ironically. "You still have that opportunity. We both know the only reason there were no Rienish here is that they are capable of disguising themselves and mixing with the people of the Maton."

Disar's eyes narrowed. Obviously he had known it, and he had hoped Adram would say nothing so he could accuse him of traitorous intent. "And they will be easily found."

Adram glanced at the truck as if the thought was only just occurring to him. "If you expect to capture them soon, why don't you hold this group here and send them all to Maton-Command on the same airship?"

Disar snorted dismissively. "I have my orders." He turned away, walking back to his own vehicle.

"So you do," Adram said softly. It was fortunate he had come prepared. He sent his patrol back to their barracks in the other truck and told his own driver to follow Disar.

Finding their way back through the trees in the deepening twilight, Tremaine kept tripping on roots. Fortunately, Calit was just as clumsy as she was, and she didn't feel embarrassed by her lack of woodcraft. *I should have brought a torch,* she grumbled to herself. But Besta hadn't had one and she hadn't wanted to risk bringing a Rienish-manufactured one. It was dangerous enough bringing the gun, and she really shouldn't have risked it. Verisimilitude was everything, Nicholas had told her.

She was fairly sure she had worked out a way to get into the city. It was going to involve some kind of distraction, stealing a truck, and waylaying a Gardier who resembled Basimi or one of the others enough that he could use his papers. The gate guards checked papers only cursorily; it was obvious they weren't expecting enemies to attempt to sneak into or out of the Maton. But getting the boat itself . . . She had the terrible feeling that was where everything was going to fall apart. Still ruminating over the details, Tremaine flinched when Calit grabbed her arm. "Look," he whispered.

She peered ahead. They were near the edge of the woods, at least she thought they were. They had to cross an open area before going back up the hill and into the deeper forest, where the others should be waiting. But there were dark shapes out there and moving figures. . . . *Gardier.* She heard Ilias yell, "Don't do it" in Syrnaic and her heart froze.

She stood in silence, waiting for the shots, until the trucks moved away. Calit shifted uneasily beside her and she realized she had been squeezing his shoulder, probably hard enough to bruise. She let him go.

She took his hand and they followed the slow-moving vehicles, staying under the cover of the trees. The three trucks reached the road that ran along the edge of the woods, taking a turn and starting across the airfield.

The trucks were slow but she couldn't follow on foot. Besides, there was no cover on the open airfield and the Gardier would spot her immediately. *Need a truck, need a truck,* Tremaine thought frantically. Most of the stupid things were on the road on the far side of the airfield, heading into the city. Then she saw one moving toward them, following the road that bordered the woods. She grabbed Calit's hand and pounded up the hill, cutting through the forest back toward the road.

"What are we going to do?" he demanded, breathing hard.

"Exactly what I say," she snarled.

They reached the edge of the woods some distance ahead of the truck as it climbed the hill with the speed of a little old lady, its makeshift engine straining. Tremaine stopped on the edge of the road and told Calit, "Give me your jacket and go collapse in the middle of the road. I'll be there in a minute."

He stared at her, aghast, and she said impatiently, "The truck won't run over you, I won't let it." Then she realized what it was and gritted her teeth in annoyance. "I'll give you the jacket back. Hell, I'll buy you a new one in Capidara."

Reassured, he pulled the threadbare garment off and handed it to her, then hurried to fling himself down in the road. She pulled her revolver out of the awkward holster in the back of her pants and chambered a round, then wrapped Calit's jacket around her arm to hide it. She knew she couldn't risk trying and failing to overpower the drivers.

The truck trundled into view as it reached the top of the hill and Tremaine prayed silently, *Let there be just one driver. Most of the damn things only have one, let this be one of those.* The fading daylight caught it and she saw only one man in the square cab. *Yes.*

With a shriek she ran into the road, flinging herself down at Calit's side. He started to sit up and she shoved him down again with a hissed, "Play dead, dammit." He flopped back, obediently squeezing his eyes shut. They were in full view of the airfield but the nearest hangar was a few miles away, and no one seemed to be outside it. The gathering dusk would also help conceal them.

Kneeling at his side, rocking and whimpering, the gun in her lap concealed by the jacket, she heard the truck chug nearer and wondered what she would do if it didn't stop. Jump up onto the nonexistent running board, maybe? But surely it would stop.

It trundled to a halt about ten paces away, and she heard the driver's footsteps grate on the gravel as he climbed out. "What's wrong with the boy?" he called to her.

She looked up at him. He was a young man in Gardier military uniform, fresh-faced and appallingly naive. "I don't know," she choked out, gesturing with her free hand.

The man obligingly leaned over Calit. Tremaine lifted the gun and shot him point-blank in the back of the head. His body spasmed as he fell, landing on the boy. She rolled the slack weight off before Calit could yell and the boy jumped to his feet, breathing hard and staring, wide-eyed.

Tremaine holstered the gun and shoved to her feet, taking a quick look around. No one was in sight. She grabbed the dead man's arm and hauled him toward the side of the road, wincing at his weight. The horrible head wound was leaving a deep red trail, but there was nothing she could do about it. Soon the night would conceal it and if they were lucky, no one would find him until morning. Calit leapt to help her and they got the man to the lip of the ditch and rolled him in. She took his gun and patted him down for more ammunition, then scrambled back up onto the road, heading for the truck.

It didn't have a starter handle in front of the engine and she climbed up to look into the cab, praying it wouldn't be too complicated for her to understand. The seat was just a hard wooden bench, though the driver had a couple of thin pillows to make it more comfortable. She shoved them aside as she slid in; the wood was still warm from the dead man's body heat. The steering wheel was metal and larger than it should have been, and the starter handle seemed to be next to it on the primitive dashboard. *Gears, gears,* she thought, pushing and pulling various clunky levers. *That must be the brake.*

As she yanked on the starter and the motor rumbled to life, Calit climbed in on the other side. The boy settled on the bench, watching her worriedly. Tremaine was a little surprised. She had deliberately ignored him, figuring he would take the opportunity to run away. "Ready?" she asked him, fumbling for the gearshift.

He nodded gravely and gripped the dashboard.

Tremaine slammed the truck into gear and they were off.

The wagon rumbled on. Ilias kept shifting, trying to find a position that didn't hurt. Huddled in the corner, Cletia had been sick from the motion and the stench. Cimarus didn't look much better when Ilias caught glimpses of him in the intermittent light. He was pushed back against the front wall of the wagon bed, bracing himself with his chained feet to stay sitting upright. Giliead was near the footboard, trying to see where they were being taken.

The daylight had died away and the only illumination coming through the chinks in the canopy was from the large wizard lights they passed under occasionally. From that Ilias knew they were moving across the flying whales' field, not down into the city.

The light grew measurably brighter and the bed swayed and tilted as the wagon climbed a slope. "We're heading up to one of the flying whale sheds," Giliead reported quietly. "They're going to take us away somewhere."

Ilias nodded, though Giliead wasn't looking at him. They wouldn't question prisoners out here; they must be taking them to some other city, somewhere inland. He said suddenly, "I'm not angry at you."

"I know," Giliead replied quietly. He glanced at Ilias, the stark light from an opening in the flap catching him in profile.

The wagon shook as it rolled from the road onto some harder surface and the sound changed; Ilias could tell they were inside now. The wagon came to a stop, the dull roar of the thing that made it move sputtering into silence. Ilias heard several sets of footsteps on stone, men calling to each other in the Gardier tongue. His injured ribs protesting, Ilias managed to sit up on his knees, bracing himself. When the Gardier lifted the flaps he didn't want it to look as if he was huddling in terror. "What do we do?" Cimarus whispered.

Giliead threw him a dark look but didn't answer and neither did Cletia. Ilias didn't want to say "nothing" aloud.

The flaps were thrown back to reveal the Gardier, all aiming the long-shafted shooting weapons at them. Ilias caught his breath, startled by the view of the vast dark shed. Only a few curse lights illuminated the great black shape of the flying whale that hung silently within. From this angle they were looking up into the cluster of jagged fins around its tail, and dust and shadows rose above the whale's back to the vast curve of the wooden ceiling. The middle portion of the whale was mostly lost in darkness but a curse light at the far end showed its nose faced two gigantic floor-to-ceiling doors. Ropes tied the whale to loops of metal set into the ground in various places and a shadowy ramp led up to the opening in its low-slung belly.

Ilias hadn't realized until just that moment how much he didn't want to go anywhere in a flying whale. The first Gardier climbed into the wagon and he slammed into him, knocking him back.

It was full dark by the time Adram's truck followed Disar and his men to the airship hangar, passing unchallenged through the gate in the wire fence in the wake of the other vehicles. The giant curve of the hangar loomed above them, a darker shape outlined against the night sky, and he directed his driver to stop in the wide dirt track. The other two trucks were entering through the cargo doors one of the men inside had just opened. The giant doors that allowed the airship to exit were on the far side and required two trucks to haul open. It would take Disar some time to summon a ground crew and prepare the ship for takeoff.

The driver brought the truck to a halt in the dim pool of electric light from inside the hangar. Adram collected the dispatch bag from the seat. "I'll be staying here for a time. Report to Benin, then return to Barracks."

It had been a long day and as Adram expected, the driver was disinclined to argue. He had been set to watch Adram for Command, but the boredom of watching a man who never did anything worth commenting on let alone reporting had worn him down over time. The driver nodded sharply and restarted the truck as soon as Adram climbed down.

Standing in the dark, Adram surveyed the area carefully. The night was already turning cool, the overcast sky masking nearly all moon- and starlight. The gate guard's small wooden shelter was about forty feet away; there was a small electric light on a post next to it. He strolled through the cargo doors.

The airship floated above the concrete floor in silence, mostly hidden in shadow except for another arc light at the far end near the launch doors. The two trucks were parked a short distance inside, near a work bay packed with tools and maintenance equipment. Men had already climbed out of the first truck and were moving to surround the one that carried the prisoners, rifles at the ready. Disar's expression turned incredulous as Adram casually joined him.

Disar snapped, "I told you I didn't need your assistance." His second, Etrim, looked away hurriedly, not wanting to witness an argument between Command and Science.

"Did you? Sorry, I thought you said otherwise." Adram was aware he had broken character, and also aware it probably wouldn't matter, not for any of the men now in this hangar.

Disar's mouth set in a thin line, but Adram knew he must want to depart as soon as possible. Disar said through gritted teeth, "Observe for Benin if you wish, but do nothing." He added with a grim smile, "We will speak of this alone later." Disar motioned for his second to follow him and started toward a small wooden building set against the curved wall of the hangar.

Adram's lips twisted in an ironic smile. "Promises, promises," he said under his breath. He knew the little structure Disar was striding so purposefully toward was the wireless room. Disar would need to report in to Maton-devara Command and to summon a ground crew. He nodded to himself. *Yes, that will do nicely.* He scanned the men who were left, seeing that all were Service except for one low-ranked Command.

Adram turned back to the prisoners' truck, where with banging, snarling in a strange language and cursing on the part of the Gardier, the natives were dragged out.

The blond man was dumped on the concrete first, two disheveled and angry guards left to flank him as the others went back for the rest. One had a bleeding wrist from a bite wound and the other the beginning of a black eye. Adram cleared his throat, stepping around to face the native. The man tossed back the mane of tangled hair and glared up at him, his blue eyes furious. Adram said in Rienish, "A distraction, if you please, when I start toward the little building on the far right. Look down if you understand me." After a startled moment, the man dropped his head, the fall of hair shielding his expression.

"Very good." Adram lifted a brow. One of the guards nodded grim approval, pleased that whatever Adram had said had cowed the prisoner. Suppressing a smile, Adram started to turn away, then paused to add, "The big one with the hooked nose and the sour expression on your left has the key to your chains."

Head down, Ilias stared after him through the fringe of his hair, paralyzed for a moment by hope. *It could be a trick.* If that was some Gardier wizard who had somehow used a curse to make himself sound Rienish . . . But if the man standing next to him really had the keys, he was willing to take the chance.

Five Gardier were wrestling Giliead out of the wagon and others had gone in after Cimarus and Cletia. There was still a circle of guards around, pointing the shooting weapons.

Ilias saw his possible ally call to one of the other Gardier, motioning him to follow, and they both started toward the little wooden hut some distance away. *Right.* Ilias eyed the guard who supposedly had the keys, deciding there was just enough slack in the chain connecting his leg shackles for this to work.

Ilias twisted, hooking his ankles around the guard's leg and yanking for all he was worth. The man flung up his arms and fell backward, his head striking the stony floor with an audible crack.

Ilias ducked a wild blow from a weapon butt, hearing Giliead's alarmed shout. The next one caught him between the shoulder blades, knocking him flat.

One of them sat on his back while another did something to his leg shackles. Ilias wheezed and fought for air, his injured side aching. When the weight moved off he was too relieved to care what they had done and just lay there, taking deep breaths, waiting for the black haze to lift from his vision. He heard someone moving awkwardly toward him, chains clinking. "Ilias?" Giliead asked urgently from somewhere above his head.

"I'm fine," Ilias assured him, the words coming out in a wheeze. He managed to roll over, realizing the guards had shortened the chain between his leg shackles so there was no slack at all. "Oh, that's great." He writhed into a half-sitting position, leaning heavily against Giliead's side.

Cimarus and Cletia were watching them, Cimarus anxiously and Cletia with a kind of incredulous admiration. The Gardier were staring down at them, some angry, some contemptuous. Glaring up at them, Giliead said through gritted teeth, "Are you trying to make them kill you?"

"He said that one had the keys, and that he wanted a distraction." Ilias's nose was bleeding and he gingerly wiped it on Giliead's shirt. "At least, I hope that's what he said. I didn't get all the words."

"He, the one who speaks—" Giliead hesitated, swallowing hard, avoiding the word "Rienish" since the Gardier would recognize it. "What for?"

"I don't—"

A dram walked toward the wireless room, the Command junior at his side. He stopped at the doorway to the windowless wooden shack. He could hear the hum of the wireless inside, warming up. They hadn't had a chance to send a transmission yet. *Perfect.* He opened the door, motioning the other officer in ahead of him. The man hesitated, but Adram ignored him, slipping the dispatch bag off his shoulder and opening the flap to dig through it. Annoyed at this inefficiency, the man stepped through the door.

Adram heard a sharp question from Disar, but he already had the incendiary in his hand. He pushed the detonator into place, held down the strike lever, then tossed it through the door. Adram bolted, one arm up to shield his head.

He made it ten paces before the blast knocked him down.

— K now." The explosion rocked Ilias back and he fell against Giliead, wincing away from the sudden flare of light. He heard debris pelting the ground not far away, the frightened shouts of the Gardier. Heart pounding, he stared at the flying whale, expecting the dark expanse of the body above them to mottle with molten orange and ponderously tip over. But the whale wasn't on fire, it was the little wooden hut against the wall. *The one the crystal wizard went into. Oh, here we go.* He struggled to sit up, savagely glad the man was dead.

Jagged sections of the wooden walls still stood but the inside was aflame and the floor around it was littered with burning fragments. Smoke boiled into the air. He exchanged a frantic look with Giliead. *This is our chance.*

Some of the Gardier had thrown themselves to the ground, others had been hit by burning wood fragments and rolled or beat at the flames. Out of the smoke the Rienish Gardier ran, shouting at the others. He spun around, pointing frantically toward the flying whale, now mostly obscured by smoke, and shouted again, desperate urgency underlying every word and gesture. The other guards bolted away, some stopping to drag the wounded to their feet. They ran past their prisoners, banging open the outer doors somewhere behind the truck.

"What's happening?" Cimarus demanded, watching the growing fire worriedly. "Are we— Is it—"

"We're getting out of here," Giliead told him hurriedly. "Just stay quiet, don't draw their attention."

None of the Gardier seemed inclined to help their bound prisoners. Then one man stopped beside the unconscious guard, leaning down to grab his jacket, obviously meaning to haul him out. Ilias froze in horror. *If we can't get to those keys—* Beside him Giliead whispered, "Just leave him, come on, leave him. . . ."

The Rienish Gardier reached the man, pulling him away from the motionless guard and shoving him on, taking him by the arm and hauling him along when he hesitated.

"Go, go, go!" Ilias urged, but Giliead was already rolling to his knees, managing to hop-shuffle-crawl toward the unconscious man. Reaching him, he twisted around to use his bound hands and fumbled for the pouches at the Gardier's belt. "Hurry, dammit," Ilias urged him, looking from the burning hut to the silent flying whale.

"No, really?" Giliead growled, head craned over his shoulder to see. The dense smoke thickened the air and Cletia started to cough. "Got it," Giliead said suddenly, elated and relieved. More twisting around, then he was pulling the manacles off his wrists.

Cimarus shouted in relief, but Ilias was still trying to watch the flying whale through the growing haze of smoke. He couldn't see how close the flames were to it, or if the fire was spreading, but he could smell it and feel the wash of reflected heat. It caught him by surprise when Giliead leapt on him and flipped him over to wrestle with the locks on his leg shackles. His legs came free, then his hands, and Ilias scrambled to his feet with a yell of triumph.

In moments they had Cletia and Cimarus free. Ilias saw one of the outside doors behind the wagon stood partly open to the night. That seemed to be their only escape route. "The Gardier will still be out there," he told Giliead, jerking his head toward the doors.

"We'll have to chance it." Giliead started for the other wagon. "Come on, they put our weapons in here."

"Why isn't the flying whale burning?" Cimarus wanted to know, peering uncertainly through the smoke as Giliead shoved back the flaps and stepped up into the covered wagon bed. "The one we had went up quick enough."

Ilias looked back and almost got beaned in the head when Giliead tossed his sword out. He slung the baldric over his shoulder, his injured ribs stabbing him as he lifted his arms, and Giliead handed out his belt knife and the other weapons. "Maybe it's got one of those crystals in it. Didn't Tremaine say they could keep it from catching fire?"

"We can't trust that." Cletia slung her sword belt over her shoulder. "We need to get out of here."

"We know that." Ilias snapped. "Why don't you—" He stopped as Giliead reappeared, ducking under the canvas. He had Tremaine's bag and their packs over his shoulder and was carrying the crystal's metal box. "Why do you want that thing?" he demanded as Giliead jumped down. "It betrayed us." It sounded like a stupid thing to say about a lump of rock and glass, but it was what had happened.

"I don't think it did," Giliead said firmly, tossing his hair out of his eyes. "Come on."

Tremaine brought the truck to a halt well away from the airship hangar. It had lights but she hadn't used them, wanting to draw as little attention as possible. If the road hadn't been free of ditches and other obstructions, she would never have made it.

In the darkness of the cab she drew her pistol, checking how many rounds were left, for once glad she had been taught to do it blindfolded. *Five. Can I do this with five?* She had left the rest of her ammunition back with their supplies. "Calit, you need to leave." She couldn't see the boy's face, but he sat next to her on the bench and she could feel his eyes on her.

"I can drive the truck," he said, a world of stubbornness in those few words.

"Will you just run away?" Tremaine snapped.

"And go where?" he demanded, gesturing to the night and the empty plain rolling away. "Everybody I know gets killed," he added, his voice trembling.

Tremaine looked away, took a deep breath. "That makes two of us." She fumbled for the latch and the door creaked as it swung open. "Don't come after me."

Running across the uneven ground toward the wire fence, she wondered how she was going to get over it. But as she drew closer she saw the gate under the electric pole was open and Gardier were running out. She halted, watching them head toward a lighted building some distance away. Some of them were carrying or helping wounded along. *The hell . . .*

Tucking her gun behind her back, she started forward more slowly. There were only three Gardier left near the hangar, though it was hard to tell in the shadows left by the stark pool of electric light. One man in an officer's uniform was arguing with two others, pointing back toward the hangar. Tremaine realized she could smell smoke on the damp cool air.

She flinched as a shot went off, but it wasn't aimed at her. One of the Gardier at the gate was on the ground and the other two were fighting, struggling over a pistol. *That's got to be one of us,* she thought, incredulous. Unable to see whom to shoot at this distance, she ran toward them.

I'm too old for this, Adram thought grimly, losing his grip on the pistol as the Gardier pulled a forearm more tightly across his throat. And anyway he had always hired people to do the physical part.

The Gardier froze suddenly but Adram felt the pistol jammed into his temple. His breath caught in his throat but the man didn't fire. In another moment Adram saw why.

There was a woman in Gardier clothing pointing a gun at them. The light from the guardpost fell across her face, but he didn't recognize her until she said, "Stop right—oh holy shit."

I was right. Pushing the last vestiges of his Adram persona aside, Nicholas said in Rienish, "For God's sake, Tremaine, take the shot."

Hearing a language he couldn't understand, the guard tightened his grip, saying, "Drop your weapon or I'll—"

The report was so loud Nicholas thought the guard had fired into his head. He staggered as the man's grip fell away, his hand going to his cheek. He felt the warm wetness of blood, but it wasn't his. He looked for the Gardier and saw him sprawled on the ground, one neat bullet hole in his forehead. He straightened up, reaching for a hand-kerchief until he remembered the damn uniform jacket had no pock-ets. Wiping the blood away with his hand, he said under his breath, "I knew emphasizing firearms training over deportment lessons would benefit in the long run."

His daughter moved toward him, lowering the pistol, staring. "It's you."

He eyed her. God, she had changed. "Tremaine, what have you done to your hair?"

Chapter 21

"My what?" Tremaine repeated blankly. She heard Ilias call her name and spun around.

Through a haze of smoke, the Syprians burst out of the open hangar doors. Sword drawn, Ilias skidded to a halt, looking from Tremaine to Nicholas. In the wash of electric light she could see he had a bloody nose and a new collection of bruises. Giliead, Cimarus and Cletia were right behind him, none of them in much better shape. Giliead, amazingly enough, still had the crystal's case. Everybody eyed Nicholas with varying degrees of suspicion. "He helped us get free," Ilias told Tremaine, watching him warily. "He sounds Rienish."

Nicholas moved casually to join Tremaine, brushing the dirt off his Gardier uniform. "I assume they're with you," he said with aplomb, nodding toward the Syprians. Tremaine just stared at him incredulously. *He's acting as if we ran into each other during the interval at the Opera.* At least she knew it wasn't an imposter using a sorcerous illusion; no Gardier could pull off an impersonation like this.

Ilias looked at her worriedly and Giliead eyed Nicholas with distrust. "Who is he?" Cletia demanded, obviously speaking for everyone.

Ah, a question I used to ask myself frequently, Tremaine thought irreverently, still dazed from his appearance. "I— He's—" A distant shout interrupted her confused attempt at a reply. She saw truck lights and the bobbing glows of hand torches coming toward them across the dark field. "Later. This way!"

She led them toward the truck at a run, Nicholas pausing to recover the dead guard's gun and shoot out the light above the gate. In the dark the truck was impossible to see but fortunately Tremaine was too overwhelmed to second-guess herself and blundered right back into it. She clambered into the cab, shoving Calit over, and Nicholas climbed in the other side. The others ran around to the covered bed.

This truck had a large panel opening between the makeshift cab and the back, and Tremaine looked through to see the dim shapes of Ilias and the others scrambling in. As she fumbled for the starter, Calit was dragged into the opening and Ilias climbed through it into the cab to replace him. Giliead leaned through, right over Tremaine's shoulder. The engine rumbled to life and gears ground as she got the vehicle turned and pointed away from the hangar; she wasn't worried about direction, just speed and concealment. Her eyes were used to the dark again and she could make out vague shapes now.

"Just how were you planning on getting out of here?" Nicholas asked calmly, still in that "casual encounter at the café" tone, as if he hadn't been given up for dead for years.

Tremaine gritted her teeth. "We were going to steal a boat." That moment under the gate's bright spotlight had shown her that he had shaved his mustache and beard and that his dark hair was shorter than she remembered, with more gray. He had always been adept at changing his appearance; she was a little startled at how instantly she had recognized him.

"You thought you could just stroll into the city and steal a ship from a military dock?" He sounded faintly incredulous.

"I stole a truck," she snapped defensively. As someone who had apparently been masquerading as a Gardier, he was no one to point fingers.

"Trucks," Nicholas said with scorn, "are easy. I have a better idea." He leaned to point across the field into the dark, toward the city. "Head that way. You should come to a road."

"We have to pick up the others first." Tremaine was gritting her teeth so hard her jaw was beginning to ache. Basimi, Dubos and Molin would be waiting for them at the meeting point. She hoped.

Facing Nicholas, one arm braced on the wooden dash, Ilias asked quietly in Syrnaic, "Tremaine, who is he? A Rienish spy?"

Tremaine took a sharp breath. "No. Yes. He's my father."

Ilias said nothing for a moment, but she could practically hear startled consternation. Giliead, braced against the bumpy ride in the opening, shifted uncertainly. Ilias shook his head slightly. "You said he was dead."

"I thought he was." *God, the Queen was right. He faked his death. Again!* Tremaine felt herself proceeding rapidly from shocked senseless to seething.

"Her father's a Gardier?" Cimarus demanded from somewhere in back, baffled.

"Cimarus, shut up," Giliead said tightly.

"That explains how he recognized your ring," Ilias continued, ignoring the interruption.

The ring she had given Ilias, the one he wore around his neck. "I'm surprised he recognized me," Tremaine snarled, realizing the Syrnaic conversation allowed her parenthetical comments.

Nicholas listened to the unintelligible conversation with his usual annoying self-possession. "I assume the big man there is your sorcerer. The Command officer who captured them was able to locate him through the avatar crystal. Was he attempting to learn how to open a world-gate with it?"

"No, he's not a sorcerer." Tremaine forced herself to explain. "Syprians don't like magic. He's a Chosen Vessel. He can see etheric traces."

There was a moment of tense silence. "You didn't bring a sorcerer?"

"Well, therein lies the problem," she snapped. "We didn't know we were coming. We took that crystal off the airship that crashed after we set it on fire. Giliead might be able to make it take us back." Had the plan always sounded that mad, or was it just the circumstance?

"If he can't," Nicholas said dryly, "things are going to be a touch awkward."

His voice urgent, Giliead asked, "Tremaine, how did he come here?"

Tremaine obligingly translated, "Everyone wants to know what the hell you're doing here."

"I was picked up by the Gardier off the island base, the one they were using in the staging world to attack Chaire." Nicholas glanced at her. "I'm assuming you're with the Rienish group that attacked it, then the outpost at the barrier mountain port?"

"That would be us," Tremaine replied tightly.

"And the Syprians are the mainland natives who objected so strenuously to the Gardier presence on the island. I see. Well, I adopted a persona called Damien Adram, and managed to convince the Gardier that I was a civilian Defense Department bureaucrat fleeing Ile-Rien due to illicit activities, and that I wished to join them." He hesitated. "Arisilde didn't tell you this?"

Tremaine couldn't answer for a moment. Nicholas pressed, "I sent him back almost six years ago. He didn't arrive?"

"Something happened," Tremaine managed. "He didn't—We didn't find out what happened to him until a few days ago. It's a long story."

"I see." After a moment Nicholas continued imperturbably, "The Gardier were anxious to know how I had managed the etheric world-gate spell; fortunately, I was able to convince them I had stolen the spell and an avatar from one of their spies in Adera, and that I had killed the sorcerer who had made it work for me, to keep from having to pay him. Part of that was true. I did steal the spell, but Arisilde accidentally destroyed the avatar when he was trying to ascertain what it was; his sphere, however, worked just as well if not better.

"I was lucky enough to fall in with the Scientist class, who are slower to jump to conclusions than Command and also have a certain liberty denied to most of the military. But it still took me most of this time to prove Adram's sincerity, though unfortunately he didn't know much that could help them. But I was able to get myself assigned to a chief Scientist named Benin. When he learned that a Rienish party had managed to gate to the staging world and how, he became determined to obtain one of the spheres. Yesterday he was able to get me assigned to the group searching for the Rienish infiltrators. I intended to find some way to avoid capturing them or effecting a release if Command got to them before I did. Then I saw the ring."

He shifted on the bench to look toward her, saying calmly, "He could have taken it off your body, I suppose. Except that at the time I left, you didn't wear it. Which seemed to imply you had given it to him. The ring isn't valuable enough—or gaudy enough—for a bribe, so it must have been a gift."

Ilias and Giliead had been tensely quiet throughout the explanation; Tremaine didn't think they knew enough Rienish to catch more than half of it. She translated a brief synopsis.

Ilias turned to look at her sideways, though she couldn't see his expression in the dark. "He pretended to be someone else?" he said softly. "All that time?"

Giliead shook his head, drawing in a sharp breath. Tremaine said wearily, "He's not crazy. He did this kind of thing when I was a child too."

"Oh." Giliead didn't sound reassured.

"So he's not crazy," Ilias repeated dubiously.

But can we trust him? was what he didn't add. *If we can't,* Tremaine thought, *God help us.*

"Now tell me about Arisilde," Nicholas said grimly.

The fire spread through the hangar, creeping from work bay to work bay, but the big beams that supported the wooden walls were slow to catch. The airship itself was unhurt; it had an avatar aboard and its power fueled the wards that protected the flammable gas cells against outside attack. But the Service personnel summoned to the hangar were working hard to remove the valuable craft; if the building collapsed on it, the wards wouldn't hold. The two trucks inside the hangar were now ablaze and others had to be brought to winch the giant hangar doors open; in the meantime the men were moving the doors by brute force. The few Command officers present were organizing a search for the escaped prisoners, but the confused reports of the survivors and the lack of any wireless closer than the next hangar hampered their efforts.

Inside, in the burning wreckage of the wireless room, the empty shell of Command Officer Disar shoved itself upright off the concrete floor and began to crawl.

The wounds in its body from flame and flying wood and metal were terrible and its clothes were blackened rags, but it forced itself forward, ruined hands clawing at the floor. It was making toward a body just outside the circle of debris, a young Command officer unconscious but with life still lingering.

Reaching him, it touched the crystal in its temple, pressing until a shard of the embedded rock snapped away. Fumbling to hold its burned fingers steady, it lifted the shard toward the insensate man's head.

Tremaine stopped the truck on the road, near the dark line of woods where Basimi and the others should be waiting. Giliead sent Cimarus out to find them and guide them in. It was still quiet near the forest's edge but truck lights were zigzagging between the distant hangars and on the road to the city.

Tremaine had explained about Arisilde as best she could. In fact, she had explained about three times, realized she was babbling, and stopped. Nicholas hadn't commented, except to say thoughtfully, "I was afraid something had happened, when he didn't return, and there was no attempt to contact me. I knew he hadn't been captured."

Then that's theory one or theory two, I forget which, of how Arisilde got into the sphere down the drain, Tremaine thought, feeling awkward. She fumbled for something to say, knowing that Arisilde had been Nicholas's oldest friend. Then Nicholas turned impatiently, saying, "There is a need to hurry. We only have a limited amount of time before another Command Liaison will be able to focus on that avatar."

But let's not be sentimental about it, Tremaine thought grimly, her fingers beginning to tap deliberately on the steering wheel.

From the back, she heard Cletia say softly, "He's really her father?"

Ilias shifted impatiently next to her. Giliead said, "Yes," with the air of giving the final word on the subject.

"Is he a wizard?" Cletia persisted.

Giliead let out his breath. "No." Ilias glanced up at him, and Tremaine realized Giliead would not exactly be sorry to stumble on another Rienish wizard they could trust. It would mean he wouldn't have to try speaking to the crystal again.

Nicholas said, "The Gardier have someone, or something, aboard your ship. The chief Scientist called it a 'presence' but I wasn't able to ascertain exactly what it might be."

"I think we found it already. It killed some Gardier prisoners. Ilias and Giliead kept it from getting the last one, and Gerard and Niles did some kind of banishing on it." She thought she could now guess what the "presence" had been so keen to stop them from finding out from their prisoners—that the Gardier home world lay elsewhere.

Tremaine saw dim shapes moving out of the trees. She could tell that the one with the long hair and the sword was Cimarus, and she assumed the three dim figures following were Basimi, Molin and Dubos. They seemed to be carrying extra packs and she hoped they had been successful in finding some supplies; they had lost almost everything else they had when the Gardier had captured the Syprians.

One of the shapes came to the truck window and Basimi's voice said, "We were able to lift some rations and a few canteens, and I found a place we could get some tools if—" His voice sharpened in alarm. "Who's that?"

"He's a Rienish agent," Tremaine said impatiently. "Just get in the damn truck before they find us."

Dubos stepped up to the window. "There can't be a Rienish agent here, how—"

Nicholas leaned forward, saying sharply, "Your voice is familiar. Were you ever in Vienne Magistrates' Court?"

"What the—" Dubos hesitated, obviously struck by that perfect Vienne-accented Rienish. He flicked a hand torch on, to a chorus of startled hisses from the Syprians. Ilias winced away from the light. "Nicholas Valiarde?" Dubos sounded incredulous.

"Ah." Nicholas sat back, smiling slightly. "Sergeant Dubos, is it?"

Tremaine leaned her head on the steering wheel, muttering, "I can't fucking believe this." *After how I had to act to get Dubos to listen to me, and now Nicholas shows up, and everyone practically wets themselves in fear and awe.*

"I made inspector before I joined the army." Dubos turned back to Basimi and Molin. "Get in the truck."

The men hurriedly clambered in and Tremaine let the gear out. As the truck rumbled forward, Dubos appeared briefly in the panel to say, "Miss Valiarde, why didn't you tell us your father was here?"

"I didn't know!" Tremaine protested, adding under her breath, "Nobody's going to believe that."

The truck trundled along in silence until Nicholas said, "When the road turns into the copse of trees up here, stop. I'll have to drive from then on as we're certain to be seen."

Tremaine squinted against the dark, peering ahead, and managed to see the curve and the dim shape of the copse. It was near the place where she had killed the truck's former driver, where his body still lay cooling in the ditch. The memory was a shock; in everything that had happened since, she had somehow pushed it so far aside it had left her consciousness altogether. Nicholas startled her out of the dark memory by adding, "The Gardier boy will have to go with you. He knows too much and we can't risk releasing him."

Tremaine shook her head, making herself focus again. "The Gardier boy had at least two chances to run away before he knew too much so he can just go with us and like it."

Ilias must have caught the gist of that because he said in Syrnaic, "He's our boy now, anyway."

"You'd better not mean that literally," Tremaine snarled back at him. She switched to Rienish to ask Nicholas, "What do you mean, 'go with you'?"

"I'm staying behind."

Tremaine sputtered, "You can't— They've got to know what you are by now—"

"The key witnesses are dead, and the others didn't see anything damning. If we manage your escape correctly, I should remain unsuspected." He shifted to face her. "When I first arrived here, I was at a disadvantage, but I can blend in now and I also have three other personas created with full documentation. If I have to leave this Maton, I can reemerge in another one as a native." He added impatiently, "I still have much to learn, Tremaine. My work here is still incomplete. These people, all that they're attempting to do, it didn't come about naturally. Something has forced this into being, has created all this for a specific purpose and I have to find out what that is."

"All right, fine," Tremaine snapped. They reached the copse and she brought the truck to an abrupt halt, putting it in park and telling Ilias, "Come on, we're getting in the back now."

He went without protest, though she could tell by the turn of his head he had thrown one more wary look at Nicholas. Tremaine found she wasn't as steady as she thought when her foot slipped on the tailgate and she would have fallen face forward if Ilias hadn't deftly caught her and handed her in. The back was dark and close, only the dim light from the opening into the cab to see by. There seemed to be benches along the sides that would make the ride less excruciating. She made her way to the front, stepping on Cimarus's and Basimi's feet to judge by the startled exclamations, and crouched down next to Giliead. "Just what is this place we're going to?" she asked Nicholas through the opening to the cab.

"It's an airship mooring site." Nicholas shifted into gear and the truck rumbled on. He switched on the headlamp, a single electric light at the front that threw dim illumination on the road. Tremaine almost protested, then saw the reason for it; it would make them just one more vehicle on the road, and the searchers would be looking for a bunch of Syprian barbarians on foot, not a truck with a single driver. "Benin's group has just completed the prototype of an airship that carries its own spell circle with it. It can gate at any point."

Tremaine winced. "Like the *Ravenna*. That's the ship we're using."

No wonder the Gardier hadn't bothered to establish a larger base on the Wall Port. *Why go to the trouble, when they had that in the works?*

Nicholas flicked a dark glance back at her. "So that's where they got the idea. It's of recent design and was just added to the airship a few days ago. You may have noticed, they aren't much for original thinking. Everything they have—the airships, their weapons—is copied from other sources. These people can't even come up with an automobile on their own. They've stolen nearly every mechanical object they own from someone else."

Tremaine frowned, though it fit with what she had seen in the little abandoned town. And it explained why the airships seemed so susceptible to accident when the crystals weren't aboard to protect them. *If the electrical wiring is slapped together as badly as this truck, it's a wonder any of them survive.* "What about their magic? The crystals?"

"To assume they haven't done the same with their magic is absurd. Where it came from," he said deliberately, "is what I've been trying to discover. It's the key to the whole situation."

"And here I thought the key to the whole situation was that they were beating the pants off us," Tremaine said, not bothering to stint the sarcasm. *And here I just used to think these things instead of saying them aloud. I have changed.* Or her incipient hysteria was preventing her from keeping her mouth shut.

Nicholas changed gears to navigate a slight rise in the ground, something Tremaine didn't usually bother to do. He said, continuing their earlier conversation, "The only thing special about that ring of yours, other than the fact that it's made of sorcerously inert white gold, is that your family name is inscribed on it. That seems to imply a particular relationship."

She took much grim satisfaction from saying, "He's my husband. We're married. And my hair was in fashion when I left Ile-Rien."

Silence, except for the growl of the truck's engine.

Ilias's night vision had been ruined by the curse lamp in the front of the wagon and he couldn't see a damn thing. But by the lay of the land, he thought they were going too near the populated area. Giliead must have realized it at the same moment, because he said quietly, "Tremaine, we're getting close to the city."

Tremaine shifted forward to speak to her father. Ilias had no trouble believing in that relationship; the physical resemblance might not be much, but the feyness and the ruthlessness were certainly similar. Ilias waited tensely, sweat running down his back. His head still ached and their bumpy progress made it hard to ignore the pain in his side, though he sat braced against the bench with his sword across his lap, using one of Giliead's legs to steady himself. The reply came too rapid and soft for him to catch. The worried reaction of Dubos and the other men told him the answer wasn't popular before Tremaine sat back with a Rienish curse and said in Syrnaic, "This airship mooring site is in the goddamn city."

Ilias wiped sweat off his forehead with the back of his arm, wincing as he accidentally touched his sore nose. "I liked the boat idea better."

Giliead made a noise of agreement and even Cimarus added, "I did too."

"Can this work?" Cletia asked, tension in her voice.

"It had better work," Tremaine murmured.

After a short time a low-voiced comment from the front warned that they were coming near the city gates. Everyone slipped off the benches to huddle on the floor, Giliead squeezing in next to Ilias, Tremaine just in front of him. Ilias curled up to make room, glad it was too dark for anyone to see his grimace. It was easier to ignore the pain when he was doing something; this sitting and waiting just gave him time to dwell on it.

Ilias heard the rumble of more wagons as theirs slowed. A voice spoke Gardier right on the other side of the canvas and he froze, feeling Tremaine flinch. The wagon stopped and Ilias took a grip on his sword hilt. Not much they could do if they were caught except fight a doomed last stand.

The Gardier spoke again, Nicholas answered, and after a too-long moment the truck moved on. Ilias let his breath out, hearing the others shift slightly in relief. But now they were in the Gardier city.

Tremaine bit her last intact fingernail to the quick as the truck trundled through the streets. She couldn't remember how far it had been to the building she had seen with the airship moored to the top, but surely the truck could travel faster than she and Calit had walked.

Finally, the vehicle came to a stop with a crunch of gears, then the engine died. Nicholas leaned back to say quietly, "Stay here for a moment."

"Right," Tremaine whispered, but as she heard him climb out of the cab she got up and stepped quietly past the others to the canvas over the back, gently lifting it aside to look.

"Where are we?" Ilias wanted to know and she waved him to silence. The truck was parked in a large stone-walled chamber with a finely worked floor inlaid with gray-green slate, now stained and spotted with oil. The lights were the customary strings of wire with bare bulbs hanging down. In contrast to the fine stonework, the wooden panel doors opening onto the dark street that Nicholas was sliding shut looked shoddy and poorly fit the opening. There were a few crates stacked on the floor and two more trucks parked nearby. It looked as if the Gardier had wanted a mews in their building so they had simply knocked out a wall and converted a ballroom or assembly room. Ilias squeezed in beside her to look out and Dubos beat Giliead to the other side.

Nicholas got the outer door closed and, as he crossed to the front of the big room, waved for them to come out of the truck. Tremaine pulled the canvas back and climbed down. The others followed her rapidly, Basimi handing out the supply bags to Molin and Cimarus.

Nicholas stood at a set of heavy wooden doors leading into the interior of the building. They were old and scarred but still bore the curlicue carving along the rounded edges that marked them as a product of the original builders. Nicholas had eased one door open and was peering out into a dimly lit corridor. He leaned back to say, "The living quarters are on the far side of the building, but there may be men working late in some of these rooms." His glance took them all in with deliberate emphasis. "Be very quiet."

Tremaine passed the warning on in Syrnaic. Ilias nodded tightly. She noticed he was sweating despite the cool air and he was carrying his sword propped on his shoulder, as if it hurt to lift it. Besides the obvious bloody nose, his shirt was torn open and there was a darkening bruise all down his right side, and the skin around his eyes looked bruised. *We need to get out of here,* she thought nervously. She could feel their borrowed time slipping away. Nicholas added, "There's a small armory on the second floor where we can find some firearms for your friends."

"The Syprians won't use guns," Tremaine told him.

He gave her that dark stare. She said with some asperity, "They won't touch anything that looks like it might be magic, even if they know it's not magic, and considering I can't even get them to press the light switches and the only one who ever touched a telephone got shot to death, I don't think I'm going to be able to convince them otherwise."

Nicholas let out his breath, rolled his eyes, then pulled the knapsack off his shoulder, opening it to take out a metal object with a heavy round end and a handle. It looked a bit like some sort of esoteric tool for ironing laundry, but knowing her father, she said, "A bomb?"

"An incendiary," he corrected. "Hold it by this end, push that into place, then hold down this lever. Then throw it and run."

"Right." She accepted the bag and followed him through the doors.

The corridor led to a wide stone stair, and though they passed several doorways, everything seemed quiet. The armory wasn't far from the second-floor landing, and Nicholas opened it with a key, revealing a long room filled with gleaming racks of weapons. Basimi, Dubos and Molin all took rifles and pistols, stopping to quickly load them, and the Syprians remained impatiently in the corridor.

Afterward they went up the stairs toward the top floor, meeting only one man who suddenly came out of a doorway onto a landing and died without crying out with Cimarus's knife in his throat. Ilias moved hastily to help Cimarus bundle the body back into the room out of sight and they continued on. The man hadn't been armed, but one shout from him would have killed all of them; Tremaine stopped counting the dead innocent bystanders.

They finally reached the top where a large archway opened onto the dimly lit landing. Through it was a room that seemed to take up the whole top floor, mostly dark except for a few pools of electric light from overhead bulbs. Parts of the space were blocked off by wooden partitions that didn't reach all the way up to the sculpted stone arches of the ceiling. In the shadows Tremaine could see worktables, cluttered with papers and drawings, fragments of mechanical parts. In the outer wall three elegantly curved stone archways mimicked the ones in the converted garage below; these might have been meant to open onto balconies, but they were closed off with old stained boards. There was an opening to the outside somewhere because fresh cold air moved through the room in a draft, gently stirring the papers. Then she heard the creak of a chair from behind the largest partition.

Nicholas eased forward, his steps silent on the stone floor. Giliead slipped past Tremaine, moving to flank him. Ilias started to follow but Giliead threw him a look and he shifted to the side instead. Nicholas took note of their movements with a slight turn of his head, but didn't object. He motioned toward the center partition. It blocked off an area directly under one of the electric lights. Giliead faded back, circling around the wooden walls, and Ilias took the other direction.

Ilias did a quick tour through his side of the big chamber, peering around the flimsy partitions, quickly checking the shadowy corners. He met Giliead again at the back, near a stone staircase that curved up to meet an opening in the roof. Giliead started up and Ilias hurried in his wake, both of them emerging into wind and darkness. The roof was a huge space, topped with a low parapet wall, but the flying whale that hung above dwarfed it. It might have been his imagination, but the huge shape outlined against the lighter darkness of the sky looked bigger than the other flying whales. The blocky outline of the crew compartments, snugged up against the belly, was much longer and there was a second small compartment hanging below. The boarding ramp was attached to it, stretching down to rest atop a pyramidal stone platform.

There was no sign of life on the roof, no other structures to conceal a Gardier, and the whale itself had no wizard lights lit inside it. Giliead went to the stone platform, stopping to listen for curses, then climbed the steps and went up the ramp. *I can't believe we're doing this again,* Ilias thought in exasperation. Trusting themselves to one of these things was mad, but it seemed it really was their best way to escape. Giliead reappeared in moments, motioning that it was all clear, and Ilias turned back to the stairs to tell the others.

Nicholas waited a moment, giving Ilias and Giliead a chance to search the room, then advanced toward the side of the nearest partition where a makeshift door stood open. Tremaine followed, trying to keep her steps quiet.

As Nicholas moved into the doorway, Tremaine hung back, leaning to see around him. She caught a glimpse of a man seated at a table, the surface spread with pages of intricate diagrams and drawings. Holding them down like paperweights were dozens of crystal shards. *Here we go,* she thought. This man surely had enough knowledge to make this whole mess worthwhile.

Ilias returned to her side, softly enough to make her jump, and leaned against her to breathe into her ear. "He's alone. The flying whale is tethered to a stone platform on the roof."

Tremaine saw Nicholas looking back at her with a raised brow. She nodded and he turned, taking the last step through the room's doorway. Speaking in the Gardier language, he said, "Benin. Working late, I see."

The man looked up, startled. "Adram?" Then he saw the pistol in Nicholas's hand and his face went still. He looked past him, his eyes finding Tremaine and Ilias in the shadows. "What is this?"

"Sorry to spring this on you, but I'm afraid my status as a Rienish criminal who sought political refuge was a fabrication," Nicholas told him, cool and just a little amused. "Stand up, please."

Arrogant bastard, Tremaine thought, annoyed all over again at his calm. At least he was on their side. She glanced away as Giliead came down the stairs, took in the situation and joined them. He said softly, "I didn't search the whole thing, but it was all dark, there didn't seem to be anyone aboard, and there was no curse crystal in the steering cabin."

"The airship doesn't look occupied," Tremaine translated into Rienish for Nicholas. "And there was no crystal."

Nicholas nodded an acknowledgment and asked Benin, "Is there anyone aboard the prototype?"

"No, my assistants have all gone to rest." Benin had pushed back his chair and stood, staring at Ilias and Giliead in a kind of aghast curiosity. "What—who are they?"

"Syprians—partisans acting for Ile-Rien in the staging world," Nicholas replied easily. "Take that dispatch bag on the floor and begin filling it with those papers, please." He turned his head slightly to tell Tremaine in Rienish, "Send the others up the stairs to the mooring platform. I suggest you hurry."

Tremaine stepped back, waving urgently to Dubos at the door. He started toward them, the others following. Cimarus stopped in the doorway to act as rear guard, but Tremaine was relieved to see Basimi wave him on and take his place. If anyone charged the door, his rifle was going to be of more use than Cimarus's sword.

Benin had recovered some aplomb. He picked up the canvas bag and obediently scooped the papers and crystals into it. He eyed

Nicholas thoughtfully. "Disar said you were a spy, but . . . he had no proof."

"That's because I'm a very good spy," Nicholas assured him.

Seeming merely curious, Benin asked, "You're going to kill me?" Tremaine was wondering about that herself.

"That would be a waste, and if there's one thing I find admirable about your military regime, it's the lack of waste." Nicholas added thoughtfully, "I'm sending you with them. You'll be well treated if you cooperate, and I suspect you'll be given full scope for your investigations."

Benin met Nicholas's eyes, as if trying to gauge his sincerity. *Good luck with that,* Tremaine thought dryly.

Dubos and Cletia passed behind her, Calit stopping to stare at Benin. Cimarus caught his arm, urging him along. As Molin reached them, Giliead stepped in, sheathing his sword and taking the crystal's box. He stopped suddenly, his face going still. "Someone's using a curse."

There was nothing in Benin's hands. "It's not him," Tremaine said, realized she had spoken in Syrnaic and hastily added, "Giliead says someone's using a spell."

Nicholas swore, gestured sharply at Benin and told him in Gardier, "We've run out of time; move now."

Giliead looked toward the inside stairwell. "It's down there," he said grimly, starting forward. Tremaine saw that Basimi was just standing there, rifle held limply in one hand. She opened her mouth to say something, to tell them to run, to shout Basimi's name, then gunfire exploded from the stairwell. Basimi's body jerked and shuddered, then fell. Frozen, Tremaine saw Giliead dive sideways and started to realize that might be a really good idea when Ilias knocked her down.

Tremaine sat down hard, already clawing open the knapsack Nicholas had given her as Ilias grabbed the legs of the nearest table and dumped it over, giving them some protection. Bullets split the wood above their heads and Ilias ducked lower. She looked across toward Benin's work area and saw Giliead pinned down behind another overturned table. Nicholas had ducked inside the partition, but Benin was stretched on the floor, a spray of blood outlining his head. From behind, the loud reports of rifles sounded; Dubos and Molin firing back from the better shelter of the stone stairway.

Tremaine pulled out an incendiary but everything suddenly went quiet. She looked up, blinking, thinking, *What the hell?* A mist had settled over the room, turning the electric bulbs into dim yellow blobs. She could barely see Nicholas and Giliead, only a few feet away, and she couldn't hear any shooting.

"They've got a wizard, of course," Ilias said with a grimace, trying to look over the top of the table.

Nicholas had come to the same conclusion. From his position behind the wooden barrier, he said, "Don't let him see you. If he can't see you, he can't cast spells on you."

"We know that!" Tremaine snapped. She heard what sounded like Dubos shouting her name, and she yelled back, "Stay down, there's a sorcerer in here!" Her voice sounded weirdly muffled and there was no answer. She hesitated, looking at the incendiary in her hand. If the mist was somehow solid and she threw this into it, it could bounce right back and kill them all in a highly unpleasant fashion. "Ilias, try to throw something. See if the mist is solid."

He glanced around, picked up a broken chair leg, and flung it over the top of the table. It bounced back, hitting the floor behind them with a clatter. He looked at her bleakly. "It's solid."

Tremaine shoved the incendiary back in the bag with a grimace. "Damn."

"Throw down your weapons!" a Gardier voice called from the doorway. "I know you are here, Adram. You killed my last vehicle, but I continue. I followed you here as if you left a trail of light."

"Oh, bugger it," Nicholas muttered, just loud enough for Tremaine to catch.

"What?" she demanded.

"The damn thing left Disar and found another host," he explained, though it still left her baffled. He raised his voice to shout, "If you come any closer, I'll kill Benin."

Tremaine stared at him. *We have a dead man for a hostage; how much time is that going to buy us?* Then Ilias whispered, sounding horrified, "What the shit is he doing?"

"I don't—" Tremaine started to answer, then realized he was staring at Giliead, not Nicholas.

Giliead, crouched behind the other table, opened the crystal's container. She saw the crystal bathe his face in light, then he sat up, looking over the top of the table toward the archway.

Suddenly the Gardier sorcerer cried out and the mist dropped like a curtain, puddling on the floor in puffs of white, then draining away like water. After a moment of shock, gunfire thundered from the arch-way.

Tremaine fumbled out an incendiary again, pushed the thingy, pulled the lever, and stood up on her knees to fling it toward the stair-well.

The impact knocked her backward like a punch from a giant hand. Flat on the ground, she realized the weight atop her was Ilias and the table, the wood shuddering from the impacts of more flying debris. Smoke choked her lungs and she heard the crackle of flame. *God, I hope Basimi was as dead as he looked,* she thought, sick.

As Ilias pushed the table aside, she saw the front half of the big room obscured by smoke. Ilias said something she couldn't hear and she pointed to her ears, shaking her head as she eased to her feet. Surely she would be able to hear gunfire.

Nicholas, one arm clutched to his side, came to his feet, motioning toward the stairs. He dropped his gun to grab the bag that lay near Benin's hand. Their companions sprang up from cover and bolted for the stairway, climbing it out of the roiling cloud of smoke, Dubos, Cimarus, Molin hauling Calit by the arm, and Cletia.

Giliead had closed the crystal's box and followed Nicholas. Tremaine hung back and Ilias tried to push her up in front of him, but she shook the bag of incendiaries, trying to tell him what she meant to do. He understood, or at least gave her the benefit of the doubt.

She followed him halfway up the steps, then stopped to arm an-other incendiary. She dropped it into the bag, flinging the whole thing out into the room, then bolted up the steps to where Ilias waited im-patiently. She took a deep breath as they came out into the clean cool night. Following the others, she and Ilias sprinted for the airship.

Then Tremaine felt the stone paving underfoot quiver as they reached the pyramidal mooring platform. She looked back to see fire blossom out of the stairwell. *That may have been a mistake.* Ilias tugged her arm impatiently and she followed him up, then across the shud-dering metal ramp. The hatch opened directly into a large control cabin, with a ladder in the center to access the rest of the compart-ments. Looking wildly around, Tremaine saw the same sort of control array as on their other airship. More importantly, the crystal's case sat open on the floor, and the crystal itself rested in the metal cage sus-pended above the steering console.

Giliead and Nicholas were already there and Dubos was at the controls. They were all bloody and bruised and soot-stained but alive. Cimarus and Cletia must have gone up the ladder since there was no room in the small control cabin; Calit's head appeared in the opening, peering down at them. Molin, waiting by the door, said something to her. Tremaine pointed to her ears and said, "I can't hear you." Her voice sounded muffled and strange.

He mouthed the words, "Where's Basimi?"

"He didn't make it," she said awkwardly, not knowing how else to phrase it. Saying it that way seemed to diminish the violence, as if he had had an operation and not pulled through. Molin turned abruptly to haul at a lever, making the ramp lift. Tremaine saw Dubos press his lips together and turn back to the wheel. Ilias stood beside her, still holding his sword, watching Giliead uncertainly.

Nicholas leaned against the ladder, looking weary. His right arm was bleeding. She read his lips as he said, "Anytime, gentlemen."

"Now would be good," Tremaine translated into Syrnaic for Giliead.

He looked back at her, his face etched with strain. *He's not going to be able to do it,* she thought, heart sinking. He looked sick.

Then she felt the deck jerk under her feet. The gondola filled with daylight, the port opening onto a view of brilliant blue sky.

Chapter 22

I'm beginning to believe this is as bad an idea as it sounds, Florian thought sourly. She was crouched in the semidark of a storage room not far from Ixion's prison. The room was warm and dank and had a lingering scent of both fuel oil and onions, which she hoped was just coming through the rattling air vent and not an indication of what had once been kept here. She had cast a concealment charm on herself to avoid anyone's notice.

She had waited for most of yesterday without any result except sore knees. She shifted, wincing, again grimly entertaining the suspicion that this was Ixion's idea of amusement. She had reasoned at first that he must be telling the truth, since no one had told him about the events in the Isolation Ward and the hospital. Gerard hadn't been convinced by this theory, however.

"Florian, I'm sorry," he had said, taking off his spectacles and resting his head in his hands. They were in his quarters and he was seated at the little desk, which was overflowing with books and papers. They had sailed away from the Walls that morning, with the new Gardier prisoners ensconced in the Isolation Ward, even more carefully warded and guarded than before. She knew Gerard felt that responsibility heavily. And Niles still hadn't gotten much usable information out of either the new prisoners or the Gardier woman. "But surely you realize Ixion is not to be trusted." Gerard sounded as if he was at the limit of his patience.

"Yes, I do realize that, but I think he's genuinely worried about this." Florian paced, since there wasn't a place to sit down for all the scrying bowls. "He's trapped where this thing can get to him and we're his only hope for doing something about it."

Gerard lifted his head. He had looked exhausted for a long time, but now he looked ill, his eyes sunken and his cheeks hollow. "I'm afraid I don't believe this 'thing' exists anymore," he said grimly. "Ixion knows Giliead is no longer on the ship; he's simply trying to maneuver us into releasing him."

"But what if he's not?" Florian threw her arms in the air, frustrated. "What if it wasn't just a construct that you and the sphere destroyed, what if Tremaine was right, and there is a second one? Or the sorcerer who created the construct is on the ship too?"

"I'm afraid Ixion's word isn't good enough," he snapped.

Florian controlled her irritation with effort; she knew Gerard was blaming himself for what had happened at the Wall Port, but she didn't seem to be able to do anything about that, either. She stopped beside the scrying bowl that held a brass grommet from one of Tremaine's boots. Even to Florian's untutored eyes, she could see the bowl held no images. Gerard had argued for using the sphere to take one of the *Ravenna*'s launches back to Ile-Rien's world, to see if the airship was trapped there. But the same reasons applied, there was still too much Gardier activity for a lengthy search in the Maiutan archipelago, the place that occupied the Wall Port region in their own world. "No luck?" she asked softly, already knowing the answer. Scrying spells didn't work over long distances, and it was especially doubtful that they would work across the barriers between worlds.

Gerard's mouth twisted and he looked away. "Nothing."

Florian hesitated, her fingers resting on the scrying bowl's rim. "One day," she said. "That's all. Just in case it's true."

Gerard was silent for a long moment, then he had shaken his head, smiling bitterly. "What else have we got to do?"

During her long watch this morning it had belatedly occurred to Florian that Ixion had said himself that he could hear his guards' conversation. If they had talked about the incident in the hospital, he would know everything he needed to make his story convincing. *Tremaine would have thought of that.* She rubbed her aching eyes. *God, I wish I knew where they were.*

*   *   *

This airship was considerably bigger than their last one; Tremaine supposed it would make a much bigger explosion when they crashed it too.

They searched it for stray Gardier first, climbing up the ladder from the suspended control cabin to where a series of compartments held the engines, the fuel tanks and large spaces for freight and bomb storage. It wasn't much different from the other airships, though everything was on a larger scale. Another ladder led up to a second level with more crew areas, or so Nicholas said; Tremaine hadn't been up there yet. Toward the bow they found the compartment that held the spell circle.

This was the only compartment that didn't have the cork matting on the deck; Tremaine sat on her heels to examine the symbols painted in black on the bare metal. The Gardier circle she had seen on the Isle of Storms base had had a holder for a large crystal in the center; this one didn't. *Nicholas was right,* she thought with a frown. *It's just like the* Ravenna's *circle.* Dommen and the other Rienish who had spied for the Gardier at Port Rel must have passed on the idea to place the circle on a large ship, giving it the ability to move between worlds at will. *Do the bastards have to steal everything?*

"Are we sure the crystal took us to the right place?" Molin wondered, coming to stand beside Tremaine. She was relieved his voice sounded mostly normal to her now; her ears were still ringing a little from the explosion, and with the buzz of the airship's engines, it was hard to tell how affected her hearing still was.

Nicholas stepped into the room behind them, saying, "We can't be certain until evening when we can get a look at the stars, but all the indications seem favorable so far." He had taken off his jacket and wore a white shirt underneath, its right sleeve stained with blood. He was occupied with wrapping a handkerchief around the minor wound in his arm. "I wasn't able to find out as much as I would have liked about the Gardier's otherworld explorations, but I did learn the etheric gates don't have unlimited options. A gate in one world can only reach certain other worlds. That's why the Gardier can't go directly from their world to Ile-Rien and must pass through the staging world first."

Tremaine thought that over, brows drawing together. "We went to a different world from the island. Florian took us there accidentally when we were trying to get back to Ile-Rien. Then Arisilde took me there to get rid of a Gardier. I think it was a different world. The sky was strange and the people were . . . a lot bigger."

Nicholas lifted a brow, frowning. "Did you. That's odd."

Molin wiped the soot and sweat off his forehead in relief. "We can work that out later, once we get that crystal back to the sorcerers. But Giliead did it, all right. He got us out of there."

Tremaine took a deep breath. "Yes, he sure did." She just hoped it hadn't done anything permanent to him.

They finished the search of the flying whale, but instead of following the others, Ilias looked for Giliead, finally going back up the narrow metal stairs in the common room to the second level. The stairs opened into a corridor with rows of depressing narrow doors for the living quarters. He stopped to look into one, seeing it was larger than those on the other flying whales, and had enough shelves for four men to sleep on instead of just two. Not that much of an improvement, as far as he was concerned.

The far end of the corridor was lit by daylight, so he was expecting windows, but when he reached it he still halted for a moment, arrested by the view. It was a common room with an array of nearly floor-to-ceiling glass panels on each side, all looking out on the cloud-studded blue of the sky and the limitless stretch of the ocean below. The windows were shaded by the bulk of the whale's belly above them, and looking up Ilias could see the dark skin of it curving away. There was a big table with the long narrow drawers that he now knew were for maps, more metal cabinets, a few chairs. And Giliead, sitting on the floor near the starboard window.

He didn't look up as Ilias crossed over to him and eased his battered body down to sit nearby. Ilias shifted gingerly around, trying to find a position that didn't make his side ache. The brown matting on the floor didn't provide any padding. He settled on curling his legs up and half-slumping over, supporting himself on one arm. Giliead glanced at him then, giving him a faintly incredulous look. "I don't want to lie down," Ilias answered the unspoken criticism. If he did, he didn't think he would be able to get up again.

Giliead returned his gaze to the sky on the other side of the thick glass. "You'll make it worse." His tone was sour.

Ilias snorted derisively, then winced at the twinge from his midsection. "Like you'd know," he said anyway.

Giliead ignored that. Ilias watched him for a long moment. "What did it feel like?" he asked finally.

Giliead let out a breath. "Like . . . shooting an arrow, except there was nothing in my hands."

Ilias considered that. "Tremaine can get the god-sphere to do things for her, and she's not a wizard."

"The god-sphere is a god. It can do what it wants. The woman in the crystal can only do a few curses, only the ones that the Gardier gave her. How to make the flying whale go to other worlds, how to make it fly back to the Gardier, how to protect it from lightning and wind and fire from the outside, and how to destroy the Rienish shooting weapons."

Ilias examined that for a flaw but couldn't find it. Even he could see that asking the thing that lived in the sphere for a favor was substantially different from using its power to make a curse work. He tried, "All the Rienish said you can't do a curse if you don't know the words that make it work."

Giliead looked at him then, his eyes dark with regret. "She showed it to me. The woman in the crystal. I'd woken her up enough that she remembered it from when she was alive. She couldn't do it anymore, but she said I could."

Ilias rubbed his eyes. It was worse than he thought. And he had thought it was pretty bad. "What are we going to do when we get home?" he asked, hoping he didn't sound as hopeless as he did inside his head.

Giliead just looked at him. "We?"

"We what?" Ilias frowned, then he got it. "Of course 'we,' you stupid bastard." He glared at Giliead, unable to do anything else because of his injury.

Giliead turned away, his face defensive and relieved all at once. His jaw set as if he was fighting for control. He said finally, "What if the god won't accept me anymore?"

Ilias bit his lip. "They'd kill us. But it wouldn't be fair. You're not crazy. The god's always been fair before."

Giliead didn't answer, still looking out at the clouds. "As far as we know."

Ilias swore under his breath. There was no one to ask what the god's reaction might be. Gerard, source of information on all things curse-related, had had no idea that the gods even existed before he had come to Cineth. "Maybe we should just . . . not go back." He knew it was a stupid idea even as he said it.

Giliead shook his head. "And never see Mother, Halian, Dyani, any of the others again? You know Cletia and Pasima will tell them what happened. I want them to hear it from me. And . . . I have to know what the god will do."

There was a small crew area just above the control cabin, though there was no furniture and nothing in the way of amenities, just metal walls and matting on the floor. Tremaine only knew it was a crew area because there was no outside door for bringing in cargo. She found Cletia and Cimarus there seated on the floor, Cletia cleaning her sword with a swatch cut from a Gardier uniform and Cimarus examining a wound in his arm. Calit was nearby, asleep, curled up with his head pillowed on one of their supply bags. There was no sign of Ilias or Giliead.

Tremaine wandered the compartment absently, finding a small room off the main area that had a tiny primitive sink. Since there wasn't anything that looked like a toilet, she assumed it was a galley.

Looking through the cabinets built into the walls, they all seemed bare. It was a good thing Dubos and the others had found some rations; if they took too long to catch up with the *Ravenna,* or had to go all the way to Capidara, they were going to need food and water.

She went back out to the supply bags and began to poke through the ones Calit wasn't sleeping on, hoping against hope that the Gardier had something like coffee. The only thing she could find was a substance in a jar that looked a little like ground coffee beans but smelled like dried seaweed. Tucking it back into the bag with an annoyed mutter, she decided to just stick with water.

She wandered back into the galley, trying to decide if she ought to occupy herself with putting some kind of meal together for everyone. It had been so long since she had eaten that she was actually beginning to regard Cletia's grain cakes as a fond memory. She studied the galley again, leaning on the metal counter, but didn't see anything like a gas ring. Then she clapped herself in the forehead. *That's right, fire.*

She became aware of Nicholas leaning in the doorway watching her. She rubbed her eyes, asking, "We are pointed in the right direction, aren't we?"

"Yes. I read the compass for Sergeant Dubos."

"That's good." Tremaine realized she had all the symptoms of crying: a prickly warm ache right behind her eyes, runny nose, but there weren't any tears. "I got everyone into this," she said suddenly, not really aware the words were out until she heard herself say them. But she had to say it to someone.

Nicholas was unperturbed. "You started the Gardier war? How precocious, at the age you were then."

His way of saying *don't be an idiot*. She glared at him, wishing she could have some effect on that impenetrable façade. "The Syprians."

"Ah. Everyone who matters."

Ouch. But it wasn't quite true. Gerard mattered, Florian mattered, even Ander mattered. Princess Olympe, Niles, Colonel Averi, Lady Aviler. The missionary woman who had been brave enough to speak to them in the Isle of Storms base, then kissed her cheek later. The chief petty officer who had given her his pistol when Ixion had escaped, various other random people whose names she didn't know or barely remembered, they all mattered. Arites, Basimi, Captain Feraim, Stanis and all the other dead mattered. "All right, so I didn't get everyone into this," she snapped. "But I made them put me in charge, then I couldn't handle it. The idea to steal a boat was stupid."

"Not stupid. Ill-informed. But it must have seemed the only option at the time." He eyed her thoughtfully. "After you entered the city and saw the situation at the harbor, did you still intend to go through with it?"

She sensed this was a question he actually wanted the answer to. "I might have. We would have gotten killed."

"The chances of dying were fairly high all along," he admitted easily. "Why did you make them put you in charge?"

Tremaine gestured helplessly. "The Syprians don't like to take orders from men who aren't part of their family. Giliead was the only one who could hear the Gardier crystal, I didn't think I could convince him to try to use it if he thought— He didn't want to do it and he did it anyway and— I don't know." She found herself pausing for the moment when a normal person would have said something reassuring. She sighed to herself. *Do I do that? No wonder I keep Florian in a constant state of distracted annoyance.* "You know, some people have fathers who just say 'there, there, it'll be all right.' "

Nicholas snorted in pure contempt. "That would hardly help, since you know it isn't true. It isn't going to be all right. The chances are good that it will never be all right again."

Well, yes. Tremaine wearily leaned on the counter, eyeing him. She didn't feel like crying anymore, at least. She felt like getting some answers. "You know Reynard Morane."

"We're acquaintances," Nicholas agreed so casually it would have fooled her if she didn't know better.

Tremaine rubbed the bridge of her nose, angry that he would still play these games with her. "He took time out during the evacuation to find me and ask me how I planned to get out of town." She had always known she had had more than one guardian, that Gerard wasn't the only one who was watching over her or the Valiarde estate, she just hadn't known who the others were. She had had a telephone number to call in the Garbardin district of Vienne for help, and had used it occasionally at the times when Nicholas's past had caught up with her. "The only way he could have done that was if the man at the Garbardin exchange reported directly to him."

Nicholas lifted a brow. "If you think that's the only way he could have done it, you badly underestimate the resources available to the Queen's Guard, especially during wartime."

Tremaine studied the ribbed metal ceiling, mentally begging for patience. "And he said he was my uncle."

"Ah." Nicholas folded his arms, conceding the point with a faintly disgruntled expression. "Yes, he was your other guardian. Years ago we made the decision to act as strangers, so association with me wouldn't damage his political career. Reynard's past was checkered enough, he didn't need me hanging about as further ammunition against him."

"I figured that part out," Tremaine told him, mock-patiently.

"Now I have a question for you." He watched her thoughtfully. "What on earth possessed you to marry that man?"

"What?" Tremaine glared at him, caught by surprise and suddenly on the defensive. "Did you pretend to be a Gardier so long that you picked up their prejudices? They don't think the Syprians are people, by the way."

As an attempt to throw him off the scent, it worked miserably. "Tremaine, don't be conventional," Nicholas said witheringly. "My objection is that by my calculations, you can't have known him more than six days."

"Oh." Tremaine rubbed at a spot on the counter, trying to collect her thoughts. The truth might be an interesting option. "It was a dare. A Syprian political opponent dared me, in front of a lot of people, and it would have been an insult to Ilias if I'd refused. So I didn't refuse. And I just wanted to." She looked at Nicholas. His expression was mildly appalled. She gritted her teeth. "Gerard said it was all right."

Nicholas regarded the ceiling, shaking his head. "Gerard was not chosen as your guardian for his status as a paragon of propriety."

This distracted her. "Gerard's proper," she protested.

"He came to it late in life, believe me."

Tremaine gestured in frustration. "Considering the decisions I was making back home before all this started, I don't think you realize how close to normal marrying Ilias was. For me." Maybe that was a sign. For someone who had wanted to kill herself not so long ago, she was doing an awful lot of things to try to tie herself to this life. Even before she had discovered it must have been partly due to Arisilde's accidental influence on her. *Maybe part of you knew that it wasn't as bad as it seemed and was trying to keep the other part from doing something stupid.* Nicholas was still looking at her. "And he's nice. And his foster mother likes me."

Nicholas let his breath out, his expression reluctantly resigned. "I suppose it's legal."

"Yes, as if that's going to matter while the Gardier are taking over the world. Both of the worlds." She knew he had no real objections, he was just trying to get a reaction out of her. Just to see how he would react, she said deliberately, "Syprian marriage is a little different. I had to buy him." After a pause for effect, she added, "I used the gold coins from the safety-deposit box in the Bank of Vienne."

Nicholas stared at her, his pose of detached comment forgotten for the moment. "All the coins?" he demanded.

"No, not all the coins." Tremaine glared in irritation. Nicholas had had hundreds of thousands of reals' worth of art at Coldcourt and yet had considered having electric wiring run on the second floor of the house an extravagance.

Nicholas shook his head, apparently willing to let the money issue drop. "At least he's not Ander Destan. I couldn't stand that little prick."

E ventually Giliead fell asleep on the floor, so Ilias found a blanket in one of the little rooms and covered him with it. Though his body ached and his eyes were gritty, his thoughts were going in circles and he still couldn't lie down, let alone sleep. He decided to go find Tremaine and see if he was still married.

He went back down the ladder into the lower crew area, pausing at a doorway to a little room off the passage, where the ship's talking curse box lived. Molin was seated inside, hunched over the box, twisting knobs and tapping on things. Ilias knew he was trying to make it hail the *Ravenna,* but from Molin's expression it wasn't going well.

He stepped away from the door without disturbing the man and turned to find himself face-to-face with his new father-in-law. They regarded each other warily. Nicholas said, distinctly and with a certain grim emphasis, "You mean to take care of my daughter." It wasn't a question.

"Yes," Ilias said, realized he had spoken Syrnaic, and repeated the word in Rienish.

They eyed each other. Then Tremaine broke the tension by stepping out of the crew area at the end of the passage. "Ilias."

Nicholas stepped out of the way, giving him a sardonic nod. Ilias moved past, not breaking eye contact until the last possible moment. When he reached Tremaine, she drew him aside into a little room off the larger common area, asking, "How is Giliead?" She kept her voice low, so Cimarus and Cletia wouldn't hear.

"Just . . . worried about what's going to happen when we go home," Ilias admitted. He leaned gingerly against the metal cabinet, trying to ease the ache in his side.

"You mean, what Visolela and Nicanor might do?"

He shook his head slightly. "What the god might do."

She frowned slowly. "Like what? It can't . . . un-Choose him." She read his expression worriedly. "Can it?"

"It doesn't happen often. Maybe once in a generation." He looked away, gesturing helplessly. Most people didn't know it ever happened at all, but the poets who kept the Vessels' Journals knew the stories. Gunias of the Barrens Pass, whose god had left him for a reason no one knew, and who had fallen on his sword. Eliade of Syrneth, who had killed her sister in a fight over a man, then walked into the sea when her god refused to see her. "I don't know. It's not like a person. Some things it cares about, some it doesn't. It didn't act any different to me after I got the curse mark—"

"But that wasn't your fault."

Ilias stopped, caught by that. He absently took her hand, noticing the nails were bitten to the quick. "This wasn't his fault either. But it was something he did, not something that was done to him. If there's a difference, that's it."

"But the god didn't mind us," she protested. "It didn't do anything to Florian or Gerard or Arisilde in the sphere."

"But it didn't Choose you either." Maybe she was right. He couldn't think about it anymore or he was going to go crazy. He let out his breath in frustration, pushing the hair out of his eyes. "There's no way to tell until we get there." He looked at her for a long moment. Her eyes were hollow and her face drawn, and her skin felt chill though it wasn't cold in here. Under those layers of sarcasm and anger she was all nerves and pain; she couldn't keep that tamped down forever. He just wished he knew how to help her. "So, how are things going with . . ." He jerked his chin toward the doorway.

"Oh, him?" Her smile was bitterly ironic. "He hasn't killed anybody or overthrown any governments or brought down any captains of industry since we've been aboard so far, so I suppose he's bored."

Ilias's mouth quirked; he hadn't understood all of that, but he was fairly sure she wasn't entirely joking. He asked carefully, "Is he angry that you got married?" He knew Rienish men had far more control over decisions made by their household. He had also known this might end with Tremaine leaving for her own land and him staying behind in Cineth, but he somehow hadn't thought that it would be soon.

Tremaine shook her head, obviously irritated. "He thinks it's impetuous of me to marry someone that I've only known for a few days from another world that I don't know anything about."

Ilias nodded. When she put it that way, it did sound a little . . . impetuous. "Karima probably already traded away the coins," he found himself saying.

"He doesn't really care, he's just trying to make me react." Tremaine gestured sharply. "It's infuriating."

He wasn't sure she was right about that.

Then from the passage, Molin called jubilantly, "The *Ravenna!*" followed by a lot of very fast Rienish Ilias couldn't catch. Cletia and Cimarus got to their feet, looking worried, and the boy Calit sat up, blinking sleepily.

"He's raised her on the wireless," Tremaine repeated for Ilias, stepping into the outer room, heartfelt relief in her voice. "God, that's good news for once."

Someone touched her shoulder, saying, "Florian."

She started and sat up, her legs aching and one foot asleep, startled to see she was still in the darkened storeroom. "Ow," she muttered, rubbing her eyes. There was no tall thin man with violet eyes and wispy white hair standing over her, that had been a dream. She shivered at the sudden chill in the air.

Then she saw something move across the threshold of the door. As she squinted at it, a breath of white mist crept in. Florian stared. "Oh. Oh, no," she whispered grimly to herself. *You wanted something to happen, there it is.*

She pushed to her feet, stepping to the door, careful to avoid the questing wisp of mist.

Like the breath off a bog, a layer of the stuff floated above the passage leading to the main corridor. *Damn it.* She thought about calling out, but the knowledge that whatever was causing this had to be here somewhere nearby squelched that impulse. She closed her eyes for an instant, going over the words of the concealment charm again, then turned the other way, moving down the corridor toward Ixion's prison. Reaching the corner, she darted a cautious look around it. Three of the guards lay sprawled in the passage, already unconscious, tendrils of mist wafting over their bodies.

The mist covered the floor on the far side of the door to the guardroom and pockets of it oozed into being everywhere there was clear floor space. *It's surrounding us, cutting us off from—* "Shit!" Florian hopped away from the mist reaching for her ankles and darted into the guardroom. Four more men lay unconscious around the empty chamber, one stretched across the table in the corner, the receiver for the ship's telephone in his hand. Florian scrambled onto the table, just avoiding a reaching wisp, and grabbed the receiver out of the man's limp hand. She tapped frantically on the cradle, but the line was dead.

The door to the inner room flew open and Florian froze as for the first time she got a good look at Ixion. He looked like an ordinary man, handsome even, wearing a set of gray army fatigues. There was a sparse dark fuzz across his skull, as if he had shaved his head and the hair was just growing back. She had expected something a good deal more horrible after the body-growing process the others had talked about, but the past few days must have completed it. His eyes darted around the room but didn't settle on her; she fervently hoped her charm was working on him and he wasn't just toying with her.

He made a ritual gesture her eye couldn't quite follow and the mist peeled back from the floor in a half circle around him. But as he stepped forward Florian caught movement out of the corner of her eye and jerked away in horror, nearly stumbling off the table.

Something was standing in the doorway, almost within arm's reach of her.

It looked like a man too, but the dirty brown rags it wore revealed gray scarred pockmarked skin, with open sores and tinges of green, as if it was riddled with disease. It was bald and the disfigurement continued all across its head and face. The truly horrible part was that in the center of many of the open sores, she could see a glitter of crystal. Florian sank back into the corner, praying she hadn't accidentally dispelled the charm by moving so abruptly, her skin crawling at the thought of being touched by the thing.

Ixion regarded it calmly. "So there you are. Whatever you are." He grimaced. "And they say my curselings are foul."

It started toward him, unimpeded by the mist. Ixion raised his hands, whispering something. A second lighter mist melted out of the air, overlaying the first, growing up into sticky gray ropes around the crystal creature. *God, let it work,* Florian thought. She had never seen that spell before, but she was willing to concede that Ixion might be the lesser of two evils here.

The creature staggered, shook its head like a wounded animal, then tore the ropes off. The etheric substance dissolved harmlessly and Ixion's mist faded. The creature plowed toward him again.

Ixion winced and Florian heard him murmur, "Damn Gardier," in exasperation. He backed into his cell as it approached, then darted to the side and she saw him grab something. A crash made her flinch and she realized he must have struck the thing with a table or chair. Ixion bolted out of the cell suddenly, the mist peeling away from his feet.

He reached the door into the corridor and stopped as if he had struck a wall. Blue light suffused the air around him; he gave a strangled cry and collapsed. Florian stared, aghast. *The ward. That was one of Arisilde's wards.* It would surely alert Gerard or Niles that something was happening, but—

Too late. The creature appeared in the doorway and lunged toward Ixion. *If it gets him,* Florian had time to think, *God knows what we'll have to deal with.*

She leapt off the table into the free space around Ixion's body where the mist had retreated. Facing the creature, she gestured her concealment charm away.

The creature staggered to an abrupt halt, staring at her. Its eyes were dark and far too human for comfort. "I've seen you," Florian said as she stepped over Ixion's body, backing away, knowing it could understand. "I'm off to tell everyone now." It lunged for her and she ran.

She got two steps before she saw the band of mist still crossing the corridor. She leapt over it but felt something touch her foot even through her boots. She landed, staggering against the wall, dizzy and sick.

The creature was in the doorway just stepping over Ixion and it would have her in seconds. Then Ixion flung out an arm and the creature staggered.

Florian pushed away from the wall and bolted down the corridor, yelling for help, hearing heavy footsteps behind her. No one answered and she knew the mist must be all through here now, blocking off help, making people unconscious. She turned down a cross corridor hoping for stairs and came to a closed hatchway.

She pulled on the handle but the door wouldn't move. *Warded, dammit, everything down here's warded!* If it was just meant to keep out curious passengers . . . She tugged with all her strength, gasping, "It's an emergency, please!"

The ward must have some kind of fail-safe to read her fear and knew she was telling the truth; the door moved under her hand and she flung it open into a half-lit labyrinth of machinery and pipes. Thrumming noise and damp heat assaulted her as she bolted down a narrow catwalk that ran next to a bulkhead. Ducking around a corner, she saw the walkway continued into the dim maze, but a byway led to the right, through a thick hatchway into a more brightly lit area. She leaned in and saw another machinery maze, with two men in disheveled crew work uniforms, their backs to her, leaning over something in the center of a mass of pipes. Relief washed over her and she stepped through the door, drawing breath to call out.

Something caught her arm and yanked her backward. Florian caught hold of a pipe in pure reflex, crying out. The dull roar of the *Ravenna*'s inner workings filled her ears; she had barely heard herself, she knew the men across the room hadn't. She hooked her arm around the pipe, twisting around, finding herself facing a gray-skinned face pocked with dull yellow crystals. Braced in the doorway, it was man-sized, man-shaped, but inhuman, foul. It wrenched at her again, hauling her nearly off the pipe. She clawed at the wall for handhold, grabbing a red lever. She saw the words "Watertight door release, do not—" and pulled it with all her strength.

Riveted metal slammed into the doorway and she stumbled back. There were body parts everywhere, an arm, part of the torso, a leg, but no blood. The thing had come apart under the door's crushing force. Past the roaring in her ears she could hear an alarm Klaxon blaring. *Finally,* she thought in exasperated relief, and decided to sit down on the catwalk.

B y the time they got the door to open again, crew and officers were everywhere. One of the engineers led Florian back up to Ixion's cell, where Niles stood, distracted and angry. He saw her and demanded, "Are you all right?"

Florian nodded. One of the boiler room men had given her a drink from something very alcoholic in a flask, and it had made her feel floaty and warm and just distant enough. "We brought the parts," she said, gesturing to the two men following who were dragging a canvas bag. "Where's Ixion? Was he killed?"

"They've taken him to the hospital. Against my advice. Gerard is going to go absolutely mad when he hears that." Niles grimaced. But before Florian could demand more information, Niles shook his head, his expression growing less grim. "You wouldn't have heard, but the wireless operator was contacted by Molin a short time ago."

"Molin?" Florian stared, the good news coming as almost a big a shock as bad. "That means they're here?"

Niles actually smiled for the first time in three days. "Very near."

T he flying whale couldn't go too near to the *Ravenna*'s deck without fouling itself in the lines that helped secure the smaller stern mast, so they had to climb down a rope ladder from the steering cabin. Normally climbing down the broad ladder in the bright sunlight, the wind pulling at his hair, would have been exciting; at the moment Ilias found it excruciatingly painful.

He had been looking forward to the sight of the *Ravenna* coming toward them across the sea, but they didn't see her until she was nearly right under them. Molin had apparently been speaking to her on the flying whale's talking curse box, and when the *Ravenna* had been assured that it was them, the curse concealing her had dropped away and the giant ship was suddenly beneath them. The view was

still fairly spectacular; the great ship looked like a giant fortress floating on the waves.

The flying whale was now temporarily moored to various secure
points on the open stern area of the *Ravenna*'s Promenade deck, including a catwalk that stretched across the width of it.

"That's actually a docking bridge, a secondary wheelhouse,"
Tremaine had explained, as they crowded up against the windows on
the second-level crew area, watching as Dubos had carefully maneuvered the airship down and sailors caught the dangling lines. He had
shouted at everyone to get out of the steering cabin and the second
level had been the next best vantage point. "The little enclosed building in the center of it has the engine telegraphs and another wheel.
The catwalk is built across the width of the ship so they can stand on
it and look down the sides when they dock, kind of like the wing
things that stick out from the big wheelhouse." Ilias had felt some vin-
dication that the ship could be steered from her stern like a rational
craft; he had pointed this out, but Giliead was still too troubled to take
much notice.

Now Ilias reached the narrow catwalk with relief, letting go of the
ladder and stumbling so that one of the Rienish sailors waiting had to
catch him. Annoyed at himself and shrugging off the help, he waited
for Tremaine to finish her descent.

She made it down safely, though she grabbed the rail as soon as she
stepped off the ladder, a little shaky. She looked sourly at Ilias. "That
wasn't fun."

"No," he had to agree. "It wasn't."

He followed her down the catwalk's stairs to the deck. There
Pasima hugged Cletia tightly and Sanior and Danias nearly knocked
Cimarus over with the exuberance of their greeting. Gerard was waiting for them and immediately caught Tremaine in a hug. *I wish he was
her father,* Ilias thought bleakly. Wizard or not, things would have been
a lot easier.

Giliead already stood with Gyan and Kias. Ilias reached them in
time to hear Giliead say, "Arites is dead."

He wished he hadn't been in time to see their expressions
change. "How?" Gyan asked, putting a hand on Ilias's shoulder.
They don't touch him, Ilias thought. *That's just because he's a Chosen
Vessel.* He didn't even think they realized they did it. When they
found out that he had let the crystal teach him a curse, it would be
so much worse.

"A shooting weapon," Giliead said, his expression stony. "He never made it onto the flying whale."

From behind them, Gerard said, "There's something I need to tell you both." Ilias turned warily, warned by his tone.

Gerard's expression was grave, his face etched with tension. "We've just had another rather startling development," he said, keeping one arm on Tremaine's shoulders as if wanting to make sure she didn't disappear. "Something happened to Ixion. The creature we thought we had banished was still aboard, and it made an attempt on him. He was caught between it and Arisilde's ward."

"He's dead?" Giliead asked sharply.

"Alive. He's in the hospital."

Tremaine watched Ilias and Giliead bolt for the stairs, frowning. "Ixion is under guard, right? And what happened to the—" She stopped as she saw Gerard's eyes fix on something standing behind her.

He went pale. "Dear God."

"Not quite," Nicholas said. With one brow cocked and a slight reserved smile, Tremaine still thought he looked insufferably pleased with himself. She rolled her eyes. *He loves this part.*

Gerard made a helpless gesture, still staring. "How—"

"It's a long and rather fraught story."

The wind crossing the stern was cool and Tremaine wanted someone to answer her questions about Ixion. Through the windows into the big room facing the stern, she saw Colonel Averi speaking to someone. She left Gerard and Nicholas to their reunion and headed for the doors.

It was one of the Second Class lounges and there was fine wood veneer on the walls, blue-and-gold carpets over tile and the sun streamed through the windows looking out onto the deck. The outside doors opened onto an area arranged as a parlor, with couches, armchairs and low cocktail tables, while the rest of it was set up for dining or cards. *Home,* Tremaine thought warmly, then felt foolish. *It's a ship, it's not your home. And you've never even been in this lounge before.*

She advanced on Averi. "Colonel, what happened with Ixion?"

"We'd given you up for—" Colonel Averi began. Then he stared past her, his expression turning faintly incredulous.

Tremaine looked around to see Nicholas strolling calmly in with Gerard, taking in the furnishings and the art on the walls as if he was thinking of buying the place. Gerard was saying over his shoulder, "—send up a crew to relieve Dubos, I gather he's—"

"Who is that?" Averi asked evenly.

It was probably the Gardier uniform that was causing Averi's consternation. She decided to be merciful and not pretend to misunderstand and formally introduce him to Gerard. "That's Nicholas Valiarde."

Nicholas chose an armchair and sat down, eyeing Averi with a contemplative air. "Colonel Averi, I presume?"

Averi looked stunned. "It can't be. He's been missing for—"

Gerard saw Averi's thunderstruck expression and came to the rescue. "Ah, Colonel Averi, this is Nicholas Valiarde. I believe you must have heard of him, he's the benefactor of the Viller Institute. He's . . . ah, been acting as an intelligence agent, spying on the Gardier."

"Can somebody tell the Ixion story from the beginning?" Tremaine demanded in exasperation.

Gerard began, "Florian had suspected—"

The door to the inner corridor flew open with a bang and Florian literally burst in, followed by Niles and two crewmen, one in lieutenant's uniform and the other in dungarees and singlet, both with the oil and sweat stains that usually marked the engineering and boiler gangs. Florian halted, taking in the array of shocked and startled faces; Tremaine saw she was clutching some long narrow object wrapped in a towel. "Are they—" she began, then spotted Tremaine. "Thank God, you're back!"

She hurried forward to throw her arm around Tremaine's shoulders in a hug. Tremaine returned it, distracted by the fact that the towel had fallen back, revealing that the long narrow object Florian carried was actually a man's severed arm. "I'm back. You have an arm."

"Yes." Florian nodded emphatically, stepping back to drop the object on the nearest table. "The thing from the hospital, it wasn't dead."

"It's dead now," Niles assured them, as Gerard stepped forward to study the arm.

The lieutenant told Colonel Averi, "He's—It's in pieces, sir. Caught in a watertight door."

"May I?" Nicholas stepped forward, picking up the stiffening arm.

He turned it over, showing Gerard the lumps of crystal set deep into the gray flesh, each in its own star of scar tissue.

"My God," Gerard breathed. He glanced up at Florian, asking sharply, "There were more?"

She grimaced in disgust. "All over his body."

"The Gardier said they had a presence aboard this ship," Nicholas said thoughtfully. "I wasn't sure what that meant, but this clarifies the situation remarkably." He glanced over at Averi. "The Gardier use those crystals to give temporary sorcerous powers to certain Command officers, called Liaisons. It also allows something to temporarily inhabit the Liaison's body." He added, with an ironic lift of his brow, "Who the Liaisons were actually liaising with, I was never able to discover. It's not something that's commonly known to all but the highest ranks." He lifted the arm, studying it thoughtfully. "But even in their case, only one crystal is implanted, usually in the temple. This is something different."

Florian stepped aside, taking Tremaine's sleeve to draw her back a step. "Who is that?" she asked anxiously in Syrnaic, nodding toward Nicholas. "Is everyone all right?"

"That's my father. We found him. He found us." She swallowed in a dry throat and finished evenly, "Arites and Basimi died."

Florian looked startled, then stricken. "Oh, no."

Gerard was explaining to Nicholas about the incident in the hospital. "I saw another one in the office, stopping the surgeon before he could call for help," Tremaine interrupted, not wanting to go into details about either Arites or Basimi. "There were two. So . . . was Giliead fighting a construct like you thought and this was the other?"

"It must have been a construct," Gerard said, frowning deeply, "But . . ."

"It doesn't quite fit," Nicholas interrupted. "Benin, the Gardier chief Scientist, said the presence wasn't able to contact them until the ship reached the mountain barrier. It would have needed access to a wireless, as they can't communicate between worlds, and I know there was no Command Liaison at the barrier outpost."

"So it must have used our wireless," Niles pointed out, adding curiously, "Have we been introduced?"

"That's impossible," Averi interrupted Gerard's attempt to explain. "The wireless room is warded and has armed men posted around the clock. It's guarded like the Bank of Vienne."

Nicholas smiled slightly. "Difficult then, not impossible." Tremaine had the funny feeling he was breaking cover too. Maybe he had been a Gardier too long; he wasn't making any attempt to hide his real self.

"Why didn't Arisilde do something about this?" she demanded. "Why didn't he kill that thing? There has to be a reason. He told me he couldn't show his hand in this, that it was a nasty spell, but interfering would put someone in danger ..." She trailed off, thinking that over. "I thought he meant put all of us in danger, in general."

Nicholas was looking at her oddly. Incredulous, Gerard demanded, "When did he tell you that?"

She gestured impatiently. "It was a dream, that night in the hospital. I wasn't sure if it was real or not."

"Put someone in danger ... Wait," Niles said, frowning. "You said the implanted crystals allow them to temporarily inhabit—possess?—the individual? Are the Liaisons aware of the possession, do they remember what they did under its influence?"

Nicholas's eyes narrowed thoughtfully. "They seem to be. But I don't know if that's an immutable condition." He eyed Niles sharply. "You think someone has been implanted with a crystal without his knowledge, and the creature used him to reach the wireless?"

Gerard took his spectacles off and pressed a hand to his forehead wearily. "Oh, God. If that's the case—"

"Why else—" Tremaine and Nicholas both began at once. He gestured with the severed arm, politely deferring to her, and Tremaine finished through gritted teeth, "Arisilde wouldn't worry about hurting the person, unless he was a complete innocent."

Nicholas nodded. "By not 'showing his hand' he may have meant that he didn't want to chance revealing himself to whomever the Liaison was reporting to. The Gardier have been desperate to discover more information about the sphere."

"It could be any one of the people liberated from the island base," Averi pointed out urgently.

"It could be one of the Syprians," Florian put in, her face etched with worry. "I guess it could be me or Tremaine, but we were always together and we were never unconscious."

"I was held too, briefly," Gerard admitted. "But I was never unconscious either, they had no opportunity to do anything without my knowledge—"

"It won't be the freed prisoners or the Syprians who were captured," Nicholas interrupted impatiently. "They couldn't have anticipated that any of them would be released, much less end up on this ship."

So that means it's not Ilias, Tremaine thought, pushing her fingers through her hair in agitation. *Besides, I would have found the crystal when we slept together.* And he had gone swimming naked twice with Giliead, who surely would have seen it. But there were others who had been taken prisoner, at Port Rel in Ile-Rien.

Florian, Niles and Ander. All three abducted by Dommen and Mirsone and the other Rienish traitors. *Taken prisoner, not killed. How long did they think they could get away with that? They should have killed Niles. They took the sphere too, and Arisilde saw what happened, kept them from using the wireless with the Gardier crystals. . . .* It all came together abruptly. "It's Niles."

"Me?" Niles stared at her. "I've never been . . ." He clapped a hand to his forehead in appalled realization. "Oh, my God."

"Surely if it was Niles, the creature would have wreaked far more havoc than it has," Averi objected.

Niles and Gerard were staring at each other, Niles sickened and Gerard in growing horror. Gerard said, "Except we put an adjuration on each other to stay conscious on the voyage. We didn't lift it until after the attack on the airship, the one the sphere destroyed, because we were both so exhausted. If that affected the crystal—"

Niles swore violently. "Giaren couldn't wake me the next morning. I could have gone to the wireless, used illusions to get past the guards, sent the operator to sleep long enough to send a message." He felt the back of his neck, loosening his tie. "I felt something back here, but I thought it was a scratch. God, I can't believe this!"

Gerard and Nicholas stepped over to look, Nicholas saying, "It's considerably smaller than the others I've seen." He raised his brows. "It's under the skin. I suspect we'll need a pair of forceps."

Tremaine rubbed her eyes to hide her expression. She could only take so much of Nicholas. *It's a good thing one of us has impersonated a doctor.* With an oath, Averi strode to a ship's telephone on a nearby table, saying, "I'll get Divies up here. You might not be the only one."

Florian looked urgent. "Tremaine, could you—"

"Yes." She took Florian's arm. There had to be a ladies retiring room or a steward's cubby or something nearby. "We need to tell Ander."

"We'll need to check everyone else who was ever in contact with the Gardier," Nicholas pointed out. He added wryly, "Including myself."

Chapter 23

Ilias reached the healer's area a few steps behind Giliead, though running to the stairs had made him breathe hard. He had known he was hurt; now he was starting to reluctantly admit to himself that he might have to do something about it.

He followed Giliead down the narrow passage into the main room and found him confronting Ander. The room was full of people, Rienish soldiers, the two healers, some of the men who he knew were high in the Rienish ranks. Everyone had stopped talking to stare. Ixion, at least, was nowhere to be seen. With the air of someone arguing with a dangerous madman, Giliead said to Ander, "You let him loose on the ship?"

Ander was planted in front of a doorway into one of the smaller rooms. From inside it, Ixion's voice called, "I've pledged my help to the Rien—unconditionally—in fighting these Gardier creatures."

Ilias took a step back in pure reflex. He hadn't really believed that the wizard was here until this moment. Giliead ignored Ixion, saying, "You can't mean to do this."

"He's still under guard. He's not going to do anything." Ander lifted his hands placatingly, as if Giliead's concern was senseless and overwrought. Ilias wanted to hit him. Now he knew how Tremaine felt, when Ander treated her as if nothing she said meant anything, as if he always knew better.

"You must be out of your mind," Ilias said incredulously. He heard a familiar metallic clicking and saw the god-sphere was sitting on a table near the center of the room, trembling a little as its insides spun in agitation. "See, even it thinks you're crazy."

"Look, this is complicated," Ander began. "I know you—"

Ixion appeared in the doorway behind him. Ilias stared, too startled to react. The wizard looked more like himself, except black stubble was just growing in on his bare scalp and he still had no brows or eyelashes. Half his face was bruised and there was a little dried blood around his left ear. As injuries went, Ilias knew he himself looked much worse. His eyes on Giliead, Ixion said, "You've cast a curse. Not just held one, like before. You've actually cast one." He smiled. "Welcome, brother."

Giliead stared for a moment, breathing hard. Ander turned to block Ixion's way, his jaw set. "Get back in there. I told you, there's no—" Then Giliead flung himself toward the doorway. Ander shouted, bracing his body in front of the opening, the door banging him in the shoulder as Giliead slammed into him, Ixion stepped back out of reach. It gave Ilias the chance to grab Giliead's sword arm and haul him around. He shoved him back against the wall with all his weight, pinning him with a forearm across his chest. "Gil, listen to me!"

Giliead glared down at him but didn't throw him off. Ilias said softly, "If he's really got another body waiting on the island, he could reach Cineth before we ever have a chance to get back there." He set his jaw, deliberately not looking toward the doorway. "Nothing's changed. We can't take the chance."

He waited until Giliead's face changed, until he could tell he saw reason again. Ilias stepped back, taking a deep breath to quell sudden dizziness. The abrupt movement had caused a flare of agony in his midsection and what he really wanted to do was hunch over on the floor. But not in front of Ixion.

Giliead straightened up, pushing off the wall, looking at Ander as if he didn't see all the other armed Rienish watching uneasily. He said carefully, "This is what he does. He gets close to people, then he kills them. If you won't be warned, then you can have him, and be damned."

He strode out of the room and Ilias followed, throwing one last grim look back at Ander.

"So the 'real' presence was the creature you saw in the surgeon's office," Gerard was saying as they walked down the carpeted corridor to the hospital. "It saw Giliead wasn't affected by the mist, so sent it a sorcerous construct in after him, not wanting to risk its own physical body."

Tremaine nodded thoughtfully. "I'm still not sure it was a great idea to move Ixion to the hospital. When are they taking him back to the warded cell?"

Gerard's mouth set in a thin line and he didn't answer. Tremaine watched him suspiciously as Florian, preoccupied, said, "When it talked to Bain and Ixion, it must have been looking for another body, since it couldn't take over Niles the way it planned to." She rubbed her arms as if suddenly cold. "Can you imagine what it would have done if it had gotten one of them?"

Tremaine snorted. "Yes." Just then they reached the hospital entrance and Giliead burst out suddenly, Ilias behind him. Giliead stopped abruptly when he saw them, then started to go past without speaking. Tremaine stepped in front of him, demanding, "What's wrong?"

Ilias, frustrated and angry, answered her, "They let Ixion out."

"No. What the hell?" Aghast, Tremaine turned to Gerard and Florian. "That can't possibly—"

"We haven't let him out," Gerard said sharply. Then he drew a deep breath. "But he was injured driving off that creature and it's— It's becoming difficult to convince Delphane and the others not to make a deal with him. I don't know how much longer—"

"But Florian killed the damn thing, not him!" Tremaine protested.

"Not with magic," Florian said, sounding uncharacteristically bitter. "I killed it with a heavy door. Damn it."

Giliead snarled under his breath and started away down the corridor. With a helpless gesture, Ilias made to follow. Gerard stopped him with a hand on his arm. "You're injured. At least let me do something about it." It was obvious Gerard felt he had badly let them down.

Ilias hesitated, looking at Giliead's retreating back. It was just as obvious that he was in pain. He had had sorcerous healing twice; the first time when a mild charm from Florian had helped a badly infected wound in his back, and again when Niles had healed a broken arm. It had to be tempting, to know he could avoid days of suffering. Giliead stopped, still facing away from them, but his head turned so they could see his profile. He said, "Go ahead. What does it matter?" and walked on down the corridor.

Ilias swore, pushing a handful of tangled hair off his face. "Come on, let Gerard help you," Florian urged him.

At least Gerard wouldn't feel useless then, Tremaine thought. She folded her arms, saying nothing, not wanting to influence his decision. Ilias shook his head uncertainly. He looked back at the hospital door, then quickly away. "Not in there."

Tremaine knew he meant not in there with Ixion. "I'll come to your cabin as soon as I finish here," Gerard told him, relieved.

Ilias nodded, still troubled, and followed Giliead. Tremaine sighed and clapped a hand to her forehead, saying, "I'd better go with them."

Florian nodded gravely. "I'll come by later."

Gerard squeezed Tremaine's shoulder. "Tell them I—" He sighed, shaking his head. "Never mind."

"I'll tell them," Tremaine promised anyway, and went after Ilias.

She caught up with Ilias on the stairs; he was taking them much more slowly than usual. Not saying anything, since there was nothing much to say, she stepped next to him and guided his arm across her shoulders so she could take part of his weight. She didn't know if it would help or hinder him, but he leaned against her with a sigh, his hair tickling her cheek. When they reached their deck he kept his arm around her. As they started down the corridor, Tremaine said thoughtfully, "If they really do let Ixion loose . . . Much as I hate the idea, we could go to Nicholas for help. Bastards like Ixion are right up his alley."

Ilias frowned, glancing down at her. "But would he go against what your people want?"

Tremaine snorted with dry amusement. "It's a very dark alley."

The cabin door stood open and when they reached it Tremaine heard raised voices—Pasima and Giliead. Ilias groaned under his breath, muttering, "She could at least let us get some sleep first."

As they went inside, Tremaine saw Pasima confronting Giliead in the main room. All the Syprians were here, Gyan grim-faced and angry, Kias standing back by the wall, his arms folded and his expression stolid. Danias and Sanior seemed wary, as if they expected Giliead to attack Pasima, but Cletia, seated on the couch, just looked tired. Beside her Cimarus stared at the wall, his jaw tight. Calit was sitting back in a corner, listening wide-eyed to a fight in a language he couldn't understand in a place that must seen incredibly strange. Tremaine had forgotten all about him; he must have been tagging along with Cimarus.

Giliead watched Pasima with a faintly contemptuous smile as she said, "I knew it would come to this. You've always been too soft, Andrien has always harbored the cursed. Now you've betrayed the god."

"If he hadn't made the curse crystal work, we would have died there," Cletia said thickly.

Tremaine looked away, shaking her head. *Oh God, this is just about getting the crystal to make the gate.* Cletia and Cimarus must not realize who had been responsible for fighting off the Gardier wizard before they reached the airship. No wonder Giliead looked like that; Pasima didn't know the half of it and Cletia's attempt at a defense meant nothing. Giliead snorted derisively. "Betrayed the god? You hate the god, Pasima, because no matter how high your councils in the city go, it'll always be above you. And worse, it doesn't care how much grain your family has or what good marriages you bought for your brothers. It doesn't know you from the lowest crippled cursed gleaner."

"We've only your word for that, haven't we?" she snapped. "Look at all the trouble that's come since you were Chosen. Ranior's death, Ixion's plagues on us, and your own brother destroyed—"

"Destroyed?" Ilias furiously interrupted Giliead's answer, stepping away from Tremaine to put himself in the middle of the fight. "I'm right here! If it happened to Cimarus, you'd tell Cletia to cut his throat and never see her again if she refused. And Cletia knows it."

Pasima was so angry she actually answered him directly. "At least I'd have done the god's will. Not fooled myself into thinking whatever I did for my own selfish reasons was right."

"That would be so much better than just living with it, wouldn't it?" Ilias retorted bitterly.

"You'd have a brother's blood on your hands, but at least the right people would still talk to you in the market," Giliead added in a deceptively even tone.

Pasima all but bared her teeth. "Maybe Ixion's vengeance on your family was just the god's way of telling you it Chose the wrong Vessel."

"You'd better hope not." Giliead actually smiled at her, though it was a bitter expression. "Ixion fought a Gardier curseling and the Rienish let him out of prison. He's lying his way into an alliance with them even now."

Cletia looked up, startled, and Sanior made an alarmed noise in his throat. Pasima stared incredulously. "You can't be serious."

Giliead laughed without humor. "Oh, I'm nothing but serious."

Pasima shook her head, stunned. "I knew you would lead us into disaster. I knew these people were lying filth, no better than the Hisians. And they've found perfect allies in you!"

Tremaine shook her head at the ceiling. *There's no point to this.* "That's it." She pushed between Ilias and Giliead, wrenched a chair around into the middle of the room, and sat down to yank off the boots she had borrowed from Pasima. Standing, she dropped them at the older woman's feet. "Get out," she said evenly. "Take your belongings, and your minions, and go. There's plenty of empty rooms toward the stern."

Pasima glowered at her, breathing hard. "This is none of your concern," she grated. "And you do not give orders to me, foreign woman."

Tremaine unexpectedly felt irritation bubble over into hot rage. She pinched the bridge of her nose until it hurt, until she could talk without screaming. Then she looked up slowly, meeting Pasima's angry gaze. "You're the foreigner here, woman, and I'm telling you to get out of this room."

Pasima took a step toward her. *Just try,* Tremaine thought, coming up on the balls of her feet, feeling that rage blossom into a dangerous calm, *Oh, do just try. You might win, but then you'd never draw an unguarded breath until the moment I put the knife in your back.*

Tremaine didn't know what her face told Pasima, but the other woman's expression abruptly went wary, and she shifted back a step. Still watching Tremaine, she jerked her head.

Tremaine was conscious of the others moving, of Cletia standing, looking uncertainly at Pasima, of Cimarus avoiding everyone's eyes as he walked to the door, of Sanior and Danias coming out of the back room carrying the packs and weapons they had brought. Pasima moved last. Leaving the boots on the floor, she stepped around Tremaine, careful not to cross the invisible line that marked the difference between defense and attack. She followed the others out.

No one else moved. Then Kias gave vent to a loud sigh, adding, "Thank the god, that's a relief."

Ilias had gotten cold feet about having sorcerous healing. Fortunately once he had lain down in the suite's main bedroom he couldn't get up again without help, so Tremaine just ignored his attempts to argue about it. Giliead just sat on the bed next to Ilias and looked weary. He seemed to have gone beyond anger at Pasima's accusations and Ixion's release and into a kind of exasperated anticipation of the next outrage. Gyan had taken charge of Calit, making the boy wash up, then going with him to the First Class dining room for some food.

Gerard arrived, bearing his black medical bag and two bottles of Gentian Great Marches '09. Following him into the bedroom, Tremaine dug the corks out of both with her teeth and the letter opener from the writing desk. She gave one bottle to Giliead.

Gerard sat on the edge of the bed next to Ilias, who had curled up awkwardly around the pain in his side. Gerard regarded him and Giliead for a moment, then said carefully, "I was very sorry to hear about Arites. He was an intelligent and engaging young man."

Giliead nodded, looking away, his jaw tight. Ilias was more occupied with eyeing the black medical bag Gerard had opened. "What's in there?" he asked, suspicious.

Tremaine took a swig of the wine, feeling she needed a cushion between her and the rest of the world at the moment. A big cushion. "You know, Niles just knocked him out last time," she pointed out. She had objected then, but right now she could see the benefits. Ilias glared at her.

"Yes, Niles's bedside manner is why he's considered an expert in etheric theory rather than medical sorcery," Gerard said in a "thank you, I'm working now" tone, his manner turning brisk. "And considering the man had a Gardier crystal in him for a week without noticing, I think I prefer my methods."

"What?" Ilias demanded incredulously. Giliead set the wine bottle down and stared at Tremaine.

"Uh, I hadn't told them that part yet," she said.

While Gerard took various powders and vials out of his bag, Tremaine explained about the small crystal and what it had done, and—fortunately—not done, to Niles. When she had finished, Giliead let his head fall back on the padded headboard and said in wonder, "That's it, Pasima's right. I'm terrible at this."

"If you say that again—" Ilias growled, shoving himself upright only to collapse on the bed again with a gasp.

True to his word, Gerard didn't make Ilias fall unconscious. But the adjurations for healing internal injuries were complicated and dull, and the heady smell of the incense and the herbal mixture he had to be talked into drinking made him drift off anyway.

When Gerard finished, Ilias was curled on his side on the gold bedcover, sound asleep, with Giliead watching him. Tremaine followed Gerard out into the main room, asking quietly, "Any idea what we're supposed to do with the Gardier boy?"

He checked his bag, then tucked it under his arm. "It turns out that under the International Accords of Warfare treaty, we're not allowed to take children as prisoners of war, so technically, you kidnapped him. Averi said he won't press charges."

Tremaine's jaw dropped. "Did I miss the part where the Gardier became signatories to the International Accords of Warfare treaty?"

"No, but we, the Parscians and the Capidarans are," Gerard said with an ironic nod. He added more seriously, "I'm sure the boy will be questioned about Gardier society, how they live, and so on, but he might as well stay with people he knows in the meantime."

"People he knows," Tremaine repeated. "His kidnappers."

"Just so."

She gave in for the moment. "Where's Nicholas?"

"He's still meeting with Averi and Delphane. The crystal has been removed from the airship and it's been packed into that lead-lined box, under wards. The *Ravenna* can't tow the airship—Captain Marais seems to think it would either be pulled down into the sea or end up impaled on one of our masts—so they're going to select a volunteer crew and it will follow along behind us. Niles is going aboard with his sphere so he can make the gate to our world when the airship nears Capidara. He's also going to provide some internal wards against fire and electrical failure, as Nicholas has advised us that this is likely to be a problem. It will only make about half our speed, so we should arrive well in time to keep the Capidarans from firing on it." He sighed. "It's also become obvious that the reason our first Gardier prisoners were killed was to keep them from revealing that this wasn't their home world. Though now that we have that information . . . I'm not sure what we can do with it."

Tremaine made a noncommittal noise. She followed him to the door. "Where are you going now?"

"Back to the hospital," he told her grimly. "To make sure Ixion doesn't kill anyone."

They sailed two days without incident, the first of which Tremaine spent sleeping, bathing and eating. The suite was peaceful without Pasima and the others and without prompting, volunteers from the kitchens brought them meals on one of the old serving trolleys. Ilias was out of pain by the time he woke the first evening, and felt up to reminding Tremaine of a promise involving chocolate pastilles. The next morning Florian came for breakfast and stayed the rest of the day. She and Tremaine listened to the others tell stories about Arites. Florian cried and felt a little better afterward. Tremaine just wished she could.

Tremaine got occasional updates on Ixion's status from Gerard, and what she heard wasn't good. Ixion was being far too canny for her peace of mind. She was fairly sure this was something he had been aiming for since first waking on the ship.

On the third morning, the ship's alarms sounded, all hatches were closed, sailors made sure everyone was off the outside decks and safely in their cabins. Then Arisilde made an etheric world-gate.

As before, the entire ship shuddered and jerked, making Tremaine's stomach lurch. *Someday,* she thought with gritted teeth. *Someday they'll get the altitude right.*

Sailing through the waters of her home world now, the *Ravenna* came within sight of Capidara in only an hour. Since Ilias still wasn't allowed to climb stairs, Giliead was still too angry for outside company, and everyone else seemed to be occupied, Tremaine went up to the Sun Deck to take in the view alone.

The wind was much cooler with a tinge of bite in it, and so far the vista was disappointing; she could just make out a dark line of rocky coastline on the horizon.

After a time Tremaine looked up to find Nicholas leaning on the railing next to her. He was wearing dark-colored dungarees and a gray pullover sweater. The clothes made him look younger, and also like one of the Chaire refugees, which was probably completely intentional. It didn't look as if he had shaved since they had arrived on the *Ravenna* and she realized he was growing his beard and mustache back. She said, "You know beards aren't fashionable in Vienne this year."

"How tragic," he said dryly.

They stood in silence for a while. More out of curiosity than anything else, she asked him, "Do you remember who you are in Capidara?"

"It'll come back to me," he replied easily. "Your friends are upset."

"Yes." She shifted, looking back out to sea. "Giliead said he won't work for the Rienish anymore." She let her breath out, suddenly willing to drop her sarcastic pose. "There might be trouble over it. I don't know what to do," she admitted.

Nicholas was silent a moment. Possibly shocked by her sudden attack of honesty. He said slowly, "Considering that he's now my—" He cocked his head inquiringly. "He's now my what, exactly?"

"Son-in-law's foster brother," she supplied, watching him carefully now.

"Ah. Considering he's now my son-in-law's foster brother, I would have to take exception to any attempt at coercion."

Tremaine just nodded, looking down to conceal her relief. Everything aside, she had the strong feeling she was going to need help. Help to keep the people she cared about alive, Syprian and Rienish both, whether they were currently speaking to each other or not. "Good. I don't think Delphane and the others realize how dangerous Ixion is."

"It's hardly surprising." Nicholas regarded the distant shore of Capidara with a faint smile. "They don't realize how dangerous we are, either."

Author's Note

The *Queen Ravenna* is loosely modeled on the *Queen Mary*, a Cunard passenger liner that made her first voyage in 1936. The *Queen Mary* is larger than the *Titanic* and survived World War II as a troop transport and hospital ship, despite the $250,000 bounty placed on her by Adolf Hitler. She is now permanently docked, but extensive and ongoing restoration has returned much of her former Art Deco glory. She is still in use as a hotel and tourist attraction and can be visited at Long Beach, California.